PRAISE FOR TRAITOR'S RUN

"Space Opera done right. Intelligent, thrilling, with heart."

Trent Jamieson, award-winning author of
The Stone Road

"… wild and expansive, and just so utterly out there."

Aurealis Magazine

"A potent SF depiction of humanity victimizing peaceful aliens." "The author's gift for xenofiction matches that of genre grandmasters like Hal Clement, Larry Niven, and C.J. Cherryh."

Kirkus Reviews

"… if you're into epic space tales with a fresh spin, Traitor's Run should be your next binge. It's got drama, heart, and makes you think twice about where humans fit in the universe."

Dirk Strasser, author of *Conquist*

"… space opera done as space opera should be done."

Richard Harland, award-winning author of
Ferren and The Angel

"… a complex and enticing web of future humanity, alien races, and murky motives…"

Mitchell Hogan, award-winning author of
A Crucible of Souls

"a vast galactic canvas with a myriad of extremely well-drawn alien societies, interstellar travel, and plenty of political machinations."

Nathan Burrage, author of *The Hidden Keystone*

THE LENTICULAR

BOOK ONE

TRAITOR'S RUN

KEITH STEVENSON

First published in paperback in Australia in 2023

by coeur de lion publishing

www.coeurdelion.com.au

© Keith Stevenson 2023

www.keithstevenson.com

cover artwork and design by Jeff Brown Graphics

Print ISBN 978-0-6481975-5-3

Ebook ISBN 978-0-6481975-6-0

NATIONAL LIBRARY OF AUSTRALIA

A catalogue record for this book is available from the National Library of Australia

For Nicola

without whom …

PROLOGUE

Talos III / neutral territory in the Earth–K-Chaan war

Volmar sprinted across the hangar and up the short ramp into the waiting shuttle.

Antwer glared at him. "It puts us on the back foot if we're late."

"Pardon, Consul." Volmar delivered a brief bow and strapped himself into the only seat left in the cramped cabin. "I was awaiting confirmation from Earthforce Command. The K-Chaan ships have indeed broken off on all fronts. The ceasefire is complete."

Antwer grunted. "For the moment." He turned to his wife as if Volmar had ceased to exist. "I still don't think you should come. The situation's too volatile."

Ellan, Antwer's wife, was beautiful and far more personable than the consul, who'd shut himself away in their cabin for the trip. She'd gone out of her way to introduce herself, and Volmar had been disarmed by her grace and friendliness. It wasn't something he was used to.

She smiled briefly at him, then shifted her focus to her husband. "You think I should be back home with our boys? *This* is the best way I know to keep them safe. A bad situation needs faultless communication if it's going to improve."

The pilot seated at the control bank completed pre-flight checks and swivelled in his chair to face Antwer. "The K-Chaan shuttle is heading for the planet surface, Consul."

Antwer clasped his wife's hand on the armrest between them. "Then let's go," he said.

Volmar watched the viewscreen above the pilot's head as the

ship lifted from the deck and moved slowly through the opening hangar doors. They were running beneath the belly of the Earthforce Heavy Carrier *Lincoln*. The long hull was studded with more weapons pods than he could count, and it was just one of twelve heavy-carrier-class ships, twenty battlecruiser-class vessels and countless single-fighter craft facing off against an equally impressive battle force of K-Chaan Empire vessels, all of them floating above the barren rock of Talos III.

The war had been raging for almost three years now, with neither side gaining the upper hand. It would go on forever if nothing changed, Volmar thought. Then out of nowhere the K-Chaan had offered a ceasefire, and Earthforce Command had dispatched Varic Antwer – a consummate diplomat – to parlay it into a more prolonged peace. It had been relatively simple for Volmar to be assigned as his aide.

The shuttle cleared the bulk of the *Lincoln* and the pilot set them on a descent to the planet. Talos III had no value other than its location in territory unclaimed by either Earth or the K-Chaan. There were no oceans, little in the way of worthwhile mineral deposits, and the only life detected was a purple lichen that grew on the red calciferous rocks strewn across the landscape, the remnants of a sustained meteorite bombardment in the planet's pre-history.

They hit atmosphere and the shuttle vibrated. Volmar saw Antwer grip his wife's hand more tightly. For all his gruffness, it was clear the consul loved his wife. What must it be like to have that kind of relationship, Volmar wondered. Was it a source of strength or of weakness? Both perhaps.

The vibration smoothed out as the shuttle descended. It was difficult to gauge height against the unbroken rock-filled panorama, but they were heading for the only structure on the planet: a prefabricated plascrete pavilion set up by remote drones operated by the engineer corps. The K-Chaan had insisted they be allowed to enter the structure first, to ensure it was free of booby traps. Earth had insisted the room be studded with remote camera and sensor feeds broadcasting to both sides to ensure the K-Chaan didn't plant their own devices during their examination.

"Do you feel nervous, Mr Volmar?" It was Ellan, leaning past her husband.

"I have very little to be nervous about. You and Consul Antwer are essential to the talks. I'm simply your aide."

"No human has seen a K-Chaan in the flesh and lived. We could all be travelling to our deaths."

"Fear won't help us now," Antwer said. "There have been wrongs on both sides."

"My husband has to keep perspective," Ellan said. "I don't."

"I *am* nervous," Volmar admitted, but it wasn't for the reasons Ellan assumed. Earthforce's generals and admirals were competent, but their minds were constrained by strict rules of engagement and cold military logic. A ceasefire or even a peace would still leave Earth vulnerable to the next threat that came along. Passion, imagination and ruthless commitment were what was required if the tide was to be turned convincingly. Volmar's colleagues were in position on the *Lincoln* and in Command HQ and EarthGov. It was almost time to act.

"Thank you," Ellan said. "I don't think we'd be human if we weren't."

The shuttle dipped.

"There's the K-Chaan ship," the pilot said.

The enemy vessel sat close to the centre of a dusky red and barren plateau surrounded by nubby hills worn down by millennia of sandstorms, the only weather the planet knew. The vessel was starfish-shaped, a much smaller version of the K-Chaan Annihilator Class ships currently hovering above the planet as part of their escort.

The Earthforce shuttle traversed the plateau, banking round the pavilion and turning to land so the structure was between it and the K-Chaan vessel. The landing skids settled gently and the pilot cut the engines, then spun again in his chair.

"*Lincoln* reports the feeds show three K-Chaan in the pavilion. Nothing hidden and no weapons."

The consul stood, exhaling loudly. "Then let's do what we came here for."

Volmar exited the shuttle behind Antwer and Ellan and walked with them across the rocky red plain. The shuttle hissed, reconfiguring its hull plates into a protective skirt around the landing skids and hatch.

Volmar saw three figures standing under the broad hexagonal roof of the pavilion, watching them approach. The K-Chaan were borderline humanoid: bipedal and three metres tall, their bodies all corded muscle beneath a thick, deep blue and mottled black hide. They wore partial armour, almost indistinguishable from their skin, and their heads were dominated by a curving tusk or horn sprouting from where a nose might have been. Their faces were blank, except for a band of mottling at the base of the horn that indicated sensory organs. Volmar thought it was impossible to tell any of them apart.

He placed Ellan's case on the circular plascrete meeting table and stood to the consul's other side. Ellan opened the case slowly – to avoid startling the K-Chaan – and activated the translator instruments. She nodded to her husband.

"I am Consul Antwer of the Earth Government," Antwer began. "This is my aide, Troels Volmar, and our translator link operator, Ellan Summers. I welcome you to this meeting. Can I confirm the translation device is functioning and adequate for understanding?"

Antwer may as well not have spoken. The K-Chaan stood together like statues.

The consul looked at his wife. She checked the equipment, running a practised hand over the contacts and tabs. "It's working perfectly," she said.

"Can you understand me?" Antwer asked the K-Chaan.

Again, no response.

Volmar studied the three figures. They didn't need weapons. Any one of them could rip a human in half with its bare hands.

Antwer tried again. "Please. We must communicate. Can you confirm our translator is working?"

The silence drew out.

"There's nothing wrong with the equipment." Ellan sounded frustrated.

"Perhaps we should send for another unit, just in case," Antwer said.

"I checked it a hundred times. It's *not* the machine."

"I'm afraid this is down to me," Volmar said. "I'm blocking the translator."

The disc he pulled from his pocket everted at his touch, the metal flowing to regain its memoryform. He levelled the weapon's barrel at the nearest K-Chaan even as Antwer grabbed for his arm. A bolt of incandescent energy lashed out, punching through the K-Chaan's chest. It dropped to the floor. The two other aliens drew weapons from their armour.

So much for the scans, Volmar thought as he grasped Antwer by the shoulders, pivoting to put the consul between him and the K-Chaan. There was a shriek. A searing wave of heat. The consul's head exploded, blood, brains and bone fragments spraying across Volmar as the dead weight of the body slammed into him and he fell.

In the sudden silence, he pushed Antwer's corpse off him and rolled to the side, coming up on all fours. Ellan crouched beneath the table, a look of horror on her face as she stared at Volmar.

"I'm sorry," he said and pushed off the floor.

Another heat blast hit a pillar as he ran and a rock fragment sliced deep across his cheek. The ceiling slumped dangerously but he didn't stop and he didn't look back.

He was outside, his lungs on fire in the thin air. The shuttle was powering up, the hull plates sliding away from the ramp. There was no cover and the K-Chaan could fire again at any moment.

Volmar fell through the hatch, covered in blood and dust. The pilot stared at him.

"Go!" Volmar shouted.

"What about the consul? His wife?"

"They're dead. The K-Chaan killed them."

The pilot hesitated. Through the hatch, Volmar could see movement in the ruined pavilion. A slab of plascrete fell to the ground and a K-Chaan rose out of the debris.

"Go. Now!"

The hatch closed and Volmar got to his seat.

The view forward bucked as the pilot engaged emergency engines, the landscape slewing around at a sickening angle as they gained altitude. Above the planet, the sky was on fire.

TWENTY YEARS LATER

1

"You're not worried about us being seen together?" I asked.

Emba paused, a still-live worm skewered on his claw halfway to his mouth. Then he sucked at the worm's tail and swallowed it whole.

"I have no reason to be," he said, the voder translating his growls and barks instantly. "But you are."

He was trying to put me off balance by choosing such a public space to dine together. It was working. I didn't like being toyed with.

"You know the risks Hierarch Czerag took sending me here."

Emba laid down the thin hook he was using to pry the worms from their coral tubes. "My only motivation is a love of good food. And this is the best restaurant under the dome. With the best views."

The room was nestled high up against the sloping crystal wall of Elysem and I could see beyond the strengthened crust plate the city sat on to the dull red planet-spanning ocean of lava bubbling and popping in glutinous slow motion. Plumes of molten rock erupted in the distance, and further out the manufactories, their hulls built completely of fabricated tekla, skimmed off the mineral wealth that floated to the surface of this tortured world.

"Besides, the clientele here is select and very discreet," Emba continued. "News of our meeting will not find its way back to your Homeworld."

It was true I wasn't the only non-Telsan in the room. And the diners seemed singularly uninterested in Ambassador Emba and his guest. Perhaps he did this all the time. But I knew he still wanted me at a disadvantage. Emba was a senior ambassador in the xeno trade and relations branch of the Telsan government and I was a messenger from Hierarch Czerag here to make a deal. In secret.

I held a woody vegetable in my mandible, tasting the sweetness of its bark while my feeder claws picked at its bitter innards. This whole journey had been one of contrasts, and now I was experiencing another: anxiety at the public nature of our meeting and the negotiations to come, and fresh exhilaration at being away from the Kresz worldmind and experiencing everything here, even the bad, solely for myself.

Emba was in no hurry to get to business. After the first course, there was a smoky broth that bubbled as we ate. It tasted like dirt, but I finished it all the same. I was determined to eat everything and show the ambassador I was happy to wait as long as he was. Longer even.

The next course was more of a challenge. It was live again, but more so: a long creature, with a dark spine-covered skin and five legs. It was served in a high-sided bowl, its legs skittering at the slippery sides as it tried to escape. Emba skewered the beast expertly with a sharp pick and pulled off its legs and crunched them between his teeth as the creature writhed around. I preferred to rip its head off and deal with it in less ambulatory fashion.

Finally Emba pushed back his plate and dabbed at his hairy muzzle with the square of cloth lying beside his glass. "And so to business," he said. He raised a paw and his grey-furred aide, who had escorted me here, joined us at the table, a thin square device clutched in its clawed paw.

"Here?" I said.

"Under ambassadorial seal, of course."

The aide tapped at the device and a force wall surrounded us. I could see the washed-out colours of the room beyond, but the dull murmur of other conversations was gone.

Emba was looking at me with his small dark brown eyes. "You start."

Here it was then. My chance to change my life completely.

"Your industries have an inexhaustible hunger for tekla and my hierarch has an inexhaustible supply," I said. "The highest quality, which we can provide at a price below the tariff you pay through our Merchants Lodge."

Emba raised a claw. "Yes, yes. The sample you provided is very pure. I'm sure you vouch it a fair representation of what you have to offer, but what happens when the lodge finds out about this? They'll cut off trade with us."

"The only commodity you buy from Homeworld is tekla. You'll have no further need for them."

Emba crinkled his snout, showing sharp incisors. "It's still a risk for us. If your supply dries up. If the quality falters. If your hierarch changes his mind because of … pressure brought to bear by the lodge, what then?"

There was truth in what he said. But it wasn't the lodge that posed danger for Hierarch Czerag; it was Hierarch Kergis. He controlled the Merchants despite the supposed separation of house and lodge and had grown rich and powerful as a result. The only way my hierarch could get a bigger share of trade profits was to go outside the existing arrangements and set up our own house's parallel agreements. If Czerag was successful, it could blow the house/lodge system wide apart. But if he was discovered before he could demonstrate to the other hierarchs that direct trade was not just possible but an attractive proposition … well, at best we'd be squeezed by Kergis and the Merchants to stop trading immediately. At worst, our house might need a new hierarch, no matter the natural and ethical barriers to assassination.

Emba took the device from his aide and tapped at the screen. He handed it to me. "For all these considerations, we think this is a reasonable price for a standard podule load."

I looked at the figure. It was low.

"My hierarch's word is unbreakable. And it's worth more than that." My feeder claws stretched wide and I tapped in a considerably higher counter offer, then handed back the screen.

Emba looked at the figure, then scrutinised me. "That's *not* a reasonable price."

"It is reasonable. And a lot less than you're paying now."

He laid the device on the table, took up his glass and drank, watching me over the rim. "If I were a Kresz, I'd know if you thought it was a good price, wouldn't I?"

"We're empaths, Ambassador. We sense feelings. You might feel that I was nervous and – given the context – infer I was lying. But it's not telepathy."

But I *was* lying. Czerag had said I could go lower. The truth was I didn't want to. Partly because I wanted to make the best deal I could, to prove I was worth more out here than hidden away in a dusty records hall. But I was also lying because I could. I wasn't surrounded by empaths, and that was liberating. At home, that feeling would mark me as a deviant. Here it was my strength.

"I suppose we could pay a little more, but not what you're asking," Emba said.

"I'm not authorised to go lower." The lie thrilled me again. "That's the deal. And at that price, the only risk you run is to become embarrassingly rich."

Emba rubbed the end of his muzzle and glanced at his aide.

"Let's make the agreement," I said.

Emba slapped the crystal table. "Hah." He turned to his aide. "Confirm the trade."

The other Telsan ran its paw over the device then held it out to me. I made a show of checking the figure was still the same, then I pressed the end of one claw against the port. The screen was passed to Emba, who looked over it, paused, looked at me, then flashed his teeth again and added his genetic imprint.

"Your Merchants Lodge is going to be furious when they discover Czerag's cut them out."

"Nothing for you to worry about. We have it under control."

Another lie. Delivery would be difficult. Ensuring my own

departure from Homeworld was undetected had presented enough problems. Not even Czerag could conceal a large off-world shipment of tekla with no lodge certification. Kergis would be alerted immediately, and he had strong links with the Defenders Lodge as well. But if Czerag had a plan to ensure delivery and keep Kergis occupied, he hadn't shared it with me. It was the way of all house hierarchs to keep that kind of information compartmentalised.

"A deal this big calls for a celebration," Emba said as the privacy screen around us fell away. He waved a paw and one of the wait staff came close. "Arga. Bring the bottle. And two glasses." He looked at his aide. "You can file those, Gratch. I won't need you any more this evening."

My feeders opened wide again and I felt my whole body relax. I'd done it. Czerag would see how useful it could be to have a Kresz off-planet.

The single sun of Telsus IV was sinking to the horizon now and the glow from the lava ocean reflected off the chairs and tables, the crystal jugs and glasses, and turned the red of my exoskeleton black.

One of the wait staff brought the liquor Emba had ordered.

"I like you, Udun," Emba said, pouring a glass and handing it to me. "You're much friendlier than the few other Kresz I've met. They're as hard to get to know as the shell they're wrapped in."

"Kresz prefer to deal purely with their own kind," I said. "By and large they see interaction with aliens as a necessary evil. And it's the same with any travel that takes them away from the worldmind."

"But you're not like that."

I replaced my glass on the table. "When I was very young, I was always running off from the escarpment to find out what was beyond the next dune. The grown-ups would catch me, bring me back and scold me. The proper place for a Kresz was in his house, they'd say. But it didn't stop me. Finally they locked me in the records hall during the day and set me to work helping the old Scholar there. They thought it was a punishment and that I'd grow out of my unKreszlike behaviour. But in among the catalogues I found documents and images that taught me about all the strange worlds spinning around the nearby stars of the Lenticular, and the even stranger beings that inhabited them. The more I learned, the more I wanted to experience them for myself. And the more the others saw that as a rejection of their way of life. In time, they came to resent me for it. With few exceptions, they still do." My mandibles stretched open. "I never thought I'd get the chance to leave Homeworld, and now …"

"Now?"

"Now I'm here, I don't think I'd ever go home if I had the choice."

Emba grunted. "I understand duty. But if you come back this way, my home is yours."

He refilled my glass and I took another sip. The arga was sweet, sticky and left a pleasant buzz.

"Even if I told you I'd have accepted a lower price if you'd held out?"

Emba drained his glass and slammed it down on the table. "Especially then!"

There was a bright flare through the window and Emba turned to look, then raised his paw to beckon someone, a creature I'd never seen before. Its head was oddly shaped, the brow ridge tapering and extending up and forward in an arc, mirrored by another bony projection below the mouth slit. The light shattered across its iridescent skin but its eyes were pure black.

It saw Emba and walked stiffly over, one of its legs refusing to bend. There were burn scars at its neck and running across what I could see of its chest through the opening of the tunic it wore. It took the empty seat at our table, breath whistling through oblique flaps cut into its cheeks.

"Udun, this is Atalna," Emba said. "Another friend from afar."

The black eyes regarded me. "You're a Kresz. I've never seen one in the flesh. Or shell I should say."

"And I've never met anyone that looks like you." The arga

pushed my curiosity past my usual reserve.

"That's because I come from somewhere far beyond your local Lenticular Space."

One of the wait staff brought another glass and Emba filled it. "Atalna, a drink. We're celebrating."

Atalna took the glass and raised it. "Celebrations are few and far between. We must cherish them."

Emba's aide appeared and bent low beside the ambassador, muttering something I couldn't catch.

"Consul Lintal," Emba said. "Now?"

Atalna shifted in his seat and I noticed the skin on the leg he favoured was brittle and cracked. His past seemed written painfully across his body and I looked away. On Homeworld, someone with such extensive injuries would be euthanised. My culture had decided long ago they had no need of medicine. The sick got better or died. It was the will of Sakat.

Emba stood. "I'm sorry. An ambassador is never off duty it seems. Please enjoy yourselves. Udun, I'll see you tomorrow at the spaceport." And he hurried away, his aide scurrying to keep up.

Atalna reached for the bottle. The movement wasn't easy for him and I imagined scorched skin protesting at the motion. He poured more arga for me and for himself, and took a sip, relaxing back into the seat.

"It's peaceful here," he said.

"Emba has been a very gracious host."

"We all deserve a little kindness." His black eyes focused on me. "There's far too much of the opposite in the galaxy. I think you've experienced some of that."

"Why do you say that?"

The slits on the side of his cheeks whistled, sending the light running across the mosaic scales of his face. "I may be a guest in the Lenticular, but I know enough to see how unusual you are – a lone, wandering Kresz. You're different, and people who are different are not always welcomed by those who consider themselves 'normal'."

"I know something about being misunderstood and facing the judgement of those doing the misunderstanding," I said.

"And yet here you are, out amongst the stars, and there they sit, huddled in their ignorance, never lifting their eyes above the horizon." It was as if he could read my thoughts. "To be normal is to be complacent. What you have is a gift."

"It doesn't feel like that. Mostly people at home are suspicious of me."

"But I'm not talking about the perceptions of others. Your presence here proves you are special. It means you see things that others of your kind don't. You think thoughts they never could. Hold onto that. It's what will keep you safe."

"Safe?" This conversation seemed to vibrate with some resonance for him, something I was missing. Again, I wondered about his past.

"Emba would say I'm scaremongering again. But he hasn't experienced what I have." He put his glass down. "You've seen the marks on my body. They were inflicted by my own people. Better they had taken my life. It would have left me easily enough."

I felt the skin tighten around my skull plate. The room was suddenly less comfortable. Less safe.

"Where do you come from?" I asked, my voice barely a whisper.

"In another life I was Atalna, prime minister of Betlaan. You wouldn't have heard of that world. I fled many light years before Emba took me in."

"Why?" I said. "I mean why did your people hurt you?"

He looked around, but we were quite alone. Still his voice dropped almost to a whisper. "Betlaan was a good world. We had our cities and our parklands. We had our devotions. One day we were contacted by a federation of worlds called the Hegemony. We knew of them, of course. They control an area of space out towards the rim, but we'd had no dealings with them. They sent a vessel to our world. We greeted them, set up diplomatic relations and welcomed their embassy – just one of their diplomats and a small staff. Life went on as normal.

"Then, six months later, a new political party arose. They spread many lies about the government, saying we were hoarding the planet's wealth for the elite and mismanaging what little we allowed to flow into services for the general population. The party didn't receive much support though it was well-funded. Elections were held and the government was returned, but a few days later there was a revolt – a thing unheard of on Betlaan. This same group, but with many, strange weapons, seized the parliament and the cabinet fled into hiding. An interim cabinet was appointed by the rebels, entirely unlawfully, and requested aid from the Hegemony embassy to quell further 'civil disorder'. The Hegemony ships and soldiers arrived mere hours later, putting any who questioned their presence to the atom blast," Atalna said bitterly. "And they have been there ever since. I was lucky to escape our world with my life. Others were not so lucky."

"So you believe this Hegemony orchestrated events?" I asked.

"I know it. I have evidence. Tri-D pictures of meetings held between members of the new party and the Hegemony diplomat before the elections. Much good that it does me now. The Hegemony has our world in its grasp, and nothing will loosen its fingers."

"But you're here now. You're safe."

He straightened in his seat. "I am not safe. None of us are. I have seen the Hegemony's ships lay waste to innocents, seen my own people turned into sadistic murderers. Since then I've made a study of the Hegemony, as much as I can. They move secretly wherever possible. They stay strong by driving outwards and sweeping aside all who might challenge them. They will never stop. And no others I have met possess their single-minded ruthlessness. Eventually, even this part of space will belong to them.

"That's the reason I survived, to spread the warning. The Hegemony always come in friendship, one hand extended but the other clutching a weapon behind their back. Now you know about them, Udun. And because you are different, because you are not complacent, I hope the knowledge will save your life one day."

Atalna sat back in his seat, watching me, and I became aware again of the conversations of others around us. I felt like I was emerging from a sharing. Or perhaps a nightmare.

"Tell me more about the Hegemony," I said.

2

"He told you his tale then?" Emba said. "I'm sorry. If I hadn't been called away I could have spared you the detail. He tells everyone he can. But Betlaan is so far away it's hard to really know what happened there."

"Are you questioning his story?" I asked.

It was early the next morning and Emba and I stood together in a private room in the government section of the spaceport, a building well away from the civil and commercial halls. Through the bubble window the landscape was dark and smouldering, with only a hint of the coming sunrise far out, through thick cloud.

Emba rocked back on his stout legs, the fur on his chest sticking out. "No, but you've seen his scars. An experience like that, it colours a person's whole view on life. He'd latch onto you if you let him. You'd be reliving war stories for cycles."

"Fortunate for me I'm going home then."

Emba grunted. "I'm not an empath, but even I can tell you don't mean that. Is it really so bad there?"

My delicate feeder claws stretched wide. "Now I've experienced what it's like out here, it's worse."

It wasn't just the thought of returning to a place where my sense of self was sometimes hard to separate from the opinions of others. Telsus IV was a wondrous contrast of technologically advanced luxury and harshly beautiful landscapes and being here was beyond anything I'd imagined when I dreamt of travelling to other worlds. But I didn't want to stop here. I wanted to see Telsus

Prime, and the moons round the methane worlds of Svesta, even the radioactive landscapes of Jantri'va if I could arrange entry. There was so much to see in the Lenticular, I could spend a lifetime just travelling. Instead I was going home.

"Well, I'm sorry," Emba said. "It's not good to feel out of place in your home."

I felt embarrassed receiving kindness from this alien who was still a stranger to me. My problems weren't his.

"I still need the details for the shipment," I said. "Location, timings, code channels …"

"Yes, and that's not something your hierarch would like to fall into the wrong hands. We must protect all our interests in this."

He walked to a table near the window and pressed a control stud. The door opened and an even shorter Telsan entered, silver-haired and carrying a small pouch. The door closed behind him as he crossed to the table and placed the pouch on the surface, then pulled out a metal instrument with a pistol grip and a thick, cylindrical body topped with a tapering tube as long as a clawspan.

"What's that?" I asked.

"The information," Emba said. "We're going to put it in your blood. Or what passes for blood in your physiology. It's a coded genetic sequence. Inert but persistent. When we know you're safely back on Homeworld, we'll communicate the structure of a particular chemical to your hierarch. That chemical, applied to a sample of your blood, will cause the sequence to express the information, decoding the data it holds."

I looked at the other Telsan holding the tube end of the device towards me. "It's safe?"

"For you personally, yes. And it's the safest way we've found to deliver the necessary information. We've used it a few times before. Mainly to circumvent our neighbours, the Svestans. It hasn't been discovered."

"All right. Then where …?"

"Somewhere in your chest," Emba said.

I kneeled in front of the small Telsan and pulled at my left pectoral plate, clearing it below the neck guard to show the hide underneath. The Telsan placed the end of the tube there. I heard a hiss and felt warmth spreading beneath my skin, but nothing else.

"There," Emba said. "It's done. Time to go home."

I stood again and we walked together into the embarkation area. The hall was completely empty.

"I had the facility cleared of non-essential personnel," Emba said. "We want this venture to be successful as much as you do."

A Telsan freighter hunkered low on the glassy apron of the spaceport field. It was covered in articulated tekla that could be reconfigured to adapt the cargo space inside to different loads. The main bulk spread up and back from the control deck in a curved hump. Both turbines were already spinning, shredding the smoky atmosphere, and the control surfaces on the rear ventrals moved with quick, insect-like flicks. The ship lock stood open for me at the end of a pressurised gantry.

"I hope to see you again, Udun. I hope you get what you want." Emba extended one paw and brushed it over the metacarpal guard above my right claws.

"Thank you. Remember me to Atalna. Tell him I hope he finds peace."

"I will. And I'll keep him safe. You have no need to worry about him."

I walked down the gantry, my hoof plates clicking on the hard decking, and entered the airlock, cycling through. On the other side, the corridor was cramped and open cabling hung from the roof, not low enough to hinder the crew member waiting to show me to my cabin, but I had to walk bent over in a shuffling gait, scraping along the metal decking and scratching my shin plates as I went. The cabin was equally confined and even though the acceleration couch was large by Telsan standards, it was a tight fit for me and the strapping barely stretched across my shell.

When I was secured, the Telsan left and I watched the smoky

atmosphere through the cabin's small port as the turbine noise grew. The ship angled, balancing now on thrusters, and began to rise, accelerating away into the brown and yellow clouds above. A jump in the turbine noise and we were going faster still, the force pushing down on me like the weight of my old life reasserting itself.

I'd go home, subject myself to everything that meant and deliver the information I carried. I'd promised that much. And in return, Czerag had promised I could leave again. That was the only thing that sustained me now.

∞

The agony of transit shocked me awake and my arm spasmed with the pain, ripping free of the couch strapping. A Telsan flight-tech was in the cabin with me. He looked wide-eyed at the broken strap, then fixed his gaze on me as if I were about to attack.

"Where are we?" I asked.

I could see through the port we were in realspace, but far out-system because djel, sura and ataz, the suns of Homeworld, were almost lost in the background of stars.

"The captain got a message to transit here instead of the Point," the Telsan said.

"Who from?" I unfastened the remaining strapping and pushed up to a sitting position.

The Telsan flashed pointed teeth. But before he could speak, the captain's voice came over the intra-ship. "Hey, Kresz. Come to the control deck. We have company."

I stood, wide awake now. My knee joints protested as I crouched in the low cabin. Had Czerag's plan been discovered?

I followed the Telsan down the cramped corridor and onto the control deck, where I could stand properly. The captain grunted at me and pointed through the curved port at an approaching ship. I'd expected a Defender Lodge striker or maybe even a battlecruiser, but this was a mining tug. The hull was rugged and angular, a squat, ugly expression of brute strength with massive double turbines hanging from the front and equally large reaction tubes running along either side. Behind it, in tow, was a mountain of ice, studded with rock. It was coming too close.

"Tell them to stop," I said. "Don't let them come any nearer."

"Open a channel," the captain said.

"No vision. Sound only," I added, but it was too late. The tug came within range and I felt the unmistakable presence of other Kresz. An ar'tet, the smallest functional group for off-world operations. They knew I was here too. I felt the sudden recognition, and then confusion when they realised only a single Kresz consciousness was on board.

A voice speaking in Kresz came over the channel. "Telsan ship. I am Bvak. I'm here to transfer your cargo."

This didn't make any sense.

"I'm near enough to your hull, so let's not play games," Bvak said. "Even close beam transmissions like this can be monitored. I'm following my orders, cargo. And you should too." He cut the transmission.

"What do you want to do, Kresz?" the captain said. "I'm not starting a war."

I didn't feel any immediate hostility from the minds in the other ship. But the strong feeling of confusion persisted. They hadn't expected to find me here. I walked closer to the port, trying to go deeper and get a true sense of what was happening on board. The strongest presence, possibly the one who spoke – Bvak – he felt … annoyed more than anything else.

The captain watched me, waiting. If anyone other than Czerag had found out I was here, they'd have sent more than a mining tug. And those on board would have known what to expect. This felt more like Czerag's doing, which meant something had changed on Homeworld.

"Signal Bvak to come alongside for cargo transfer," I said. "I think your voyage is over, Captain."

A ring of jets flared briefly from the other ship as it disengaged from its ice mountain for close manoeuvres.

I made my way back along the corridor to my cabin and grabbed my travel pouch, then retraced my steps to the lock. The inner door was open and through the port in the external hatch I saw the mining tug turn, halt and then move closer.

The floor shook as the docking ring engaged. The Telsan captain was still on his control deck and no one had followed me down. No doubt they'd be glad to get back to Telsus ahead of time. If Emba's deal fell through it was no great loss to them.

The lock closed behind me and even before the outer hatch opened I felt the common sending that meant both "well met" and "farewell".

A Kresz stood in the other lock, waiting for me. He was the same body type as me but his plates were a deeper red, and he was dressed in flight skins with the bronze square in a clasp at his neck. An Adept pilot then. And from my own house judging by the length of brown cloth woven through the flight-skin strapping at his neck guard, but I didn't recognise him. Still I didn't feel threatened.

The annoyance I'd sensed was washed away by renewed astonishment as the evidence of his eyes confirmed I was completely alone.

"I'm Bvak," he said. "I'm here to take you home."

"Why should I come with you?" I asked and felt his annoyance flare again.

"You could stay with the Telsans, but you already know that's a bad idea. Otherwise why would I have been sent?"

Still I didn't move. I wanted to understand why he was here, but it was possible he didn't know either.

"Are you working for the house or the lodge?" I asked.

"Does it matter?"

"My shell's hard enough, you know. And I don't like people who trade questions with more questions."

He'd have felt my anger in those words but I sensed only amusement from him.

"You've a suspicious nature," he said. "Good. Nurture it. But we all do what we're told. Your shell's hard enough to understand *that*, I hope. Come or don't. It's up to you. If you won't, I can get back to my mining."

I walked into Bvak's lock and the hatch sealed behind me. The inner door swung aside and I followed him into the ship. It was old but built to Kresz dimensions at least.

"I'm Udun," I said.

"I'm sure I shouldn't know that," Bvak said. He stopped and turned. "One look at you and I can tell I won't be getting back to mining anytime soon. I shouldn't ask, but I'm going to anyway. How is it you've been on that ship by yourself?"

I sensed the same suspicions I'd endured most of my life welling up in him. I was more sick of it now than I'd ever been before. I'd borne the opinions of other Kresz because I'd accepted they were right about me. But things were different now. I'd been out amongst others who took me at face value and I'd been successful in my mission, so far at least. Why should I accept less from my own kind?

"I'm different," I said.

He blinked slowly, tasting my anger. "That you are. Come aft. There's no need for the rest of the crew to see you."

I followed him to the end of the dim corridor, into a narrower one and up a flight of steps into a broad mess room, then through that to another corridor and finally a small cabin with a single sling that looked far more comfortable than the Telsan couch I'd endured.

I sat up into the sling and Bvak leaned against the wall, watching me.

"Why are you here?" I said.

"I told you. Orders." The breath hissed through his spiracles. "We've been out here mining for the best part of two cycles, when an outbound prospector comes alongside, invites himself onboard and tells us to come to these coordinates to pick up some cargo and deliver it directly to Czerag without any outside interference. So, we drop everything because that's what the hierarch wants. Only when we get up close to the Telsans, we realise the cargo is not what we expected."

He was deeply puzzled. I could feel it. He was as much a puppet of Czerag's will as I was. And he wasn't happy about it either.

"You could ask me what *I'm* doing out here," I said.

His feeder claws stretched wide. "Now you're just being cruel."

That much was true. Only the hierarch and his closest advisors were allowed to see the whole picture. Everyone else knew only what they were told and didn't ask questions. It wasn't often I was in a position to know more than another member of my house. But I still didn't know why my return trip had been interrupted.

"Has anything happened on Homeworld?" I asked.

"I told you, we've been in the outer system for two cycles."

The thrusters started up and I was pushed gently back into the sling. We were accelerating. Presumably the Telsans were already gone.

"How long till we make planetfall?" I asked. This ship looked considerably slower than the Telsan craft.

"Five days," Bvak said. "We could go quicker, but that would look unusual."

Five days stuck on a ship with a group of Kresz who didn't have much to think about except the stranger they'd picked up. A Kresz that was obviously odd and not to be trusted. There was no way I could block those feelings out for the duration. But it was only a taste of how it would be in the escarpment. Distrust bred fear and suspicion. It was all depressingly familiar. I was trapped in a feedback loop from which there was no escape, and I was headed back to a planet full of Kresz who couldn't help but react the same way to me. I'd accepted it before, but I couldn't now.

I should have forgotten my mission and stayed with Emba. But Czerag had given me this chance and I felt that debt. It made me angry at him and angry at myself. But it was anger without purpose. It wouldn't change anything.

3

Rhees feathered the throttle on the Typhoon ramcraft to hold formation. Petar was visible through the canopy to starboard. Jute flanked her port nacelle. The tac display spread over her forward view showed the rest of the force in textbook formation, a tight pyramid, the apex pointing towards the trailing Trojan moon on the dark side of the ring.

Comms chatter was hushed and sporadic. Everyone was keyed up, looking for signs of the opposition force, wanting to get the first shot. Well, they could have it. It was all very well being the first. But Rhees planned on being the best. Ace this last training flight and she'd have her pick of postings, and she could insist Petar come along with her.

The chat spiked and the flight commander spoke up, silencing the others. "Settle! We have them."

It was faint on tac – the barest of contacts – but there was definite movement near the Trojan. The moon was big enough to conceal a fair few ships; the Typhoons were barely twice as long and wide as the gee capsule that held Rhees rigid. Of course, it could be a trick.

"Gamma Wing," the commander said, and Rhees caught her breath. "Peel off and do your thing. I want to see some real damage out there."

"Aye, sir," Rhees said.

Petar gave a thumbs-up through the bubble and Rhees punched for full thrust, turning tight and leaving the formation far below, with Petar and Jute trailing her all the way. They flew up out of the orbital plane, looping over and away from the Trojan moon, and then diving towards Neptune.

Petar was keeping close watch on the tac feed from the main force. "Definitely contact," he said. "Showing a sizeable force. Pretty much all of them. Looks like they want to make a stand. Very old school."

"Very stupid," Jute said.

"Wouldn't count on it," Rhees said. "They want to win as much as we do."

They were tracking down to the ring, but significantly behind the main force now. Rhees wanted to go further, brush the cloud deck and shake any contact the enemy tac might still have on them. She wanted them to be ghosts.

They passed beneath the twisted ring and paced for a hundred or so klicks, skimming atmosphere.

"Lost contact," Petar said.

"Which means we're gone too," Rhees said.

"So how much damage do you want to do?" Petar asked.

"All of it," Rhees said.

"Leave some for us," Jute said. "It's rude not to share."

Rhees kicked the thruster up another notch. The craft shot forward.

"Partial," Petar said.

"Got nothing but the main force. What's your calibration?" Jute asked.

"Closer than you're looking," Petar said.

Rhees accepted a feed from Petar's ship. Pattern was degraded this close to the magnetosphere, but it looked right. Six singleships, bogies for sure. She pulled back almost to coasting. Sons of fuckers ... They were stationary. Buried in the ring.

She switched to sector view. Their group was still moving in pyramid formation, more than halfway to the moon now and closing. These bogies were well behind the action. Their intention was clear. Wait until main engagement and then swoop down behind and start picking off ships. The formation would break up, trying to cover two fronts at once, and the bogies would win.

"They haven't seen us, I'm sure of it," Petar said. "If we wait till they break and start their run we can come in behind. We'll be covered in glory."

"If we wait," Rhees said, "they'll be in open space and there's six of them."

"So?" Petar said.

"If we go in after them we'll still have the element of surprise. More so, and they won't be able to manoeuvre."

"I don't think –" Jute began.

"What?" Rhees said.

"It's risky. We won't have room to manoeuvre either," Jute finished.

"Yeah, well, we won't need room. We're the better pilots."

"C'mon, Jute," Petar said. "We can do this. The bigger the risk, the bigger the party afterwards. Those guys won't know what hit them."

"Form up on me," Rhees said, already plotting an insertion. "And heat up your cannons."

Neptune's ring – more like a twisted necklace – was skinny compared to Saturn's, and packed with icy debris. But it was stable and the comp could handle it. The cannons were primed with hollow alloy pellets for the training run, not deuterium, but they still vibrated the gee capsule as they powered up. The shots would be enough to rattle the ramcraft, and onboard comps would tally damage, deactivating "dead" bogies.

Tac showed countdown to commit. She flicked the abort option aside.

"We're gonna be heroes," Petar said.

The counter reached zero. Even through the gee capsule she felt the push of maximum burn as the ramcraft leaped up and twisted together into the transient gaps in the ring. The hull rang with minuscule hits, dust-sized debris creating a rainfall of impacts. Larger rocks speed-blurred past the canopy.

The bogies showed red, centre screen and closing. Holding position.

Petar and Jute pulled close in the tight space, noses to Rhees's nacelle tips. One klick and closing.

The ships veered as one, missing larger debris as microwave processors continued to plot the optimal path. Five hundred metres.

"Weapons hot!" Rhees said.

Still no visual. Space ahead was too crowded. Should be something soon.

Another dip. A twist. The debris cleared. Bogies dead ahead. But facing them. They must have turned. Massed cannons.

Pellets peppered her hull. Not enough for real damage, but the sudden barrage tipped her. A shriek of tortured metal from starboard. The nacelle.

She looked through the canopy. Saw Petar staring at her. Shock on his face. His ship veered. Hit rock. Spun.

Her own ship registered the final hit that deactivated her engines. Safeties kicked in to keep her stable.

Petar was still spinning. Then he ran out of room. Silent flash. Ramcraft breaking up and the gee capsule smacked down. Straight into a big rock.

Dead eyes stared at her through a broken faceplate.

Rhees screamed and sat bolt upright in bed.

The sheets wound around her were slick with sweat. She cradled her head in her hands, breathing heavily. "Fuck," she rasped.

Her breathing slowed, but that didn't ease the pain in her chest. Petar was dead. She should be in jail. She would be if her father wasn't an admiral, hadn't interceded even as he made it clear how disappointed he was in her.

She took a long shuddering breath and wiped the sweat-slicked hair from her forehead. The image floating above the holodisc on the bedside table showed her and Petar, hugging, laughing, alive.

She went to the head and washed her face in the basin, cinched her blonde hair back. In the mirror, her eyes showed dark rings beneath. She and Petar had been on the fast track. Good career ahead of them; everything starting to make sense. All over in the blink of an eye and nothing made sense to her now. Her life was playing out around her and she didn't have the power to change it.

Today was the first day of the "new start" her father had brokered for her. The past was to be laid to rest. No chance of that. But she had to do one thing before she at least tried to move on.

Throwing on a fresh skivvy, she walked back into the main room – the only room – and sat on the couch, pulling her legs up off the floor.

"Open call," she said.

A holo dilated at eye level and she selected the call-matrix on her wristband. It was a sequence she hadn't used since Petar had given it to her three years ago for "just in case".

Lines of numbers rolled across the holo as the comps searched Voss Space comms connections for the unique codestring. He might be unavailable and that would be fine. She would know that she'd tried.

There was a flash. The screen blanked again, then the number scroll continued. She waited.

The Hegemony Diplomatic Corps badge – the infinity symbol – faded in. A light blinked in the corner of the image. There was no location ident. It could have been anywhere in Hegemony space. A man sat in a darkened room looking sleep weary. It was Petar's face: the same sharp nose, strong dimpled chin. But the hair was straight, not curly. And the eyes were different, older. Denev, Petar's brother. He looked as shocked as Rhees felt.

"Rhees …" he said, but seemed unsure what to say next.

"Denev. I'm sorry to disturb you. I … I've been meaning to call. Since … I'm sorry I haven't. Been too much of a coward."

Denev's dark eyes were fixed on her. She wished he'd look away.

"I just wanted to say ..." Her throat felt like it was closing up. She pushed on. "I can't tell you how sorry I am about Petar. What happened. It was my fault. I killed him."

She stopped. It was done.

"I know," Denev said.

She tried to see the emotion behind his words, but his face was unreadable.

"I always tried to keep him safe," he said softly. "You put him in harm's way and now he's gone."

"You must hate me," she said.

"At least you know what you've done. At least you admit it to yourself."

The holo blanked.

She felt empty inside. Sixty-seven days since Petar died. She'd been back on Earth for eight of those. And every night was the same.

She pulled off the skivvy and climbed into the shower booth. The water was tepid but it washed away her tears.

Back in the main room, she opened her wardrobe and hesitated. Did she really want to do this? She dismissed the thought. She should wear the patterned onepiece, but she'd never felt comfortable in civilian clothes. She'd be Fleet right up until she was HDC. There was nothing in-between. She took out her dress uniform pants and jacket and dressed quickly.

Her apartment was on the 916th floor of a building in the Twenty Thousand Block. The buildings this far out from the centre grew close together and the blue sky, peppered with flyers, was shrunk to a thin ribbon directly overhead. As she stood on the smooth plascrete outside her building, people passed her by as if she were barely there – a ghost. She needed to prove that she still existed. That after Neptune, she wasn't broken.

She stepped onto the band that looped up from the entranceway to her building, and skipped through a series of accel strips onto the main slidewalk that carved its way through the apartment block canyon. The strip was close to empty this early and she walked along the fastest band, quickly leaving the residential sector behind.

The sky above widened through the business sector and finally opened up above Vigilance Plaza, which was lined with faceless, low-rise buildings that led to the Hegemony Diplomatic Corps Datahive: an unbroken grey egg supported on a single oblique column of plasteel.

Rhees positioned herself for the next split, then took the slidewalk down, stepping quickly onto the decel strips until she disembarked at ground level and the entrance to the Datahive. She pulled at her uniform jacket to straighten out the wrinkles, took a last look at the cloudless sky, and walked into the reception area.

A single slab of obsidian formed a desk running the full length of the foyer. Just as large and floating above it near the ceiling was a silver infinity symbol. The shape shifted as she approached the desk, looking from this angle like a moebius strip – two dimensions twisted into a third – and then a snake swallowing its own tail.

The young man behind the desk wore a standard Diplomatic Corps onepiece, black and nondescript except for the same infinity symbol embroidered above the left breast. He was concentrating on the obsidian surface and Rhees knew she was being subjected to a broad spectrum of security scans. Finally he looked up at her, taking in her uniform, the brass clasp on the jacket and the broken threads circling a darker patch of blue cloth on her upper arm, where her squadron badge had been.

"Rhees Lowrans," she said. "I have an appointment."

"Come this way, please."

She followed him into a waiting elevator, but instead of going up, they went a long way down.

The doors opened directly onto a vast chamber. The floor was polished plascrete, a perfect circle, maybe a couple of hundred metres in diameter; the walls receded into the darkness above, lined with walkways and shadowy figures. The space was filled with a layering of hushed voices like an ocean tide.

A man stood waiting for her. Thin. Old but not feeble. Silver hair swept back in a receding peak. His cheeks were sunken, and the right one carried a long scar – a straight line of puckered white skin from just below his earlobe to the edge of his thin lips. His eyes were in deep shadow. This was Troels Volmar, Comptroller of the Hegemony Diplomatic Corps. Her father had made it very clear: do not fuck with this man.

"I expected you nine minutes ago," he said.

Rhees stepped onto the hard floor. The click of her boot heels echoed in the emptiness as she crossed the distance between them and snapped to attention.

"Rhees Lowrans reporting for duty, sir." She didn't offer an apology. She almost hadn't come.

"Duty is it?" Shadows flowed across Volmar's face as he shifted. His eyes were the blue of an iceberg. "I'm not sure you understand the meaning of the word." He looked her up and down. "What use will you be to me, Lowrans? What use will you be to Earth?"

After Neptune, she wasn't sure she had an answer.

But Volmar didn't wait for one. "I have no time for dead weight here. Your record shows you're insubordinate and lack discipline. And people around you die."

She looked down sharply, biting hard on the inside of her mouth, tasting blood. Don't give him the satisfaction. When she looked up again her face was impassive.

Volmar was still watching her. If he was enjoying this, he didn't show it.

"Everyone in this facility has been hand-picked by me after rigorous and lengthy training. Because the work we do here is of the utmost importance to the continued survival of Earth. This," he looked up into the darkness, "is where the real power of the Hegemony lies."

She couldn't control her expression this time.

"You don't believe me?"

She was still standing at parade attention. With a brief nod from Volmar she stood at ease.

"I don't recall the K-Chaan war machines being turned back by a terse diplomatic memo," she said. "And it took the Fleet to vaporise every one of their colonies afterwards."

She expected Volmar to explode, to send her packing, and that would be fine. Nihilism was very attractive right now. But the comptroller's lips thinned into the approximation of a smile, and on the walkways circling above them, the quiet murmur of data interpolation faded to silence. Rhees wondered how many of the staff working above had unplugged from their datanooks to listen.

"I was on the front line when the K-Chaan almost overwhelmed us," Volmar said. "You were probably busy getting born then. And I know if HDC had been active then as we are now, that situation would never have been allowed to develop the way it did."

He strode towards the centre of the chamber, where a safety rail circled a deep pit set in the floor. "Come here."

Rhees looked up. White faces spiralled above her. Some pulled back from her gaze; others continued to stare down. She joined the comptroller.

Below them, a holotank displayed the galactic spiral arm and, out near the tip, the hazy border marking Hegemony space. The stars close in to galactic centre were rendered simulations – placeholders at best – but the suns in and around the Hegemony were displayed in realtime, or as close to it as the network of Voss Space relays allowed.

"Look at how small we are," Volmar said, gesturing towards Hegemony space. "A tiny island of order in the midst of unending chaos. It's no small feat that we've survived and flourished despite what almost happened with the K-Chaan. But it's not because we have a strong fleet."

Rhees glanced at him, but Volmar's eyes were focused on infinity.

"The Fleet you served has its uses, but they are very limited," he said. "Confined to pitched battles or intra-system disputes. The real struggle for survival takes place without a shot being fired and it's the Corps that makes it happen. We don't just collect data here. We use it. We use it on a thousand worlds through a network of countless operatives. A thousand tiny wars are waged and won every day, each one in plain view of an unsuspecting citizenry." He cleared his throat, straightening again. "It's the only way to ensure our continued survival. And it's not something the Fleet is well suited for."

He took her by the upper arm and turned her to face him. It was such an unexpected move she didn't know what to do. He stepped closer until he towered over her, his gaunt features illuminated by the faint glow from the holotank. His grip was firm, but she didn't pull away, refusing to be cowed.

He bent his head to her ear and his voice dropped to a whisper. "I know you don't want to be here. I don't want you here either. It's only because your father has pull with Central Administration that you're not rotting in a stockade where you belong."

She pulled back then, breaking his grip, but Volmar's face remained unreadable.

"However," he continued, "talk to me again as you just did and you'll wish it was *you* splattered across the rings of Neptune. Understand?"

It took everything she had, but she took a step back and saluted. "Yes, sir."

Volmar's thin lips pursed and he gave the slightest of nods. "Not so much as a sparrow falls in the Hegemony without our express permission. You could be a part of that. But first, get rid of that Fleet uniform. You're HDC now. God help us."

God help *me*, she thought. This was her life now.

4

Petabytes of information flowed through the Datahive every millisecond: observations from the Voss Space relays, reports from HDC operatives working in the field, intercepted communications from systems far beyond the Hegemony's influence, and – closer to home – surveillance data on every human being in the solar system.

It wasn't really a secret. Everyone knew monitoring was widespread, but individuals believed surveillance was what happened to other people who had something to hide. It was a comforting lie people told themselves so they could sleep at night. But just three weeks working the datanooks had shown Rhees that the HDC was interested in everything and everybody, so it observed everything and everybody.

Her job was simple. Humans excelled at pattern recognition. So she played wingman to the computer algorithms sifting the data; a simple biological conduit ascribing significance values to multiple intel streams. It was stultifying work.

The information flow throttled back suddenly and the neural brake was lifted, even though the overlay showed it was well off shift end. Her eyes and ears were her own again and she heard the jarring bass of the general alarm. Vestiges of the datastream melted away and the chair disengaged, pulling Rhees out from the datanook.

At first it had been hard to move straight out of immersion. She'd become an extension of the machine; pure consciousness without a body. But you can get used to anything, she thought.

Other nooks were disgorging her colleagues onto the

concentric walkways around and above her. She followed dark shapes across the floor to the guardrail of the holopit: the source of the alarm. The others made room for her, keeping their distance as if she carried a disease.

It had been this way since she'd been dumped here. She felt completely cut off from the world around her, both because of the unreality of the datastreams and the fact that no one spoke to her unless their work required it. Every night she woke drenched in sweat from nightmares. And every day it was harder to believe she deserved more than being buried in this mausoleum to other people's lives. Something had to change and soon. She had to break out of the lethargy that pulled at her like slowly setting amber. If she didn't, her sanity would seep away.

In the holotank, one of the suns in Hegemony Space flared so bright she had to look away. It lit up the whole inside of the Datahive for a handful of seconds. When she looked back it was gone, replaced by a dimly pulsing icon.

"An interesting turn of events."

Rhees didn't acknowledge the remark or the speaker standing directly behind her. The cultured euro-bloc accent was unmistakable. He'd barely spoken to her since her arrival. But whenever he did, he made it clear how much he disapproved of her presence.

"Magnify the strike zone," Volmar said, coming to stand beside her at the rail and speaking to the pit AI. "Tactical mode."

The image dilated into a dizzying streak of onrushing stars. Then the newly ruined system lay mapped out before them. The devastation was as complete as it was inconceivable. The inner planets had been entirely vaporised. Ghost images, labelled in red, showed their last tracked positions. Huge chunks of debris – all that remained of the outer planets – tumbled away from the epicentre. Rhees followed the progress of one continent-sized mass as it fell into the frozen darkness.

"And what does our master Fleet tactician make of this, eh?" Volmar's tone was as dry as a desert wind.

Rhees still held onto enough of her old self to feel a slow burn of anger as she turned to face him. "I'm not Fleet any more. And I wasn't a tactical officer."

"But you were trained in tactics, yes? And presumably you were also trained in how to address a superior officer. Or is Fleet discipline as lax as everything else it does?"

Any remark she made would only elicit more of the same. Volmar let the silence stretch.

"You'll have to develop a thicker skin if you're going to survive in the Diplomatic Corps, Lowrans. And I'm still waiting for your tactical analysis."

"There was a nova – sir. What more is there to say?"

Volmar blinked once, slowly, like a reptile. "Not good enough. You've had an easy run here so far. It's time you started contributing something more than your body heat."

Rhees turned back to the holo. Volmar had gotten under her skin and she'd spoken without thinking. She might hate him, but she'd learned he was precise in everything he did and he expected no less from others.

The precursor stages of a nova would have been observed and reported long before the sun actually blew. But it had triggered the alarm, so this event was unanticipated. That left deliberate intervention. Nothing on this scale had happened since the K-Chaan war. The Hegemony had no current threats in the sector, not even civil unrest. There were the Hanloi out towards galactic centre. The Hegemony mission to Hanloi space had been lost without trace three months ago, but there'd been nothing from that region since. And this was too far inside Hegemony space to be connected.

Her eyes followed that massive chunk of rock again, almost a small planetoid, cartwheeling lazily into oblivion. Directly in its path, a few hundreds of thousands of kilometres further out – so far from the devastation she'd almost missed it – she saw a tightly bunched group of small green dots. They carried no transponders, but there looked to be about fifty of them. As she watched, they began to wink out of existence.

"I'm not certain," she said, "but those unregistered vessels out past the heliopause look to be worth investigating."

Volmar sighed. "You may have a brain after all." He stepped up to the guardrail. "Replay time sequence 8924110. Same magnification. Time factor eighty."

The image blurred and resolved. The dead sun and planets were reborn. Rhees's attention was drawn to the second planet. The space around it teemed with intra-system traffic, each ship showing up as a blue point labelled with a transponder code.

"What system is this?" she asked, looking at all those ships.

"One of the Brell colonies," Volmar said absently. "Total population thirteen billion."

Thirteen billion dead, Rhees thought. They just didn't know it yet.

The green points of light began to appear all across the system, making Voss Space transition inside the gravity well – some instantly exploding as a result. Blue ships moved to engage the green. Even at the increased playback speed, the battle resembled a deadly slow-motion ballet of vectors and accelerations as ships moved, turned and died in silence.

"Here it comes," Volmar said.

Rhees saw where he was looking. A small group of green-flagged ships transitioned well past the orbit of the innermost planet. At least half of them disintegrated immediately as tidal forces ripped them apart. The rest accelerated towards the sun. She watched their progress, expecting them to veer off at the last moment. But they plunged into the photosphere and were gone. If they were piloted, she thought, whatever this was had been a suicide mission.

All across the system the attackers broke off from their multiple skirmishes and disappeared into Voss Space. The blue ships hung there, perhaps confused at the sudden turn of events.

Rhees looked at the sun again. Everything seemed normal.

Seconds ticked by. The attackers transited out where she'd first seen them. Then an ominous darkness spread across the face of the sun. It shrank in on itself, seemed to stabilise again, then burst outwards, the sum total of its mass changed to pure energy on a cataclysmic scale. Rhees exhaled loudly, the tension in her finding sudden release as the shockwave from the mother sun embraced each one of her children in turn and tore them apart. Within seconds there was nothing left.

"A very effective operation," Volmar said.

"Effective? We just watched thirteen billion die."

"Grieving won't bring them back," he said. "It may insult your sensibilities, but I think our energies would be better spent making sure this doesn't happen again. We need action, not tears. Enhance one of their ships; let us see what they look like."

The tank image blurred as the image processors constructed a representation of the raiders' ship design: a central cockpit with weapons pods overhanging above and below, like a horseshoe balanced on edge.

"Interesting," Volmar said.

"You recognise it?" Rhees asked.

"No. But it's not Hanloi." Clearly Volmar had been thinking along the same lines. "And their willingness to transit inside a gravity well without a Voss bridge … Clearly it's a species we haven't encountered."

"Anyone can transit in-system if they don't care about the risk of blowing up. But there's not much the Corps can do about this," Rhees said. "Fleet gets the same feed. They must be mobilising a task force as we speak."

"And what's Fleet going to do in this situation, Lowrans? There's no way to trace those ships through Voss Space."

"That battle group means business," she said, refusing to concede the point. "At some stage we're going to have to fight them. And that means a Fleet deployment."

"Despite your opinion, the Corps is much better suited to

dealing with this type of threat. You don't understand the extent of our power."

"Then teach me!" she said, the frustration of endless days in the datastream bursting through. "I've been here for weeks now sifting data."

Volmar regarded her through half-lidded eyes. "Immersion's a bit below you, isn't it, Lowrans? You fancy yourself as a woman of action." The cold smile was back. "But we've all seen where that leads."

"Let me do something worthwhile," she said, ignoring him. She couldn't stand the thought of another day lost in this building.

"All right," he said abruptly. "I'll give you a chance to prove yourself. But if you fail me, it won't matter a damn who your father is friends with."

Rhees hesitated. Things were moving too fast and she felt suddenly unsure. Was Volmar manipulating events to get rid of her?

"What do you want me to do?" she asked.

"It's simple really." His tone was conversational again. "There's a commercial yacht leaving tomorrow for the planet Herakli. Our sector office is there, a mere three parsecs from the strike zone. You'll join the staff, do what you're told and assist in the investigation of the attack."

She realised they were now completely alone by the holopit. She looked back towards the datanooks where the others were busy sifting intel again. There wasn't really a choice.

"I accept the mission," she said.

5

The ship shuddered and through the small port in my cabin I could see our mountain of ice floating free with others of its kind into a gravitationally stable orbit where it would sit until it was broken down to its constituents. We continued our turn and there was Homeworld and, above it, the Hub lanced by the skystalk that reached down to Aktiuk spaceport. The central sphere of the station was ringed by docking bays, each a different house colour. Not that they denoted ownership of any kind. The Merchants Lodge ruled here, and behind them House Kergis.

The station slid past and I lost sight of Homeworld. Our ship was giving the Hub a wide berth, preferring a slow orbit down to the planet's surface, well away from the main traffic between the Hub and Aktiuk.

Up at the front of the ship, the businesslike mood I'd been vaguely aware of changed. Something was threatening us.

I slid out of the sling and stood indecisively near the door. I had no weapons. I wasn't a trained fighter. But the feeling was tense, worried and growing more so. Then it broke and I recognised Bvak's presence growing stronger, moving aft towards me.

The door opened and he held onto the frame, breath whistling through his spiracles. "We're about to be boarded. Defender patrol."

I took a step back. I couldn't be found.

"Sakat!" he swore. "I knew you'd be trouble. Come on."

I grabbed my travel pouch, made sure I'd left nothing else behind, and followed. But where could I go? This close to

Homeworld an escape pod would be quickly spotted and captured, and Defenders would easily detect me if I tried hiding onboard. I could no more stop feeling than I could breathing.

I rushed to keep up, hoping Bvak had a plan. We passed the lock, then up a ramp and finally onto the flight deck. Two of the crew were there: the pilot and navigator judging from the stations they occupied either side of the main vuscreen. A Defender cruiser was approaching, still some way off.

"Look to your instruments, not him!" Bvak shouted at his crew.

The intensity of their concentration on me diminished as they turned back to their stations. The navigator was Cultivator caste, her elongated arms reaching up to engage relays over her head.

Bvak kicked at the base of his command chair and pushed the seat back over the deck plates. He hunkered down and looked up at me, anger and desperation heavy in the air between us. He clawed at the seam of the plate below where his chair had sat and levered it up, revealing an empty space lined with a bluish alloy. It was the same metal that covered the walls of Czerag's shielded chamber.

"Don't ask," Bvak said. "Just get in."

Despite the danger, I hesitated. What if I was found?

"Come on," Bvak urged, his anxiety washing over me in waves.

I looked up at the vuscreen. The Defender cruiser was closing fast. I climbed down and lay in the space with my legs folded up under me.

"Don't make a sound," Bvak said. "There's air enough in there for a short inspection."

Set into the side wall was a smaller vuscreen that showed the flight deck and the back of Bvak's head as he leaned down and settled the deck plate over me. As the lid sealed, my sense of the others on the ship was suddenly gone. Why would an asteroid miner have a shielded box – something no one but hierarchs could afford – installed on his ship?

On the screen, Bvak reinstalled his chair to the central position then moved to stand beside the main vuscreen, talking to his crew. I waited. I could hear nothing of what was being said above me.

The ship shuddered and I imagined the Defender cruiser's bulk locking onto our docking ring. I didn't know if the search was standard for ships that had been out for a while, or if we had been singled out because Czerag had been betrayed.

On the screen a Defender walked onto the flight deck. His body plan was different to mine: the armour plating was thicker, and Defenders were the tallest of males, despite lacking a second knee joint and mid-calf. But the most noticeable difference was the oversized arm – usually the left – which ended in a massive pincer, good for crushing enemy shells in the time before our empathic sense evolved with the Emergence. The Defender wore standard combat skins bearing the lodge sigil – a miniature stylised gaszti blade – on his shoulder. Bvak stood looking up at him, talking, indicating something with his claws.

The Defender half-turned as another came into view. I could see their feeders moving as they spoke. Then the first Defender turned back to Bvak, said something and disappeared with the other.

Bvak looked directly at my screen, or wherever the feed input was located, but without the empathic contact I had no idea what was happening. Then the deck kicked jarringly again and Bvak was lifting the deck plate. Sensation flooded in. Relief from Bvak and his crew.

I climbed out of the hiding place and helped him reposition his chair.

"We made it," I said. Half-statement, half-question.

"They knew something was wrong, but they searched the ship and found nothing to hold us on. No doubt they suspect I have some contraband on board," Bvak said. "I expect we'll receive extra scrutiny next time we head out. I hope you're worth it."

"We all do what we're told," I said, echoing what he'd said to me when we first met.

"Sit." He indicated an empty chair near the bulkhead. "You may as well stay up front."

The crew's attention was like claws scrabbling at my hide, insistent, distrusting.

Bvak tapped the pilot and took his seat. "Both of you can go to your quarters," he said, and the pilot and the long-limbed navigator left us alone on the flight deck.

I looked at the deck beneath his chair. No one would guess what was beneath it.

"Why does a simple cargo hauler have a concealed chamber lined with expensive shielding?" I asked.

Bvak's emotions were a mix of guilt and annoyance. "You're not the first favour I've done for Czerag. And you won't be the last."

Homeworld was dead ahead: a brown ball, streaked with cloud, and I thought again of what that meant to me now. Soon I'd be back at the escarpment among Czerag Kresz who thought they knew me all too well. And then there'd be Isza. We'd argued the day I left.

Bvak glanced my way. If he picked up my ambivalence about returning home he kept quiet.

I watched the view as he piloted us down. I was tired and I caught myself slipping into a fuzzy kind of communion with Bvak. I pulled myself out, fighting to stay awake. Then we hit atmosphere, the turbines kicked in and the thrum of a planet full of Kresz burst over us. There was no way to block it. It was like a sound you hadn't realised you'd been straining to hear until it started again.

No outworlder really understood. They pictured the Kresz as some kind of composite hive mentality – a bunch of characterless drones – not fully formed individuals with our own thoughts and desires. But the sensation of others' feelings was natural for a Kresz, as natural as looking up in the sky and seeing the suns, and just as reassuring – unless you were different like me. Despite my difficulties however, I could still appreciate the deep connection it enabled. It was something I'd certainly shared with Isza. With touch, the augmentation of our engorged mantles, and full communion, that sharing could go deeper still. An intimacy with the self as other and the other as self. I wasn't religious, but it was hard to argue against the Priests' insistence that the Emergence was evidence of Sakat's plan for us.

We settled into a slowly descending flight path, buffeted by air currents, and as we cleared a bank of cloud I saw we were already fairly low, on approach over the Inland Sea. Even at this height I could make out the white peaks of waves whipped up by the wind. The faraway coast curved out of view.

We dropped further, approaching a broad jungle of blues and greens, and off to the north-east, pushing through the canopy, the towers of Aktiuk, the Treaty City. It passed behind us and we crossed lush growth, broken here and there by settlements – probably Kergis holdings by the latitude – following the path of the Ruhaku River that drained from the mountains into the sea. Gradually the undergrowth thinned and we banked, heading directly over open desert. It seemed Bvak preferred navigating by sight rather than instrument. We passed over a sandstorm, a big one extending as far as I could see and blurring the landscape a deep ochre.

Finally I saw the escarpment: a broad, flat expanse of bare rock standing above the top of the storm. I knew every dip of that rock, its cataracts, tunnels, open and secret entrances and scuttleways, the oases at its foot, the deep chambers beneath and further back into its stone heart. A lonely youngling had plenty of time for exploration.

The wind was still blowing hard and throwing up a blinding torrent of sand as we closed on our destination: a small landing field near the main entrance to House Czerag. Then the ship bucked and leaped upwards. At the same instant, my mind screamed – almost a physical shock. I was fighting for consciousness. Despair and anger. A bitter taste in my mouth. Then another assault driving through my skull.

Bvak wrestled the controls to stop us pitching over. "Engaging landing sequence!" he shouted.

The turbines began to cycle down. It was all I could do to sit rigid in my seat. Images, mimetic representations of feelings that were not my own, played across my inner eye: a vertiginous plunge, an ah'lok I'd once seen devouring another weaker than it, pulling the head off in its beak. And all of it coming from below.

I tried to withdraw from the flow. It didn't work at first. The lights seemed too bright, the sounds too deafening, the feelings too abrasive. But I kept trying – hovering on the brink of madness. Then it abated just enough to let me think my own thoughts again, and suddenly it was gone. Nothing but the sound of the storm.

"Trouble?" I said. My head was pounding. I wished I was back in the shielded box.

Bvak keyed the communicator. "House control. This is the mining tug *Czakut*. What in Sakat is happening down there?"

"Control," said a voice. It sounded as dazed as I felt. "Reports aren't making sense right now. House Defenders are alerted. There's a detachment on its way to meet you. Control out."

Bvak looked at me and I could feel his puzzlement. "Come," he said.

The ship was settling as we stood. The lock was already open and we descended the ramp into the rushing, sand-laden wind. The storm's violence would help to conceal my return. The others in the escarpment had been told I'd been sent by the hierarch on an errand to the deep desert, but they didn't know where.

My secondary eyelids flicked across, protecting my eyes and changing wavelength perception so the whirling sand in front of my face faded out and I could see past my outstretched arm. Bvak felt guarded beside me. Sand scratched against our shells and the gale howled. Bodies were moving towards us quickly, the hulking shape of Defenders holding lanterns. The sense out here was muted and a little dreamlike. It was like the reaction of an animal badly hurt but safe for now, curling around its wounds and trying not to think too hard about what had just happened. There were still aftershocks, almost like a re-imagining of whatever the inciting event had been, but they were lessening in intensity.

Bvak and I waited as four house Defenders came alongside and fell in behind us. They didn't speak. They were here to protect us from whatever had happened, but I didn't think they knew what that was.

We walked across the sand to the shadow of the escarpment and then into the wide fissure, following it until it twisted left and the wind dropped. There was light up ahead. The opening into House Czerag. Someone was standing there, shorter than most and bent so low by thickened dorsal plates he grasped onto a thick staff to stand. The plates on his arms were deeply etched with whorls and interlocking spirals inlaid with brassy metal. It was Tzek, Czerag's chief advisor. I felt his sending in greeting and responded.

"Come with me, both of you." He turned and stalked into the entrance hall and we followed.

Two more Defenders were waiting inside, their gaszti blades unsheathed, and they joined our group, leading us. Everything was in motion and sensation crowded the air, all of it ill, so that our surroundings seemed washed out of any meaning at all.

I briefly recognised faces among the knots of people standing or moving quickly through and into corridors or up stairs carved into the rock. Even in the near panic, I felt their recognition and, just as quickly, their reaction to seeing me again: confusion, as if they weren't sure I was someone they could trust, then the hurried covering as they tried to mask what they felt.

We passed into a length of corridor at the back of the hall. "Tzek!" A voice rang out from the far end. Even before I looked I recognised the presence. Hierarch Czerag.

He was flanked by two more Defenders, their physicality far less imposing in his presence. The skin beneath his skull plate was black, the patterned spots completely joined together, and his shell was a midnight purple, with individual plates so thick that his movements were slow and rigid. He was missing a feeder claw on the left of his mouth opening, which always made me think he was frowning.

We hurried to join his group, and together climbed a short flight of steps, then crossed a breezeway that was open to the sky: a thin band of starlight cut into the darkness of the surrounding rock. The emotions from the group around me were conflicting and I concentrated on my own thoughts.

We moved into another passage that angled down and then levelled. There was a shout ahead and a renewed sense of urgency. I saw an Adept run through a doorway. There was such a feeling of horror and disgust coming through that opening, I didn't want to go any further. But there was something familiar too.

A crash, and a Defender appeared in the doorway, huge arm coming down on a figure that skipped aside. Suddenly Reka was rushing towards us. But it felt nothing like him.

My thoughts were dashed aside by waves of anger and hatred. The Defenders in front of our group closed in, but the corridor hampered them. Reka passed between them, heading for Czerag.

I thrust forward, my instincts taking over, and grabbed at Reka. As my claws closed on his torso plates, I almost lost myself, caught in a sudden rushing sensation of madness as if I'd become untethered from the world.

We clashed together and fell. Everything stilled. I rolled on my side as Reka was plucked off me, lifeless or just unconscious, lifted in the strong pincer of one of the Defenders.

Tzek's wooden staff struck the ground beside me and I grasped it to haul myself up. "You should have been a Defender," he said, his anger flaring at the nearest of the guards who had failed to stop the attack.

I couldn't understand what was happening. I knew Reka as I knew my own self. He was my divide, from my first moult as an instar after breach. He would never hurt anyone.

Tzek brushed grit and dirt from my shoulder plates before I stood, and the Defenders formed up again in front of and behind us.

"Come," Czerag said.

We entered the side room. Everything was covered in a miasma of senses: dull pain, the half-remembered horror of a nightmare, a dense protective sleepiness.

The Defender behind me still held Reka in his pincer. He was only unconscious. I could hear the breath in his spiracles.

The room was badly lit, a lantern lying on its side on the floor, element damaged and sputtering. Someone – a Priest, I realised from his robes – was squatting beside a female. There were things on the floor around her head like wooden pegs, glistening in a wet pool. Her carapace was slick with wet too. It was her own rusz, thick and yellow and splashed across the stone floor. The way her arms were spread out looked strange. She moaned and her head fell to one side. The numbness in my own head faded, the lantern flared brighter and the full horror of the scene hit me. Those things by her head – they were her feeder claws and larger mandible, cut or ripped from her face. Most of the rusz was coming from there, but there was a wooden shaft sticking from her abdominal plates. The haft of a gaszti blade. And then I realised her arms and legs had been severed from the rest of her body, making it look like she was lying awkwardly. It was a wonder she still lived.

The Defender holding Reka spoke, his voice deep and surprisingly soft. "Hierarch, this male invaded the female's place and attacked this female in a most vicious way. There was no warning. Suddenly his mind was screaming evil. I came as soon as I could and subdued him, but I was too late."

"And failed to keep your hierarch safe from a similar attack," Tzek said.

The Defender's horror and guilt at failing to prevent either attack was a sick pounding behind my eyes.

"Who is he?" Czerag asked.

"It's Reka," I said.

Tzek planted his staff on the ground and looked from Reka to me. "Your budding from the instar stage?"

The focus of the other Kresz in the room shifted towards me, making it feel even more oppressive.

Czerag gestured at the unconscious Reka. "Take him to a shielded area where he will not disturb the house when he awakens."

The guard stalked out the room carrying Reka.

"She lives, Hierarch," the Priest said from the floor.

"Give her what comfort you can," Czerag said. "Bring her family to be with her. I will visit later. Bvak?"

The pilot stirred behind me. "Yes, Hierarch."

"Take my message to those in the entrance, have it passed through the house. Tell them to go to their chambers and dormitories, look to their own families and make sure they are safe and comforted. Let the peace of the house return."

Bvak left quickly.

I looked down at the injured female. Rusz flow from major trauma was quick to stop – it was how our bodies were made. A legacy of our brutal past, and the only reason she'd survived. But survival like this wasn't a blessing. How could Reka do this? Why?

Czerag led the way back into the passage, retracing our steps through corridors back to the entrance hall, then striking out through a wide arch into a bare corridor, then a small reception area ending in a stout door of endar wood. Tzek held a metal sliver to his ear gap, speaking into it as we walked. All the Defenders except one left us on the way, going at Czerag's direction to take up stations and reassure the house that the threat was over. The last one took up a position behind us, effectively blocking further access to this vestibule.

Tzek pulled on the door handles and swung them outward. At the same time, the blue metal shield barrier behind the wooden doors rose into the rock above us. We walked through the entrance, round a partition wall that blocked the view from outside, and into Czerag's chambers. The strange and restless feeling of the house abated as the shield closed behind us.

Czerag sank onto a stone bench in the centre of the room as he gave in to the full horror of what we'd seen. I stepped forward but he waved me back. "What has happened here?"

"It's as the guard reported," Tzek said. "An unprovoked attack, sudden and without warning. But furious for all that. The things he did to her …"

The air was thick with Tzek's anger, sadness and confusion. And I felt suspicion too when he looked at me. He was struggling to make sense of something that defied rationality.

"Details, Tzek," Czerag snapped and I felt the rebuke. The old advisor calmed immediately.

"Reka worked with me in the records hall under Scholar Idke," I said. "But …" I couldn't reconcile the picture I had of Reka in my head with the creature in the tunnels.

"He left for Aktiuk yesterday morning," Tzek said. "He must have stayed overnight because of the storm, but no one saw him return. The weapon – the gaszti blade – was no doubt taken from the armoury. They're checking the tally now, but the haft identifies it as one of ours." He took the sliver from his ear gap. "Could this be connected to Udun's trip? The timing is suspicious."

"Perimeter check on all entrances, including the hidden ones. And the mines," Czerag said and Tzek repeated the orders into his relay.

"Did he know the female?" Czerag asked me.

"He kept himself to himself. He never mentioned anyone else." Reka was even more isolated than I was: a divide of someone who was already half an outcast.

"She's training as an Adept – or was," Tzek said. "No family ties or mutual friends. It was completely unprovoked. He should have been killed outright."

"That's a mercy he doesn't deserve," Czerag said. "The forms will be followed. For Reka and the female."

I knew what that meant. Reka's fate was sealed.

Czerag's attention shifted. "I need your preliminary report," he told me.

It felt like an age since we broke atmosphere, but it was less than a span of hours.

"The mission is complete, Hierarch. The agreement with the Telsans has been made and I carry the information on manifest requirements, signals and timings, credit arrangements and delivery points encoded in my body. The Telsans said they would send data on the chemical structure required to extract it. But once that's done …" I paused, but there was no subtle way to say it. "I'll be ready to leave again. As you promised."

"Even if that were possible before," Tzek said, "there's what just happened with Reka to consider."

"I don't know what you mean." There was nothing I could do to help Reka.

"He's your echo."

"He's my divide," I said, annoyed that Tzek would spout lore the Scholars had discredited long ago.

"It speaks to a weakness, perhaps shared," he said. "An instability in character. We can't risk you travelling outside the house. Particularly now."

"Hierarch —"

"Things are at a delicate stage," Czerag said. "It was hard enough to bring you back undetected. Kergis already suspects us. And even in Aktiuk our people are stopped regularly on the streets for 'security checks'."

I could feel the intention building in him: he was going to tell me no. The anger I'd felt all the way home flashed between us.

"It's not how I want to live any more," I said, my voice sounding louder than I intended in the small chamber.

"This is not —"

"You promised me," I said, then stopped suddenly. No one interrupted the hierarch.

His own anger was like a cold block of stone in my mind, forcing out anything in its path. "This is nonsense. Alien nonsense. You cannot leave now. There is no time to indulge you further."

It was as if he'd struck me.

"And later?" I was bargaining now. I could hear the tone in my voice. Weak.

"I will decide." He turned away from me to activate one of the vuscreens set in the wall behind him. "Now go. Tzek will arrange the data extraction. Tomorrow."

I stood for a moment, caught by a feeling of helplessness.

Czerag looked down at the ground, then shifted to look at me again as his anger left him. "You have served your house well. Put these other thoughts from your mind."

It had been a mistake to come home. I could see it now. Czerag had promised me whatever was necessary to progress his plan. But he didn't feel bound by that promise.

"I want to see Reka," I said.

"That's not advisable," Tzek said.

"He's my divide. If that's to be held against me, I need to understand what happened."

"The Defenders will give you entry," Czerag said. "Try to get some rest, Udun."

"Yes, Hierarch." I walked around the partition, where the shield wall opened for me, then closed to cut me off from Czerag and Tzek.

The Defender at the far end of the vestibule stepped aside to let me into the passage. "You're Udun."

The voice startled me and I turned.

"You don't know me," the Defender said, then pulled himself up, his head almost brushing the bare rock above him. "I'm Gurud. We'll talk later, I hope."

"Yes," I said, too distracted for anything more, and walked on.

In the entrance hall, the lights were dimmed and only a few people were still up, huddled beside the large firepit flued through a natural opening in the rock. But they were too wrapped up in their own thoughts to notice me. There was a wary fatigue about the place that matched my mood.

I'd realised on the journey back that Homeworld would never feel the same to me. Not now I knew what life was like elsewhere. But even without that, this place had changed. No one had defiled the safety of the escarpment in living memory. It was unthinkable.

And yet gentle, quiet Reka had done exactly that. It took a deep madness to inflict those kinds of injuries on someone when that suffering instantly became your own.

I retraced my steps past the females' quarters. There was no sign now of the violence that had been done there. The corridor angled up then down, before splitting. There were only a few shielded rooms in the house and this was the closest to where Reka had been subdued. Two Defenders were stationed at the entranceway. The image of a gaszti blade came to mind, the steel freshly passed across a sharpstone. They were still keyed up and ready for battle, but Tzek must have told them I was on my way. One turned and pushed the heavy door open, following me inside and sealing the room again.

A single dim lantern showed Reka slumped in the far corner. I could feel nothing from him. I kneeled beside him and placed my claws on his skull plate.

Despite what Tzek implied, Reka was nothing like me. When the others in my breach began to push me away because of my strange ideas, I resented him. Because he was an outward signifier of just how different I was. We were never friends. Not like Isza and me. But I was always aware he was "of me". I cared about him.

He stirred and I bent closer, trying to catch his words. A feeling of complete exhaustion washed over me. There was a sound behind of steel against leather as the Defender pulled his gaszti.

"Reka. It's me," I said.

He mumbled again. I couldn't make it out, but I fancied I could hear a wind howling across the end of a tunnel.

"Can you sit? You're safe now."

The wind rose as he came fully awake. "I was in the library," he said. He was looking at me but his eyes were unfocused.

"Yes. And?"

I felt fear and wasn't sure if it was my own. The wind grew stronger, pushing at me.

"I was in the library," he said again. Louder.

I felt buffeted as the wind turned around me, spinning faster. Closing in.

"What happened to you?"

It was getting hard to think. The wind was so loud now and so strong and I knew it was Reka. It was the madness inside him, taking hold again.

"I was in the library!"

He grabbed my claws, pushing me back, and I fell to the floor. He rose up, leaning over me.

"I WAS IN THE LIBRARY!"

The Defender loomed above me, his huge pincer swinging over my head and smashing into Reka's face, throwing him against the back wall. The wind stopped.

I scrabbled to stand, still confused by the sudden violence of Reka's attack.

The Defender opened the door and I stepped out into the calm of the corridor, trying to make sense of what I'd felt in there. Reka's mind was gone.

I gave the common sending to the Defender in thanks and turned down the passage. This place was a trap and I was stupid to have come here. Tzek believed it was only a matter of time until the same madness that gripped Reka surfaced in me. He'd make sure I never left the escarpment again because of it.

I had to go. Now, before Tzek or Czerag could stop me.

6

Back in the entrance hall, even those who'd sat by the firepit had gone to their rooms. I passed the Defenders at the door. They didn't stop me and I walked back along the cutting. The desert was at peace again, as if the earlier storm had manifested with the violence in the escarpment and stilled when Reka was subdued.

A trail of lanterns dotted the foot of the cliff and I followed the path, my hoofs sinking into the sand, feeling it run between the small articulated plates. I didn't feel tired, though I knew I should be. Events had been packed very closely together for some time now. Rounding a jutting point of rock, I came to one of the oases fed by a deep cataract in the cliff face. A thin stand of udek fronds clustered along the opposite bank. I kneeled to drink, sucking at the cool water.

I could get to Aktiuk by mid-morning if I travelled all night; after that I wasn't sure. It wouldn't be easy to get off-planet, but I'd think of something.

I stood and walked into the darkness of the desert.

∞

My empathic sense was fully alert, seeking the contact that would tell me I was being pursued. But no one came. I moved across the dunes in an easy gait, my legs flexing to compensate for the uneven ground, feeling exhilarated by the physical activity. Feeling free, but knowing that for the lie it was. Not yet.

At some point, the escarpment behind me was lost from

view and eventually I saw the first glow from the lights of Aktiuk on the horizon. Was I doing the right thing? Czerag needed the information encoded in my rusz. But if I'd hesitated after leaving Reka, someone would have felt my unease and become suspicious. If I was leaving it had to be now.

I thought about sending Czerag a sample when I reached Aktiuk, but there was no way I could do that without raising too many questions. He would have to contact Emba another way. He'd betrayed my trust in him. He should expect no better from me.

I paused in the lee of a dune, hunkering low while I caught my breath. Something skittered away in the dark, its body rasping over the sand.

There was another sound. Low at first, but rising quickly in intensity. Turbines in the distance and coming closer. I pressed my body against the curve of the dune, but if the craft was flying low enough ...

A flyer shot over the dune ridge just above me and the engines caught, shrieking as the ship's long snout suddenly dipped and slewed round to face my hiding place. Sand was thrown up in two whirling columns as the craft levelled and sank lower, the turbines cycling down as it drifted to land in the depression at the foot of the dune. I could feel the pilot inside. Even if running would help, I couldn't run from her.

Isza leaped from the open door of the flyer, covering half the distance to me. "Just what do you think you're doing out here?" she called.

I stood and walked down to meet her, already sensing anger, hurt, confusion.

"It's best you don't know."

Her anger blossomed, pushing everything else aside. "Another errand for Czerag? Has he got you so ... No. It's not that, is it?"

This close, my immediate emotions were open to her and she pressed at them, tasting the nuances. I wasn't sure what sense picture she saw, but we'd shared enough in the past for her to work out exactly what I was doing.

"You're running away? Are you insane?"

Would I even know if I was?

She held my arm in her claws, magnifying our connection. Her mantle was rising, pulling me towards full communion. I fell back on the sand, breaking the contact.

"I can't," I said, feeling her hurt even more keenly. "There's too much I can't share with you. It's dangerous."

She hunkered down in front of me and swore. "I told you not to get involved with him. The escarpment is nothing but secrets now."

"Czerag promised if I did as he asked, he'd let me go off-planet again," I told her.

"And he broke that promise," she said, her anger giving way to concern. "So you just turn your back on everything else?" Including her.

"I can't live here now, not after what I experienced out there." I waved my claws at the night sky.

"It was what you wanted?"

Isza had always supported me, even when others criticised the things I said or the way I felt. Even when she couldn't understand me either. But there was no sense picture I could share to explain how it had felt to finally leave Homeworld.

"At first, I was terrified," I said. "That shock of really being alone for the first time in my life. But then I got to Telsus and started looking around, talking to people … It didn't matter how I felt on the inside. No one could know unless I told them. And that felt good. I belonged to me only. I'm not going to give that up."

The breath sighed through Isza's spiracles. "If what you know is so dangerous, Czerag can't just let you leave. And there's no point running if you have no way to get to where you're going. How will you use the skystalk without a hierarch authorisation? And what will you do on the Hub if you get there?"

"I had to leave. If anyone suspected, I'd be locked up."

"The only way to escape Homeworld is on a ship with orbital capability and a tenspace drive. And for that you'll need a pilot."

Her resolve was like a cool, smooth stone.

"I can't get you mixed up in this," I said.

Her feeders splayed wide. "I already am. But this needs careful planning. If you get caught they'll bury you so deep in the desert, you'll never get away again."

"And what happens to you?"

"That's why we need a plan. And why you need to come back home with me. Now."

I looked up at the stars of the Lenticular in the night sky. The Telsan home star shone bright blue-white. All of it was out of reach.

Isza touched the flesh beneath my neck guard and flowed through the contact. I felt the hurt in her again. That I wanted to leave. Leave her. But her strength was there too.

"There's another reason to stay," she said. "Reka still needs you."

I looked away. "There's nothing I can do for him."

"You can *be* there when Czerag passes judgement. You can do that much for him."

I thought of Reka screaming at me in the shielded room and Isza's grip tightened on my shoulder as she sensed some of that encounter.

"I don't think he'd know if we were there any more," I said.

"That's not the point." She paused, and I felt the intention building in her. "We need to find out what happened to him."

"Tzek thinks Reka's madness was caused by some instability inside him. And because he's my divide, there's a good chance that weakness is in me. It's another reason to keep me here."

"Tzek is wrong. Something else caused it." She stood and held her claw out to me. "Come on. It's late. Or early, and I didn't exactly get permission to take the flyer. I'll drop you off out of sight and you can walk back to the house. You had a lot to think about, that's why you were out all night. Meet me back at my room and we'll face the morning together."

I looked up at her. I'd go back. For all the reasons she said. But it felt different now. I wasn't alone in this.

She pulled me up and we walked together to the foot of the dune.

"How are you going to explain taking the flyer?" I asked.

Her feeders stretched wide. "It's not exactly my first time." She stopped at the door and looked at me. "I mean it: I will help you get off-planet. Just promise me you won't run off on your own again."

I felt the tension drain from me. "I can wait for a while."

And if Reka's madness *was* caused by something external, I could prove Tzek was wrong about him. And me.

"You mentioned secrets," I said as I sat in the co-pilot's chair and Isza powered up the turbines. "What's been happening?"

She snapped some switches overhead. "I don't know. People come and go. The mine's working at full capacity but they keep sending more workers there. Those that go are told not to talk about it. And now I can't fly decommissioned ships to the reclamation facility any more – increased security, they say – so I have to leave them on the other side of the escarpment and jump a transport back. No one knows why and no one asks. No one sees the whole picture except Czerag."

I didn't know anything about the reclamation work – only that we recycled tekla from decommissioned hulls and sold it to the Merchants Lodge along with refined tekla from the mine. But the rest of it had to be connected to my Telsus trip.

We rose on a flurry of sand, gaining height rapidly until the escarpment climbed above the horizon.

"And there's no other work around," Isza continued. "The deeprange ship *Might of Gnow* was lost at the beginning of last season. All House Kergis pilots. The lodge is short now, but does that mean I get more flights?"

We shot forward and I was pushed back into the chair.

"They haven't even called for replacements," she said. "But I can tell what's going to happen. They'll be training up some Kergis cadets to slot right into the space jobs."

We were coming up on the escarpment fast and she dropped speed until we were flying just above the tops of the dunes.

"Maybe you could get a space job flying for the Telsans," I said.

I felt her amusement. "Exile's not for me. Not unless I have no choice."

But it may come to that, I thought. She was willing to risk everything for me.

Isza left me in the shelter of a ring of dunes, rising quickly to fly the rest of the way to the escarpment.

The sky behind me was already lightening and I ran quickly until I came close to the string of oases near the house entrance. Through the cutting, the Defenders were as alert as before, but it seemed my absence hadn't been noticed.

Back in the entrance hall, it felt as if most of the house had found sleep, but it was a strange kind of rest, as if this place was no longer the refuge it had been to those who lived in its depths. I walked across the breezeway again and into another passage, past openings in the stone walls to my left and right covered with woven hangings. I heard the sounds of sleep, felt the steady rhythms of unconscious emotion.

One opening was still lit, the door covering pushed to one side. Isza was already there. I entered, closed the hanging behind me, and undressed quickly. We unrolled the sleeping mats in silence and lay side by side. Isza brushed the top of my skull cap with the tips of her claws, tracing a line down the brow ridge to the edge of my feeders, and I felt the comfort of her closeness. Then she dimmed the lantern and I closed my eyes and realised how tired I really was. Even so, for a while I just lay there, disjointed images running through my head. I could tell Isza was still awake too, captive to her own thoughts. Stray sense impressions from her mixed with those of others resting nearby – the meaning, if there was any, impenetrable.

At some point, sleep came and I crossed into the worldmind.

An almost pre-historic place, it was a fundamental expression of the Kresz species informed by race memory, genetic predisposition and who knew what else. No one had measured how far it extended across the surface of Homeworld as empathic fields overlapped and bled into one another. But it was always there, an undercurrent to our dreams and memories. A type of collective unconscious where the individual was lost in the multitude. There was no chance my secrets would be discovered there.

∞

I woke in the still dark room to morning sounds and the feel of others stirring nearby. Isza stretched awake beside me, and our shells clacked together.

"Morning," I said.

"Morning." She grabbed her clothes and started dressing. She was focused. Eager. "Sooner we're all there, the sooner we can get this over with."

I pulled on my travelling robe, thinking I should pick up a change soon, and we stepped together into the corridor, almost walking straight into Zael. The young Adept had shown a lot of interest in Isza last time I was here. An interest that clearly hadn't been mutual.

"Udun," he said. "I heard you were back from the deep desert."

His feeders were open in greeting but there was that sense of pulling back that meant he didn't trust me, that I was strange. My own reaction was to pull back in exactly the same way, which reinforced Zael's reaction. I was a prisoner of my own strangeness.

"Just last night," I said, though I was sure he knew that. I was uncomfortable with the lie Tzek had put out about my whereabouts, but that feeling was indistinguishable from how I always felt around others.

"It's a terrible business with Reka," Zael said, "but perhaps it was inevitable."

"What do you mean?"

"Well, you know what he was like."

Yes, I thought, like me. But Zael was oblivious to my reaction.

"He'd just gotten worse lately. He was difficult to be around. More than usual, I mean."

"Did you ask him what was the matter?"

Zael blinked. "He barely spoke on a good day. And he wasn't exactly a friend."

Typical of Zael. "When did you notice this change?" I said.

He thought for a moment. "Maybe halfway through Luk'ri."

Only a few weeks after I'd left.

"So, just what were you up to in the deep desert?" he asked.

Isza pulled at my arm. "We should go." As usual, she was acting to protect me. "Bye, Zael."

We joined a steady stream of Kresz moving deeper into the tunnels. All around us was a kind of unwanted expectation.

"Zael's still unhappy because I've chosen for the next cycle and it's not him," she told me.

"He was hopeful?"

Isza's feeders stretched wide. "Just more proof of his overinflated ego."

"So ..."

"Who? His name's Gurud."

"The Defender?" I remembered the guard who'd introduced himself outside Czerag's chamber. Now it made sense. "We met briefly last night."

It wasn't often I could put my breach-sister off balance.

Up ahead, another corridor joined our own. The crowd was growing and I started thinking about what Zael had said.

"Did you notice any change? In Reka?" I asked Isza.

"You know how he gets. I thought he was missing you. I tried to talk to him about it."

"And?"

"He said his work was taking him to the Academy more and more and he didn't like being away from the escarpment. I told him not to worry so much." The breath hissed in her spiracles. "Maybe I could have done more."

"He'd been to the Academy before the attack and no one had seen him return. But when I spoke to him –"

"You saw him? After the attack? How was he?"

I paused, remembering the howling wind. "He's lost his mind. He kept screaming he was in the library."

Isza sensed something of what I'd experienced. "At the Academy?" she said.

"He wasn't making sense. Don't blame yourself. No one could have anticipated what happened."

The corridor was brightly lit now and all but deafening as chitinous hoofs smacked and scraped along the hard floor. The narrowness didn't help, but slowly the corridor widened and then angled upwards until it became quite steeply raked, and finally we stepped out onto the bare rocky plateau of the escarpment. It was already bright day outside and my second eyelid compensated for the glare. It was warm too. The flat rock stretched away to either side and in front of us. Behind us lay the escarpment's edge, the desert beyond and, further on, Aktiuk hidden by distance and heat.

A hot wind flowed up from the sand below and pushed at our backs as we walked with the other House Czerag Kresz to a broad stone platform. The crowd fanned out to either side, circling it.

Czerag stood in the middle, flanked by Tzek and two Defender caste, their gaszti blades held high in the bright light of sura and djel. As we waited, ataz – the third sun – broke over the lip of the escarpment. The shadows deepened and the hot wind stiffened.

I heard running hoofsteps behind me – felt a blade bearing down on my exposed back. I almost tripped but Isza steadied me. Through her grip I could tell she was shaken as well by sudden fears. There was no invisible attacker: Reka had been taken out of his shielded cell. It was his madness we were feeling.

Unease grew among the crowd. Isza pushed to the front and I followed.

Reka emerged from behind the stone platform, half-carried, half-pushed by another two Defenders, each with a firm grip on his elbows. His head whipped violently from side to side, taking in the assembled crowd. He looked directly at me for an instant, but there was no hint of recognition.

Drummers off to one side began to rap on small tympans. The sound was a welcome distraction, because the feelings coming off Reka were as unsavoury as they were strong. Violent hatred fuelled by animal fear assaulted me, threatening to draw me into a circle of paranoia. I should lash out, kick, bite, break, do whatever I could to get away, and then wait like the cunning setzla for an unguarded victim so I could kill again.

Isza's grip tightened and that helped me push the impressions away a little and focus on the drums again.

The Defenders brought Reka to the front of the platform and pushed him into a kneeling position. He struggled, but his arms were bound and his captors' grip was too much even for strength born of madness.

He started to shout. "Leave! Leave! Get out of my head!"

The drums leaped in intensity, drowning out his howls. The rhythm sounded like the steady beat of pulse points beneath chitin, waiting for a blade to penetrate and spill their essence on the desert. I tasted rusz.

No. Those weren't my feelings. I thought of home, of Isza, of Bvak meeting me at the edge of the system, anything to push Reka out of my mind, but he only receded a little.

Czerag was standing behind Reka now, holding a blade across his chest, speaking the words of excision. The drums were suddenly louder again, their rhythm more insistent, filling the world with their sound.

"No house. No caste," Czerag said. "No family. No lodge."

Reka's mantle began to rise and he screamed at us, the words unintelligible but the feelings all too obvious and suddenly magnified as he approached full communion: murder, loathing, hurt, fear, despair. His shouting grew, each sound, each sense pounding into my head. I felt I would go mad if something didn't stop this now –

"Outcast. Excised," Czerag said, his voice low behind the noise, and then his knife came down, the blade slicing into and through Reka's mantle in one swift motion. The flesh slid to the ground. The evil filth pouring into my mind stopped.

Reka screamed on. Louder even. But it was just noise now.

The drums stopped. Reka stopped too. His body was bowed over. The Defenders pulled him up and led him back the way he'd come.

Czerag handed the blade to Tzek, who sheathed it. I shuddered, feeding on Czerag's quiet calm like someone starved. Reka was gone and I felt empty in a way I wouldn't have believed until this moment. Isza felt it too. The unexpected absence.

The hierarch turned and walked off the back of the flat stone, the crowd behind parting to let him pass.

We flowed around the platform to follow him. No one spoke. We were all too shocked, instinctively drawing together for comfort after Reka's assault.

As we walked across the escarpment, the wind dropped behind us so the air became as still as the minds surrounding me. We were in the hiatus between one awful moment and the next.

The ground rose and we came to a wide dip, almost a natural amphitheatre, with broad landings on either side leading down. A cloth canopy covered the centre of the area, shielding a wide stone table from the glare of the suns.

Czerag was there, and we filed down the landings until we were close to the table. The young female was lying on top of it, her torso supported so she could sit up a little and look around. She was attended by a Priest. The female's face was horribly mutilated. I doubted she could even talk properly let alone feed. Her arms had been laid alongside and then bound onto her torso with fine cord. A wide cloth was draped over the far end of the table with something bulky beneath it. I realised that was her legs.

We waited until the whole house was assembled. Czerag raised his arms and what little noise there was from the crowd hushed.

"The perfection of this innocent has been shattered through no fault of her own," he said. "She has spent the long night with those who love her, with her family and her house. He who caused her harm has been removed from the communion and we will not speak of him again. Her essence will now be offered up to Sakat."

The Priest raised his staff and shook it, the bells hanging from it ringing out across the hot silence, then he laid it down and took up a wooden cup and passed it to Czerag. The hierarch raised it to the female's mouth. She drank, though much of the liquid spilled onto her tunic. He then helped her to lie more comfortably.

The Priest shook his staff again and held it over his head. The tinkling of bells ceased, replaced by a swift rustling noise as the gathered Kresz raised their mantles. Rows and rows of circular hoods, all facing the female.

I hesitated. But not to join in would have singled me out and insulted the family. There was no danger to me here: the female was the sole focus of those assembled. My hood engorged and my feeling of self expanded and fell away into the communion.

My attention was drawn inexorably to the female. She seemed to shine out at us. I felt her pain, but also her love, the love she had for her family, for Czerag and, by extension, for all of us. The minds around me were like points in a vast constellation, joined by imperceptible yet powerful forces. We sensed together the sadness of farewell but the acceptance of it also, the rightness. What Czerag had said was true – her broken body would only be a prison for her now. She sat in the centre of this matrix, open to us, receiving so much but giving so much, until the sense of her began to drift as the poison took hold, a personality defocusing, spreading through us all, touching us in a way we would remember forever.

The feeling ebbed slowly. And then she was gone. The mantles relaxed, the connection unwound, and we were together but alone on top of the plateau.

Czerag bent and lifted her up and the Priest uncovered her legs and took those up too. Her lifeless body was carried to the flared metal spikes set into the ground behind the table. Each was half the height of an adult and the points were broad and honed fine and sharp.

More Priests appeared to help. Czerag and the first Priest took the torso, holding it high and bringing it down on the middle spike until the female's head was severed from the neck guard. Then Czerag took the head alone and broke it open on the second spike. He raised the breached brain pan to his feeder claws and supped at the flesh inside, then passed the head to the Priest who carried it to the family to taste.

One group of Priests were busy with the other spikes, breaking into the pectoral, abdominal and pelvic plates, and pulling out the innards onto large stone platters. Another group cracked the femoral and upper and lower patella sections of the legs, and the bicep, radial and metacarpal shell, with gaszti blades to get at the meat inside.

Soon I joined the line filing past the bench so each Kresz could receive a piece of the flesh.

"The flesh rejoins us as does the essence," the Priests said as they passed out the remains.

The meat was yellow in my claws. I lifted it to where my feeders could grip it and tear off morsels, pressing them into my mouth. It tasted as always: bland with a slight floral taint.

Those Kresz I had eaten of before had died naturally at the end of a long span of cycles. But the female had no such opportunity. Her potential had been wasted by someone who had once been a part of me. It was hard to retain a sense of peaceful transition, of leave-taking, in the wake of all that.

7

The surface of Herakli was nothing more than a yellow blur to Rhees as the ship spiralled down sunside. The planet was closed for the off-season and the commercial yacht was more than half-empty. Those citizens who could afford it had moved to the asteroid habs, or to worlds in a completely different system, to avoid the razor storms.

She sat on an overstuffed chair in the observation deck tapping at a ship tablet. With no dedicated HDC dataport on board, she couldn't access the dossier on the attack that was no doubt being continuously updated. The newsfeed reports were scant on detail and too concerned with downplaying what had happened. The Central Administration was keen to control the narrative for the human population of the Hegemony. The Brell colony was "well away" from any human settlement and no humans were in the system at the time. The colony was small – a direct lie – and poorly defended. Investigators were on the scene and the attackers, thought to be a relatively small renegade group, were expected to be neutralised soon. So go back to whatever you were doing before you were so rudely interrupted by thirteen billion deaths, Rhees thought.

At least she'd been sleeping better since she came onboard. Her nightmares were less defined and harder to remember when she woke, and last night she'd slept right through. It was something else to feel guilty about: that she might be "getting over" Petar's death. She told herself she never would, but she knew that in the long-term she couldn't survive the intensity of grief she'd been feeling. She needed her life to mean something now. Not to make sense of what had happened or make amends. That could never happen. But she'd trashed every opportunity and every good thing she'd had. It was time for a new way to live. And this mission was a start.

Nevertheless, her last conversation with Volmar played over in her mind. He was counting on her to fuck up, and the odds of that were good. She wasn't a field operative. Fleet had trained her well, but this was far outside piloting a ramcraft and shooting a cannon. Perversely, that took the pressure off a little. If Volmar had so little faith in her, it meant he'd have others on the ground who were much more capable. They were probably already well into it while she wasted time cruising Voss Space in a pleasure craft. At least she could watch and learn. And there may be some part of her Fleet training that could be useful. If nothing else, she might bring a fresh perspective to things.

The spaceport was on the nightside of the planet and close to Adjubon, capital of the main landmass. But as the ship came in to land, she saw that beyond a sprinkling of lights from the spaceport buildings and main thoroughfares, the city was in darkness.

She'd already grabbed her bag and was entering the main elevator as the yacht settled on the landing grid. A few more passengers joined her, business types she guessed. She'd dressed in civilian clothes during the trip and she caught more than one sideways glance at her uniform now. Everyone had something to hide, she supposed, and HDC had a reputation for knowing everything.

The lift fell the short distance to the surface of Herakli. Gravity was five per cent above Earth normal. The yacht had acclimatised its passengers incrementally during the trip, but even so Rhees knew she'd tire more quickly here. The triple door slid down, aside and up and a sweet-scented breeze cooled her skin. Insects chirped in the dark.

There was a scattering of port personnel and officials around the grid, but her uniform would make sure she wasn't bothered. She *was* meant to be met however. She looked around, craning to see another HDC onepiece. Nothing, but there was a tall man walking towards her clothed in a white djellaba, loose cotton trousers and knee-length boots.

He slowed and she realised who it was. Denev.

He looked just as shocked. *"You're the operative?"*

Fuck Volmar. Rhees felt rooted to the spot.

Denev dropped his head and the folds of the djellaba cast a shadow across the lower half of his face. It was Petar standing there. Get back onboard, Rhees thought. But she'd run out of options. Do that and Volmar would have the excuse he needed.

"We can't talk here," Denev said. "Follow me." He turned and picked his way across the grid towards the spaceport buildings, the wind pulling at the hem of his cloak.

The elevator door stood open behind Rhees. The other passengers were queuing to board the ground transport to the city. She shouldered her bag and followed Denev.

The inside of the spaceport looked nothing like she'd expected. It was almost rustic: low ceilings with a central area under a broad atrium, and small shops and eateries set into the walls. It was all but empty. Denev was waiting for her at the entrance to a tearoom. His expression was unreadable.

A waitperson greeted them and, after a word from Denev, showed them to a small, dimly lit booth with fat cushions and a low table. Denev ordered tea for them.

"I –" Rhees began, but Denev raised a finger and glanced at the waitperson's receding back.

Rhees threw her bag into the corner and they sat across from each other in silence. Denev watched her calmly as they waited. Rhees looked at him, looked away, focused on the wall hangings, the scattering of other customers, looked back, tried not to catalogue the similarities and differences between his face and Petar's. Finally the waitperson brought a tall pot of tea, a jug of honey and two stoneware cups, and pulled a curtain across the booth as he left.

"I should go," Rhees said. "You don't need me here." She didn't want to hurt him any more than she already had.

He reached over and repositioned both their cups until they sat exactly opposite each other on the table, moved the jug and pot to the side within easy reach, then sat back and looked at her again. He was so hard to read.

"I've caused you enough …" She trailed off. Just what was the right word for what she'd caused him already? This time she saw the tendons tighten across his jawline. She couldn't begin to imagine how he felt. How much he must hate her.

He took the lid off the pot and stirred the contents with a long silver spoon, which he wiped on a linen napkin before replacing the lid. He sat back into the soft cushions, watching her again.

"I used to be stationed here," he said. "But I was moved to Prox about a year before …" He hesitated but she knew what he meant. "Volmar ordered you to come here and help out with the investigation."

"Yes, but –"

"Volmar ordered me to meet the operative he was sending in person. He was very insistent that we work together closely and deliver a successful outcome for the investigation."

"He's fucking with me. With both of us."

"The point is: you leave now and I'll be held just as responsible for failing to follow his orders."

He poured tea for them, added honey to his cup, then held the spoon up, looking at her. She shook her head and took a sip. It was bitter. That seemed fitting.

"Regardless of why both of us are here, there's still a job to do," he said.

"It's not that simple. Volmar wants me to fail."

"He doesn't think you deserve a chance," he said. She glanced at him. He was staring at his cup. "Do you?"

She already knew this was the only chance she had. But how could she say that to the man whose brother she'd killed?

"I don't see how we can work together," she said.

"I can be professional if you can. We don't have to like each other or the situation."

"This is what you want?" she asked.

Finally she saw the anger she'd been waiting for. Then he looked down, reached for the pot and topped up both their cups. He was just as trapped as she was.

"Can you do what we have to do?" he said, focusing on his cup again.

"Yes."

He took a long breath and looked at her. The mask was back in place and he was just as unreadable as before. "Good."

He leaned forward and put his elbows on the table, cradling his cup. "So, details. I've been on the ground the last two weeks, renewing my connections with our network. Nothing yet, but it's just a matter of time. There were no survivors of the attacks obviously, which makes our job harder, and the Voss Space relays round the Brell colony were severely compromised by the nova. Analysis section is trying to reconstruct what it can from them, possibly get an entry or departure vector for the enemy ships, and in the meantime new relays have been deployed. Disaffected citizens across the sector are being rounded up and subjected to interrogation. That's a long shot, but something may shake loose. But there's more."

"Another attack?"

"Nothing as bad as the Brell colony, but the raiders have been active in the sector. So far there's been three hit-and-run attacks. Two on trade vessels and the destruction of an orbital station. We're analysing the data but there's a lot. We can use another pair of hands."

More immersion? She hoped not. But if Denev needed to make this work, she wasn't about to argue.

She drained her cup. "I'm ready if you are."

∞

Rhees barely slept that night, and it wasn't because of the gravity or the strange smells and sounds of a new planet. Volmar wanted her to fail and Denev ... She'd seen the hatred in his eyes even though he hid it quickly. She'd been hoping for a fresh start, even if it *was* with the fucking HDC. But she'd been fooling herself about that as well. There was no one she could count on out here. Even Denev might have another reason for keeping her around. To punish her? Fuck, in the right situation he could even kill her – take his revenge – and no one would be any the wiser.

She lay on her back. Pile on the paranoia why don't you? But she *was* alone. And no one had her back. This wasn't about building a new life. It was about survival.

She groaned and rolled over, stared at the blank wall, then screwed her eyes shut. Clear your mind. Focus on the quiet. But she was afraid to sleep. Because of what she might dream.

When a knock came at her door in the pale morning, she was already up and dressed.

Denev looked the same as he had last night, but his djellaba was open, revealing a deep blue silk shirt shot through with copper wire. He didn't seem the dandy type, so Rhees assumed this was standard streetwear.

"You need to eat?" he asked.

She didn't feel hungry. "Coffee would be good."

He turned towards the entrance vestibule and Rhees followed, aware of the incredible distance between them. Petar had never opened up about Denev, or anything else about his childhood. But she knew his parents were both dead, killed while he was a baby. Which meant Denev would have been about four and much more aware of what had happened.

Rhees's mother had died in the war too. She'd been too young to understand at the time, and her father had never been around much because he was in the service. It was only later she realised that he'd pretty much given her up after her mother died and she was passed from relative to relative for years. She'd just turned fifteen when she tried to initiate contact. Her father was rarely on Earth so holofeed was the only option. It was awkward – not just because of the physical distance between them – and the conversations always stalled. When she was accepted into Fleet she thought that at least would please him, but things hadn't turned out so well and the disappointment he'd shown when he'd been pulled into the whole sorry mess seemed now to define their relationship.

Petar's history with his brother had obviously been just as difficult, because the few times Rhees had probed him about it, his deflections had bordered on antagonistic. "Wound too tight for this galaxy," was all he'd say about Denev. Rhees could see that for herself now. But he had plenty of reason to be while she was around.

Sand crunched under the soles of her boots and lay in little piles in the corners of the vestibule. Nothing could keep it out apparently. The main door hissed open onto a Herakli dawn. Green-tinged wispy clouds lay spread across the sky, radiating out from the rising sun, which was a little redder than Sol. The street was lined with low buildings, no more than three storeys high. Most of them were shuttered, but one ground-floor cafe was open across the street. Tables dotted the walkway in front of it, and a fat man in a turban, rich red tunic and sporting a substantial moustachio stood by the counter.

Denev and Rhees crossed the deserted roadway and sat at a table. There were no other customers around. The fat man came out with a pot of coffee, cups and two plates of what turned out to be pastries dripping with clear honey. He deposited everything on the table between them without a word and withdrew to the counter.

"You come here a lot," Rhees said.

"I'm the only reason he stays in business."

She looked at him but he didn't seem to be joking. He had a very effective poker face.

"We can review the data we have today," he said. "Tomorrow

I'll show you around. There's not much to the city, but there are some people you should meet."

He moved her cup so it matched his – just like the previous evening, she thought – and poured coffee for them both.

"Other operatives?" she asked. It was a relief to focus on business.

"Some. Some informants too, and others that it's just good to have a relationship with."

"You work fast."

He shrugged. "Like I said, I've been here before. It was just a matter of reintroducing myself."

She took a sip. The coffee was thick and strong. "You enjoy working for the Corps?" She had meant it as harmless conversation, but it came out sounding like an accusation.

He sat back, cradling his own cup. "If I had a harmonics detector right now I could pick out a whole range of emotional tags from that statement. You prefer Fleet."

"That's not an option any more." She didn't want to get into that this morning. "But I'm having trouble adjusting to a different *modus operandi.*"

His face cracked in a brief smile. It suited him, and she wondered if she'd imagined that flash of hatred the night before. Or maybe he was just very good at being a spy.

"That's very diplomatic," he said. "Maybe you do have a calling in the Corps. But I'm aware of the low regard most Fleet personnel have for HDC operatives."

Two other uniformed HDC personnel crossed the road from the Corps office and sat at the next table. One was tall, broad-shouldered and very blond with a ruddy complexion, broad nose and thick lips. The other was shorter and much thinner with black close-cropped, but still curly hair. He looked like a child by comparison. The owner brought out coffee for them.

"We're both competing for resources from the Central Administration," Rhees said. "It doesn't encourage cooperation."

"That's the way the CA likes it. It keeps us on our toes."

"But it goes deeper than that," Rhees said. "The underlying philosophies of both organisations are diametrically opposed."

"Sometimes I think Petar chose Fleet instead of HDC purely because he didn't want to be like his big brother," Denev said and a shadow passed over his face.

"We can never make choices for others," she said. "Not the ones that matter."

"That's interesting coming from someone who blames herself for my brother's death."

Rhees foundered. Was he accusing her again? He'd said he wanted her to stay, but surely she reminded him too much of what had happened. He certainly reminded her of Petar. The set of his shoulders as he sat, the way he placed his hands on his lap, the slant of his eyes – all conjured a strong sense for her of the man she'd come to love still living and breathing. It was painful, but it was also something like a gift to think that Petar wasn't completely gone from the universe. That something of him, however differently expressed in Denev, persisted.

"I don't want to get into that again," she said. "Not here."

"I shouldn't have brought it –"

"Hey, horsey-boy! Where you going in such a hurry?"

Rhees looked over Denev's shoulder. The blond HDC guy was shouting at an alien across the street. A Brell: tall, long-necked and long-headed, with ears sticking up and covered in fine brown hair. The alien walked faster.

"Giddy-up, horsey-boy," the blond shouted and laughed.

"Really?" Rhees said to Denev. She leaned past him. "Hey. Shut the fuck up. How old are you – *twelve?*"

The blond stood up quickly, his chair toppling behind him. His friend was already standing too, laying a hand on his arm.

Denev jumped up, turning to meet the oncoming blond, and pushed him back. "Calm down!" he said.

The blond glared at Rhees. "Who the fuck are you?"

Rhees stood too, all the stresses of the last weeks bubbling up inside. She was ready for this. She brought her fists up. "Let's find out."

Denev kept one hand on the blond's chest and turned towards Rhees, holding up his other hand to ward her off. "Calm down, both of you, or I'll report this."

"Come on, Killian," the smaller man said, still holding his friend's arm. "I want to eat. This isn't worth it."

Killian didn't move for a moment and Rhees tensed. Then he looked down at his friend pulling at his arm. "You'll keep," he said to her, then turned away to pick up his chair and sit again.

"What is wrong with you?" Denev said.

I'm the crazy bitch that killed your brother, Rhees thought. She felt suddenly overwhelmed by every bad choice that had led to Petar's death and every slight and insult she'd endured since she joined HDC. She wanted to scream. Instead she dropped her hands and let her breath out. She tapped her band to pay for breakfast and walked back across the street, Denev following her for a change. The Brell was long gone.

Denev caught her arm. "I mean it," he said. "What's wrong?"

She was still riding the sudden wave of anger at Killian. "*This.*" She slapped at the HDC sigil on her chest. "The difference between this and Fleet. Fleet protects; HDC controls. That's the opposing philosophies right there. And your friend just demonstrated the result."

"Come on, Killian is an idiot."

"He's not the only one," she said and instantly regretted it. "No, I didn't mean you."

Denev dropped her arm and took a breath. "Look, I understand. You don't want to be here. You don't want to be HDC. But you said you could work like a professional. Was that a lie?"

Rhees sighed, the anger flushing out of her. "Fuck." He was right. She felt trapped: she lashed out. Sadly predictable given her track record.

"Not all species are happy citizens of the Hegemony, you know," he said. "The Brell Conglomerate only joined after we neutralised their spaceyards. They couldn't fight us so they were forced to join us."

"But now they have, how smart is it to treat them like shit?" Rhees said. "It just makes them hate us more when we should be showing them the benefits the Hegemony brings."

"Sounds great in theory. But operating on the ground is very different to flying around in a ramcraft."

"It's all part of the same thing. We're here to keep Hegemony citizens safe. It doesn't matter what species they are. We're judged by our actions more than our words. That's important." But she was calm enough now to know she couldn't change HDC one fist fight at a time. "Forget it. Let's get started," she said.

They walked together back through the vestibule, past the front office and the corridor where her quarters were, and down a ramp to a large circular room that was bare and open. A platform ran around the wall above their heads and she could see datanooks set at regular intervals on the next level. It was like a mini version of the Datahive, which meant they were standing in the holotank.

Denev activated the projectors with his band and they were surrounded by the ruined Brell system. It was even worse now than Rhees remembered. Red wireframe ghosts outlined the sun and the orbital positions of the nine planets that used to make up the system. The mountainous chunks of outer planet she'd seen on Earth were long gone, spinning through frozen infinity now. The remaining debris was well out towards what had been the heliopause. Larger pieces were tagged and linked to their ghost world by thin orange lines.

"How could this happen?" she said, almost whispering.

"It was daytime when light from the attack made it to Prox Base," Denev said. "We went outside. The sky blazed so bright we couldn't see the sun." He pulled the image back until they passed through the shell of expanding gas still glowing brightly in a ghostly spectrum. "That's still visible from Prox now, day and night."

"It would be beautiful if we didn't know what was there before. What about the other attacks?"

The image pulled out again to a sector view floating around them with an overlay showing arrangements of star clusters and colonies.

"Most of the habitable systems are divided up between the Brell Conglomerate, the Sissilak and the Totek," Denev said. "They co-exist peacefully enough. There have been three new incidents, all occurring in Sissilak space."

Glowing purple icons marked the sites. Rhees couldn't see anything to link them spatially. They didn't form a linear arrangement and there was no obvious central point they were clustered around. Denev focused in on the first icon, closest to the ruined Brell colony. It was open space.

"Nothing around," he said. "About six hours out from a transit point. A group of cargo transports and a single Sissilak patrolship. They didn't have a chance, and we didn't have a relay nearby so our data is limited. The ships were all blown apart in seconds. The raiders weren't interested in whatever they were carrying."

"How do you know it was the raiders?" Rhees asked.

"The patrolship sent this along with their distress call." A window opened up with a blurred image of a ship, the configuration instantly recognisable as one of the raiders' horseshoe craft.

The view pulled back and zoomed in to the second icon. Again there were no planets, no moons, nearby. A smoke-ring nebula was tagged at two AUs from the attack site.

"Three days later, the same thing," Denev said. "Sissilak ships again, although this time they had one of their militia destroyer escorts with them and a wing of Talon fighters. The attack took longer but the result was the same. Debris scatter indicates the attackers came in from the direction of the nebula. We've had teams through there since and they haven't found anything. No base, no ships."

"And the last one?" Rhees asked.

"Happened two days ago. This system is newly annexed by the Sissilak. It has no habitable planets, but they're setting up survey and mining operations."

The image showed a dwarf star, dull orange with a broad ring of asteroids about half an AU out accompanied by some bigger shepherd moonlets. The last icon was centred above what looked like the largest of those.

"This time there were survivors," Denev said. "A survey team sent down from the orbital mining rig. We've got vision of the whole attack."

"I'd like to study that," Rhees said. She paused, thinking about the string of raids. "It's weird. They start by destroying an entire star system and follow it up by picking off a few cargo ships and a mining rig. It's like they wanted to get our attention and now they have it they've throttled back to see how we react."

"It's exactly like that." A tall woman was standing by the entrance, elegantly dressed in a teal-coloured silk jacket and mid-calf skirt. She had short grey hair and looked to be in her mid-sixties, but her blue eyes were sharp and the lines on her face spoke more of laughter than age.

"Consul Demain, this is Rhees Lowrans, newly attached to the HDC unit," Denev said.

The consul nodded. "Nice to meet you, Rhees. I wasn't informed of your posting. Or your arrival."

Rhees wasn't sure what to say. The consul was a political appointment and not part of the HDC hierarchy. It hadn't occurred to her to report anywhere.

But Demain was smiling. "It's all right. I like to pretend I have some real authority here from time to time."

"I'm sorry, Consul," Rhees said. "I've jumped right into the current situation."

Demain crossed to stand beside her and looked at the last attack site. "As you should. The Brell Conglomerate, the Sissilak, even the Totek, they all want to know what we're doing about it. But the pattern of attacks … It's hard to fathom." She looked at Rhees. "Are you a tactical expert?"

"Rhees is a field operative," Denev said. "But she has some experience with Fleet."

Demain's finely shaped eyebrows lifted and Rhees tried to hide her annoyance at Denev.

"A brief spell," she said.

Demain was waiting for more, but when the silence stretched past a few seconds she nodded again and said, "In any case, I hope you get results soon. My counterparts are demanding a resolution and the longer this goes on the more they demand."

"We're doing everything we can, Consul," Denev said.

"I'll leave you to it then. Good luck."

"Please don't tell anyone else I was in Fleet," Rhees said to Denev when Demain was gone. "I don't need anyone fishing around in my background."

"I'm sorry. I was just thinking your experience might bring something new to the data analysis."

Rhees glanced up at the datanooks and sighed. "I'll certainly try."

8

The priests collected what was left of the female's flesh. Nothing would be wasted. The crowd broke into smaller groups to discuss what had happened at the escarpment since the suns last rose. No one seemed in a rush to re-enter the tunnels.

"There's Gurud," Isza said. "You should say hello properly."

I didn't feel like socialising but Isza pulled me along behind her, through the crowd towards a group of Defenders.

In the cramped vestibule outside Czerag's chamber Gurud had all but filled the available space. Outside in the open air he seemed just as improbably large. He was as tall as Isza but easily twice as broad. His chest plates were burnished a bright red and incised with the sigil of the house Defenders. With his over-large left arm ending in a viciously sharp pincer he looked like a lumbering but deadly behemoth. But as I focused on him through the overlapping jumble of feelings bleeding through the crowd, I also had the sense of a quick mind. There was a flurry of conflicting impressions as he saw us closing on him: surprise, happiness with a strange mix of nervousness, and something approaching mistrust. It was fair enough to guess I was the cause of the latter.

Isza reached out and grasped his pincer, the knuckle bigger than her whole fist. She was protecting me again, moving to dampen Gurud's reaction with her own sense of me.

"You two have met, I hear," Isza said to him. "So now you can start becoming friends." It sounded more like a command than a suggestion, mainly to Gurud but also to me.

His feeling of mistrust blossomed at Isza's words. But now I was close to him, it didn't feel absolute. He'd become more nervous when Isza mentioned our incipient friendship. His relationship with Isza made him more disposed to understand me. He just wasn't sure how to do that.

"A distressing homecoming," he said to me, shifting uneasily.

"Yes. But the worst is past now, I hope. Things can return to normal. You two have chosen, Isza says. I'm glad you make her happy."

I felt him relax a little as he realised I could at least appear normal. I saw Isza give his pincer a little squeeze of encouragement. It was very sweet, this huge Defender and my sister. An unlikely pairing but it felt right; to Isza as well obviously.

"Isza says you want to travel. Not just to the lands of other houses but beyond the reach of our suns. Why is that?" Gurud blurted.

Isza's claw dropped away from his. She was annoyed, but it was a question I'd been asked many times before in many different ways. I didn't feel any malice from Gurud. He was embarrassed at his clumsiness but he genuinely wanted to know. He was trying to understand me, making the effort for Isza's sake – although she didn't see it that way. I liked him for it. It was a refreshing change from the minds that wouldn't or couldn't understand me.

I couldn't tell him that I'd already been beyond our own suns, but I could answer him honestly enough. "I don't really know why. It's not something I chose. The feeling's been with me since I was an instar. To see things no one else has seen. Some people think that's not a right thing to wish for. Right or wrong, I can't help it. The thought of travelling further than any other Kresz has always excited me."

He mulled that over. "Czerag's seed expresses itself in many different ways," he said finally. And I felt clearly that he accepted my answer and – whether for Isza's sake, mine or something else – we were friends.

I thought I'd be forthright myself; after all this was my breach-sister he was seeing. "How long have you and Isza been together?"

"Am I in the way?" Isza said.

"Since the season of Kareee," Gurud said, ignoring her. I wasn't sure this was a wise long-term tactic. "We will mate at the next house communion."

He said it with certainty, as if talking about ataz rising only after sura and djel were in the sky. It seemed to me that fierce, independent Isza liked this about him, though it was probably a character trait destined to annoy her in the long run.

The Priest's bells were ringing again and Gurud shifted his bulk to look over the crowd.

"I must accompany the remains," he said, and I stepped aside to let him past. "We will meet again over the evening meal." And then he was gone.

"I suppose I don't have a choice in the matter," I said quietly to Isza and she rapped my chest plate.

"Don't be like that. He's a good person. He's just a little brusque."

The crowd was dispersing, heading back into the escarpment. Over by the stone table, the female's carapace was picked clean and laid out ready to be burned, though at least one piece would be kept by the family.

Some thought the essence of the dead rejoined the worldmind, spread too thinly to be sensed, until – if the god Sakat deemed it worthy – it was reborn in a new nymph's body. It was all part of his plan for us – the steady progress towards perfection that began before history. I preferred to think that when we ate the flesh of the dead, they became a part of us; and when we died and were eaten in turn, we and they would become a part of the next generation, and on and on. Maybe it wasn't so different but it felt more natural, less ordained.

"We should go," I said to Isza, and we retraced our steps back towards the tunnel into the network of passages.

Tzek was waiting at the tunnel entrance for us. I thought it was me he wanted but he turned to Isza. "You're needed in the hierarch's chambers. House business."

Isza looked at me, but I had no more idea than she did why she was needed.

"I'll come down with you," I said.

"No, Udun. You have an appointment with the Scholars. South tunnel in their chambers."

"It's fine," I told Isza, feeling her sudden concern for me. "I'll meet you in the entranceway afterwards."

We parted, and I joined the groups of Kresz filing down the corridors into the cool passageways deep under the escarpment. The south tunnel connected from one of the main refectories near the base of the escarpment and ran down into bedrock that had been worked and shaped into a series of rooms now occupied by the Scholars. I left the crowds behind, my hoofsteps echoing down the empty, lantern-lit passage. The air was much cooler down here.

Finally, I pushed a curtain aside to enter a brighter chamber. The Scholar who greeted me was typical of the body type: short as an instar, with thin and delicate claws, and longer feeder claws used for manipulating fine instruments as much as for eating.

She led me to a padded chair, then opened cabinets set into the wall and assembled her tools. What she held up was nothing like the elegant Telsan device used to inject me. It was a simple metal tube, sharpened to a point at one end with the other attached to a shallow cup.

"Your pardon," she said.

Of course, I would have to do this to myself. No Kresz would cause pain to another if it could possibly be avoided. I took the instrument, guided the point between my pectoral plates to the pulse point there, then pushed it through the hide. The Scholar winced and pulled back as she felt the pain of the insertion. The rusz flowed into the cup and I pulled the tube out again and handed it to her. I pressed on the wound with one claw as she took the sample to her bench and began to decant it.

"You can go now," she said.

The rusz flow had sealed over, so I stood and retraced my steps to ground level. I knew the Scholar would have no knowledge of why she was taking my rusz, and was sure the sample would be handed to another Scholar who had no knowledge of where it had come from. Another Scholar would apply the chemical compound transmitted by Emba's people with no knowledge of its origin. And another would read the results; or perhaps only partially, leaving the work to be completed by yet another. No single step or piece of information in the process would be enough to reveal the full picture. And none of them would question why. Only Czerag would know the full results and he commanded complete obedience and secrecy.

In the entrance hall, the double doors were open and the fissure that led out to the oases was bathed in full sunlight. As I reached the doorway Isza emerged from the tunnel to Czerag's chamber.

"There you are," she said, out of breath. If feelings were visible, she'd have been glowing.

"What did Czerag want you for?"

"I have a job. Finally. A decent one. A tenspace run. The Defenders Guild asked for *me*." Her feeders spread wide.

"Can you talk about it?" I asked as we walked together out to the cutting.

"It's quite a mission actually. I'll be piloting one of three ships, accompanied by two Defender craft."

I was suddenly concerned. "It's dangerous?"

"I don't think so. They're just being cautious after the *Might of Gnow* went missing. One of our other deeprange ships encountered an unknown vessel a few days ago far out beyond the Lenticular. You know what the protocols are. They didn't attempt contact."

Of course, I thought. Why talk to unknown aliens? It wasn't the Kresz way.

We left the cutting and walked along the base of the escarpment.

A group of instars were sitting in a circle with their carers over by the oasis, playing a game that involved one of them running to a nearby bush and bringing back a leaf to pass to the next youngling in the circle.

"The deeprange crew prepped to leave," Isza continued, "but just before the tenspace jump, they received a transmission from the alien vessel – a string of numbers in a base system very different to ours. They translated to spatial and temporal coordinates."

"An invitation," I said.

"The Council has decided these aliens are to be met and politely told that their contact is unwelcome and is not to be attempted again."

"And the Defenders are accompanying you to make sure the aliens understand?"

"Something like that."

I spread my feeder claws wide. Isza couldn't help but feel my amusement.

"What?" she said.

"I really don't fit in here."

"I suppose you'd want to get to know them. Maybe become friends?"

"Terrible, isn't it."

She paused. "It feels wrong to be leaving you now. I'm not going back on my promise – it'll just be –"

"It's a good job and you need it. I'll manage. Did they say who these aliens are?"

"I think they're called 'Hegemony'."

It was as if I was back on Telsus IV with Atalna, experiencing again the nightmare he'd conjured with his stories.

Isza grasped my wrist guard and the essence of what we were both feeling flowed between us.

"They're dangerous. Far more dangerous than some random alien encounter," I said. "We need to tell Czerag."

"He's monitoring the Council session in his chamber."

"Was Tzek with him?"

"No."

"Come on then."

∞

Back at the entranceway one of the Defenders told us Tzek was likely still on top of the escarpment. We followed the passages back up. The rocky plateau was all but empty now and hotter than before, and we found him at the end of one of the deep channels eroded high up in the face of the escarpment. The opening looked out into the desert, which was painfully bright under the combined glare of sura, djel and ataz until my desert eyelid compensated. Dunes rippled away to the horizon, distorted by heat shimmer.

"He's out there, you know," Tzek said, recognising us without needing to turn from the view. "Reka. None of the desert tribes will help him. They'll drive him from their camps." He turned then to look at me. "Why would a Kresz choose to cut himself off from everyone and everything that might save him?"

"What you describe is the consequence of his act, not the reason behind his choice to act," I said. "We can't know what that was without asking him. And he didn't seem inclined to talk."

"Perhaps," Tzek said simply, and shifted his gaze to Isza. "You seem excited, or ..." he paused, "you were. Now you're not so sure."

"Isza told me about her mission," I said. "To the Hegemony. I've heard about them. They're dangerous and we should have nothing to do with them."

Tzek looked at Isza and I could feel his mind calculating. "And have you told your breach-sister how you came by this information?"

"He has not," Isza said, her anger flaring. "He's served his hierarch and told me nothing."

Tzek blinked briefly. "In any case, Udun, you appear to be in complete agreement with the Council."

"No, I'm not. We shouldn't even be meeting them. If there's any chance they could trace us back to Homeworld, it could be the end for all of us."

He could see how strongly I felt about this. He looked from me to Isza. "There's no way we can halt the mission without raising questions in the Council. We couldn't explain how we came by such intelligence." He blinked. "No, we can't afford any additional scrutiny. Not now."

"We can't afford to ignore it," I said. "Tzek, this threat transcends any house rivalry."

"And where is your proof? Do you expect the hierarch to endanger his plans on your say-so?"

"Then let me go out again. A quick trip to Telsus IV. I can get you all the proof you need."

Air sighed through his spiracles. "And so it comes back to this. Your own desire to leave Homeworld. Is that what's behind your 'danger'?" He leaned on his staff and stood straighter. "The hierarch is grateful for what you have done. But we both think it best that you fade back into the life of the house after your journey."

So Czerag had made his decision.

Tzek felt my rising anger and snapped, "Or if you prefer, there are boltholes in the deep desert where no one could find you."

I wouldn't fester in some hole in the ground. Just the thought of it made me feel sick. Tzek watched, probing my reaction. I didn't trust myself to speak.

"Udun," Isza said. She was worried for me. She knew as well as I that Tzek's advice carried a great deal of weight with Czerag. If he said bury me, I was as good as buried.

I took a step back and looked out across the desert. "I'm sorry," I said.

"Be careful on this mission," Tzek said to Isza. "The Defenders Lodge asked for you by name and we don't know why. It may be they know about Udun and your connection to him."

"But I don't know anything," Isza said.

"Then you'll be perfectly safe," Tzek said. "But I expect you to keep your eyes open. I'll want a complete report when you return.

Safe journey."

He turned back to the view over the dunes.

Isza and I retraced our steps into the escarpment, walking together through the branching corridors until the feeling of others around us masked Tzek's presence.

Isza stopped at a junction. "My orders are to leave immediately for Aktiuk to join up with the mission crew. I'll need to get ready."

"And tell Gurud he'll have to delay his plans for you both."

Her small feeders spread wide. "Poor Gurud. He's been very patient. And you have to be patient too. Keep away from Tzek and wait till I get back. Then we'll see about getting you off-planet."

I held her close, and could feel how concerned she was for me when she should be worried for her own safety.

"Be careful," I said. But I remembered Atalna's warning, that the Hegemony came with one hand extended in friendship while the other concealed a weapon.

9

Adjubon City, Herakli / Cygnus Sector / Hegemony

Space flowed through Rhees and around her: planets dancing, ships flitting like fireflies, there then gone, datatags flashing by, terminating at transit points, reappearing systems over. Trans-sector, local system, extra-sector patterns of movement. Months of voyages matched with flight plans, transponder records, manifests, docking rolls. It was easy to lose time, lose a sense of where you were in physical space, lose a sense of self. This was what Rhees hated so much about immersion. The data was seductive because there was so much of it, and one piece of information led to layers of data beneath, and more layers after that leading down to forever. She'd catch herself, as if she was falling asleep standing up: a mental head jerk to bring her back to self-consciousness. The reflex made her feel sick to her stomach, but she couldn't bring herself to surrender completely to the dataflow. Volmar would say this was indicative of a stubborn egocentricity that proved she was ill-suited to Corps work. There may be some truth to that but, despite the nausea, she was making progress.

She pushed on, moving from the primary transport hubs and lanes to secondary and tertiary routes, data passing through her in a timeless flurry, before turning her attention to the raider attacks. She spent only a short time on the Brell colony; what really interested her were the smaller raids. She recreated each event, tracking debris scatters in reverse, reassembling shattered vessels, freezing the simulation each time a partially reconstructed hull registered a hit to look at energy yields, diffraction patterns, impact angles, and then backtracking the blast, adding in what they knew of the raider ships to extrapolate likely attack vectors and formations. If there had been only a single attack, the modelling would be pure guesstimate, only one of a double handful of possibilities, and so next to useless. But she had three attack runs in similar circumstances to review, and through all of them she felt she had a picture approximating the raiders' preferred tactical deployment, the way they moved together to minimise their profile to enemy ships, and how they targeted vital systems then looped back to mop up. It wasn't too dissimilar from patterns she'd studied in Fleet. There were only so many ways to approach, disable and destroy a vessel in space.

She was completing a fifth run on the orbital mining facility attack when the datastream halted abruptly, lifting the neural brake, and a window opened up in the virtual space. An incoming transmission, numbers running across and down her field of vision, then a flash and the HDC infinity symbol appeared, fading out to Troels Volmar looking directly at her.

"Hard at it, Lowrans?"

She was still feeling vaguely nauseous and wished she could cut the feed. Talking to Volmar was like engaging in unarmed combat.

"I'm reviewing the data, Comptroller," she said warily.

"Analysing information that's already been catalogued by people who are much more skilled at it than you. You have no better idea of what you should be doing?"

"I've been here less than a day." What did he expect?

"And your next steps are?"

She had no idea what came next. "Formulating. Once I've finished my review, they'll be a lot clearer."

His eyes narrowed; he clearly wasn't fooled. There were no obvious leads in what she'd analysed so far. Though she had a feeling there was something there. Something waiting to fall into place for her.

"Our own analysis has been more fruitful," he said. "We've isolated what we think are raider transmissions, ship to ship during the attacks. We're working on a translation and we'll send that to your field supervisor." He paused. "Speaking of which, how is Antwer?"

Fully aware of her body again, Rhees settled back in the padded womb of the datanook. "He's been very helpful." You fucker, she added silently.

"I'm sure he'll be able to make up for your inadequacies. You begged for a mission, Lowrans. I don't just expect results; I expect you to impress me. We both know what will happen if you don't." The window closed.

Rhees activated the sequence to cut the datanook's visual and auditory feeds so she could fully rejoin the real world. She'd been just about ready to finish her shift before Volmar's call, but he had a special way of getting under her skin and now she was keyed up.

Her band told her it was 10 p.m. local time. Herakli ran a twenty-six-hour day. She stood on the platform above the empty holospace and wondered what Denev was doing. It was a strange thought. He could never be a friend, and she was sure her presence was at best uncomfortable for him. But today he'd been true to his word. They'd worked together like professionals.

She made her way to the entry vestibule and out into the street. No one around. The cafe over the road was shuttered and the street was in darkness. She could go for a walk, but it didn't feel particularly safe outside. The place was so still, like a ghost city. No moons lit the gloom.

"Fuck Volmar," she said. Then her stomach rumbled and she remembered she'd skipped lunch. Turning back inside, she took the corridor past her room. There was a commissary further along.

As she rounded a curve in the passage she almost ran into Killian. He towered above her, big-chested and broad shouldered, practically filling the passageway.

"Can I get past, please?"

Killian took a step forward. Physically threatening.

She looked up at him, repeating, "Can I get past, *please?*"

He glanced past her and said, "Look, Jorn, it's the Fleet bitch."

Jorn had come up behind her. Maybe they'd been waiting for her. There was no way this could end well, but she tried. "Just let me pass. This doesn't need to happen."

"You don't tell us what to do, Fleet," Killian said. "We found out all about you. Killed one of your own team."

"Washed out," Jorn added. "Needed your daddy to make it all better."

Rhees let out a slow breath, relaxing her shoulders and distributing her weight more evenly on the balls of her feet. "You guys can read. I'm impressed. Let's see how you handle numbers. You have to the count of three to get out of my way."

Killian grunted and said, "Or what?"

Rhees shrugged. "Three." She pivoted and punched Jorn in the face with a hard left hook. He dropped like a stone.

Behind her now, Killian hesitated and she brought her elbow back and up and rammed it into his nose, felt the cartilage give as his head snapped back. She turned to see blood flowing over his lips and chin.

His head pitched forward again as his right fist swung round. Rhees ducked so the fist flew over her head, driving into and through the wall up to the elbow. She'd brawled with big guys before, some of them deceptively fast. Killian wasn't one of those. Standing again, she thrust her knee three times in quick succession into his gut, forcing him to keep doubled over so his arm was still trapped, then delivered two more vicious blows to his nose. He straightened, pulling his arm free, and staggered back until the other wall stopped him. Fuck, he wasn't down yet. But he was angry.

Roaring, he ran at her, both arms wide and high to grab her in a bear hug. She waited, then dropped to all fours and pushed up, arching her back so her hip connected with his, lifting him off the ground. His momentum carried him on, pivoting over her, the roar turning to a scream that cut off as his head smashed into the floor and he fell in a heap, looking like a discarded rag doll. He was out cold, but still breathing.

Rhees stood and straightened her onepiece. No one had come to see what the racket was. Still tingling from the rush of sudden close combat she made her way to the commissary, walked past empty tables and stood in front of the dispenser wall, waiting for her breathing to calm.

The food was heavily skewed towards local dishes: spiced grilled meats, simple salads and dips. She took a selection, arranged it on a tray and grabbed a bottle of water, deciding to eat back in her room.

In the passageway, Jorn was gone but Killian was still out cold. Had his sidekick just left him here? It said a lot about their friendship if he had.

Rhees kneeled, placed her tray on the floor and put her ear against Killian's chest. Heartbeat strong and steady. She hauled at one arm, turning him on his side into the recovery position. As she straightened, he started to snore.

"Next time, pick on someone your own size," she said, and took her tray back to her quarters.

10

A storm front was moving in and night was falling early across Adjubon. Rhees hadn't seen Denev all day, and that was just as well. When she'd woken and thought about the fight in the cold light of day, she'd realised how poorly it would play in his eyes. So she'd kept a low profile, eating in the commissary outside normal dining hours and staying locked in the datanook the rest of the time. Knowing she was just delaying the inevitable.

She'd finished reviewing the raider material an hour ago, and had come up to the roof to watch impossibly tall cloud formations pile up along the horizon then advance on the city. And to reflect on her mistakes.

The access door opening behind her made her turn and her heart sank. Her luck had finally run out.

"This is where you're hiding?" Denev said, advancing on her. "Didn't I tell you we don't brawl in HDC?"

She backed up against the railing. There was no excuse. She knew that, but she tried anyway. "I didn't go looking for it. They wanted it."

"And you gave it to them! Jesus, I'm meant to be your supervisor. I'm responsible for you, and this is just the sort of out-of-control attitude that –"

"Don't you think I know that?" She couldn't bear to hear him say the words. "I fucked up. Again!"

Tears pricked at her eyes and she blinked them away and turned angrily back towards the storm clouds. She wasn't going to pieces in front of him. Not after what he'd already endured because of her.

"I'm trying to change." She took a long, ragged breath. "But it's fucking hard."

Harder still because she felt so *alone*. Maybe Volmar was right. No. She wouldn't give that fucker the satisfaction.

"I'm sorry," she said. "I'll do whatever it takes to make this right. I'll apologise to Killian."

There was a pause and for a moment she thought he'd gone. Out in the distance there was a bright green flash in the growing thunderhead.

"I don't think Killian wants to even acknowledge what happened," Denev said behind her. "It doesn't really fit with his self-image."

She laughed, but it sounded bitter and still tinged with tears.

"But …" Denev cleared his throat. "He's in no shape to help me tonight, so I'm a man down."

She wasn't really sure what he was saying. She turned to face him.

He looked down at his calfskin boots, as if considering, then back at her. "I have some fieldwork if you're up for it. *If* you can keep from getting into a fight, that is."

"I can be diplomatic. You said so yourself."

"One of my contacts, a member of the Sissilak trade office in Adjubon, wants to meet tonight. He has some information."

"About the raids?"

"He didn't say, but I've had good intel from him before."

"I can help. I'm ready," she said.

But Denev was looking at her critically. "No. You're not. Come with me."

She followed him back to ground level and a room beside the holotank. The door slid open at his touch. There were racks of clothing, open shelving with boots, sandals, satchels, and other shelves with hardware. Some of the tech she recognised, including some surveillance gear and a mini-comp; other items she wasn't sure about.

Denev moved among the racks, sorting through and selecting clothing. "If we're moving among the locals, it's best not to flash the HDC insignia." He looked at her. "It's not too popular with some of the species."

"You surprise me," she said.

He smiled at that and she felt the tension drain out of her. God knows he owed her nothing, but he was giving her a chance.

He disappeared in the racks for a moment, then came back with an armful of clothes. "These should help you fit in." She took the bundle.

He grabbed a pair of soft leather boots from the shelves. "And these."

Handing her the boots, he picked up two items from the tech on display. One was an earpiece translator link, a trink. It linked with her band to provide instant translation. The other piece she didn't recognise. It was like a copper ring, but designed to fit around two fingers.

"Mobi," he said. "Immobiliser. Non-lethal. Just push it against whoever you want out of your way."

"You're expecting trouble?"

"If I was expecting trouble I'd get you a blaster from the armoury. It's just for insurance."

She took the trink and the mobi, and looked down at the clothes and boots cradled in her arms. She'd never been dressed by a man before.

"I'll just be a minute," she said and walked quickly back to her room.

She shed her onepiece and washed her face in the basin, then pulled on the loose silk pants and thick linen shirt. The natural materials felt luxurious against her skin after the synthetic of her HDC uniform. The boots were perfect, the soft leather moulding to her feet. She walked back into the ensuite and looked at herself in the full-length mirror. She had to admit he had taste.

She pulled on the djellaba he'd selected, a midnight blue with overlapping circles of copper thread that went well with the dark maroon pants and white shirt. She gave herself a lopsided smile in the mirror. She'd gotten out the habit of wearing anything more than uniforms since Petar died.

She fitted the mobi over the middle and ring finger of her right hand and walked back out to the vestibule to meet Denev. The look in his eyes when he saw her – she'd seen it before from other men. But it was a little unsettling coming from Petar's brother.

He looked away, clearing his throat self-consciously. "You look good. Like a true local." He pulled at a fold in her djellaba, held up a section of the hem. "The cloak has autonomous shielding built in. Just in case. And some other tricks. To deactivate it, just press this stud."

"Handy," she said. She wouldn't have seen the contact if he hadn't pointed it out to her.

They walked out into the night. The clouds had settled over the city now and the wind was picking up, blowing in gusts that pulled at her djellaba.

"It's meant to hold off for a couple more hours," Denev said, looking up at the sky.

They walked the length of the street, then turned left and an immediate left again into a side street, then right into a narrow lane. The grid pattern of the main streets broke down completely here, the laneways meandering and branching, opening into small communal squares surrounded by apartment dwellings. The streetlighting was dim and the alcoves and columned arcades that were typical of the local architecture made for a shadowy landscape ideal for any kind of wrongdoing that took one's fancy, Rhees thought.

"Much street crime?" she asked, ducking behind Denev as they passed through a narrow arch.

"Not as much as you'd think. The residential areas are pretty much single species and the communities are close-knit. Besides, when it's not storm season most of these streets are crowded. The Herakli treat the pavement outside their houses as extra living space."

The twists of the lanes sheltered them for the most part, but every so often they'd turn a corner, cross a broader street and get pushed by a strong gust of wind. Looking between the buildings at the sky, Rhees could see the clouds were taking on a greenish tinge, like a days-old bruise.

"It's down here," Denev said, leading them into a dim alley and relative stillness. A single lamp at the far end lit up a sign: *The Fortunate Wanderer.*

Denev stopped at the taverna door and leaned close, his lips brushing the hair above her ear. "Just follow my lead inside. The Sissilak knows me but he doesn't know you. He might be a little brusque."

Rhees nodded. "I can handle brusque."

He pushed open the door and she followed him into a small vestibule, then through another thick door into a noisy barn of a place. It felt like the entire population of Herakli had crowded in here to wait out the razor storm building outside. Booths lined the walls and it was standing room only around the central bar. As they pushed through the crowd, the low ceiling – hung with pierced lanterns – opened up to show two more levels above, just as crowded, built around an atrium.

Denev half-turned. "Upstairs," he said, nodding towards the far wall behind the bar.

They pushed their way through knots of people. Rhees looked at the faces she passed. They were majority human, and for the most part reflected the ethnicity of the human settlers that had originally colonised this sector. The aliens she saw were mainly Brell, easily recognisable with their oversized heads and long necks towering above the humans. There was a booth of Sissilak near the foot of the stairs. She'd only seen holos before. They resembled snakes but with four arms, and the scales that covered their human-sized bodies were thick like an armadillo's plate armour.

The stairway was less crowded. Denev stopped on the next level, craning to look across the crowd, then touched Rhees's hand briefly to follow him. They cut diagonally through more drinkers. The noise was more subdued here but punctuated by shouts of laughter.

Rhees could see where they were headed: a Sissilak near the balustrade at the edge of the atrium. It reared up as they approached, its scales rattling, and the small group of humans near it moved away to give it some room.

"Ix'la," Denev said, "this is my associate, Rhees Lowrans. A little out in the open for a meeting, isn't it?"

The Sissilak responded with a series of short barks that the trink translated for her. "Best to be in open. Safer."

"Safer from who?" Denev said.

"This for you. It is what you asked."

Rhees saw a slip of plastic in the Sissilak's claw. Denev took it and tucked it quickly into his djellaba. He glanced at Rhees. Was that guilt in his eyes?

"I thought this meeting was about something else," Denev said.

Rhees wondered what was going on.

"It is." The Sissilak's head ducked and rose again, the scale plates shivering down its back. "First you guarantee. Two million credits. And you take me in now. Safe place. I can't go back to trade mission."

Rhees looked around at the room full of drinkers and up to the next level above, which was just as crowded. She drew closer to Denev, suddenly wishing she had a blaster.

"What do you mean?" Denev said, the tension clear in his voice.

The Sissilak sank lower on its coiled body, one arm reaching into a fold in its belt. It pulled out a datacrystal and held it between them. "Two million credits. This intel." Its mouth opened wide, crowded with needle-sharp teeth.

A beam of light hit the Sissilak, capturing its whole body in a red glow and instantly vapourising it.

A wave of intense heat passed over them. Rhees threw her arms up, trying to see through the glare. "Denev!" she shouted.

The light was gone. She blinked away the afterimages. Denev was still there. Alive. He had a blaster in his hand, but he hadn't fired. He was looking around for the shooter.

There was a shocked silence in the aftermath of the blast. Then chaos broke out. Rhees heard screams and roars of anger as people rushed for the exits, pushing others out of the way, fighting. There was nothing but ash where the Sissilak had been.

Rhees felt terribly exposed at the balustrade, but then she saw the datacrystal lying on the floor where it had fallen. She bent quickly and scooped it up, pushed it well down in her pocket.

Denev was beside her. "I can't get through to HDC. The storm."

A body flew over a table near them and crashed to the floor. There was a mass of brawling bodies between them and the stairs. Then the hiss of a blaster. Someone screamed and fell near the top of the stairs. It was impossible to tell where the shot came from or if it was the same shooter.

Two men, locked together in a struggle, crashed against Denev. He pushed them off and looked over the balustrade.

"Jump," he told Rhees. "I'll cover you."

Rhees looked down; the drop was about six metres.

"Let the djellaba take the impact," Denev said.

She looked into his eyes, then grabbed the handrail and leaped, twisting as she fell to land on bent legs then roll onto her side. The djellaba stiffened and somehow cushioned her at the same time. She came up on her feet. Denev was still above her. The bar-room floor was less crowded, but those still here seemed locked in a deadly struggle. Rhees didn't know who were potential attackers and who were simply brawling bystanders.

She ducked to avoid a chair that smashed against the bar and kept low, dodging clutching hands and flying fists. But the higher gravity was beginning to take its toll. Someone grabbed her from behind. She twisted and kicked out, heard a shout and was free again.

A powerful grip on her throat pulled her upright. He was big, broad, full-bearded and angry. She pushed the mobi towards him, but his fist swallowed her hand. She slammed the elbow of her other arm into the bridge of his nose and a knee into his groin. He released her hand with the mobi and she thrust it against his gut, freezing him. She spun past.

Denev jumped, but he fell awkwardly and stayed down. She lost sight of him.

"Denev!" she shouted, ramming the mobi into the back of whoever was blocking her view. The body fell and she saw Denev on the floor. He was in danger of being trampled.

She pushed forward, using the mobi indiscriminately to clear a path. Faces turned to her in terror, screaming, trying to get away from the mad woman who appeared to be killing everyone in her way. Then she was kneeling beside him. His face was stiff with pain.

"Fuck! Twisted my ankle."

"Come on." She slid an arm under him, levering him off the floor with some effort. She managed to get him standing, leaning against her and favouring his left foot.

A red-faced man spun to face them, roaring. Denev raised the blaster, pointing it right at his chest. The man's fist faltered and he fell back.

Others saw the blaster and cleared a space for them to the exit. Rhees didn't hesitate, half-dragging Denev into the vestibule. He leaned against the inner door, breathing heavily.

"Just your ankle?" she said. "You weren't hit?"

"The ankle's enough!" He looked pale.

"We need to get back to HDC. Can you make it?"

He nodded.

She opened the outer door. The wind was howling. She looked back at Denev.

"The djellaba will keep us safe," he said and pulled the hood over his head, closing the material around him.

Rhees did the same and slid an arm around his waist.

They followed the twisting lane back to a wider road. As they left the relative shelter of the laneway the wind slammed them against the wall. Rhees's djellaba stiffened instantly, closing around her as a protective repulser field extended over her face. A heads-up display showed her the street, with a side display plotting the route to HDC. She tried her band. Still no comms.

The wind pulled at them as they kept to the wall and made their way along the street. The air was full of sand, but it was nothing like the full force of a razor storm that could strip the flesh from you in seconds. Still, visibility was down to nothing but the HUD kept her on course.

Another alley gave them some shelter. Denev was quiet beside her, but she could hear how heavily he was breathing with the effort to keep moving.

They were forced to cross two more open boulevards and a square, the wind pushing them in a drunkard's walk that couldn't have been easy for Denev. What streetlights there were brightened and dimmed with the intermittent sheeting of sand. The journey seemed to take an age but finally they turned the corner into HDC's street. Ten metres from the entrance, they passed through a repulser field and the wind dropped to nothing.

The fabric of Rhees's djellaba softened and the visor deactivated. The door opened at her touch and she helped Denev into the reception area, where he eased himself to the floor, leaning against the wall. She slumped beside him, exhausted.

A door opened and a tall, thin man in an HDC onepiece walked over quickly and kneeled beside Denev.

Denev straightened his leg out. "This is Taj," he managed, sounding out of breath. "You haven't met. Taj. Rhees."

"Never mind that, how's your foot?" Rhees said.

Taj peeled the boot off gently, cradling Denev's ankle. "Not broken. But we should get you to the infirmary."

"Just get me to my room," Denev said.

Rhees pushed herself up and, with Taj's help, hauled Denev upright and helped him to his quarters. The room was bigger than hers and decorated Herakli style. Dim glowglobes cast a warm light across silken wall hangings, a large dark-wood desk with a dataport, and three easy chairs clustered around a small combustion stove. An opening into another room showed a bed, wardrobe and an entry into the ensuite.

They eased Denev into an armchair. He was looking better now, Rhees thought; he'd been deathly pale in the vestibule.

"I'll get something for the pain," Taj said and left.

"I don't understand," Denev said to Rhees. "Ix'la was a minor functionary in the trade mission. Not high enough up to know something worth getting killed for."

"I did manage to save this." Rhees pulled the datacrystal from her pocket, then noticed one facet of it was blackened and melted. "Fuck, it must have caught some of the blast."

"Try it." Denev nodded towards the dataport.

She swivelled the unit to face them, fitted the crystal in the port and activated the terminal. Nothing.

"Give it to the analysts," Denev said. "They might be able to extract something."

Taj re-entered and looked at the active dataport. "You're finished for the night, Denev."

Rhees switched the port off.

Taj pressed a hypospray against Denev's neck, then kneeled beside his foot and pulled a flexible strap around the ankle. "I'll strap this up. The spray should help you get a good night's sleep. And take one of these." He held out a blue capsule to Denev. "It'll target the sprain and promote cell regeneration."

"I'll get you some water," Rhees said and went into the bathroom.

Denev took the pill and the glass of water from Rhees and swallowed.

"Come on," Taj said. He helped Denev to stand and, with Rhees's help, walked him into the bedroom and sat him on the edge of the bed.

Rhees took Denev's djellaba and draped it over a nearby chair.

"Get some rest," Taj said.

"You've got your orders," Rhees said. "We'll pick this up in the morning."

She and Taj parted in the corridor, and she walked back to her quarters. She wasn't sure she'd sleep tonight, and not because her ears were still ringing from the blast at the bar. For one horrible moment back there she'd thought Denev was dead. Next time she'd carry her own weapon.

11

The records hall was set deep into the base of the escarpment where the air was cool and dry, all the better to keep the older texts from rotting on the shelves. Even so, it wasn't a dark place. Incandescents were set into the walls, and light was diverted among the close-packed records by burnished metal reflectors fastened into the rocky ceiling. The main entrance was wide and open, and crowded with far too many metal tables for the number of Scholars and Adepts that used the library. The Academy in Aktiuk was close enough that most preferred to use the superior facilities there.

It was one of the things I'd liked about the place after I'd been "forced" to work here. Hardly anyone visited so I was usually left to myself, alone with the collected knowledge of House Czerag, the histories of life before the Emergence – the battles and conquests, truces and treacheries – and a sizeable collection of scientific treatises, starting with the earliest experimental theories of house Scholars, giving way to more enlightened works when Aktiuk was founded after the House Wars, and incorporating the knowledge of alien species once the Kresz took their first voyages into the wider Lenticular. I loved it here when I was growing up. It let my mind roam free when everything else I knew seemed designed to hold me down and force my life into a design I neither wanted or cared about. Now it felt like just another prison.

"Tzek told me to expect you."

It was Idke, coming through the stacks to stand at the edge of the study area. He was more bent over than I remembered, the thickening plates forcing his body into a configuration more suited to sitting at his desk than standing. His head was pushed back against the folds of his hood and angled as if he were listening to some faraway sound.

"He said you'd want your old job back and I'm more than happy for that to happen," he went on. "I find myself short-staffed after yesterday."

The words sounded callous but there was no such feeling behind them. The sole purpose of life for Idke was the conservation and curation of knowledge. Everything around him was a tool to be used for that purpose. If Reka was no longer part of that endeavour he no longer mattered.

Tzek had told Idke I would come. It was clear he wanted me to blend back into my nondescript life, buried beneath the stacks of the records hall again. For the moment, until Isza returned, it was the right thing to do. I'd be out of Tzek's way and he'd think I was doing as I was told. But it wasn't the reason I'd come here this morning.

"What happened to Reka?" I said.

The breath hissed through Idke's spiracles. "You *saw* what happened to him."

He turned and walked back through the stacks and I followed. The shelves twisted this way and that to best take advantage of the reflective surfaces above. Idke moved with a painfully slow gait and I wondered how long he'd be able to keep going. His life would be at an end when he could no longer track down some connection or other among the records.

Finally we emerged into Idke's workspace. It was wedged between stacks crammed with old books, scrolls and papers that spilled onto his broad wooden desk.

He sat in his well-cushioned chair and closed his eyes for a moment. "You're here to help me?"

"Yes." It was true for the moment. "But I'm still worried about what happened to Reka. I'd heard he was distracted, even more withdrawn than usual lately."

"Moods are for the young and no interest of mine. He functioned adequately. If anything was the matter it didn't affect his work."

"Isza told me he was doing some work for you at the Academy."

Idke pushed at some papers on the desk in front of him. I could tell he wasn't really interested in discussing Reka. "He was. I still contend our records are superior on evolutionary matters, but there are some treatises at the Academy that could prove worthwhile. He was sourcing those for me. That will be among your duties now."

Of course, I thought. But a trip to Aktiuk could be useful. Perhaps someone at the Academy could tell me more.

"When did he start travelling to Aktiuk for you?"

"Does it matter?" Idke focused on me for the first time.

"It does to me."

He thought for a moment. "One-three weeks ago. That was his first trip. His last … Well, he never returned here from his last. Sakat knows where the scrolls are he was meant to bring back."

One-three weeks. About halfway through Luk'ri. The same time Zael said he'd noticed a change in Reka.

"Do you need me to travel to the Academy?" I asked.

Idke's feeder claws stretched wide. "And what would you do blundering around the stacks there? You have a lot to review and learn here before I inflict you on anyone else."

I found the scrolls Idke wanted later that day. They were on top of a pile of rubbish dumped with Reka's other belongings when his sleeping quarters were cleared. I sifted through his few possessions but there was nothing to suggest a reason for his madness. I needed to go to the Academy if I was to find out anything else. But that would have to wait until Idke felt I was ready.

∞

Life fell into the normal house rhythm around me. The familiarity was harder to take when I thought of the brief taste of real freedom I'd had on Telsus IV. So I kept out of the way among the stacks, only surfacing to check with Idke or to sleep in the room I'd shared briefly with Isza.

On the third day Isza sent back a package of information to the records hall, including datalogs on her flight plan, an image reel from the deeprange ship the Hegemony had contacted, and a copy of the transmission. The Hegemony vessel was large: a blocky prow projecting half the length of the ship forward of two large triangular weapon nacelles coloured orange at the front. The whole assembly was backed by massive engines angled above and below the main superstructure. The transmission message was just as she'd said: a time stamp and spatial coordinates.

Past the first two banks of shelves and hard up against where the raw stone of the cave curved inward at one side, there was a bench set with readers for the later texts, held in microcells, and an antiquated processor. I used the processor to call up that region of space and overlaid the tenspace network. There were a number of openings close by: some simple loops or dead ends, but two of interest. One was a narrow channel that fed into the primary network, including the main junction through Kresz space into the Lenticular that looped off towards the galactic core. The other was a wildly tangled channel, wide but dangerous to navigate. It was hard to tell, because our own tenspace maps didn't extend far past that point, but it looked to be heading in the direction where Atalna had told me his planet, Betlaan, was.

I pulled the display back so the curve of the galaxy was visible. Hegemony space was meant to be out near the tapering end of the galactic arm. Atalna's world was further in and near the outer edge. The Lenticular was closer to the midpoint, both in distance from the arm's frayed outer edge and from galactic centre. The Hegemony ship was wandering far from home. If their goal was conquest, they either had inexhaustible resources and vast fleets that had subdued all space between their origin point and here – and if so, why hadn't we or any of the other Lenticular planets heard anything? Or they'd skipped many, many worlds and civilisations just to come to an

unremarkable piece of space leading to the Lenticular. I couldn't
see a reason why. But the more I thought of Atalna's words, his
broken, scarred body, the pain in his eyes, the more I was sure there
was danger here.

Another disquieting possibility occurred: Atalna's world had
obviously been under surveillance before the Hegemony made
contact. Did they already know where Homeworld was? I could
imagine stealth-run scan packets, transmission listening stations and
all kinds of exotic devices that could be deployed in Homeworld
orbit if that was the case. But perhaps it wasn't that complicated.

I walked back into the stacks. Idke was tireless in his devotion
to the records hall, making sure to secure a copy of every report
and survey issued by any of the lodges. An entire bank of shelves
was devoted to the Scholars Lodge, and it wasn't hard to find the
report on the *Might of Gnow*, the missing deeprange ship Isza had
told me about. I took the microcell back to my bench and loaded
it into a reader, flicking through the report until I found the last
known coordinates of the ship. I copied those into the processor
and the image zoomed into a region of space close – in relative
terms – to the upcoming rendezvous point. It was no more than a
day away by tenspace.

I stared at the screen, my mind racing. If the Hegemony had
taken the *Might of Gnow*, they could have tortured those onboard
and extracted all kinds of information about us. Now they wanted
to meet out in the open. But why?

Isza's ship was due to leave later today. Tzek had ignored my
warnings. But perhaps what I'd found here was enough to make
the Council think twice about the rendezvous without revealing
Czerag's plans.

∞

Gurud wasn't on guard in the antechamber, but the Defender there
recognised me and let me pass. The wooden doors to Czerag's
chamber were already open and the shield-metal barrier rose into

the rock ceiling after only a few moments. Tzek appeared around the partition wall. He felt very guarded and I almost made my excuses to leave again and come back when Czerag was alone, but he said, "Come in, Udun. We've been talking about you."

Czerag sat on his stone bench, his blackened plates shining with a deep lustre.

"I need to talk about the Hegemony," I said.

Czerag blinked slowly. "Tzek mentioned your concerns to me."

I looked at Tzek, wondering how he'd portrayed the information I'd provided.

"It's more than a concern, Hierarch. I just reviewed the location of the rendezvous point. You know of the deeprange ship that went missing, the *Might of Gnow*?"

He considered for a moment, then blinked once.

"It's only a day's travel by tenspace from where Isza and the contact ship is travelling to."

"So?" Tzek said. I felt the resistance in him.

"The Hegemony would think nothing of capturing one of our ships and torturing the crew if they were interested in us. They could already know the location of Homeworld, the disposition of Defenders Lodge forces. I think the meeting is a trap."

"It's conjecture," Tzek said. "Stories to frighten instars."

I ignored him, focusing instead on Czerag, trying to make him feel how certain I was. "These aliens are dangerous, Hierarch. They take entire worlds. If you could speak to the alien I met – Atalna – you'd be as concerned as I am."

"Then show me," Czerag said, his mantle already rising. He held out his claws, took my own in a firm grip, and flowed through the contact. I kneeled, powerless, and my mantle rose in response.

The sight of Czerag fell away as the essence of that night gripped me. The sense of dread Atalna had conjured was palpable between us as our conversation played out across the inner eye. My words and his coming from my mouth in Czerag's chamber like whispers of memory. Finally it was done. Our mantles relaxed and I leaned back, breaking contact.

The only sound in the chamber was that of Czerag's thickened plates rasping over one another as he shifted on his bench.

"If what Atalna told you is true, then the appearance of the Hegemony so close is worrying," he said at last.

"If my analysis on the missing deeprange ship's proximity to the meeting site was sent to Council, they may reconsider the rendezvous," I said. "It could give them – and us – some time to prepare."

"Prepare for what?" Tzek said. "There is no proof we can give them that wouldn't raise questions about what we are doing –"

"Tzek," Czerag said quietly.

I stood again, waiting for the hierarch's decision. He considered telling the Council. But then I felt him turn against that course.

"The Council is doing the right thing," he said. "These aliens will be met and told that we do not wish further contact. Our knowledge would not change that or whatever comes after. If there is to be war, it is the will of Sakat."

"You have to *do* something, Hierarch. Please."

But he was implacable; I could feel it. There was nothing I could say that would make a difference.

"Which brings us to you, Udun," Tzek said, and I felt the venom behind his words. "We are entering a delicate phase in our preparations for trade. We can't risk anyone finding out about your trip off-world, even by accident."

I knew what was coming. The sense impression was of walls closing around me, the suns blotted from the sky.

"You are to travel to one of our hides in the deep desert. Just until we send the first shipment. You will be safe and secure there. And when this is over you can return to the escarpment and your duties."

I should have been angry, but all I felt was numb. "When do I leave?"

"Immediately," Tzek said.

"I'll pack my things."

I nodded to Czerag, who gave the common sending, and retraced my steps past the Defender to the main entranceway. I knew I should get my things, return here and wait for whatever transport arrangements Tzek had made. Instead I kept walking, through the door and out into the sunlight. Past the cutting, the desert spread out all around me. Wide. Open. But not free. Not that.

I turned right and walked past the small landing field and onto the vehicle racks. Gurud was there, fitting a half-track on one of the newer speeders. His head turned towards me as he felt my presence.

I reciprocated the sending and said, "Where are you going?"

"Aktiuk spaceport. Final documentation for Isza. I volunteered to take it to her."

"I'll come too. I have an errand to run at the Academy."

It was the truth. The errand was my own. I had this one chance to tell Isza what I'd learned – warn her at least and tell her what was happening to me. Then I'd use what time I had left to find out what happened to Reka before Tzek had me caught and sent to the deep desert.

Gurud looked at me. He could tell I was upset, but he didn't know why and – thankfully – he wasn't about to ask. He lowered the half-track part of the speeder onto the sand and stood. "I suppose it's all right."

"I'll stay out of your way if you need some time alone with Isza."

He climbed onboard the speeder, almost tipping it, and slid over the bench so I had enough room to sit.

"Spaceport first. Academy second," he said.

"Of course."

12

The half-track crunched through the brittle top layer of the sand and thrust us across the dunes quickly and smoothly. Gurud didn't have much to say, and I sat quietly and watched the landscape, feeling as if I was in uncharted territory. I should have been worried, but I felt better away from the oppressiveness of the house. I was determined to make the time I had count.

Eventually the sand gave way to scrub and then, at some arbitrary divide, a forest sprang up around us. The ride wasn't nearly as comfortable on the rough forest floor but Gurud didn't seem inclined to slow down, and we bounced around, dodging tree trunks.

"As much as you've been missing Isza," I said above the noise of the turbine, "she won't be happy to see you with a cracked shell."

Gurud gave a low, rumbling grunt. "I feel rather hurt you don't trust my driving skills."

We swerved again to avoid a particularly thick endar trunk.

"A dead breach-brother is also going to annoy her," I said.

The half-track slowed, but not because of anything I'd said. As we brushed through a stand of bushes onto a clearer path we joined a stream of all kinds of traffic. Speeders like ours and larger maglev-assisted transports jostled and edged past more traditional carts pulled by slow-moving yoqs and, in some cases, Defender-caste Kresz. We were entering the outer suburbs. Like a rising tide, buildings appeared among the trees and dense foliage. They were simple dwellings at first: this residential area belonging to House Haketiug for the most part.

Aktiuk's suburbs radiated out from a central hub and were loosely defined along house and lodge lines. For most Kresz there was a curious doubling of loyalty, or halving perhaps. We all belonged to a house – that was our family – and house needs and considerations generally came first. But we were by body plan, brain structure and disposition suited for different functions in society. That's why the lodges were established. I was of the Scholars Lodge, though I'd never formally joined and I didn't think they were too worried about that. Anyone could see Gurud was of the Defenders Lodge, and Isza's skills suited her for work as a pilot in the Adepts Lodge, which included most of the professional disciplines. The other lodges were the Cultivators and Merchants and, of course, the Lodge of Sakat to which all Priests belonged. So as well as house loyalty, we had a feeling of comradeship towards our fellow lodge members, regardless of their house origins, because they were like us. And those who joined a lodge held allegiance to the lodge's dean, who advanced the lodge's interests at Council, just as the hierarch cared for the interests of the house. Theoretically the structure provided balance between familial ties and broader societal needs. Where it all fell down was that some lodges and houses were more traditionally aligned than others, forming a voting block in Council and a power imbalance.

The lodges had been set up to support the diversification of traditional trades within the houses when the House Wars ended. So, for example, House Ukat had always bred Cultivators to fish the Inland Sea, which they owned. But when the House Wars ended and Kresz were no longer confined to their lands, individual choice increased. Not every Cultivator-caste Kresz from Ukat wanted to spend their life fishing, which meant Ukat had to source Cultivators from other houses to join the fishing fleet. So the Cultivators Lodge grew up to act as a broker between the houses to ensure labour supply. But because House Ukat had by far the largest population of Cultivators on Homeworld, Ukat Cultivators still tended to dominate the Cultivators Lodge – the senior lodge officers and the dean were all House Ukat – so the lodge was predisposed towards the interests of House Ukat. Despite the best intentions, we hadn't freed ourselves from a house-based monopoly at all. We'd just driven it behind closed doors.

Just as House Ukat dominated the Cultivators, House Kergis controlled the Merchants Lodge. All off-world trade had to go through them and that's what made Kergis so powerful. Czerag was about to challenge that.

We were coming closer to the main city hub now and the traffic was heavier. The Treaty City had never been planned; it grew up as a natural result of the end of the House Wars. That made for an "intuitive" road system that wound erratically through and around huge rooted endar trees and stonewood trunks.

Taking advantage of a gap in the traffic, Gurud swerved and accelerated onto a broad-cut channel and we emerged into a patch of sunlight. Up ahead, a giant trunk of stonewood had fallen across the road years ago. Rather than move it, a tunnel had been cut straight through. Lean-to dwellings were built against the trunk on either side of the roadway, their walls bowed against its girth. And some enterprising Adept had flattened off an area along the top of the fallen trunk and built a two-storey house there with good views of its surroundings.

The traffic quickened through the tunnel and the buildings grew more dense as we sped towards Aktiuk. Then we entered the network of city streets and the traffic thinned as individual vehicles turned off towards their destinations. We cut off into the Merchants Sector. The canopy of trees above gave the roadway a night-time feel, the sunlight bluish through the foliage. We flew past shops, some built from wood, others made from mud-brick, all with their wares on display: lamps, baskets, pottery, furniture. Gurud had to brake often for pedestrians: an old Kresz crossing the road, or a nymph who had broken away from its carer.

And then we were at the perimeter fence of the spaceport, following the tree line away from the main entrance down towards the shore of the Inland Sea. To our left, through the fence, the smooth landing strip curved around the edge of the water. Far off there were the port buildings and the tall control tower; between the tower and the fence were parked transports, atmos-flyers and some Defender craft; and beyond was the sleek needle of the skystalk, which carried the bulk of trade goods up and down from the Hub. An inverted cone of cloud clung to the upper section – a permanent feature – as if the atmosphere was being siphoned out where the cable pierced through to space.

We were waved through a small gate near the water.

"I'll get off here," I told Gurud. "Just tell Isza I'm down here to say goodbye."

He slowed the vehicle long enough for me to jump off, then tore away towards the ships.

I walked down to the edge of the apron. The aggregate was crumbling where the water lapped at it constantly. The view across the green waters was beautiful, with the forest sweeping away to the right and – after the break for the spaceport – to the left as well. You couldn't see the far shore; in fact, for a long time the Inland Sea was thought to be part of the Kedisz Ocean to the south. White spindles sloped along the horizon: the fishing fleet out in the deeper waters. Next month they'd move closer to shore after the dark-fleshed luk'ah that gave its name to that time of year. There was nothing else to be seen on the water. The surface was choppy, whipped up by a stiff onshore breeze, but it felt changeless, like the infinite reaches of space. Behind me lay the Treaty City, packed with Kresz trading, learning, loving, quarrelling; always changing, not always for the good. I wanted to be gone from here. To anywhere.

I sensed Isza approaching. She was angry.

"What are you doing here?" she said. "If you want me to help you escape now, I can't. There's too much –"

I placed my claws on her chest plate and she stopped. She could feel I was calm. I wasn't about to ask her to do the impossible.

"It's okay," I said. "But I want you to promise me you won't take any risks out there."

"You know I won't."

"The *Might of Gnow* – I think it was taken by the Hegemony, which means they know everything there is to know about us. I want you to hang back when you meet them. It could be a trap."

I felt her mood shift as she heard my words. "You're sure they're that much of a threat?" It wasn't really a question. She could sense how I felt. "All right. I'll take extra care. If anything happens I'll pull us back immediately."

I relaxed a little and let her go. "When you come home, I'll need you to find me. Tzek is sending me to the deep desert hides."

She rested her claws on her pelvic plates. "Don't worry. There isn't a deep enough hole they can put you in that I can't pull you out of."

I felt something else from her then. An anxiety that hung beneath everything else.

"Are you all right?" I asked.

"I don't know. I'm nervous about the flight. Even without this hostile Hegemony of yours." Her breath hissed through her spiracles. "I have to get to the ship. It's in final prep." She looked into my face. "Be careful, Udun."

"You be careful. Come home safe."

"Here you are," a voice said.

I hadn't thought it possible for Isza to feel more tense. I turned to see a Kresz approaching. Shorter than me, he seemed younger as well from the colour of his shell. He wore a Kergis-green flight harness, all pockets and loops, and looked innocuous, but the feel of him was less than pleasant. I imagined things moving under the Inland Sea, half-glimpsed, sharp-toothed and malevolent.

"More pre-flight nerves?" he said to Isza. "Not what we'd expect from a pilot with the experience you claim you have." He swept one palm across the other. "But this is a big mission for you. So many ways to mess up."

"Udun," Isza said, "this is Erdjis, Defence Force Liaison."

"And who is this?" he said, turning to me. "A well-wisher? A lover perhaps? But no. More than that."

I felt his mind probing at mine, more than the simple surface scan when meeting someone new. I'd been wrong to come here.

Isza felt it too. She moved a little in front of me, distracting Erdjis.

"Udun is my breach-brother. I thought you were seeing to the final loading," she said, clearly hoping he would go away.

"All done."

"Then there's nothing more to keep us," she said. "Goodbye, Udun."

We touched claws briefly and then she turned, taking Erdjis with her.

He half-turned back to look at me, brought a claw to his feeder tips and then pointed at me. I felt the standard farewell, but there was a coldness to it.

∞

Gurud was talking with another Defender at the front landing strut of an old freighter. He broke away when he saw me.

"Isza wasn't too happy to see me," he said.

"That makes two of us. She's nervous. But I'm sure she'll be fine."

The speeder was parked near the fence. We walked back to it and climbed in. Gurud was lost in thought and I felt sorry for him, separated from Isza when their relationship was at such an early stage.

"The Academy," I reminded him.

He gunned the engine and we took off jerkily towards the same gate we'd entered. We drove back through the Merchants Sector and turned to head into the city proper. There was more traffic but the roads became wider and easier to navigate.

The Academy lay to the north of Treaty Mount and we skirted the souk near the Council Chambers before turning onto a broad boulevard lined with endar trees that took us all the way to the campus: a chaotic grouping of buildings clustered around a broad but well-shaded park. Gurud pulled the half-track up beside a stone building with an imposing arched wooden door twice as tall as any Kresz. This was the Academy library where Reka had been sent on his errands for Idke. There was a chance whoever he met here might have something useful to tell me.

"I won't be long," I said, dismounting from the speeder.

"Take as long as you want. I'm coming with you."

Gurud followed me up the stone steps. There was a smaller side door beside the grand archway and we entered through that into a reception area, its walls hung with banners from the time of the House Wars. A small Kresz sat just inside the door, wearing a tunic the blue of House Ukat and fastened at the neck with the silver ring of the Scholars.

"Idke of the House Czerag records hall sent me," I said.

The Kresz peered at me and I could see his inner eyelid flicking back and forth across his eye as if trying but failing to focus.

"Room three-four-two. The stairs down are over there." He indicated an opening in the side wall.

The stairs were narrow and wouldn't be easy for Gurud.

"You don't need to come down with me," I said.

"I will anyway."

Perhaps Isza had asked him to keep me safe. Or maybe he'd decided for himself, knowing she wouldn't be happy if anything happened to me that he could have prevented.

I felt his unhappiness at each scrape of his carapace against the stone walls as the stairs turned. At the bottom I looked for our room number and turned left, walking along the corridor that was, thankfully, wider than the stairwell.

The door to room three-four-two was ajar and I pushed it fully open. The female inside looked up from her desk and I sensed the common greeting. The room was lined with records, pamphlets, almanacs stacked against the walls, and well lit by incandescents.

"Have you lost your way?" she asked. She wore Scholar's robes and the silver ring as a clasp.

"I'm Udun from House Czerag," I said. "I work with Idke. And this is Gurud."

"I'm Gehaki, librarian responsible for intra-house studies. Has Idke sent you on one of his errands?"

"Actually I'm here about another of his assistants, Reka. Have you had anything to do with him?"

She blinked and ushered us into the room, but there wasn't much space.

"I'll wait out here," Gurud said.

I removed a pile of papers from the visitor's chair and sat.

"Yes, I met Reka. Very quiet, but a good listener. I haven't seen him for …" She stopped to consider. "Well, it's been quite a while, but his helper is the more frequent visitor. I haven't had much to do with him. Reka told him where the items were that Idke wanted."

This didn't make sense. Idke had no other helpers. "Did he have a name?"

Gehaki sensed my confusion and I felt her own concern in return.

"Everything borrowed is signed out," she said, pulling a ledger from the shelf behind her and laying it on her desk. She turned the pages to about midway. "This is updated daily." She ran a claw down lines of close-spaced writing. "Here. One-zero days ago."

She turned the book to face me, her claw pointing to a column and the name "Daek". I'd never heard of a Daek in House Czerag.

"What's wrong?" Gehaki asked.

"Daek is not Idke's assistant."

"I don't understand."

"I don't either. But if he comes back, can you contact Idke?" I stood up. "You've been very helpful."

She didn't know what to say and I took the chance to leave. I had as many questions as she did, but no more answers.

Gurud followed me back along the corridor. "Idke didn't send you, did he?" he said.

"No. I'm sorry. But you heard what she said. Something strange has been happening. If Reka wasn't coming to the library, where was he going?"

We stepped outside again. It had begun to rain.

"So what now?" Gurud said.

"I don't know. Home, I suppose."

I had to tell Tzek what I'd learned. And then he'd send me away.

∞

We walked together back down the steps to the roadway, and started across it to the speeder. I caught the movement before I heard a sound. Quick, dark and too big to get out of the way. A vehicle bearing down on us.

I stumbled as Gurud half-turned to me, pushing me backwards. Then the crunch as he took the full force of the impact on his exoskeleton. His pain flowed through me like fire and I fell to my knees. He was thrown in front of me, skidding along the roadway. He lay still and I felt nothing from him, the pain suddenly gone.

A shadow fell across me. I was lifted up in a strong grip, the feeling of the other battering at me, driving out all sense. I was reeling from Gurud's last sending and couldn't resist as I was pulled towards the vehicle. Its turbine was still screaming. No, this was something else. Others were around me, more claws on me, lifting me. A jangle of sense pictures and emotions. My head felt heavy, filled with too much. The sky spun around me and I saw a blocky shape gliding down to land beside me. Gurud. What was happening?

I was dropped and fetched up sharply against a metal wall. Others around me. A door closed and the floor tilted and bucked. I cried out and it tilted more, pushing me against the wall. A window above me showed ground then sky then ground. We were flying. Isza? No, this wasn't her. Did she know what had happened? Was she with Gurud?

I looked around the small cabin. There were three Defenders crowded into the space with me. One looked directly at me and I shied away from the violence I felt there. They were hunkered together, braced against each other to keep steady in the cabin, which was levelling out but still moving faster. We banked again, the Inland Sea flashing beneath us. Then a thick bag was pulled over my head.

Robbed of vision, the feeling of the others so close was almost overwhelming, but I became aware of subtler elements in the general sense of menace. There were echoes of what I'd experienced when Gurud was hit by the vehicle, the pain and shock. They'd done this. They hadn't been immune to the experience – no Kresz could be – but they'd done it just the same. There was a seam of anxiety too, whether from guilt, fear of failure or something else I couldn't tell. But they were committed to whatever this was. There was no turning back from here. That was the sense I felt the most.

We were landing. With so many sensations pulling at me, I didn't know how much time had passed. Enough to cross the Inland Sea? There was a final bump and the others were moving around me. Claws wrapped around my upper arm and helped me out to the ground. Each time one of them touched me I felt bludgeoned.

Dirt beneath my hoofs. Insect noise. Sunslight filtered through the cloth of the bag.

They led me over rough ground and then the light changed and the sounds echoed around me. I could tell we were in a building. I kept walking, guided with nudges and taps. They seemed as unwilling to touch me as I was to be touched.

I was spun around and pushed to sit in a chair. Wooden. It didn't move as I sat. Was it secured to the floor? Chains ran across my pectoral plates, pulling me against the chair back. More chains scraped around me, securing my arms and legs.

"Where am I?" I said.

I sensed amusement but no one answered. The sound of steps, then a heavy door sliding shut and I lost all sense of others nearby.

I was in a shielded room.

Now at least I could think. I'd been grabbed outside the library. Was this connected with Reka? And was Kergis involved? He was suspicious of Czerag. Suspicious enough to use his influence to increase Defender patrols in orbit. If they found out what I'd been doing for Czerag in the Lenticular …

I forced myself to calm down. Wild thinking would help no one. I'd been taken but I didn't know why or by who. It may be unconnected to Reka or Kergis and they'd taken me because I was easier than Gurud to subdue. I hoped he wasn't dead but the crash had felt … I'd never experienced anything like it.

I reached out with my feeder claws, picking at the weave of the cloth bag over my head, trying to break the individual strands. The cloth parted a little and I pulled back my feeders, which were aching from the effort. I couldn't see much, even when I tilted my head. The dull blue of shield metal on the floor, dirty but smooth. The walls were the same but featureless. And the door. It looked thick, with no handle on this side.

Looking down I could see the chain across my chest, and thinner chains wrapped around my arms. Escape was impossible.

If they'd brought me here to question me, they'd know if I was hiding something. But what they asked would also reveal what they suspected.

I had one line of defence. I was terrified and I could use that to block them. Focus on the fear that they meant to harm me. They'd already harmed Gurud.

I focused on my fear. Feeding it. But hours passed and no one came.

13

Denev woke early feeling muzzy-headed, and remembered Taj had given him something to sleep. He lay back on the pillow and closed his eyes. Last night he'd been ready to send Rhees home to Earth and screw the consequences. But then he'd seen how much she was struggling in the aftermath of Petar's death. Just like him.

A voice echoed across the rooftops, too distant to make out words but the singsong lilt was easily recognisable. The Muslim faithful were being called to prayer.

Denev didn't believe in Allah or God. There'd been no comfort in Petar's death, and when Rhees called from Earth, he'd been in so much pain he'd lashed out at her. But he was really the one to blame. Keeping Petar safe had become all that mattered after their parents were killed. But he'd been too much the controlling big brother and not enough the friend Petar needed. *That* was why he'd failed.

He reached over and grabbed his djellaba, which was draped over the chair beside the bed. His fingers found the pocket sewn into the folds of the cloth and closed around the sliver of plastic Ix'la had given him. He read the words printed on it again: *Troels Volmar.*

When Petar died, Denev had started to question a lot of things about his life. Like what had really happened to their parents. All he'd been told at the time was that they died in the line of duty. But when he went looking for the files, he found they'd been sealed, even to an HDC operative with his clearance. The name of the person who'd sealed them was classified too. So he'd used his contacts to approach the problem from a different angle. Ix'la had finally given him a name. But Denev couldn't just question Troels Volmar, and Ix'la was dead.

The bells from the nearby Kathedrikos Naos Makarios rang, drowning out the call of the mu'addin. Gently Denev placed his foot on the floor, testing the ankle. It felt okay and he stood with only a little discomfort. He showered quickly, and pulled on an HDC onepiece and boots. His head felt clearer. The ankle was paining him some, but he'd be fine. He had work to do.

Out in the corridor he almost ran into Taj.

"How's the ankle?" Taj asked.

"I'm fine. Thanks for your help last night." They stood in awkward silence until Denev said, "Anything from the Sissilak trade office?"

"Not much." Taj smirked, adopting a formal tone: "*It's regrettable one of our staff should be caught up in a random attack.*"

Denev didn't laugh. "It didn't feel random."

"They've advised their people to keep out of the human part of town."

"What about surveillance data?"

Taj shook his head. "It's patchy at best. And we had nothing from any of the street relays. But it's impossible to cover all the routes through that warren."

Two mysteries: the raiders and Ix'la's murder, and no progress on either front, Denev thought.

"I'm heading to the holotank," he told Taj. "Maybe I'll come up with something."

"Good luck," Taj said, and he walked off towards the mess.

Taj had been appointed as Denev's unofficial aide when he'd first arrived, but Denev hadn't been able to break through the veneer of professional formality between them. It was entirely his own fault. He didn't do small talk. It always felt like a waste of time.

He shook his head and made his way down to the holotank, where he stood in the centre of the empty space and addressed the

AI: "Download the data from the djellabas we were wearing last night and commence playback from the time we entered the taverna."

The entry vestibule and the crowded bar appeared around him and he watched Rhees and himself enter and make their way to the stairs at the other side of the room. She moved with a powerful grace he hadn't registered before, though he'd seen the results in the fight last night. He wondered how Petar and she had met. What had they been like together? He really didn't know who his brother had become. His strongest memories were of the little boy he'd bossed around. But the last time they talked, Petar was a man who knew his own mind.

Rhees was a lot like Petar, he thought. And not simply because she hated HDC. She'd surprised him with her strong views about respecting aliens and keeping them safe. If she knew the mission here had nothing to do with protecting the Brell or other alien species in the sector, she'd be outraged. Thirteen billion beings had died on that colony. The right response would be to throw the full force of every agency of the Central Administration into this volume of space to prevent more deaths. But there were no significant human population centres in Cygnus Sector, save for Herakli, and that was all but deserted right now. The unspoken dictum of HDC was that they served the interests of the Hegemony, but, within that, the interests and safety of humanity were paramount. The Battle for Earth could never be allowed to happen again. Thirteen billion aliens had died. Too bad. The question wasn't, how do we prevent it happening again? But rather, how do we prevent it happening in human space?

Denev had been in HDC long enough to know that classifications like right and wrong were unhelpful. None of that had mattered to him because the Corps was the one place he knew he could keep his brother safe. But now … somehow he'd lost his way.

He felt tears prick behind his eyes as the holos of Rhees and him stood beside Ix'la.

"Halt," he said, trying to push away the feelings that were overwhelming him.

"Where did you get this?"

The voice startled him. Rhees was standing on the threshold.

He coughed and rubbed at his nose, but it was clear she'd seen his reaction, even if she didn't know the cause.

"I can come back if you like," she said.

"No. Come in. It's fine. The djellabas passively scan their environment. I'm reconstructing last night." He paused, not sure how to continue. The last day had changed everything. "I wanted to thank you. For saving me."

"Don't worry about it."

"And I know it's overdue, but ... I ... regret what I said to you on the comm. I wanted to hurt you because –"

"Please. Don't apologise to me. You agreed I was to blame. You were right then and you're right now."

He shook his head. "I know what my brother was like. I'd worried about him for a long time. He was impetuous."

"So was I. So am I," she corrected. "I was in command of that flight. I'm ultimately responsible. That's certainly the way the court saw it."

"The court needed someone to blame. Military justice doesn't allow for much in the way of nuance."

"If you're saying you forgive me, please don't. I can't forgive myself."

She walked into the room and circled holo-Rhees and holo-Denev frozen in front of Ix'la. "Do I really look that ..." She stopped.

"What?"

"Over-wound," she said.

"To the djellaba you did. At least, last night."

"Everything's subjective," she said. "We see what we expect to see until we're forced to shift perspective. That's been bothering me all night. You said Ix'la had some intel on the raiders."

Denev looked away. If Rhees found out meeting Ix'la wasn't entirely HDC business, it might complicate things. "I assumed he did. Apart from the raids, this sector has been quiet for years."

"But that's just it. I know the raiders have taken a step down from star-killers to hit-and-run tactics, but individual assassinations?"

Rhees was right. But who would kill Ix'la in such a public place? Certainly not his own people, even if they'd suspected him of selling secrets. They could have simply disappeared him with no fuss.

"No. This is about something else." Denev addressed the AI: "Step forward, same time factor."

Slowly, holo-Rhees looked up at the balcony level above, then drew closer to holo-Denev. Ix'la sank on his lower coils, one hand reaching towards holo-Denev, holding the datacrystal. Then the beam of light.

"Freeze," Denev said.

The bolt floated in the air, just touching the Sissilak's back between the lower shoulders. It was almost too bright to look at directly. The trail pointed back and up.

"The next level," Rhees said.

"Step back. Follow the beam," Denev ordered.

He watched as holo-Rhees and holo-Denev fell away through the floor and the image centred on the energy bolt, backtracking the flight up towards the next level of the bar. But as it flowed backwards, ghost images sprang up, multiplying into an inverted cone that grew to cover half the balcony. The image froze again.

"The further from the djellaba, the more we need to extrapolate. They're not really built for surveillance, just local recording," Denev said.

"So who was up there? Display the balcony area indicated by the blast pattern," Rhees told the AI. "Extrapolate body type based on scans if necessary."

The balcony above them descended to floor level until Denev was standing in the transparent crowd.

"Run backwards and forwards on the same time factor between the extrapolated firing time and the moment the blast hit the Sissilak," Rhees said.

Denev looked at the crowd around him. Most people were relatively static, standing in groups; some moved, carrying drinks or heading to or from somewhere.

Rhees stood on the wrong side of the balustrade, apparently floating in mid-air, scanning the movements near the edge. "There," she said, pointing at a Brell.

At the moment of firing the creature was near the edge of the balustrade, then it turned and pushed through the crowd, heading to the back wall. The AI repeated the action.

"I see it," Denev said. "But he could be doing anything. Looking for a friend?"

"He certainly stands out," Rhees said. "He's the only alien close to the balustrade."

"So he would stand out."

"Freeze the image," Rhees told the AI. "There's something about the way he moves. He reminds me of that Brell Killian shouted at."

"How many Brell have you come across? We see what we expect to see, remember?"

"I suppose," she admitted.

"Did we get anything off the datacrystal?" he asked.

"It's completely fucked. Enough energy to disintegrate a Sissilak will do that." Rhees blew her breath out between pursed lips. "Come on, I'll buy you a coffee."

They walked slowly together towards the front of the building. Denev's ankle was aching again and he tried not to put too much weight on it.

"Still hurting?" Rhees asked.

"A bit. But I'll live."

Outside, sand lay in drifts and piles against walls and light poles, but the cafe was open and the area around the tables was swept clean. Denev made for his usual table and sat gratefully, stretching his leg out to one side.

"I suppose if it's not connected with the raiders, HDC won't be interested," Rhees said. "It's only an alien that died."

Denev grimaced. "There's always the chance they were shooting at me. Or you."

"No one wants me dead. In this sector anyway."

"If Ix'la was drawing me out so his accomplices could take a shot, they did a poor job of it. The Sissilak *had* to be the target. He had intel that someone didn't want passed on. He knew his life was in danger. He thought he was safe in the bar."

"How long did you know him?"

The question was asked innocently enough, but Denev knew Rhees had seen Ix'la hand him the slip of plastic before all hell broke loose. She wasn't coming right out and asking him about it. That was something at least.

"Quite a while. It's a big sector but the same faces keep coming up if you move in the same circles. He's been helpful before."

"Well, whatever he knew, someone thought it important enough to risk shooting him in public."

"And they got away with it."

The cafe owner brought a tray with a pot of coffee, two cups and two plates with the local pastries. Rhees arranged the cups and plates on the table to mirror each other. Then Denev realised she was copying him. He raised his eyebrows at her and she smiled in return.

"Tell me about the sector," she said.

"Before the Hegemony assumed control?"

"Nice euphemism, but yes."

He took a sip of coffee. "The three main species are the Brell, the Sissilak and the Totek. The Brell are the most technologically advanced, close to Hegemony standards. What the Sissilak lack in tech they make up for in aggression. They were involved in a lot of territorial disputes with the Brell before. Both species are expansionary, but the Totek acted as peacemakers. There's something about them – maybe it's cultural, biological, we haven't been able to find the reason – but the Brell and Sissilak both defer to them. Which is strange, because they're no more advanced than the Brell and if you've seen one – they look like walking kettledrums – they're no physical match for the Sissilak. Still, over the years they've brokered a lot of agreements for the other two and generally kept the peace."

"The Brell folded when we took out their spaceyards," Rhees said. "What about the Sissilak?"

"They rolled over after the Brell."

"Not so aggressive after all?"

"This was five years after the Battle for Earth. The Hegemony had already built a reputation that it was not to be fucked with. The Totek took the pragmatic approach and petitioned to join the Hegemony as soon as we showed up."

"Is there still some friction between the Brell and the Sissilak? That might explain why the Sissilak got killed," Rhees said.

"Nothing that we've heard of."

"So maybe HDC isn't as in control of this sector as it thinks?"

"And that's what worries me." He picked up his cup and sat back, looking down the street and sipping at the strong coffee. Just what was Ix'la into?

"We still have nothing on the raiders," Rhees added.

Denev put his cup down. "That's the other thing that worries me."

Over Rhees's shoulder he saw a tall Brell dressed in heavy robes edged in red and black brocade stepping out of an auto on the other side of the road. He nodded towards her. "Look."

Rhees turned. "Who's that?"

"Delegate O'Dran. She's the chief Brell diplomat on Herakli." He stood and his ankle twinged sharply. He'd need to rest soon. "Let's go see what she wants. You still have your trink?"

She pulled the earpiece from her pocket. "Haven't had a chance to return it."

Despite his ankle, Denev walked quickly back across the street, Rhees following. O'Dran was already in the vestibule of the HDC building when they entered.

The Brell towered over Taj, her long ears almost brushing the ceiling, but he was speaking firmly to her. "The consul's not here. She's on her sector tour."

The Brell let out a nasal bray. "Who's in charge in her absence?"

Something didn't feel right. O'Dran was on the Sector Council so she'd know Demain was on her regular tour off-planet.

Denev stepped up. "I can help, Taj. Delegate O'Dran, I'm HDC Operative Denev Antwer. This is my associate Rhees Lowrans. Please, come to my office. I'm sure we can help you, or at the very least ensure the consul gives your matter serious consideration."

"Thank you," O'Dran said.

In Denev's rooms, the Brell folded her attenuated frame into one of the armchairs and Denev and Rhees sat too.

"I know Consul Demain communicated the Administration's shock and anger about the unprovoked attack on the Brell colony," Denev said. "I'd like to add my personal condolences for the losses you've sustained. The HDC and the Central Administration are doing all they can to bring the guilty to justice."

A long ear twitched. "Yes, we Brell have had all the platitudes we can stomach for now. They make for poor feeding."

Okay, Denev thought. Clearly the normal diplomatic niceties weren't required. "I appreciate your anger. What else can we do for you?"

O'Dran's lips vibrated, but the sound went untranslated. Then she said, "We have sent repeated requests to the sector administrator to bring in more Fleet ships. The attacks on Brell and Sissilak space cannot be allowed to continue. What good is the Hegemony if you can't keep us safe?"

"You know how big this sector is," Denev said. "And how wide-ranging the attacks have been. There aren't enough ships in the entire Hegemony to effectively cover that volume."

"But our largest population centres are still exposed. The Hegemony limits the number and size of our militia units. You need to do more now we are under attack. You need to bring in ships."

Time to push back and see what gives, Denev thought. "Ships are not the answer." Two black eyes glared at him. "The entire instrumentality of the Hegemony is working to eliminate this threat. You have to be patient and trust us."

"Words. I should have expected nothing more." O'Dran stood quickly. "I can find my own way out."

"I will inform the consul of your strong feelings in this matter, Delegate," Denev said.

The door scissored shut behind her as she left.

"That could have gone better," Rhees said.

But Denev was staring at the glowing embers in the stove. "No, it couldn't ... I feel like I'm missing something."

"*We're* missing something," Rhees corrected. "I had the same feeling in the holotank ... Fuck, two days ago. But she has a point: a few more Fleet ships *could* help, no matter how big the sector is. We'd have better first response."

Denev looked at her. "Volmar's orders. That's not going to happen."

"Fuck Volmar! We have no way of telling if these raids will escalate again. Can we really risk them dropping another star-buster in a populated system?"

"It's not our call. But O'Dran doesn't want more Hegemony ships. She wanted to know how we'd react to her request." He touched his band. "Taj?"

"Yes."

"Step up surveillance on Delegate O'Dran."

"On it."

14

The blast seared Rhees's skin, burning her eyeballs, but she could still see the alien writhing in the corona of heat. Petar looked right at her, then he was burning too.

She sat up in bed. It was 3 a.m. She took a long breath, blinking away after-images. She'd dreamed about the taverna, but it had been Petar there instead of Denev. And the alien burning – it had been a Brell not a Sissilak.

She closed her eyes, remembering her dream. Everything was mixed up. There was something she couldn't quite remember. But she knew where to look.

She pulled on her onepiece and walked out into the corridors. No one was around at this hour. The datanook above the holotank was waiting for her and she sank into the padded darkness, keying the synapse link. It didn't take long to sort through the records and find what she wanted.

The majority of sector travel stayed very close to established flight lanes because they offered the most energy-efficient route and if something went wrong with the ship another vessel would be along soon enough to help. The exception was prospecting and scientific missions. But every ship filed a flight plan that included a personnel and cargo manifest. And these were checked by transit officers on departure and arrival, with in-flight spot checks fairly common.

The thing about immersion was that even though you experienced the dataflow on a subconscious level, the information stuck and connections were made. The name O'Dran was familiar even though Rhees had only heard it spoken yesterday. And there it was.

A Brell vessel, registered as a mineral survey ship, coming out of the colony on Endikar had passed out of the Voss Space relay network and was untracked for a day and a half. Not that unusual. But what was Delegate O'Dran doing on it?

She set up another search to see if O'Dran's name popped up in any more unusual places. The Brell did a lot of trips back and forth between her home world and Herakli, which wasn't unusual, but nothing else stuck out.

Some extra Fleet resources would be useful if something was happening outside the relay network, but Volmar had shut that down. Rhees thought she knew why and it sickened her. She remembered his reaction when they'd watched the Brell colony incinerate back at the Datahive. There'd been no emotion. Volmar was like Killian, but not so obvious about it. He didn't care what happened to the aliens here – or anywhere else for that matter – and that sentiment riddled HDC.

Did Denev share that view? And what had Ix'la passed him at the taverna? Denev knew Rhees had seen but he hadn't volunteered an explanation and she didn't want to push him with questions. Their relationship was still too fragile. She couldn't get a handle on Denev. She hadn't expected to like him, not from the little Petar had shared with her. But he'd been more than fair to her. And after yesterday it felt like maybe they could be friends.

She pushed back from the nook and stood. She was exhausted. Broken sleep, higher gravity, it all added up. She needed a coffee.

It was still too early to venture outside, so she made her way to the mess … and stopped in the doorway. Denev was sitting at an otherwise empty table, a mug in front of him.

She got a coffee from the dispenser and dropped into a chair across from him. "Is this the early shift, or the late, late, late shift?"

"I'm too tired to remember," he said.

"I'll drink to that." Rhees clinked her mug against his.

"All we have is questions on top of questions."

"I have a fact if you'd like to hear it," she said. "Though it leads to more questions."

"I'll take a fact."

"After Delegate O'Dran visited, something shook loose in my head. Turns out she was on a Brell survey ship that went 'off grid' for a day and a half. I take it she's not a mineral specialist as well as a diplomat?"

"Not that we know of," Denev said. "When was this?"

"The ship lifted four hours after the first hit-and-run on the Sissilak cargo transports."

She took a sip of coffee while Denev mulled this over.

"If there's a connection between all these events, I can't see it," he said.

Rhees nodded. "Meanwhile we're overdue for another attack. Volmar's going to be pissed. Not that I care about his mental state, but I'd rather not be at the receiving end so soon after the last time."

"This is on me," Denev said. "I'm the local lead." His band vibrated and he lifted it to his lips. "Yes, Taj?"

"Thought you'd like to know. Delegate O'Dran is on the move. Heading to the spaceport."

Rhees stood, feeling a jolt of excitement. "Are you thinking what I'm thinking?"

"Auto in the basement," Denev said.

She followed him to the nearest elevator.

The auto was prepped and waiting for them, moving off as soon as they'd both strapped in. It glided up the ramp onto the laneway that ran behind the HDC offices, accelerated to the end of the lane, then made a series of rapid turns, losing barely any speed. The fact the streets were empty helped and they were soon on the main roadway to the spaceport.

Denev stared at the onboard dataport. "Taj has the flight plan. Lodged half an hour ago."

Rhees leaned in to read the words scrolling across the screen.

"She's headed to Brell Prime on 'government business'."

Denev tapped at the screen. "It's not that unusual. She's made … sixteen trips back to Prime in the last year."

"At short notice?"

"Some."

Rhees looked out the window. They were running at top speed now along the darkened roadway, buildings passing in a blur. The display on the windshield showed they were five minutes from the spaceport.

Denev flicked at the list of trips. "Here's her mineral survey trip. Part of a fact-finding mission as chair of the Brell government minerals subcommittee."

Rhees sat back. "Well, there you go. Everything's accounted for."

"Still doesn't feel right."

Rhees smiled. This was more like it. "I'm glad you said that. We follow?"

"There's a scoutship on continuous standby at the port. It can handle the Herakli to Prime run – it's only a nine-hour trip. I'll have Taj alert the pilot."

Fuck that, Rhees thought. She grabbed his forearm. "You *have* a pilot. Besides, three in a scoutship is a tight squeeze."

Denev called Taj to have the pilot bring the scoutship up to ready status. Rhees saw half a smile playing on his lips.

"You look like you're starting to enjoy yourself," she said.

"Maybe I am."

∞

The auto pulled to a halt and Rhees jumped out before the door was fully open. The scoutship was small, with a short nose projecting forward above two combination turbine landing skids and a bulbous rear section that curved up and behind the top of the windshield to accommodate the bulk of the powerful main drive. It would do.

In the pre-dawn gloom the pilot stood with a buggy full of

gear at the scoutship entry. "You're rated for this?" he asked Rhees. The snark was obvious in his voice, but she wasn't biting today. She just smiled and sorted through the collection of vacuum suits on the buggy until she found her size.

The pilot looked at Denev. "This ship's my —"

"We'll be fine," Denev said, but the pilot still looked stuck between worried about his precious scoutship and pissed at Rhees for brushing him off.

"It's got a full inventory?" Denev asked, picking out a suit.

"Of course," the pilot said, seeming to settle on pissed.

"Then you can go," Rhees said, pulling on her suit.

The pilot glared at her and walked off in disgust.

"I think I'm getting the hang of this diplomacy thing," she said.

"I can see that."

Rhees clambered past a small benchseat squeezed into the limited space between the top of the lock entry on one side and the curving bulkhead on the other and sat in the pilot's crash-seat at the front of the cockpit. Denev took the co-pilot's crash-seat to Rhees's left while she flicked at control interfaces. The lock was sealed behind them and the ship moved slowly away from the hangar.

She read the clearance on the dataport. "Nice to have friends in high places. Our flight plan was lodged two days ago and we have immediate clearance to lift."

"Just one more perk of working for the HDC," Denev said before he was pushed violently back against the crash-seat.

The scoutship leaped into the sky — Rhees loved how responsive it was to her touch. She felt the stress she'd been holding in her body fall away as the clouds shredded past them. It had been too long between flights.

Out to the side the horizon curved more and more until they crossed the line where they weren't flying above the planet any more, they were in orbit around it.

"And here's O'Dran's ship," Rhees said.

It was one of several craft in their field of vision, but the only

Brell vessel. They were all headed for a higher orbit, where the giant torus of the Voss bridge flattened out local spacetime for in-system transit.

"We'll need to punch it if we're going to get close enough before transit," Rhees said. "Otherwise we could lose them. The chamber on the other side is huge."

"Don't do anything that will draw attention. You're in an HDC ship. Covert surveillance is what we do best."

Rhees kept the scoutship on its current heading, joining the line for the bridge. She spun up the transit engines.

"I'm establishing a secure link to the torus," Denev said, looking at the dataport. "We could be wasting our time. The spaceport database shows O'Dran's booked on a return flight to Herakli departing three hours after she arrives at Prime. That's a quick turnaround."

"What's so important it requires her physical presence?" Rhees said.

"It has advantages over the Voss relays. We can hack their feed."

"Which suggests she's up to no good. Or am I just buying into HDC's standard paranoia? Trust no one."

"What do your instincts tell you?"

Rhees sighed. "That she's involved in something."

O'Dran's ship entered the Voss bridge and transited.

The scoutship was moving up in the queue. Four ships ahead of them.

"Another benefit of being HDC," Denev said. "The in-Voss Space side of the bridge will track her till we get through, at least within line of sight."

"You people have all the best toys," Rhees said, willing the ships ahead to hurry.

Finally it was their turn. The bridge synced with the transit drive and balanced their entry into Voss Space; as smooth a jump as they could hope for.

15

The chamber was lit by strobe-lightning flashes that dwarfed the ships floating within. Tracking sensors were useless in Voss Space, but Denev counted ten ships in the immediate vicinity. Others farther off moved through the darkness. He got a ping from the bridge and marked O'Dran's embassy clipper on the heads-up display.

"There she is."

Rhees manoeuvred their ship around the nearest vessels to follow.

Denev had been here many times before. The chamber was shaped like a long funnel, with two major channels leading off the wide end. If O'Dran was headed to Brell Prime, her clipper would take the lower channel.

Rhees maintained relative distance from O'Dran's ship. "That's it," she said, easing the thrusters back a little. "We're all just one happy Hegemony going about our business."

Some vessels moved past them to the 'mouthpiece' end of the funnel that led to the main network back to Sol system. O'Dran's ship moved further ahead and dipped into the channel network towards Brell Prime, trailing a Totek transport.

"You'll lose them," Denev said.

Rhees glanced at him. "You stick to the spying and I'll do the flying. I'm not going to lose them. Flight data shows it's only the Totek transport and O'Dran's heading to Prime. I don't want to crowd them in the channel."

They reached the lip of the opening. The channel curved down and to the right. O'Dran's clipper was nowhere in sight.

"Don't worry," Rhees said. "Where else can they go?"

They fell into the gradient, Rhees riding the engines to control their descent without affecting the local field potential. Around the curve the channel flattened out and O'Dran's ship was visible in the distance, moving at a steady rate. The Totek transport must have pulled ahead.

Rhees shifted in her seat. "Nine hours. What do we do when we get there?"

"Taj is coordinating with our network on Prime. We'll be met. What happens after that depends on O'Dran."

The walls of the channel narrowed around them and began strobing energy. Denev watched the instruments, but the field potential was nowhere near problematic. At least for the moment.

He settled into his chair, dividing his attention between O'Dran's ship, which was almost but not quite out of sight, and Rhees. The scoutship responded smoothly to her economical movements, and her focus seemed absolute. This was another side of her, one he hadn't expected. During the short time he'd spent with her, she seemed to always be in motion, a bundle of nervous energy, not always under control. But here was a quiet centre, completely consumed in doing what she was good at.

Two hours passed in comfortable silence and Denev was feeling the effects of a sleepless night. He sat upright, rubbed the sleep from his eyes, then drifted off again. This time when he opened his eyes it took a moment to realise O'Dran's ship was gone.

He snapped awake. "Rhees."

"I'm on it. They dipped around a curve."

The scoutship accelerated, slowing as they reached the bend in the channel. But when they rounded the curve, O'Dran's ship was nowhere in sight. Rhees accelerated again, flashes of plasma chasing them along the tunnel. They rounded the next curve. Still nothing.

"Fuck," Rhees said. She pushed the ship harder.

Denev watched the field potential rising, but it stayed just under the danger zone. The ship rounded another curve and there was a vessel ahead. Rhees throttled back.

"It's the Totek transport," Denev said.

"Did O'Dran's ship transit out of Voss Space?"

"We'd have picked something up in the local field if we passed a transit site. Besides, how can they make their scheduled arrival at Brell Prime if they've transited?"

"Maybe they don't care about that. I'm turning around."

She flipped the ship and they started backtracking. Denev watched the Voss Space field readout, looking for any sign of an in-channel transit. If O'Dran's ship *had* transited, it was a near-suicidal manoeuvre. Voss Space position bore only a hazy correlation to coordinates in normal space. The transit chambers – both natural and artificial, like the one held in place by the Voss bridge above Herakli – were relatively stable and well-charted, but the corridors that spanned the space between them drifted according to their own weird physics. A channel could cut through empty space or the heart of a star, and that correlative in normal space changed from minute to minute.

They were almost back at the point they'd lost sight of the ship, and nothing had registered on the field readout.

"No transit," Denev said.

"We look again," Rhees said and flipped the ship. "Forget the sensors. Let's use our eyes."

The ship moved slowly along the channel. Denev was painfully aware that every second they wasted, O'Dran – wherever she was – was putting distance between them.

The channel walls were uneven, their topography determined by the local energy gradient and nearby dimensions occupying parallel branes. Some parts shone brightly while others were cloaked in shadow. Rhees set the scoutship's searchlights to play over the walls in a regular pattern as they advanced. They navigated the first curve and entered a straight section.

"What are we looking for?" Denev asked.

"I hope we'll know when we see it."

They moved in silence to the end of the straight and started around the next curve. Rhees brought the craft to a halt and focused the searchlights on the ceiling.

"What's that?" she said.

Denev saw that the ceiling bowed above the curve.

Rhees manoeuvred the scoutship past the projection and angled up so they were looking at the back side. There was an opening. Small, but not too small the scoutship couldn't fit through.

"O'Dran's ship's too large for that," Denev said.

"It's shrinking. Look at the edges."

He saw they were contracting, pulling in slowly like a sphincter. Soon the opening would be too small to enter. But there was nowhere else O'Dran could have gone.

"Let's go," he said.

∞

Rhees wasn't sure there was enough time to get through the opening cleanly, but as the nose of the scoutship entered the channel the strangely shaped plasma opening pulled back, allowing them to pass.

"I've never seen anything like that before," Denev said.

"Voss Space is weird. Could be a natural phenomenon."

"I hope so. If the Brell are able to manipulate Voss Space in ways we can't, we have a bigger problem than we thought."

The rear view showed the opening continuing to contract. "I just hope we can get back out," Rhees said.

She'd been as keen to enter as Denev. It was the best option – fuck, the only option – to find O'Dran. But if it proved to be some strange Voss Space dead end, they could be trapped. None of this would have fazed her six months ago; she'd been so confident in her own abilities. A lot had changed, and it wasn't just her life she was gambling with now. But they had to find O'Dran. There wasn't time for second-guessing.

The corridor ran almost perpendicular to the main channel

they'd left. The field potential was lower and the walls a little tighter, and they had no way of knowing where it might lead. They climbed for twenty minutes, until the way curved gently forward, finally arriving at another sphincter that opened into a small chamber.

The space was lit by a single stable column of energy, cold blue like ice. Rhees brought the ship to a halt on the threshold.

"It feels like a destination," Denev said.

Rhees hoped so. "What does the compensator read?"

Denev modulated the device, searching up and down the bandwidth. "The chamber's stable in three-dimensional space. No stars nearby. Reading a mass. A single planet. Half the size of Earth."

"We're not waiting for an invitation, are we?" Rhees said. Eager to be out of this part of Voss Space, she primed the transit drive, using the compensator to choose an entry point wide of the planet, and engaged. The colours of the chamber walls drained out around them and they were back in space.

Denev conducted a sensor sweep of the area. "We're well outside the Voss Space relay network. Too far out for comms either."

"A blind spot."

"Getting a fix." He paused. "That's strange."

"Stranger than a secret Voss Space tunnel and an unidentified planet?"

"We're over halfway to Brell Prime. Well off the main route, but …"

Rhees had seen another exit on the far side of the chamber. "A shortcut? Keep working those sensors. I'm taking us in to the planet. We don't need any more surprises."

The world was airless, dark and frozen. Perhaps ejected from its system by some cataclysmic event aeons ago and left to wander between the stars. But it wasn't entirely lifeless. Six ships were nestled together in what looked like a small extinct caldera: two Brell craft – O'Dran's embassy clipper and another identical ship – and four Sissilak mining ships.

"Care to guess what they're all doing here?" Rhees said.

"Reading no one on board. But there's an airlock built into the caldera wall."

"Any sensor contact?"

Denev shook his head. "I'm getting nothing."

"There's a break in the rim. I'll set down there."

The small craft sank quickly and silently, settling onto the rocky ground as the engines cycled down.

"No automated sentries, no sensor satellites," Rhees said. "They're not expecting any visitors."

"I'll take what luck we're given," Denev said, keying a locker below the control console and pulling out two blasters. He handed one to Rhees. "But let's not trust entirely to luck."

Rhees grabbed her helmet and followed Denev, hunkering down while she waited for him to cycle through the small lock before she could enter. She was used to the stiffer high-gee suits worn in ramcraft. This one was more flexible, but looking out the port at the dark landscape she could have used something with a bit more shielding. They could die out here and the Hegemony would be none the wiser. She checked the charge on her blaster.

The inner lock opened and she cycled through, joining Denev on the planet surface. Gravity was much weaker than Herakli. A little less than being on Mars. The sky was full of stars but there was barely enough light to see Denev standing beside her. Infrared wasn't much use in a terrain that was close to absolute zero. She toggled her visor to ultrasound and watched as Denev opened a hatch in the side of the scoutship and took out a small rigid equipment case.

They walked over the powdery ground to the break in the caldera. Keeping to the wall, Rhees edged around until she could see the ships grouped together. She waited for a full minute, making sure there was no movement, before walking into the open. Still nothing.

She looked back. Denev's voice came over the helmet feed.

"Nothing scanning us."

She took a deep breath of suit air and they covered the ground in long strides to the lock in the caldera wall, coming to a halt beside the door mechanism. She felt dreadfully exposed.

Denev kneeled and opened his equipment case, selecting a pen-shaped device with one flat surface that he stuck to the lock controls. They waited. A light flashed once and the door slid silently open, flooding them with visible light.

Rhees switched her visor over and the world came back in full colour. The floor of the chamber inside was covered in dust showing multiple footprints. None of them human.

"Drag your feet," Denev said. "No prints."

Rhees liked his optimism. It suggested they'd make it out again in one piece. Or maybe he was just being thorough. She checked the charge on her blaster again, then stood to the side of the inner door, ready.

The outer door closed and the inner door cycled. The corridor it opened onto was empty. The walls were smooth, as if the tunnels had been cut with a laser.

Denev kneeled down over his case again. "We wait here in case we need to make a quick exit," he said, and held up three grey pellets in the palm of his gauntlet. They lifted from his hand and drifted down the corridor out of sight.

Rhees hunkered beside him, keeping her blaster trained at the point where the pellets had disappeared. Denev took her left arm and pressed a contact on the gauntlet. The view on her visor split, the top half showing three feeds moving down the corridor. Pellet-eye views. The rest of the corridor was empty and she relaxed a little.

The pellets split up, one heading down another passage at a junction, one floating up to the rough ceiling, while the other skimmed along just above the floor like a singleship buzzing a planet surface. And Rhees could hear sounds now. Voices, becoming louder.

The view from the pellet near the ceiling expanded as it turned a corner and hovered at an opening into a large cave. There were aliens there. An assortment of Sissilak, Totek and ... She saw O'Dran, standing with four other Brell.

One of the Sissilak was talking, the words instantly translated by her helmet trink. "You *kill* Ix'la."

O'Dran raised one long-fingered hand to the Brell around her and stepped away from the group to face the Sissilak. "Not me personally. But I would have if I'd been able. Your 'colleague' was about to sell us out to HDC."

The Sissilak reared up to match O'Dran's height. "So you say."

"Stop this posturing, Needra. I know your own people have confirmed Ix'la's treachery. I have an arrival to make at Brell Prime and I don't have time for this."

Needra swayed a little, its plates shivering. Rhees was reminded of a cobra preparing to strike. "Still want our ships back."

O'Dran's group began to protest, but she waved them to silence. "That's not the smartest move right now. We're more effective together. And it's safer for all concerned."

"Easy to say," Needra countered. "We suffer three raids in last demi-month. You lose tiny colony. Nothing since."

"I wouldn't describe thirteen billion Brell as a tiny colony. No other species has borne such heavy losses against these raiders. But that is not my point, if you'll allow me?"

Needra sank slightly, coiling its main body.

"No one knows where the raiders will strike next. And there's no point deploying the ships we've worked so hard to conceal without a clear target. Surely your militia ships are sufficient to patrol your borders."

"Ships are our ships," Needra snapped. "Don't need permission how and when we use them. That not deal."

"But your actions would get you and us into more trouble than you could handle," a grating voice said, an odd clicking noise beating a tattoo to accompany the words.

Needra and O'Dran turned as a Totek shuffled forward. Rhees had seen a couple of images in the briefing pack and Denev's 'walking kettledrum' description was right. The alien was short, with three legs supporting a bulbous body with a flat expanse of skin – almost human-looking – stretched across the top of its skull. The skin tightened and slackened as the Totek's claws tapped out a rhythm on it.

Needra rose again, its sharp teeth clearly visible. "What you mean by that?"

"Simply that the appearance of so many 'new' ships across Sissilak space would almost certainly draw the attention of Hegemony bureaucrats. That attention would spread to the other species located close by as their investigations proceeded in the manner of all methodical paranoids. And our precautions, sufficient to deflect long-range observation, would not long stand up to that amount of scrutiny. All our work, all our hidden ships, all our planning would be for nothing. And you can be sure the Hegemony would concoct a unique 'reward' for our considered treachery."

"Don't care," Needra hissed. "Want ships!"

"Then you can have them," O'Dran said, cutting across the Sissilak. Some of the others began to protest. "But," she continued, loud enough to drown them out, "let's keep them together a few days longer. I've been to the HDC offices and they confirmed there's no additional Fleet presence expected so we're still free to act. Another raid must be coming very soon now. And the ships we have are much more effective as a single attack group. Let us take advantage of this window and keep the ships on battle alert for another tenday. The raiders don't have unlimited resources and their supply base must be situated close to us and be of a reasonable size. Between us we cover a large amount of space. All we need is time. Someone, somewhere, will hear or see something that will give their location away. If we can find their base, we can send in our ships in one swift surgical action, which would rid us of this threat and avoid detection by the Hegemony."

"I agree," the Totek rapped out.

"If nothing happens I'll gladly break up the ship group and we can go our separate ways until the emergency is over," O'Dran said.

Needra rose up on shivering plates, glaring at her. "You have tenday."

The view pulled back as the pellet withdrew and Rhees blinked the feeds away. She looked at Denev. "We need to get out of here. Undetected."

Denev closed his case and stood. "I've vapourised the pellets."

They stepped back into the lock, the inner door closed over, and they waited for the cycle. Rhees watched the readout as the air pressure bled out. A secret fleet of ships … It seemed the aliens in this sector weren't as ready to acquiesce to Hegemony control as the Central Administration thought.

The outer door opened onto darkness and they made their way quickly across the regolith. Rhees looked back often, expecting to see the lock open, hear the alert being raised, shots fired. But they made it to the break in the caldera wall undetected.

Back in the scoutship cockpit, she pulled off her helmet and stowed it under her seat. "Fuck. This is big."

"Not quite what we expected," Denev said. "We need to work out how HDC can best leverage the intel."

"I can think of a few options," Rhees said, activating the lifters and bringing the ship into a shallow ascent angled away from the caldera.

"The obvious reaction isn't always the most useful. Confronting the Sissilak, Brell and Totek about this could go very wrong, very quickly. We need to contain the situation."

Spoken like a true diplomat-cum-spy, she thought. But this was a threat she could understand.

She punched for more thrust and they shot away from the planet, vectoring towards their last transit location. They still had to make it to Herakli in one piece.

16

The door slid heavily back and, instantly afraid, I tilted my head to look through the bag. It wasn't a Defender but someone from the Cultivator caste; a female from the way her skull plate tapered above her neck guard. She turned to look at me as the door closed. Smiled. The sense of her was like cool water on hot flesh.

She moved forward, her elongated arms reaching out to me. I flinched. The bag was lifted gently from my head and she kneeled in front of me.

"I can feel your fear," she said. "It's not necessary. You are safe."

"I'm in chains."

"No one will hurt you. We have questions. That's all."

Here it is, I thought. This will tell me how much they know.

She was dressed in a plain smock, her plates darkening red, older than me. But she wore no house colour or lodge sigil. She walked back to the door, knocked on it. It slid open and I felt others outside. A Defender handed her a platter and the door closed over again, cutting off my sense of anyone other than her.

"Would you like me to feed you?" she said. "You must be hungry."

"I can feed myself," I said, wondering if she'd loosen my bonds.

Her feeder claws spread wide. "You can't leave until we say."

She kneeled beside me again, placing the platter on the floor. It held a stone bowl with some stew and a ripe blue gahe fruit. She loosened the chains on my lower arms enough so I could eat, and placed the platter on my lap.

I wasn't sure about the stew. Would they drug me? I lifted the gahe fruit and ran a claw through the thick rind, splitting it in half and picking at the pulpy seeds inside with my feeder claws. I looked at her as I ate, imagining what they could do to me. I was helpless. The fear rose again.

"Don't," she said. "We only want to know what is happening in House Czerag."

"The House is the House," I said, quoting the old saying. "It is not for outsiders."

"And still we ask." She was calm. Confident she would get what she needed. That too was a frightening concept. "Your hierarch has plans, like all of them. But these plans we would know."

"Why?"

"Because we have seen Sakat's true path and nothing can be allowed to prevent it."

Was that where her confidence came from – some kind of religious fervour? Or perhaps it was the kind of faith a strong hierarch instilled. All hierarchs had plans, as she admitted. What were Kergis's?

She rose. "You will tell us what we need to know."

I laid the empty gahe husk on the platter. Maybe I'd been awake too long. I felt weak, the feeling leaching from my claws. My arms were heavy.

"What have you ..." I began, but I was too tired to finish the thought. My eyes closed.

∞

My head jerked up, eyes snapping open as my mind screamed with pain and anger. Reaching out to me, not a claw span away, was some mad creature. It roared at me, each shriek like death given voice. I tried to pull away, straining against the chains. The chair was solid.

Claws lashed through the air, reaching for me, but never quite close enough. My mind was on fire, yearning to be free, so I could maim, tear, consume.

The room around me twisted in garish colours. I shouted out, my voice blending in a death yell with the creature.

∞

Blackness. Quiet.

What *was* that? Something like Reka, before his excision. Chained like me, but close. Too close.

My head felt strange. My body was gripped by a sensation like sudden acceleration. Like a tenspace transit. But the chair was still beneath me.

A pinpoint of light ahead, rushing at me. Expanding. Swallowing.

The scream. It was there again, howling frustration. Raking the air between us. Burrowing into my mind. Madness taking everything. Wiping out every thought. Wiping out me.

Pain coursed down my side. Unable to reach me, the creature was ripping at its own hide beneath the plates. I felt every tear in his flesh and looked down, expecting to see gashes opening along my side.

I flinched as it tore off a feeder claw. Exquisite pain running across my mandible. Too much to bear.

∞

The female kneeled in front of me as if she had never left. The creature was gone. No, not a creature. Another Kresz. But insane. A monster.

She touched my leg and her presence instantly magnified. "There is a truth you are not telling us."

My mandibles spread wide. I felt like laughing but I couldn't think why. "We can all say that."

"If you stay here, you will go mad. I can feel it. You are slipping away. We are not meant to feel the things that you are feeling."

"I don't know anything," I said.

"Ah," she lifted her claws away, "that is a lie."

"I don't know anything!" I screamed at her, sounding to my ears like the creature.

"I brought you food."

I hung my head, wishing her away. "I'm not hungry."

She stood. I heard the door open.

∞

The creature hurled itself at me, its hatred dashing against my mind. It howled and I howled too. She was right. I'd be mad soon. I wanted it to break loose from its chains so it could kill me. It strained towards me, its eyes fixed on mine, its thoughts fixed on a single idea. To end me. Life was madness. Death was peace.

Time slipped away and the world with it. I ran through the endar woods, the creature behind me, unseen but I could hear the snap of branches as it ran full pelt. Why not stop? But my legs were not my own.

I leaped high, higher. High above the treetops, reaching for space.

A claw wrapped around my hoof, pulling me down, and a gaszti flashed in my eyes.

∞

"Drink."

I was still chained to the chair. There was a gourd at my feeders. Water. I lapped at it.

The gourd was pulled away. "Not too much. Wait."

I looked at her, noticing how golden her eyes were. She was so kind. Kind. My mind was moving slowly. That didn't feel right. Only Isza was kind.

"No more," I said. "Please."

Again the creature, mandibles wide.

Then the female –

Creature –

Female –

"No more!" I screamed.

∞

The room was empty. I was slumped to one side on the chair, leaning heavily against the chains.

"You're awake," she said.

The door slid closed behind her. Were there others outside? I could no longer tell.

She kneeled in front of me as always, but reached out and grasped my upper knees in her claws. She flowed through the contact. Her mantle was rising.

"Stop," I said. "What are you doing?"

It was a violation, but I couldn't resist. My mantle rose. The contact intensified.

"You betray your people."

It was impossible not to react to that word. Kergis would see Czerag's actions as betrayal. Many others would too. She picked up on my response, the focus of her concentration shifting.

"Tell me what you've done."

She pushed. A powerful force. The room faded. I felt pulled down below conscious thought. I couldn't let that happen.

"I'm different," I said. "You can't understand me."

"Tell me and you'll be saved."

Sunslight fell on me and I knew I'd lost the fight. We were in the communion space. I opened my eyes.

"Tell me," she said.

We stood face to face in the open desert. But we weren't alone. A multitude of Kresz, all body plans, all houses and lodges, surrounded us. They were waiting for me. I could feel it. They wanted to accept me. Take me in. Love me for what I was. All I had to do was tell them what I'd done. Then I'd be at peace. Saved.

"That's not right," I said.

"It is right. Tell us. Join us."

"No." It felt wrong. "This isn't right. This is not how it is."

"It can be. It's what you want."

"It can't. You can't understand. I'm different."

"We love you," she said. "All will be one. Open yourself to us."

I could see it. A universality of Kresz, united in a way we had never been before, with a place for everyone.

I looked past her to the edge of the crowd. A face moved behind the others, disappeared as a shadow fell across the assembly. Then the suns came again and I saw. Reka. He was there. And he had a warning for me.

I pulled back. I could feel the female stretching to hold me, willing me to stop. To turn back to them. To the gift she offered. Why couldn't I see? All I had to do was tell them.

Something was building inside me. I could feel it pushing up through my thorax, growing. I clamped my feeders tight shut, but nothing would stop it. My head was burning. I was in a speeder, going faster and faster. It couldn't stop. Wouldn't stop. I had to let it out.

I screamed, and kept screaming, wrenching at the chains, on and on without cease.

I opened my eyes. The female was gone. The room was gone. My chains were gone. I was lying on the forest floor.

I rolled over and pushed myself up on shaky legs, slowly rising to stand. I began to walk, concentrating on the rhythm of the steps. Nothing else mattered. Just walk.

I didn't know how long I went on like that, but the sky was lightening when I realised the woods were thinning out and giving way to scrabbly bushes. I could see the beginnings of the desert ahead.

I fell to my knees. I couldn't go any further.

∞

My vision cleared. A head, dark against the sky. Broad, thick skull cap, curving around the eyes.

"Gurud. You're alive."

"*You're* alive," he said.

He pulled me quickly upright and I was alert for an instant, sensing danger. There were three other Defenders with him. I could see a deep crack running down the side of his pectoral and abdominal plates. He broke contact and I felt myself sliding back into a place where nothing much mattered.

"You've been drugged," he said. "Do you know how you got here?"

I blinked. "Where are we? The woods?"

"We're on the border of Czerag lands. We've been looking for you everywhere. Come on. Get onboard."

He gestured behind me to a large half-track truck with another Defender at the drive control. I was weak but steady on my hoofs. It felt like I'd slept for a long time. I climbed on and Gurud helped me with the harness. My claws were too numb to manage.

"Sorry," I said.

He touched me again and the feeling flowing through the contact was unmistakable. He cared about me; was worried about me. Almost as much as Isza.

"You'll be home soon," he said.

The turbines roared into life and the platform lifted, tilting as the rest of the small force of Defenders climbed aboard. We moved off through the trees, then broke out into brilliant sunslight and accelerated across scrub. Everywhere I looked had an unreal cast to it.

The others were focused, watching their surroundings. I could feel the tension running through them, but from a great distance. I remembered the room, the female, the creature, my walk through the night. It felt like it had all happened a long time ago, if it happened at all.

The hardpack ground gave way to desert and the engine

stepped up a level, throwing a plume of sand behind us as we accelerated. There was no one and nothing around us as far as I could see. But the Defenders didn't relax. They stayed watchful all the way to the escarpment.

Gradually I began to feel more grounded in my surroundings. Gurud was right: I'd been drugged. Details of my interrogation were coming back. But why had they freed me?

As we pulled to a halt near the cliff wall, a voice called my name and I felt disoriented all over again.

"Udun!" Isza jumped onto the platform, but as soon as she touched me she pulled back. "Sakat, what happened to you? I thought you were going to the deep desert. But I can feel –"

"What are you doing here?" I said. "Was the mission cancelled?"

She unbuckled my seat harness. "I've been *on* the mission. I got back two days ago. I've been debriefing in Aktiuk since then."

I paused. "How long have I been gone?"

Gurud grunted and I felt something like guilt. "You've been missing for two-four days."

Two-four days. It felt like maybe two or three. Somehow I'd lost time.

"What do you mean 'missing'?" Isza said. "Gurud, why didn't you tell me?"

She was angry and I understood now why Gurud felt the way he did.

"Czerag's orders," he said. "We had to keep his abduction secret."

"Abduction!"

I grabbed Isza's shoulder plate and her anger stalled as she sensed how weak I was.

"Gurud was nearly killed when I was taken," I told her. "Don't blame him. But we have to see Czerag. Now."

She cast a glance at Gurud and something passed between them. Something not meant for others.

"We'll all go together," she said.

I looked towards the fissure in the high cliff wall. Another group of Defenders was approaching. They formed up with Gurud and the others surrounding us.

"They're here to take you both to Czerag," Gurud said.

As we walked I tried to reconcile how much time had passed with my memories. But I couldn't.

We turned into the fissure, and I saw heavily armed Defenders stationed along its length. The entranceway had been fortified too: a low wall stretched across the opening with more Defenders behind it.

We passed around it and into the main hall. Kresz were coming in and out of the galleries, carrying equipment podules, sacks of food, antiquated blasters. There was an air of tense purposefulness.

It felt like we were preparing for war. But war was unthinkable.

17

Our escort peeled off in layers as we walked the short corridor to Czerag's chamber. By the time we got to the other end there was only me, Isza and Gurud.

The heavy shield door ground open and Tzek stood in front of the partition wall, beckoning us inside. The feeling from him was a confusion of emotions. But as we entered and Czerag stood stiffly to greet us, I had no difficulty in reading what the hierarch felt. He was relieved to see us.

"Udun. You are unharmed?"

"Yes, Hierarch."

"Where were you?" Tzek asked, his emotions resolving into impatience.

"I don't know. I only just found out how long I've been gone."

I stumbled and Isza was there, holding me. "Let him sit," she said, and helped me to a stone bench. Czerag sat again, facing me.

"Why were you at the spaceport with Gurud anyway?" Tzek asked.

I felt the accusation, but Czerag waved the question away.

"Later, Tzek. We've been searching for you since Isza left," he told me. "Gurud joined the group as soon as he was able and I don't think he's slept since."

I looked up at the big Defender standing beside Isza and sent him my thanks.

"I was taken when they attacked Gurud," I said. "They flew me somewhere but I couldn't see. I thought they were taking me across the Inland Sea …" But if that had been the case, I could never have walked to the edge of the desert. "It must have been to confuse me."

"Did you recognise them or anything about them?" Tzek asked.

"No. They wore nothing that suggested a house or a lodge. I only caught a glimpse of the Defenders who took me. But there was a female. A Cultivator. She was a strong empath."

"She questioned you?" Tzek asked.

"She tried. They drugged me. And … they locked something up with me. A Kresz, but mad. He filled my mind with his hatred. Thoughts of killing. Madness. I felt myself slipping away."

Isza kneeled beside me, her arm resting across my shoulder plate. I drew strength from that.

"Hierarch, I know they took Reka," I went on. "I was forced into communion and I saw a memory of him there. It was the only reason I was able to resist. I think he'd been taken and questioned repeatedly."

"Gurud told us what you'd learned at the Academy," Tzek said. "We've found nothing on this Daek. But if Reka was taken, why didn't he say anything after the first time?"

"I don't know. But if they did to him what they did to me … They may have been trying to put him under some compulsion to spy for them, but it sent him mad instead. I felt my own mind slipping away while I was there."

"And what did you tell them?"

I looked up at Tzek. It was obvious he was thinking the worst. Czerag simply waited.

"Nothing," I said.

"They had you for two-four days!" Tzek said.

"You resisted?" This from Isza.

"At first. Yes. They knew I was keeping something from them. The drugs, the creature – they were trying to break me down. And then the female was there and we entered full communion. But … it didn't feel right. They told me …" I felt ridiculous saying it out loud. "They told me they loved me. That they wanted to accept me.

It was so obviously artificial to be so wanted by other Kresz."

"Oh, Udun," Isza said.

"Then I saw Reka and I knew I'd become like him if I didn't resist. I told them it wasn't right. That I was different. But they kept at me. I think I did go mad then. All I remember is a scream. And then I woke up in the forest."

"What do you think?" Czerag asked Tzek.

Tzek stared at me, probing at the edge of my consciousness. "He's being completely open. He believes what he says. Communion wouldn't help." One claw pulled at a feeder. "It's possible that whatever empathic strategy they used just didn't work on Udun. He's not like the rest of us."

I wasn't hurt by Tzek's words. It was the truth.

"What exactly did they want you to join?" Czerag asked me.

"I don't know. They had to be Kergis's people. He's already suspicious. But what she was offering … it didn't feel like a house or a lodge. It was more than that. Something … She said, 'All will be one'."

"Sounds like religious nonsense to me," Tzek said. "Kergis is hardly religious."

"But he's not above using whatever tool is available," Czerag said.

"Why take Udun at all?" Isza asked.

"At first I thought they knew I'd been off-planet," I said. "But they never questioned me about that. I think I was just out in the open and unlucky. Whatever they'd done with Reka had failed and they needed a new subject. We could have been followed from the spaceport for all I know."

"Where you should never have been in the first place," Tzek said. "We can't risk him being taken again, Czerag. He must go to one of our deep desert hides."

I refused to be held prisoner again. But before I could speak, Isza tightened her grip on me and her anger mixed with my own.

"No," she said. "He's not going anywhere. Udun stays with me."

The feeling of her was implacable, countered by an equal feeling from Tzek. And then Gurud placed his thick arm around Isza protectively. He didn't say anything. He didn't have to.

Isza took the knuckle of Gurud's oversized pincer in her other claw. Because she was still touching me I experienced strongly how they felt about each other in that moment. I'd never felt that way about anyone. But there was a physical undercurrent there too. Coming from Gurud, but suddenly reciprocated. Isza let go of me and I pulled back before I was overwhelmed.

"You and Gurud will keep Udun safe," Czerag told Isza. "There's no time to send him away even if I wanted to. He has more work to do now. We all have. But I need to hear your report, Isza. What happened on the contact mission?"

Isza let go of Gurud's claw. "If Kergis's people took Udun ... it must be significant. Kergis was on one of the Defender battlecruisers that accompanied us. He took control of the mission."

"What?" Tzek said.

"We need to know everything, and now," Czerag said. He held out his claws to Isza.

"With Gurud here?" Tzek said.

Czerag blinked. "They will be joined soon."

His mantle was already rising, Isza's too.

I reached a claw out to Tzek. He flowed through the contact, and then Isza was there. And Gurud. I'd never experienced close communion with more than one person. There had been moments like the one on the escarpment when we'd joined to farewell the mutilated young female, but those tended to blend the individual into the mass. Here – although Isza was the focus of attention – I could still sense Czerag, Tzek and Gurud as differentiated personalities. But as we sank deeper into communion and Isza began to recount her journey, it was as if I saw events through her eyes, maybe not as they actually occurred but as she experienced them. Feeling how she felt.

∞

She's exhausted, on edge, and worried about what comes next. The ship, leased from the Jantri, is nothing less than miraculous, but even so the tenspace crossing has been arduous, with days spent strapped to the acceleration couch careening down energy gradients. Even that is nothing to the constant attention of Erdjis, picking at her and undermining her confidence.

For now they are stationary and Erdjis is busy on comms with one of the escort ships. The diplomat is coming aboard before the final transit to realspace.

She waits at the lock with the rest of the crew: K'la, the House Ukat xenolinguist and ship's communications officer – nervous, well aware of how much the mission's success rests on her – and Djnc, House Akczek ship's engineer, whose only interest is his engines. He's clearly unhappy about being dragged away from them to greet some xeno-office functionary. Erdjis joins them, unable to conceal his excitement. Isza has no time to ask him why before the lock starts its cycle.

And then she feels it as the outer lock opens. Something like the dawning of a sun rushing over the horizon of an airless moon. Something stark and all encompassing, so that there is no shade, no refuge. No escape.

The inner lock slides aside and Kergis stands there: thickened shell, black cap plate. He is bent over as if the ages weigh him down. It's a physicality at stark odds with the force of his personality, lighting up the room.

Kergis looks straight at her, and it's as if her personality is peeled away beneath that gaze.

And then Erdjis steps forward, burning with devotion like a little moon circling Kergis's sun, and the all-consuming glare is blunted. Isza feels her wits returning and realises Kergis doesn't possess supernatural powers over her. He is a hierarch, yes, but still only a Kresz. Normality reasserts itself; there is work to concentrate on.

"We should prepare for transit," she says.

Kergis is flanked by two aides who she only now registers. They help their hierarch onto the nearest couch and the padding draws tight, holding him firm in its embrace. There aren't enough couches for the aides, so they withdraw down the short stairs to the galley to use the benches there. It's not ideal but better than standing up for transit.

The rest of the crew take to their couches. The engine is ready, the lightboard hovers above her, responsive to her touch. There is a tension inside her, drawn out like a wire. She wants this to be over with. The ship starts moving towards a tenspace corridor near the apex of the chamber – a split in the violet cloud with a sick tinge of dark green through it.

Around her, she can feel the others concentrating on their tasks, wanting to do a good job, needing to. Erdjis whispers to the escort in battle language. Djnc flicks through drive data and sensor reads. K'la arranges major phonemes on her lightboard.

But now they are committed, all this is background. Isza is pure focus. She is the ship made Kresz. It moves only as she wills it.

She is sucked upwards into the tunnel as if caught in a vacuum. Perspective shifts and instead of climbing, she's falling again, twisting left and right, following folds in the path. The speed seems out of control, but there's an easing back and the tenspace walls begin to brighten, seeds of blinding golden light coalescing on all sides.

"Watch the braking, Djnc," Isza says.

"I'm watching it. We're not going to cause a discharge. Look."

The ship slows further and the lights fade; the tunnel returns to brooding darkness. Somewhere up ahead the escort ships are transitting.

"There's the signal," Erdjis says and Isza pushes the ship forward again.

The hull shudders, so violently her head shakes in the restraining couch, blurring her vision. Shots of energy race along the corridor past them, and up ahead there's a darker patch in the black, swelling as she races for it. It's the end of the tunnel. The terminus. Implacably dark and solid.

The ship leaps forward and the end becomes darker still. The blank wall rushes towards her. She waits for the impact. Her body spasms, skewered on an ecstatic wire piercing her limbs. The air is sucked through spiracles in explosive decompression and she's helpless to draw breath.

And then the universe detonates in her brain, stars unwinding, novae searingly hot, and darkness, soft, peaceful darkness, rising up, wrapping her in its cool folds.

The ship appears precisely between the two escorts in a clear space surrounded by rocks. A distant, bluish sun shines weakly, playing its light over them. She pushes back the sensation of transit, alert to the danger around them.

"We're in an asteroid field," she says to Erdjis. "Why in Sakat didn't the Defender ships know about this?"

"Our charts of this area aren't complete," Erdjis says.

"Well, it's not a tactically smart area to be meeting in. We can't run through rock. Transitting is the only way out. We should leave. Now."

"Your concern does you great credit, Isza," Kergis says, pushing upright on his couch. "But we do not run from aliens."

"Picking up some fairly exotic emissions ahead," Djnc says. "I'm guessing it's a different type of transit effect."

On the viewscreen, an elongated mass, lit by the blue sun, is twisting out of a hole that isn't there. It's different to the Hegemony ship in the holo of the deeprange ship encounter. This one is smaller, sleeker, and snaps into shape as the last of it exits into realspace.

"Passive scan," Isza says, fascinated by the sleek lines of the ship. Its beauty almost rivals the Jantri design.

"They're scanning us," Djnc says.

"Move to active scanning. Ready with the language primer, K'la."

"Incoming transmission," Erdjis says.

She feels suddenly tense. And then realises the emotion is not her own. "What is it, K'la?"

"The message. It's not a primer like ours. It has Kresz words and what I suppose are correlatives in the alien's language."

"They know our language?" Erdjis says.

[I almost break out of communion at this, and I feel Isza move closer to me, worried.]

"It's not perfect," K'la says. "But it's a fairly good grounding."

"Like any civilisation, our broadcasts travel outwards unchecked in all directions," Djnc says. "We're still well within the transmission shell."

"Assuming you are right, Djnc," Kergis says, "and I do not dispute it, the real question is why show us they know our language, even in a rudimentary form? Are they trying to scare us or reassure us?"

"We have a language lock," K'la says.

"Then let us regain the initiative," Kergis says. "Open communications with the ship; voice only." K'la does, and Kergis says, "Kresz diplomatic ship to Hegemony vessel. We have responded to your invitation. We are ready to communicate."

[Tzek's curiosity magnifies but Isza felt nothing from the hierarch that is out of step with his words.]

"Sensors can't penetrate their hull," Djnc says.

"This is the Hegemony First Contact Vessel *Olive Branch*. I am Troels Volmar. Are you able and willing to meet on our ship? Our atmosphere is benign to your species."

The voice is a machine translation so it is hard to infer any emotion from it.

"How do they know what we breathe?" K'la says.

"Our hull didn't block their scans," Erdjis says. "I wouldn't read too much into it."

"Calm yourself," Kergis says. "There is no immediate threat. We have two heavily armed battlecruisers. And I doubt this Hegemony would lure us all this distance just to destroy us. Isza, bring us forward."

The ship looks like an engorged Kresz mantle: a concave disc with thickened edges and a bulging central cord standing out along the spine. Its hull is a dull grey; no markings except for two circles side by side across the top of the disc near the front. The circles are elongated on the facing edges where they join each other, more like a twisted cord than two separate shapes.

Isza feathers thrusters, coming in at an angle, moving around the face of the other ship to one side where a docking ring extends unlike any other. The end moves forward, raw and ragged, questing like some giant mouth. It changes shape as it closes on the Jantri hull, matching port shape and sticking to the metal where it touches.

Kergis stands. "Isza, K'la – you will accompany me."

K'la slaves her mini-processor to the ship's linguistic banks and passes out voder links. She's fighting to control her fear. Kergis places his claws on her pectoral plate and the effect is instant. Isza can feel the flow of calm even standing on the other side of the cabin.

They enter the lock together, the inner door closing behind and the outer lock cycling open. The docking tube looks like an organic plastic: flexible and shining wetly, it dries quickly and draws tighter, the folds along the inside wrinkled and irregular.

Isza takes a first tentative step. The floor is firm and she walks forward, held by a thin, exotic sheath across an endless fall.

"There's gravity here," she says. "A definite down."

"What kind of creatures use living tissue as technology?" K'la asks.

Erdjis's voice sounds in Isza's ear. "We've been able to partially scan the ship ahead. There are two beings waiting for you past the other door. They appear to be unarmed."

They enter the other lock. K'la is still nervous, despite Kergis's influence. The hierarch is impassive, facing the unknown with equanimity.

The inner lock opens. Two creatures stand in the corridor beyond. They look small and soft. They have fur on the top of their heads and one has fur on its face. Their skin is pink and softly gelatinous. The effect is unattractive. Both wear garments that cover most of their bodies: identical, black, with that double circle over a pouch near where a Kresz's pectoral pulse point lies.

"Welcome. Follow us, please," one of them says. Or that's what Isza hears through her voder. The actual sound is more like the mewling of a nymph wedded with the screechy call of an ah'lok.

The walls of the corridor are painted metal, the ceiling metal too, with recessed lighting. Every so often the walls are broken by a closed door or an electronic panel of some kind, perhaps a control junction. It's no more impressive than the inside of any other ship. Still, she is hungry for detail and looks at everything, trying to divine its function.

A large doorway stands open ahead. The aliens stop on either side and usher them in. The room is large, dominated on one side by a flat image of a starfield running the length of the wall. There is a long table flanked by chairs. Another of these soft Hegemony types is standing at the far end, one of its stubby arms stretched out towards them. It is taller than the other two aliens. Thin like an endar tree trunk.

"Welcome," it says in perfect Kresz, both in the voder and in her naked ear gap. While well-pronounced, it is the greeting of a youngling before its empathic ability emerges. That fact undercuts any attempt to impress.

"I am Troels Volmar. Please, be seated," it says, again in good Kresz.

Kergis sits first, flanked by Isza and K'la. There is a small black cone on the table, which the alien picks up and fits to its ear gap.

"Forgive me," the voder says in Isza's ear, but it's the same mewls she heard from the others that come from Volmar's mouth now. "My understanding of your language is basic at best and all but exhausted."

K'la lays her mini-processor on the table, integrating the new data and correlatives as Volmar speaks.

There is a clear jug on the table, holding a colourless liquid and surrounded by cups. Volmar motions to it. "For all the species we have encountered in our travels, this beverage – water – is commonly drunk. I think perhaps all life in the universe can drink water."

"Thank you," Kergis says. "We will not drink with you."

It is difficult to interpret Volmar's expression. Isza doesn't discern any change from what she presumes was a welcoming look.

"I thank you for your presence," Volmar says. "You have travelled far."

"As have you," Kergis says. "There are no civilisations in this part of space, or anywhere near here."

"It is true we are explorers. We venture far from our world to learn and share our knowledge with like-minded intelligences," Volmar says.

"And is that why you have invited us here?" Kergis says.

Isza doesn't dare focus her attention on the hierarch too closely, but all she feels on the surface is that same calm, backed by strong purpose.

"I represent a group of worlds and civilisations collectively termed the Hegemony," Volmar says. "One of our guiding principles is to seek out and contact new life wherever we encounter it, to offer our friendship for mutual benefit."

"And where do you originate?" Isza asks. It is not protocol and she feels Kergis's annoyance, but under the circumstances it seems an innocent question and one that could prove useful to her breach-brother.

Volmar indicates the wall display, which tilts until the viewpoint is oriented somewhere above the galactic plane. The thick band of stars forming the spiral arm is clearly visible.

"Here is our meeting place," Volmar says and a purple circle appears in line with the Lenticular but close to the arm's edge. "The Hegemony is located in this part of space."

A golden shape appears near the extreme tip of the arm. By galactic scales it is small, but she estimates it encompasses at least fifty suns. Of course there's no reason to believe this is a true representation of the Hegemony's borders, or even its correct location.

"That's a long way from here," she says.

"It is indeed. Please, I have not learned your names."

"I am Kergis," the hierarch says. "This is Isza." She catches the hint of displeasure again when Kergis says her name. "And K'la."

Isza takes advantage of the pause to press her point. "So why travel so far from your home? I would think there were civilisations enough in the space between us to keep your explorer ships busy for a long time."

"We have a great many explorer ships and we have been exploring for a very long time. We go where our travels take us. And they have brought us here."

"And this returns us to my question," Kergis says, taking control of the discussion again. "What you would like this meeting with us to achieve."

"Contact with alien species is an end in itself," Volmar says. "We learn so much from each other and it benefits both sides. With diplomatic agreements come the sharing of technology, ideas, information."

Isza can clearly feel Kergis is nonplussed and it's easy to understand why. What do Kresz want with alien knowledge?

"Our people do not seek contact," Kergis says. "We do not wish relations with you or others at this time or at any time in the future. Our way does not require it."

"That is unfortunate. But understandable," Volmar says. "Each species must walk its own path towards the end of the evolutionary process, that ultimate expression of its fundamental reason for being. It is an ambition worthy of our respect. In our experience, those aims are sometimes frustrated by the intrusion of unwanted external aggressors. It is a hostile universe. The Hegemony also exists to provide mutual aid and protection for its member species."

Kergis is implacable. "I am sure your Hegemony's goals are as you say, but it is not for the Kresz. We have our own path. And so I must ask that you no longer pursue diplomatic ties with us. We wish only to be left alone."

Volmar's head moves up and down in an odd gesture. "It is a pity, but I respect your wishes. We shall not seek further contact."

The group stands.

"Farewell," Volmar says and they are escorted back to the lock. The meeting is over.

18

Slowly I came into myself again as the communion dissolved. My mind was reeling at everything I'd experienced through Isza. But I was more certain than ever that we were in danger.

"Did Kergis return with you all the way to Homeworld?" Tzek asked Isza.

"No. He transferred to the Defender escort while we were still in realspace. We transited first. The Defenders waited to ensure we were not followed."

"Why would Kergis go in person?" Czerag asked.

Tzek considered for a moment. "He's certainly not just playing the diplomat. Any formally empowered speaker could have done that job. But this is the first time in a long time we've been contacted by outsiders. By rejecting these aliens in person, Kergis increases his standing with the conservative factions across all the houses and lodges, not just his own."

"Has he made any announcements?" I asked.

"Nothing," Tzek said.

"You got back ...?" I asked Isza.

"Two days ago. I've been busy with system checks and lodge debriefs since then."

"Kergis was at the council meeting this afternoon," Czerag said. "He didn't mention it. I wasn't even aware he'd been off-planet."

"Perhaps he plans to make an announcement later," Tzek said.

"Hierarch," I said, "this has to be connected. The Hegemony is a threat. Kergis is a threat. And now the two have met."

"Kergis rejected the aliens," Tzek said. "What are you suggesting?"

"That we're in more danger than you suspect."

"There may be something in what you say," Czerag said. But he was distracted, looking over at Isza and Gurud.

They were holding claws again. Isza had been away for a long time, and their joining had been postponed because of the mission. I felt embarrassed by the emotions I could sense. This was not something I should be experiencing with my breach-sister. Then I noticed the smell in the chamber: part pheromone, part precursor. It was the smell of softening carapace. Isza was preparing herself for ... well, for Gurud.

"Isza," Czerag said, "we can talk more later. I think you and Gurud should take some time to be together. May Sakat bless your joining and may you breed true."

Isza was embarrassed. Gurud was more stoic. "Thank you, Hierarch," he said, and they both left.

"We can't draw attention to ourselves. Not now," Tzek said.

"Hierarch, I know how things are here," I said. "I felt it in the corridors. I know you're at a delicate stage in your planning. But I'm convinced we must do something to protect ourselves from the Hegemony threat."

He held my gaze for moments, weighing my feelings as much as my words. Then he blinked.

"Udun, you bring me problems I would rather not consider. The decommissioned ships the houses and lodges sent to our reclamation facility have not been stripped down for their tekla. I've had them refitted. Some as cargo carriers and others as armed escorts. Some look like cargo ships but have hidden armaments. It is necessary. I intend to see our cargo delivered safely." He straightened and I felt the hard steel within him. "No one must be allowed to stop us."

"You'd fire on ..." I couldn't finish. It was impossible to imagine Kresz firing on Kresz ships.

"If I have to. We must succeed, and we must endure until the other houses see that they can do what we have done and force the Merchants Lodge and Kergis to back down. There is no other option. I am evacuating the house to keep our people safe."

It was clear the danger from Kergis and the Merchants Lodge was more immediate than some nebulous threat from the Hegemony. Czerag was contemplating a civil war, however limited.

"I am not a fool," he added. "Breaking the trade monopoly isn't going to be much good if we are overrun by aliens in the meantime. The unknown is always threatening. Sometimes because we just don't know enough, but sometimes because it actually *is* a threat. What you – and now Isza – have shared is enough to make me err on the side of caution. We are stretched. But we will do whatever we can within our current operations to monitor for this Hegemony." He paused and I felt his concern again. "I have another job for you."

I sensed a sudden ambivalence from Tzek.

"We prepare for the worst, but I want you on the transport with Isza. When you arrive at Telsus, I need you to press our advantage. You will use your contacts to negotiate new markets for our tekla in the Lenticular. The more attractive I can make this to the other houses, the weaker Kergis's position will be in Council. But it all depends on you."

"Of course, Hierarch." Under the circumstances, it felt wrong to be happy. But I finally had what I wanted.

"I must prepare for Isza's secondary insemination," Czerag said. "Are you well enough to get back to your room alone? I can call a Defender."

I stood, still weakened but steady enough. "I'll be fine. Thank you, Hierarch."

The shield door lifted and I was among the sensations of House Czerag once more. I didn't feel like resting, despite what I'd endured. Or maybe because of it. I walked out the main entrance and along the cleft through the escarpment, past the many

Defenders still at their posts, and onto the desert floor. The suns were setting behind me and it was already dark at the foot of the cliffs. But there was no feeling that the day was drawing to a close. I made for the oasis. It felt good to be out in the open air. To be alone. Or as alone as I could be on Homeworld.

The air passing through my spiracles was cooler closer to the water. I had no idea what would happen next. At least Czerag was alert now to the threat of the Hegemony. It would be better if the whole planet were ready. But that wasn't possible under the circumstances. In the meantime, Czerag had a private fleet of ships, some with offensive capability, hidden out there in the deep desert. It was amazing that he'd been able to carry his plans so far. Homeworld was about to change irrevocably. I wondered what shape this new order might take and how well we would survive it.

I sat with my hoofs in the water, letting it find the gaps in my carapace and cool the flesh beneath. The last tendrils of sunlight were touching the sky and the stars were becoming visible. I could make out the hazy, squashed circle of stars that formed the Lenticular in the east. A pinprick of light passing overhead glinted briefly: satellite or spaceship, I couldn't say. Whether it was Kresz or Hegemony was also unknown.

Darkness fell as I watched the stars slowly wheel across the sky. Behind me I sensed the activity in the escarpment, but here it was quiet and still. The Lenticular reached its zenith and still I didn't feel tired. It was good to be here with the wind gently passing over my body, and the sounds of the night: insects, night creatures slithering across the sand, the quiet rippling of the water.

I thought of the communion I'd shared with the female. It was a strange thing; I couldn't quite understand the sense of it. The Priests taught that the path of Sakat would bring us to a state of perfect Kreszhood where all would be as one. The political situation on Homeworld showed we were far from that divine consummation. Kergis was one of the most powerful hierarchs on the Council. Did he really need to enlist the help of religious zealots?

I didn't know how long I sat there, listening to the wind rustling the bushes nearby. But then I heard another sound, hoofs on sand, and I felt Isza approach. She sat beside me and pushed her legs into the water. She was quiet, but agitated. It was hard to get a fix on her feelings. They were jangled, disturbed.

I touched her gently. "Isza, what's the matter? Has Gurud …?"

"No. Gurud's been perfect."

Thank Sakat for that at least. If Gurud had been less than perfect I wouldn't know how to confront him about it.

She stood up again, paced partway around the pool. I got up and followed her, not sure what to do or say. Not wanting to pry, but liking the emotion coming off her even less.

"It's nothing he's done," she said again. "I just – I couldn't sleep, that's all."

This was more than some post-joining nerves. Isza had joined before. She'd breached three times. "There's something more, isn't there?"

She turned on me then and for a moment I thought she was going to hit me. "You're not the only one allowed to have secrets, Udun."

I couldn't say any more. She was right. But she knew I cared about her. She could feel that I wanted to help her. That she could count on me. Slowly her anger ebbed and she sat by the pool again.

"It was my mating. After Gurud."

"You mean with Czerag?" I paused, embarrassed. Joining details weren't openly discussed. But I could see she needed to talk about this.

"Gurud and I joined," she said, "but when Czerag came and I asked him to make the pupa a Defender, he said no. He said these times called for something else." She looked from the water to me. "I'm carrying a hierarch. And I don't think I'm the only one."

My first instinct was to ask if she was sure. I kept quiet.

"What does it mean?" she said.

Hierarchs were a breed apart. There was only one to each

house, because as well as leading, it was the hierarch who performed the secondary insemination to determine the body type of each fertilised pupa. The hierarch chose whether it would be born a Defender, Cultivator, Adept, whatever, to balance the diversity of the house. Czerag wasn't that old. Why would he sire a hierarch? And why more than one?

"I don't know, Isza." But I thought I did. Czerag was ensuring the house would have a leader if he was killed.

Isza stood. "I have to get back to Gurud."

"I'll meet you at the ship later."

"You're coming with us?"

"Czerag's orders."

A complex set of emotions passed between us. Life had seemed simple once.

Isza left, and I sat for a while longer before going back inside. Walking through the corridors it felt like the whole house was in motion. They were packing to leave.

I took the main passage up to the top of the escarpment and sat on the edge, looking down. Lines of Kresz stood by the landing field at the foot of the cliff. One transport took off in a light flurry of sand and another moved down to take its place. With my desert eyelid I could see other groups of Kresz far out, walking into the desert in all directions. There were so many Kresz on the desert floor now that the house must be almost emptied.

"Quite a sight."

I turned. Tzek stood behind me, leaning heavily on his staff.

"Do they even know why they're leaving?" I asked.

"They know enough. They trust their hierarch to know the rest," Tzek said. "You're disappointed you didn't know everything ahead of time."

"I know why I wasn't told. But it doesn't make it any easier."

Tzek was quiet, the feeling from him neutral.

"I know," I said eventually. "Making it easy for me isn't a priority. Are we really just going to fly through the Point unchallenged and deliver our cargo without any trouble from Kergis?"

"No one expects it to be that simple, Udun. We have weapons, but I don't believe we'll be fired upon. No house has attacked another in one-one generations. There is a chance, I know, and if it happens the results would be terrifying. But I believe the real battle will come in the Council chamber."

If Czerag was creating new hierarchs, he didn't share Tzek's optimism. Or was I simply being fed the official story to keep me calm?

"I hope you're right," I said.

"And I hope you find whatever it is you're looking for out there." He glanced at the Kresz at the foot of the cliff, then back to me. "I admit I had my doubts about you, Udun. I thought you were weak, but you've proved me wrong. If things go badly, I'll leave a sign for you under Czerag's seat. You'll know where to find me if you need me."

If things "went badly", I didn't expect to live through it. Nevertheless, I said, "Thank you, Tzek. I hope we'll meet again."

I left him to his thoughts and took the tunnel down into the house. Every chamber I passed was empty and my hoofsteps echoed ahead of me.

Inside what had been Isza's and my room, I activated the lantern. At the end of my sleeping mat was a small metal box with my few possessions. I grabbed my pouch, then considered the gaszti Isza had given me when we finished school. Its handle was endar wood and so was the sheath, inlaid with glass mosaic. I'd left it behind on my last trip, thinking a weapon wasn't really the thing to take on a journey of discovery. This time was different. I fixed the twine so the gaszti hung at my hip.

A quick scan of the room. I may never return here, I thought. Tzek's words had left me feeling morbid.

Out by the landing field, I joined what looked like the final group boarding a particularly old-looking transport. We hunkered near the bulkheads and clung to the cargo webbing as the ship lurched into the sky and headed for the deep desert. While those Kresz I'd seen walking across the dunes were heading for the hides, we were going to the transports to fly away from Homeworld. Perhaps to die in space.

I thought of how scared I'd been the first time I left. But the overwhelming feeling from the others in the transport now was a kind of subdued anticipation. I didn't know how much they knew, but they weren't fearful or resigned. Something was awakening in them. It wasn't a familiar feeling. I tasted the sensation, trying to get an image that might lead me to a better understanding. But nothing came. All I was left with was a vague echo of Reka in the final moments before the gaszti cut him off from us.

We disembarked into a dusk-filled sky and I saw what Czerag had been hiding in plain sight all this time. Rows and rows of ships: transports, couriers, one or two corvettes. This was meant to be a graveyard, a place where craft at the end of their serviceable life came to be stripped of tekla. But these ships weren't dead. The air thrummed with engines in warm-up. Behind the ships stood the twisted metal towers and pipes of the tekla plant, and beside that the mine head. Beyond was nothing but empty desert.

The others in my group moved off down the nearest row of ships, presumably to whatever craft they'd been assigned. I heard Isza calling. She stood in the door of a squat, beaten transport, her arm raised to me. I was glad to see her after the sad, strange feelings at the escarpment and the even stranger sensations from the others on the flight here. She was a reassuring anchor in a place that suddenly didn't seem to be the Homeworld I knew.

She took my arm as I came level with the ship and pulled me up into the entrance. "I thought you'd be keener to leave," she said.

"Are you sure this thing can get us all the way to Telsus?"

I had to shout to be heard. The noise from the ships around us was growing and the wind from their turbines whipped the sand into an artificial dust storm.

"Us and the hold full of refined tekla we're carrying," she said.

"It won't be a swift ride and it won't be comfortable but it can get us there."

"Tzek didn't seem to think there'd be any trouble from Kergis on the trip out."

Isza blinked. "You see that battlecruiser two rows over?" She pointed to the largest ship on the field, bulky and black, with a Defender sigil on its nearest weapons nacelle. "That's the ship we're staying closest to. Call me a pessimist if you like, but I'll be a live pessimist. Come on, let's get inside."

"Is Gurud here?" I asked as the door closed behind us, cutting off the noise and the wind.

"It's just you and me. He has another mission, which he refused to tell me about."

The flight deck was cramped and the plastic on the co-pilot's seat was worn and cracked, the flight restraints frayed. There was only one vuscreen, set below a two-piece window, thick acrylic gone milky on the edges. The ceiling and walls to either side were closed in and studded with toggle switches and readouts.

Isza strapped in beside me and placed a comm in her ear gap, a stick pickup looping around her mandible. She began flicking toggles and activating nondescript consoles. This was the type of ship that needed a real pilot. No friendly processor to interpret your commands and make sure you didn't fly into the nearest mountain. The sound of the turbines spinning up behind us was surprisingly quiet.

"Don't let the sound fool you," Isza said. "The only reason you're not plugging your ear gaps and shouting to be heard in here is the tekla in the hold dampening the noise."

"Then I'm glad I won't be taking the return trip with you."

"Return? You're as optimistic as Tzek." She looked at me sideways. "So you'll be off wandering again." The feeling accompanying her words was happy and sad.

Through the whipped-up sand, the sky was dark. A tone sounded in the cabin.

"That's our signal," she said.

I felt her anxiety spike and my own matched it. There was an answering echo from outside, presumably the other ships. I wondered if the sense of our preparations was strong enough to make it to Aktiuk.

The sound behind doubled and the transport wobbled as it lifted off the ground, Isza riding the controls to keep it steady.

Other ships were taking off beside us. The big battlecruiser lifted above the other transports, accelerating ahead.

"That'll reach orbit before us and warn off any Defender ships," Isza said. "I hope. We're going to show up on Aktiuk spaceport's scans any second. Czerag will have some explaining to do."

"Do you know where he is?" I asked.

"Hunkering down in one of his alternative shielded chambers in the desert while the rest of us risk our lives."

"You really don't like him."

She blinked. "Look where he's brought us, Udun. This is a rogue move. Nothing good will come of it."

"He's trying to change things. He's trying to break the monopolies, the lies about how our society operates. You've complained yourself about not being given proper opportunities by the lodge."

"I know things need to change. I just don't agree this is the best way to do it. It's too aggressive. There are other ways, less direct, that take more time. But they're more legitimate: building public opinion, lobbying through the Council, counting votes. It might take a two-cycle or three but the result will be the same and there will be less likelihood of rusz being spilled."

"It won't come to that."

"Don't fool yourself." The space between us filled with sudden anger. "Czerag thinks it will. Why else would he sire more hierarchs?"

"Insurance?" I said, but Isza was right. We were headed for trouble.

"My way he wouldn't need insurance," she said.

We were well above the desert now, rising into the atmosphere. It was dark. None of the other ships showed running lights and the only illumination was a curve of light on the horizon. As we lifted higher, sura rose over the planet's edge, a reverse sunset bathing the cabin in pale blue light.

"Wait. There's comms traffic." Isza touched the device at her ear gap. "Yes," she said, then looked over at me. "Aktiuk port has ordered us to turn back."

"And?"

"We go on."

On the vuscreen in front of Isza, we were part of a swarm of ships all tagged with Czerag signifiers, crowded together in a messy formation. If I closed my eyes and concentrated I could feel those points of light – not the ships, but the Kresz inside them. A small community leaving the worldmind. And because we were all House Czerag, united in a common cause, we were ready – Sakat help us – for whatever came next. That was the feeling I'd picked up in the transport. They didn't want to fight, but if the fight came to them they wouldn't back down.

"What has Czerag started?" I said.

"You see it now," Isza said. "Cycle after cycle of peace, of putting up with slights, struggling against the day to day. Being reasonable, considerate. You see how easily that can be swept away when we put ourselves in a position where we'll be threatened? This goes deeper than breaking some trade rules, Udun. This can tear us apart."

"There have to be two sides willing to battle for that to happen."

"You think House Kergis or the others are any different?"

"More reason to get to the Point and then to Telsus as quickly as possible," I said. "Once this is done it's done. There'll be no reason to attack us then. There's only dealing with the fallout – the trade block on Council falling apart when they see they've lost control."

"You're right. Now we've been seen, that's the only choice we have. It's the only option Czerag's left us."

19

Denev was quiet on the way back and when Rhees looked over she was surprised to see him dozing. She was still coming down off the adrenaline high from not getting caught.

They'd been able to access the shortcut tunnel again, and once again the sphincter at the far end parted as they approached. It was a phenomenon the Hegemony techs would no doubt love to study.

Loops of purple energy strobed down the corridor, making the scoutship appear to be travelling faster than it was. But the field potential was fine. They were an hour out from the transit chamber and Denev was still sound asleep, making a not very endearing nasal whistle on every out-breath.

Rhees thought about what she'd learned since arriving at Herakli. The HDC investigation was thorough. Perhaps too thorough. Plodding and futile would be another couple of fitting descriptors. At least in terms of tracking down the raiders, though the store of intel on the attacks was vast. The locals had the right idea protecting themselves from the raider attacks. Fuck, they'd been pushed to it by HDC inaction, although their secret battle fleet had clearly been built to attack an entirely different enemy.

She looked at Denev again. He was out for it. She knew what she *should* do: keep her head down and stick with the program. With luck and time Volmar might forget he wanted rid of her, especially if he thought she'd been domesticated. Declawed. But people were dying. So what if they were *only* aliens? She was determined some good would come out of the fucked-up mess she'd made of things.

She reached under her seat, pulled out her helmet, fitted it on her neck ring and twisted it shut. The suit's systems came online. She opened a comms channel and a virtual window appeared across the upper segment of her faceplate. She entered the familiar codestring on her gauntlet keypad. Lines of numbers rolled across her faceplate as comms linked to the nearest relay and searched for a connection route. The image flashed once, then settled, displaying the Fleet insignia and a number of icons below for different channels. She selected the Communications Department, a euphemism for the covert intelligence arm.

A few seconds later a smart young officer appeared wearing immaculate dress whites. "Submit your ident code, please, citizen," he said in a clipped, nasal voice.

Rhees hesitated. "I have some urgent information for Fleet Command –"

"The ident code," the officer interrupted, making eye contact for the first time.

There was no point arguing. This was Fleet. There would be no communications access without a valid ident code.

She entered her code.

He looked down, reading information off another screen. Rhees knew it would be her Fleet record. The man's eyes widened as he looked up sharply and broke the connection.

"Fuck!"

There was a tapping sound on the side of her helmet. She twisted it off. Denev was wide awake.

"What do you think you're doing?" he said.

She felt instantly guilty. Then angry at feeling guilty. "Contacting Fleet. They wouldn't listen to me."

"Are you trying to get yourself executed?"

"I'm trying to stop these fucking raiders. What are HDC doing?"

"What do you mean by that?"

"All this fact-finding and analysis they've been doing, without actually *doing* anything – like calling in some help from Fleet. HDC isn't interested in protecting the Brell or the Sissilak or whatever. They're gauging the strength of a new enemy out in open territory so they can fine-tune the defences around Sol."

At least he had the decency to look guilty, Rhees thought. But he wasn't about to roll over.

"And if we are? What do you care about some Brell and Sissilak?"

"That's HDC talking, Denev. You're better than that. These people are in danger and we're lying to them about the protection we're offering."

"And we've just discovered those same people have been plotting against the Hegemony all along."

"And why do you think that is? Do we treat them as equals? No. They're subjugated. Second-class citizens, made aware of that fact at every turn. Fuck, they're not even allowed to set foot on Earth. How do you think humans would react to that kind of treatment?"

"You're sounding like an Inclusionist."

"Maybe I'm starting to understand their point of view," Rhees said. "Is there no room for simple human decency any more?"

Denev opened his mouth to argue, but paused. "I believe that you believe there is. Tell me, if Fleet *had* listened to you, would you have told me what was happening?"

Rhees stared at him, feeling her anger rise again. "Are you going to tell me what Ix'la passed you before he got vapourised?"

"That has nothing to do with this."

"But it wasn't HDC work either. I saw the look on your face."

Denev took a ragged breath and she could see she'd hurt him. Again. She regretted bringing the whole thing up.

"I'm sorry."

"It's okay."

He looked out the port at the strobing lights of the Voss Space corridor. Seconds passed and Rhees thought that was all she was going to get. It was only after she turned back to the controls that he spoke again.

"You know my parents were killed in the war. No one ever told me the circumstances. And by the time I was old enough to understand, it didn't seem right to ask. But after Petar died, I wanted to know. Then I discovered the files concerning their deaths had been sealed and I couldn't find out who had ordered it. Ix'la got the information for me."

"Who gave the order?"

"Comptroller Troels Volmar."

Fuck. Volmar was into everything. "Do you think he was involved?"

"I don't know, but it's not something I can ask and there's no way those files will be released without his say-so. I don't even know *why* it's important to me."

"You're trying to make sense of your life. I can relate to that." She focused on the instruments for a moment and increased thrust. "I'm sorry I went behind your back."

"Were you trying to get Fleet to take you back? Use this intel as a bargaining chip?"

She snorted. "You really don't know anything about me. Fleet would never take me back."

They lapsed into silence.

When Denev spoke again his voice was almost a whisper. "I should still report you for contacting Fleet."

Rhees looked at him, trying to understand what was going on in his head. "You do what you have to do," she said. "And so will I."

∞

Denev stared out at the Voss Space corridor. Rhees had a point. There was no way HDC's current trajectory would end in anything other than more death and suffering for the Brell and Sissilak. When he was little, he'd convinced himself his parents had died because he'd lied to his nanny when they were away. After that it didn't really matter what he did; things could never get worse than they already were. Rhees lived in a world that still allowed for a moral compass. You're better than that, she'd said. He wasn't so sure, but Petar had said the same thing the last time they met.

Denev had travelled all the way back to Earth to see him, to the education facility he'd left four years before. So much had changed for him, but the dorm Petar occupied looked as if it had been frozen in time. Same scuffed wall panels. Same view over the playing fields.

Petar had filled out, grown tall, but his face was leaner, more defined. His voice was deeper too when he said hello. Denev had missed his nineteenth birthday a month before.

He hadn't been sure how to start. "How've you been?"

Petar folded into the armchair without answering, but Denev had seen a trace of that boyish smirk that used to infuriate him.

"Where did you haul in from?" Petar had said. "Or is that 'classified'?"

The temptation had been strong to match Petar's tone, fall into familiar patterns. But that wasn't why he'd come. Denev had seen how dangerous the outside world could be. Now Petar was leaving school, he had to keep him safe.

"Not classified, no. I've been at the listening station in the Kuiper Belt. It's an amazing facility. State-of-the-art Voss Space observation and comms."

"I'll bet." Petar had looked at Denev through half-lidded eyes, as if he'd rather be anywhere else than here, talking to his fuckhead brother.

Denev had tried to show they could be friends. That he was genuinely interested in his brother. But it was hard. His words sounded flat and dead even to his ears. "So what's been happening for you?"

Petar had looked out the window, looked back. "Why are you here?"

Again he'd resisted the urge to snap back. "I'm visiting my brother."

"I haven't heard a single word from you since you graduated from this dump."

Four years. "I meant to keep in touch. It's not always possible with the Corps."

"What? With all that 'super-secret-agent' business?" Again the hint of a smirk.

"It's not like that." The conversation wasn't going as planned, so Denev had decided to just get to the point. "Look, you've graduated now. Good marks, I hear. It's time to choose a career."

Petar had slumped further in his chair, chin on chest, watching him.

"I want you to join me in HDC."

He thought he'd been prepared for any response. But when Petar burst out laughing he hadn't known how to react. Instead he'd ploughed on. "I've arranged a spot. On my project team. It'll be a steep learning curve at first. But the work is interesting and we'll be together again."

"So you can tell me what to do all the time?" Petar shook his head slowly. "That's not going to happen."

"You'll need a job."

"With HDC?" He'd made even the idea sound ridiculous.

"It's a good career. Just take some time to think about it."

Petar was wilful, but he'd always done what he was told in the end.

"I've thought about it. I'm joining Fleet."

Denev heard the words, but couldn't process the concept. "No, you're not."

Now the smirk was there in full and Denev gripped the arms of his chair to stop from leaning forward and slapping him.

"I'm not your little brother any more," Petar said. "I've already been accepted."

"Do you know the life expectancy of Fleet grunts? You're withdrawing your application."

"The fuck I am. At least Fleet fights its enemies out in the open. I know all about the dirty tricks the Corps plays and it makes me sick. It's bad enough you're with them, let alone thinking I'd join you."

"You don't know what you're talking about. It was HDC pay that kept you in this school."

"I didn't ask for that, and I'm finished now. I feel sorry for you. You're better than this. I hope one day you realise it."

Denev's patience had snapped then. At the ungratefulness, yes, but also the pity he'd heard in his brother's voice. "If that's the way you feel, I won't interfere in your life any more."

Petar stood, lanky and relaxed. "I'll let you know how I'm going. Bye, Denev."

He'd left and Denev had never seen him again.

Since then, Denev had thought of a million things he could have said to persuade his brother to come with him, to change the course of his life. To *give* him life. But it was all too late.

∞

The scoutship entered the transit chamber. Traffic was sparse and they were at the Voss bridge and through into space far quicker than on their outward journey. Soon they were settling to the landing field through the dusk of a warm evening.

Denev could tell Rhees was still angry by the way she slapped at the control surfaces and shut down the scoutship, descending to the lock without a word as soon as that was done and exiting.

He transferred the surveillance logs from his suit to his band and cleared out the buffers on ship comms and sensors, then followed her out. She was already in the auto, her suit lying in the open lock. He shucked his own off and threw it down beside hers. He keyed both suit systems for a full log erase, then joined her in the auto and they rode back to HDC in silence. He wanted to tell her everything was going to be okay. But clearly it wasn't.

They left the auto in the basement and rode the elevator up still in silence. When the doors opened, Troels Volmar was waiting for them in the corridor.

"Well, well, Lowrans, you have been busy. Bar-room brawls, assassinations, Voss Space pursuits. HDC's budget may be large, but it's not bottomless. I hope you have something useful to share." He focused on Denev. "Has she been causing you trouble, Mr Antwer?"

Rhees was staring at the floor, but Denev could see the tension in the set of her shoulders and the tightness of her jawline. He knew what she was thinking. By HDC protocol, he should now denounce her attempt to contact Fleet, or be found just as guilty as she was when it was discovered. Nothing escaped the notice of the Corps. It was why he'd deleted the buffers on the ship and the suit logs. That may raise suspicions of its own, but nothing he couldn't explain away. He paused. It looked like he'd chosen a side.

"It's been a busy few days," he said. "Shall we go to my office, it's more comfortable. And I could do with a coffee."

In his rooms, Denev saw the staff had arranged a fresh pot on the small stove. Volmar sat across from Rhees and Denev, watching them both as Denev poured the strong brew into earthenware cups.

"So have you found our raiders, Lowrans?" Volmar said.

What was it between Volmar and her? Rhees made to speak, but Denev cut across her, diverting Volmar's attention away.

"Not exactly. We followed the Brell delegate O'Dran through an unknown Voss Space channel and recorded a secret meeting between her and representatives of the Sissilak and Totek."

He tapped his band, linking it to the dataport, and a holo appeared in the space between them. The meeting played out, ending with the Sissilak's concession.

Volmar had watched the holo intently, chin resting on steepled fingers. He dropped his hands to his lap. "We suspected some kind of resistance, but nothing this organised." His gaze shifted to Denev and Rhees. "Good work."

The compliment sounded grudging to Denev.

"What do you think we should do with the information, Lowrans?"

Rhees cleared her throat. "We should prepare a full report to go to Fleet HQ. They'll be able to deal with this secret force before they move against us."

Volmar sighed and picked a thread of lint from his onepiece. "Oh, I don't think we need worry the Fleet about this."

"I don't understand," Rhees said.

"Everything's black and white with you, isn't it, Lowrans? As a result, you miss opportunities. Effective government means using the resources you have to hand effectively, not dismantling them simply because they're nominally controlled by someone else. No, the Fleet is not the answer to this problem any more than it's the answer to the attacks. But, unlike yourselves, I have not been diverted from the main game. I take it you haven't gleaned any actual intelligence on the raiders?"

"Nothing yet," Denev admitted.

"Can you see the solution to the problem? Oh, come now. The answer's so simple even your Brell friend could see it. It's obvious the raiders must have a base within striking distance of this sector. All we have to do is find it and destroy it."

"So you admit we need a military solution?" Rhees said.

"In a sense. We need a lever. But we don't need the Fleet blundering across half the quadrant."

"No Fleet?" Rhees said. "You mean …"

"Now you understand. I mean this secret group of rebels will do our work for us."

"You have the location of the raiders' base," Denev said.

"I do. As I said, I haven't exactly been sleeping. There is a base, but it won't be there for much longer. You will ensure this information finds its way to O'Dran in a manner that won't raise suspicions. Your network should be up to that task, Mr Antwer. Then we sit back and watch events unfold."

"And then call in the Fleet to mop up the leftovers?" Rhees said.

Volmar was silent for a moment, then stood. "If it's necessary,

Lowrans. If it's necessary."

There was no arguing with Volmar, Denev thought. He had everything planned so all the pieces fell his way. Was it the same twenty years ago? The only way he'd find out was to break into that sealed file.

20

One of the controls chimed. "We're out of atmosphere," Isza said. "We're moving off now. Best speed."

Out the window, I saw the other transports move together in the black. We drifted with them, sliding between ships when a gap opened, moving towards the front and beside the battlecruiser. Comms traffic was minimal. What was there to say?

Down on Aktiuk the houses and lodges would be watching us. Some wondering what we were doing; others already guessing. Comms would be sent from one boxed and shielded hierarch and dean to another. Queries and protests would be aimed at Czerag. Would he dissemble to buy us time? Or would he take the opportunity to push his manifesto, using our mobilisation to show that with this single act the old ways were over? What would the reaction be?

"Something's coming," Isza said.

I looked at the screen. Beyond the jumble of Czerag ships there was a fast-moving point heading at an angle to our flank. By its speed and trajectory, it would intersect with the leading edge of the – well, what would you call it? We weren't a fleet. More like some nomad desert caravan.

The point was a neutral grey colour, then the signifier sounded and the point shifted to green: Defenders Lodge.

"None of our ships can move that fast," Isza said. "There's only one that can. Here it comes."

On the screen it was starting its run along our leading edge. I looked out the window and saw a thin blade of ship that flared out into a disc section backed by outsized engines. It flashed by in bare seconds, looping around us on the screen and heading back the way it had come.

"It's the ship I flew on the contact mission," Isza said. "Leased from the Jantri."

"You flew that?"

"It mostly flew itself. We're lucky it's not armed."

"It had a Defender signifier," I said. "So where are the Defenders?"

"Nothing on the screen yet. But they'll be coming."

"And then what?"

"It depends on who gets to the Point first; and if it's us, how much time we have to get through. But I know one thing."

"What?"

She felt so calm. Or maybe resigned. "If they do get there first and decide to fight, this battlecruiser we're nestled against like an ah'lok chick won't hold out against them for long."

We watched the screen, waiting for the first sign of company. The Jantri-built ship would have relayed telemetry to the main Defender contingent showing our deployment and our almost complete lack of armaments. I thought again of those hierarchs and deans down on Homeworld. The angry words they would be throwing around; the threats and other pressures being brought to bear. All those violent emotions behind us, and here we drifted in a kind of false calm. This was where all those words would finally come to rest.

"There," Isza said. On the very edge of the screen, a first pinpoint of green.

"One ship?" I asked, optimistic. Then another green signifier joined it. And another. "How far to the Point?"

"Far enough."

"Will we get there first?"

She looked at me. "It's going to be close."

I alternated between watching the moving lights on the screen and peering ahead hoping to see the satellites of the Point. But I couldn't see anything except black and stars, and the ships behind us were gaining.

The thought suddenly occurred that the Point wouldn't be the end of the race, not even a halfway marker.

"Would they follow us into tenspace to try to stop us?" I asked.

"There's nothing to prevent them, but they'd be mad to fire on us in there, if they intend to fire on us at all. And once we transit back we'll be in Telsan space and they risk causing a diplomatic incident if they attack. Assuming that bothers them."

"Can you stop being so optimistic," I said.

Her small feeders rattled. A momentary lightening of the tension in the cockpit.

Finally, I was sure I saw something ahead.

"Yes. That's it." Isza flipped some toggles and the engines took on a different tone. "Spinning up the tenspace drive. It'll be ready by the time we get there."

"How long?"

"I think ..." She paused. "Something coming through on the comms."

More switches flicked and a voice rang out in the small cabin. "Udun?"

"Tzek," I said. "Where are you?"

There was a rush of static, then, "... fine. But the science vessel we sent out to scan inside the tenspace corridor just picked up something large moving towards the Point. We lost contact. I think you should pull back."

"Isza here, Tzek. We can't. Defenders are almost on us. What does the battlecruiser commander say?"

More static.

"Repeat, Tzek," I said.

"Long-range comms are being jammed and that ex-Defender ship seems particularly affected. There's no time. Make them veer off. Make it convincing. Now! We're going offline. You won't be able to contact us."

"What?" I said. "What's happening down there? Tzek!"

"Tell the group to move back! Tzek out." The line went dead.

I looked at Isza.

"I'll try the short-range comms laser," she said. "Jelad! Isza here. We have to veer off."

I could see the Point ahead now: a loose arrangement of satellites. On the screen the Defender ships weren't far behind. I wished I could read the scan in more detail. I didn't know what the scale was. But if it was going to be close before Tzek's call, then any deviation would buy them time and make it more difficult for us. What was happening on Homeworld? What was coming through the Point? Sakat ... what was coming through from tenspace?

"No. Now!" Isza was shouting. "Something's on the tenspace side and we have to get out the way." A pause. "It was *Tzek* who told me! Now relay the order!"

Changing course wasn't a simple thing for our jumbled collection of ships. We were packed close together and the ships weren't crewed by military pilots. Most were cargo captains; some weren't pilots at all. A ship cut across behind us, just missing our engine vent. At least we were close to the battlecruiser, which protected that flank, and Isza kept with it as it turned slowly away. But where could we go? We were horribly exposed.

Over by the Point, space began to twist in a direction that didn't seem possible.

"Something's coming through," I said.

Isza and I watched a long black snout push through the fabric of space like the bill of a luk'ri larva surfacing for its first breath of air. The snout broadened into a large block flanked by orange-tipped triangular weapon nacelles. I'd seen this ship before. It looked like the vessel that had contacted our deeprange explorer.

I felt like I couldn't breathe. "The Hegemony is here," I said quietly.

"What?" Isza shouted. I wasn't sure if she was talking to me or to Jelad on the cruiser.

The first Hegemony ship moved towards the loose weave of the Point satellites, and another snout emerged. Not a 'diplomatic' mission then. This was an invasion.

"We have to get out of here," Isza said. "We're no match for them. Let the Defenders deal."

The Defenders. I looked at the scanner. They were almost on us. They couldn't miss this incursion into Kresz space.

Isza followed the curve of the Point.

More Hegemony ships were emerging. The first was through the Point satellites now and waiting for others to form up alongside and behind it into an offensive wedge.

Past them, coming from Homeworld, were the Defender ships, close enough now to see with the naked eye.

Isza touched a switch and the vuscreen schematic changed to a magnified view. The Defender ships were drifting away from each other, taking a concave formation to try to contain the invaders and give each ship an unimpeded firing line.

Another large cruiser was emerging from tenspace. Just how many were coming through?

"I wish we had something more powerful than a comms laser," Isza said.

"Why? I don't think that would do much good against —"

"To knock out the Point! Wreck the gravitational equilibrium."

"And stop them coming through?"

"Or slow them at least. Any others would have to transit further out and then cross realspace. It would give the Defenders time."

"We could ram the satellites," I said. "Even if we only took out one or two it might be enough."

She looked at me with an odd mixture of horror and excitement. "I'm not ready to die quite yet, Udun. But there's another way. Hold on."

She punched a series of toggles above our heads. There was a grinding noise from behind. Then she took the controls again and veered the ship away from the Point, almost crashing us into another transport.

"What are you doing?" I shouted.

"Watch," she said, and touched the scanner so our view shifted aft.

I could just see the back of our ship at the bottom of the screen, but the shape was wrong. The cargo hatch was open and streaming out of it was a line of cargo podules. They drifted away from us with our sudden change in course, heading towards the Point. As I watched, the podules drifted into the Point network. Most sailed through and into the enclosing space. But then one podule connected with a satellite. There was a brief, soundless flare. Then another podule hit. And another.

A Hegemony ship was emerging from tenspace as the collisions happened. Its snout twisted violently, thinning and bulging until the vessel exploded. The plasma ball was intense and my desert eyelid cut the glare as the blast front-kicked the podules back out of the Point and then blew the remaining satellites. There was a frightening hammering as pieces of debris smashed against our hull. Then silence.

Isza checked environment and I strained to hear the deadly whine of hull breach. Unbelievably we were still in one piece, as were all the other ships in our convoy. But the advance of Hegemony ships had halted. And still no shots had been fired.

The Defenders looked to be in position, spread in a hemisphere pattern across the space between the Hegemony ships and Homeworld.

The scanner switched back to tactical with a warning bleep. A small point detached itself from the lead Hegemony ship, heading towards the Defenders at first, then looping back and passing over the invading vessels. It was a missile, heading our way, twisting as it moved to avoid any answering shots. But we had nothing to shoot with. The battlecruiser was ahead of us, with too many transports between it and the missile for it to take any evasive action.

"I don't think our actions went entirely unobserved," Isza said and got on the comms again. "Disperse the ships, Jelad!"

We accelerated, but sluggishly. Some of the cargo remained inside our ship, throwing off our centre of gravity, making it hard for Isza to pilot.

I could see the missile through the window now – not just a point of light on a screen but a deadly physicality. It twisted its flight path again and smashed into a transport just below us, destroying the ship. As the missile impacted there was a death scream from the Kresz onboard that burned more keenly than the flames billowing past us. Followed just as devastatingly by an emptiness in the loose collection of minds that had formed since we left Homeworld. They had died horribly and we all experienced that violence. This wasn't like Reka – a swift excision cut away from the worldmind. This was much more visceral. My body tingled from the ghost experience of blasting heat and tearing decompression. My thoughts jumbled as I tried to piece together the truth of my eyes – that I was alive, intact – and the truth I had felt of a fiery and painful death.

"Udun?" It was Isza, speaking hoarsely.

"I'm here," I said. "Did you –"

"We have to get out of here."

Our ship had been sent into a slow spin by the explosion. It was a miracle we hadn't hit any of the others. Isza brought the spin under control.

Out the window I had a skewed view from below and behind of the Hegemony fleet. I watched as a Sakat Class battleship blasted the lead ship with a particle weapon. Fierce blue energy played over the Hegemony ship's hull. It seemed – ludicrously – to be absorbing it.

Then there was an explosion, silent but brighter than sura for an instant. It was like a signal. Suddenly the space between the opposing ships was filled with energy, explosions, ships disintegrating. More

Kresz deaths battered at us, driving out conscious thought, filling up the emptiness with hate and pain and fear.

"Go!" I managed. We had to put some distance between this and us or we would go insane.

Isza pushed savagely at the thruster controls. The ship pitched, pushing us back into our seats, responding quicker now because of the empty hold.

Pain lanced through my skull. Another death. Or maybe more than one. Was it possible to quantify the pain of each murdered Kresz? Was the measure equal to each, or did some suffer more than others? Did many feel worse than one? Jangled nonsense thoughts flooded my brain among fresh thrusts of pain as the battle raged behind us.

We looped in a wide arc away from the Point to eventually head back to Homeworld. Where else could we go? With distance came a measure of sanity again. I felt Isza relax a little and shared her relief. The killing was still going on behind us but at least it was bearable, if that was the word.

"Is there anything on comms? Anything from Homeworld?" I asked.

Isza flipped a switch and voices flooded the cabin, layered over each other, some tense and clipped, others close to shouting. Mostly battle language.

"Nothing from Homeworld," she said. "Not on an open channel anyway."

The screen showed an aft view. Miniature ships, moving in a slow dance, tiny flares marking their passing. It would be beautiful if I didn't know what it meant.

"It looks like we're containing them," Isza said.

I looked again. The Hegemony ships were almost lost within a spread of Defender ships. They'd lost some. So had we. But those left were now coming under concentrated fire, their shields flaring in the dark.

A shout over comms. Not battle language this time. "Erdjis!

What are you doing?"

"Erdjis?" I said to Isza. "What's happening?"

She pulled the magnification. "The Defenders are splitting. Look."

Some of our ships had pulled back behind the others, leaving a hole in the defensive shield. The Hegemony ships, seeing their chance, accelerated for it. Other Defender ships moved to close the gap and were fired on. By our own ships.

"Erdjis!" A scream over comms, then a hiss of dead air, a blossom of fire on the screen and a crushing feeling of death that passed, thankfully, just as quickly.

The Defenders were shooting at themselves. Or rather, two distinct sides were emerging, one aided by the Hegemony ships, which, though fewer in number now, still had considerable firepower.

I thought of Atalna and those Hegemony ships appearing so quickly around his planet, coming to the "aid" of the alternative government; the secret treachery that must have occurred for that to happen. I thought of Kergis meeting in person with the Hegemony on the contact mission. He hadn't left with Isza. He'd stayed behind to betray us.

"Get on the comms," I said.

"Aktiuk control," Isza said. "This is House Czerag convoy ship."

We were putting distance between ourselves and the battle, but I could see the Hegemony and the newly allied Defender ships were winning. Formations broke apart, shielding flashed and hulls were breached. Kresz died. I hoped I'd never get used to that feeling.

Isza was explaining what we'd seen. She finished and the channel was silent.

"You need to relay this to the Defenders Lodge now!" she said.

"Hierarch Kergis commands now," spaceport control said. "Best you land and give yourself over to our forces or we will shoot you out of the sky."

"Can you raise Tzek?" I asked Isza.

She pushed a contact, but there was nothing but dead air. "I don't know where he is," she said.

On the screen, the battle was all but over. The remaining Hegemony ships joined in formation with what had to be Kergis-controlled ships. Smaller vessels emerged from the Hegemony hulls: fighters, which swarmed over and between the ships, manoeuvring past the floating debris around the Point and accelerating towards us.

"There's nowhere left to run," Isza said as they closed on us.

We couldn't transit without being torn apart by gravitational forces. We'd never make it back to Homeworld before they caught us, and it wasn't certain what reception we'd get there anyway.

The fighters were sleek and black like their larger carriers, but with stubby wings projecting either side, and what looked like gun ports on those wings and studding the nose. They were built to fly in atmosphere as easily as in space. I thought of the undefended residential areas around Aktiuk. It would be a massacre. Perhaps it would be better that we didn't survive to see it.

"Don't," Isza said. "We're not giving up now."

"We're in a salvaged cargo ship with an alien fleet bearing down on us and no cover. We've run out of choices," I said.

"Not quite, but it's not going to be pretty," she said and activated the transit engines again. They were still hot from our aborted jump.

"We'll be destroyed."

"We will be if those ships get to us."

21

Our group of ships was scattering. Some were heading into deep space; others, like us, were looping around the main battle site to make for Homeworld. Our single battlecruiser had turned back towards the fight. The commander must have known it was futile but he might slow the enemy enough to give us a few more moments of life.

On the screen, the fighters were closing on us. They had phenomenal acceleration. The Hegemony clearly wanted to make sure no witnesses survived. What the Kergis ships thought about that, I couldn't imagine.

The battlecruiser fell further behind us, facing the oncoming fighters. Puffs of vapour close to its body marked missile launches – bright daggers streaking towards the enemy ships. An energy beam lanced out and the missiles exploded, the smaller ships looping through the expanding flame and bringing their guns to bear on the cruiser.

Our transit engines shrieked.

"Isza, what are you doing?" I shouted.

"Saving our shells."

On the vuscreen, the cruiser exploded and the Hegemony ships started firing on the transports. My carapace was throbbing with the transit build. The fighters came closer.

"When the Point blew, spacetime didn't just snap back into shape," Isza shouted. "There's a ripple of null gravity. It's moving towards us. Look." She pointed at a dial with numbers rapidly counting down.

"Are you sure?" I asked. But there was no alternative.

The dial hit zero. Isza grabbed the transit control, pushed it forward, then just as quickly pulled it back.

My body felt like it was being crushed and stretched at the same time. Everything went black. A sharp pain pierced me behind the eyes. Then the seat harness jammed into my thorax and my head hit the edge of the controls. There was a bright light. A plume of smoke and a collision alert.

The alert stopped, followed quickly by the hiss of gas choking off. I heard switches being flipped. I focused. Isza was still in control. Black space outside the window and no ships that I could see.

"Isza ... what did you ..."

"We transitted with the ripple. When it lost cohesion it dropped us here. The ship's still functional. Mostly. Hull integrity's fine."

"I'll never doubt your piloting skills again," I said. "Can we still make it home?"

If we couldn't, we were dead. With a full-scale invasion taking place, it was unlikely Homeworld could send help even if they wanted to.

"Wait. Checking systems," Isza said.

I wondered how long it would take for the other Hegemony ships stuck on the tenspace side of the Point to get to Homeworld. If they had anything like the speed of their small fighters, it would be sooner than we'd hoped. But what about the Lenticular? Would the Council have time to get off a distress signal through the broadcast spire? Even faced with imminent invasion, would they ask for help from others?

Telltales on the board above our heads lit up and our ship began to turn. The screen flickered and showed a tactical of the immediate area. No other ships in sight. Through the window, the sharp blue point of sura drifted across our field of view.

"We're still in the Kresz system at least," I said.

"Oh, yes. If we'd bounced hard enough to end up in open

space, we'd be in pieces. Look." A small yellowish cloud-covered planet was nearby. "That's Rux'dal. Which means …"

We continued to turn until a sliver of brown and blue planet was dead ahead, the rest of it in darkness. Homeworld.

"How long?" I asked.

Isza tapped at the controls. The ship moved forward sluggishly. "We've been lucky. Two hours to orbit."

"What more can possibly happen in two hours?"

On the screen, the nightside of Homeworld was magnified. I remembered that view from space when I'd left for the Lenticular. The darkness had been strung with lights, concentrated in settlements and more diffuse along the powergrid. There was nothing in that inky blackness now. At best it meant people had gone into hiding.

Isza touched my shoulder and the strength of her presence anchored me. I looked at her. Her mantle was engorged and I could feel my own responding.

"Udun, you have to share with me now. I don't know when we'll get another chance."

She was right. The communion with Czerag at my homecoming, and with Isza in his chamber later, had been a one-way, incomplete thing, focused on a single event. True sharing was all-encompassing. There was no reason to keep secrets any more.

Our essences reached out, tentative at first, then twining one around the other. The horror of the last hours melted away. We had survived and we were together. That was all that mattered. Isza had proved herself at the Point. We'd face whatever we found on Homeworld together. There was no one I'd rather be with.

We went deeper, past the side of ourselves we turned outwards. I was still me but I was beginning to access a complex series of feelings not my own. An image came to me of an endar tree, its strong smooth limbs twisted, some almost bent around others. The main trunk, topped by the tree's crown, was strong and straight, bathed in the light of the suns. One of the smaller branches up high was topped with blue shoots and as I looked at those I was reminded of Gurud. The branch, though thin at the end, was thick and strong where it joined the main trunk. Lower down, one of the branches was rough and hollowed out in places where the bark had crumbled. It smelled of decay. I thought of the nymph Isza had lost in breaching nearly four cycles before.

I moved past the tree or into it. It faded from my sight to a neutral grey. I knew Isza was experiencing something similar, touching on my surface feelings then closing around some image that represented my core essence to her, and now we were entering the true sharing. I couldn't tell if the images that came to my mind were exact representations or associations from my own mind that matched what I was hearing and feeling from Isza. We were both talking, almost unconsciously, the words wrapping around us.

She spoke of how she'd worried for me when I left, her suspicion about Czerag, her sadness. She talked about Gurud and I saw their first meeting, felt the charge she had felt being near him and her frustration that he could make her feel that way when what she really wanted to do was concentrate on her flying. She'd tried to get a place on a trade flight to the Lenticular – these were very rare – just to feel she was closer to me in some way. I hadn't known that. I knew how much we meant to each other, but I was touched that with everything going on in her life I had still figured so prominently. She spoke of Czerag in the mating chamber and I felt the resistance from her, his overwhelming presence, and the strange feeling of violation when it was over – strange because I'd never thought of secondary insemination in those terms; it simply was – and then the fear when he told her the pupa would become a hierarch.

I was talking too, about my journey into the Lenticular – a mixture of anxiety and elation. The first aliens I encountered. How excited I was to see Svestans and Telsans and Jantri. How strange they'd been at first, but how similarities emerged with greater exposure. The customs I'd witnessed, and the mistakes I'd made. The feast of new thoughts, sights, sounds that greeted me each morning.

The deal I'd made on Czerag's behalf. The way that made me feel useful; me, Udun the strange, who was looked on with suspicion by most. I felt a response from her at the mention of Czerag, one that reiterated her own feelings for him but also validated mine. Finally, she felt the guilt I harboured about my reluctance to return, my worry about merging again, the fact that I wanted to be out and alone again at the earliest opportunity. She could see that it wasn't personal. It was just a fundamental part of who I was. She accepted it and me, and I felt grateful and stronger for that.

At some point, by mutual agreement, we began to climb out of the sharing, our minds unwrapping with a kind of sweet sadness that we were returning to the everyday sensory experience of one another after experiencing something much greater.

We were back in the transport's control cabin, staring out at the space around Homeworld. The Hub was close now and completely untouched. With Kergis's treachery revealed, I suspected his supporters had moved quickly to capture the station and imprison the others there. Or had they killed them? Could they do that?

"How did Kergis, Erdjis and the other House Kergis Kresz keep this from the rest of us?" I said. "This isn't some typical Council subterfuge. How did none of us feel anything of this betrayal right up until the moment it happened?"

"I have no idea," Isza said.

"Perhaps no one but Kergis knew what was going to happen," I continued. "Does he have such complete control that his house will follow his orders blindly and instantly, even to kill other Kresz?"

Isza blinked. "No. You saw the way the Kergis portion of the Defenders moved back and turned on the others while forming a corridor for the Hegemony ships. That kind of manoeuvre takes careful planning and coordination. They knew what they were doing beforehand and they acted together when the time was right." She eased back the thrusters, moving the ship into a slow turn. "We should get down. If Kergis does control the Hub, they'll scan us soon if they haven't already."

We'd been lucky so far – more than lucky – not to have encountered any other ships. The Hegemony's heavy cruisers were nowhere in sight, or the smaller fighters. But as we angled down I could see evidence of their passing. Large plumes of smoke hung over Aktiuk. The comforting feeling of sharing with Isza left me completely. People had died down there. Some with no idea why.

Then we touched atmosphere and the worldmind shrieked. Self was all but obliterated in the misery and madness, anger and pain. Isza grasped my arm and I held hers. Together we rode the anguish, drawing as close together as possible without full sharing. She was as shocked and fearful as me, but it was personal: the emotions of one person, not a multitude in crisis. It was something I could encompass in my understanding.

The ship shook as we ploughed through the air, the hull heating quickly.

"We should head for the desert," I said. "We can lose ourselves there."

I felt Isza's opposition immediately. "No. Gurud is in the city. I have to find him."

"Isza –"

"We're landing at the port. We're too easy to track over open desert. We can lose ourselves in the confusion below."

She felt less convinced of that than she sounded, but she had to find Gurud. She'd saved us both. I couldn't refuse.

"The Hegemony may already control the port," I said.

"If it looks quiet, we'll land there. Otherwise we'll land in the streets. We have to get out of the sky. Our luck can't hold."

On the screen I could see details of the attack now. A huge area of jungle to the north of Aktiuk was burning. The Academy precinct was covered in thick, roiling smoke. Smaller columns of smoke dotted the city and threaded through the tree canopy in the outer suburbs. Treaty Mount was untouched. Was Kergis there, I wondered. Had he installed himself on the central podium? If he'd made a deal with the Hegemony, how far did it go? Did he consider himself our ruler now?

Isza took us lower, skirting the edge of the city. The landing field lay ahead. Some areas looked untouched: ships parked in orderly rows, the spaceport tower and administration buildings, the facilities crowded round the skystalk. But then I saw the long black gash across the main runway, and the tumbled and smashed ship, big enough to be a cruiser, in flames at one end.

There were other ships parked near the sea end of the apron. Not Kresz design or anything I knew. Black circles huddled together, each one with multiple ramps leading from the main hull to the ground. Isza steered away from those, though there was no sign of life around them.

"We'll land over there." She indicated a warehouse area ringed by transports like ours, only newer.

"Then what?"

"Udun, I don't know," she said, fear and irritation in her voice and in my sense of her. "We find Gurud. We survive. We fight back."

22

The ship dipped, almost crashing, then levelled as Isza brought us under a canopy fixed to the side of a large warehouse and settled to the ground.

"With luck we're off any satellite imagery now," she said. "We walk from here – under cover if we can. I don't want us tracked."

We both peered outside for any movement, then checked the tactical display. Nothing. Isza pulled something from a box beneath her seat. An antiquated blaster, black with a tapered snout. I felt sick.

"You know how to use that?" I asked.

"How hard can it be?"

The turbines had wound down. As we walked outside there was a distant roar, punctuated by sharp cracks. I heard a scream far off. But the immediate space around us was still.

Isza and I kept close together. We couldn't block the turmoil or horror in the worldmind, but focusing on each other helped. We kept to the warehouse wall, under cover of the canopy, and moved quickly to the corner of the building. Our luck was holding. There was a covered walkway connecting this warehouse to another closer to the perimeter. The entrance Gurud and I had used was near that part of the fence.

We ran, keeping a sharp lookout, but there was no one in sight. The fighting had moved on from here, although there was evidence enough of it: the wreck of the downed cruiser loomed to our right, still on fire; cargo podules scattered across the apron. A few had fallen under the walkway cover. Rather than skirt around them and risk being seen from above, Isza jumped on top of the largest, beckoning me to follow.

She disappeared from sight on the other side and then I heard her scream and felt a shock run through my body. Without thinking I jumped as hard as I could, sailing right over the podules and landing badly, jarring my left hoof, slipping and falling hard on my side.

"Isza!" I shouted.

She was kneeling at the edge of the nearest podule. On the ground, half-hidden, I saw an arm. I stood. My leg was painful but I wasn't badly hurt.

"Isza," I said more quietly. "Are you all right?"

The body lay between two of the fallen podules. His shell was the bright red of youth – I doubted he was even out of the Academy. But across his chest the chitin had been seared black. The top of his head was missing.

"He didn't even have a weapon," Isza said.

"Come on." I touched her lightly on her shoulder plate. Grief flowed through me and I drew my claws away. My Isza. So capable and self-controlled on the outside. But we needed to keep moving and there would be more horrors to witness. I touched her again, trying to force a sense of urgency. "We have to go, Isza."

Finally she stood, turning away from the body. She held the blaster tightly. "Let's find help. If it still exists."

We moved off along the walkway again until we got to the next warehouse. Rounding the corner of the building, we looked across the field to Aktiuk. One of the small Hegemony fighters was hovering over the city, its cannon firing sporadically at a building or the street, I couldn't tell from the angle. Bricks and stones erupted upwards with a fresh plume of smoke and the fighter slid on jets or repulsers or whatever it used to avoid the smoke and started firing again. Two beams in the unmistakable signature of mantle energy – black at the core but crisscrossed with bright blue – shot up from below, each one targeting the fighter's wing. The engines burst apart and the fighter careened down and disappeared from sight. There was a loud crash and then nothing.

"That's where we need to go," Isza said.

I thought it was probably where we didn't need to go.

We'd run out of cover between the walkway and the perimeter fence. But at least we could see the gate. We ran across the wide open space. As we ran, the worldmind was an inescapable awful presence dominated by hatred, pain, fear, anger, a desire to kill. Reka's madness was nothing compared to this.

We reached the fence. The gate was unlocked. We passed through and stopped under cover of a broad endar tree, the breath whistling in our spiracles.

"No destruction raining down on us from above," I said.

"Not yet anyway. But let's not make it easy for them. We'll cut through here, come out on a different street." She indicated a narrow laneway passing between two high-walled houses. Trees overhung the lane from both courtyards. "And we need to get you a weapon."

I looked down at my hip. I still had my travel pouch, but my gaszti was missing. There was no way I could go back and look for it.

We walked briskly, not ready to run again yet, until we came to an entrance in one of the walls. The door hung open and we could see the courtyard and another open door leading into the kitchen. There was no one around. Objects were scattered on the stone pavers: a cooking pot, a youngling's toy. Whoever lived here had left in a hurry.

We moved on and came out of the lane into a winding street with high buildings close together. This was one of the poorer areas: the road was hard-packed dirt.

"The fighting is over this way," Isza said, jerking her head up the street that rose and curved to the left.

I had no idea what we were going to do when we got there. And I got the same sense from Isza. But I wouldn't be separated from her again and hoped we'd still be alive by next sunrise.

We ran up the road, keeping to the sides, passing shop after deserted shop. The familiar was suddenly unfamiliar – it was like a dream. The road joined a broader street and we turned along it. I stopped. I could hear voices, shouting. They were definitely speaking Kresz.

We ran faster, up another rise. Finally we could see other Kresz. A large group of them. They had built a barricade blocking all four entrances to the crossroads at the bottom of the hill. It didn't look very defensible, but they were there and alive.

Halfway down the road between us was the ruin of the Hegemony fighter we'd seen earlier. It had ploughed into a workshop and was stuck in the second storey, still ablaze.

Isza lifted her claws and shouted. One of the Kresz on the barricade shouted back and we felt the welcome sending. We started down the hill. And then I stopped.

"Isza," I said, "listen." There was a low, deep-throated rumble behind us. "A ship. No, more than one."

We turned to look the way we had come. Hegemony fighters, two lines of them in formation and coming in fast. The engine sound grew deafening. They screamed over us, heading straight down the street. The dirt road in front of us erupted in flame and dust. Kresz ran towards the barricade nearest us and blaster fire and mantle energy shot into the sky. Another explosion of flame and dirt and another, marching down the road. Buildings erupted. The ground shook and we fell to our knees. Smoke choked the air.

And then the first missile hit the barricade. The wood erupted. Bodies flew broken into the air. The screams were terrible, but nothing to the screams inside my head.

More missiles hit. Nothing could live through that. And then it was over. The fighters flew on, not even stopping to verify the kill, and disappeared from sight over the city.

In front of us the dirt of the road had been pushed up into mounds that teetered over deep pits. The walls of the buildings were broken open or cracked, some in flames. At the crossroads, the barricades were smashed and burning freely. I could see bodies in the flames. No one lived. I could feel that.

Isza lay beside me in the dirt, still gripping the blaster that now seemed useless after the firepower we'd just witnessed.

"Why?" she said. There was no anger in it, though she could have been angry, at the waste of life, the hope we'd just seen killed. But no, she felt almost resigned. If a Hegemony soldier had come upon us then, I think we would have both surrendered. That is, if it didn't just kill us because it could.

Isza pushed herself into a sitting position. We were dreadfully exposed in the middle of all this destruction, but it didn't matter. Suddenly I felt a rush of – what? Joy. Overpowering joy. Why would I … Then I saw a large Kresz emerge from one of the ruined buildings, running faster than his bulk would suggest, one huge pincer held out to us. To Isza.

Gurud. He caught her up in his clawed grip, pulling her bodily into the air and holding her close. Despite her size, she was like a toy in his arms. She clung to him fiercely. I looked away.

"I hoped you'd escaped," he said. "That you were far from here."

Her voice was muffled, pressed into his shoulder plate. "The ships stopped us. We got away. But so many are dead. In space. Down here."

"What happened at the house, Gurud?" I had to know.

He looked at me, but still held Isza close. I doubted he would ever let her go if he had a choice.

"It was completely evacuated by the time our ships left. Most went into the deep desert. I was on a detail to meet a small group of Czerag students at the Academy. We were to escort them to one of the safe places before Kergis or one of the other houses seized them for hostage. Then the aerial bombardment began and our transport was damaged." I felt his frustration and something more. "We ran into the streets, trying to find somewhere safe. We ended up here."

"The others?" I asked.

"All dead when the barricade was destroyed. Their bodies are down there with the rest. Sakat knows why I survived." He looked long into Isza's eyes, then said, "Come on."

He started away from the destruction, still carrying Isza.

"Gurud," she said, "I can walk. I'm not injured."

Reluctantly he put her down, but still held her claws in his.

We were walking through a nightmare. The dead lay crushed beneath the rubble of fallen buildings. The smell of burning flesh hung in the air. The city was broken and haunted by phantasms of feelings even more horrible than what we could see around us.

"Where are we going?" I asked.

"Those of us left are gathering at Treaty Mount. We heard the news just as those ships came."

"Gathering? Why?"

He stopped and I could feel the iron in him. "To fight, Udun. To kill or die."

"Haven't you had enough of that for one day?"

"Udun," Isza warned.

"Fighting isn't optional when your home is in flames," Gurud said.

He walked on, pulling Isza with him. I followed, trying to understand the essence of what I was feeling from him. He was angry, yes, but it was anger under tight control. Anger harnessed and put to work fuelling resolve. Purpose. Yes, purpose, that was it. Gurud was Defender caste. But they used to be called Warrior caste.

The Emergence had made war on Homeworld obsolete. Before then, the Warriors had fought for their house, battle on battle. Generations of fighting, with one house dominant for a while, then its strength waning as another rose. Victory and defeat. Death and glory. But not any more. Not since the Emergence. The Defenders did nothing but defend now. And defend against what? The odd insane creature like Reka? Infiltration of the house by spies? Hardly fitting work for what they used to be: the relentless, crushing pincer of their hierarch's will. But now came an adversary that threatened us all. A non-Kresz that could be hurt and killed without any ill effects. Cynically I thought it was a wonderful opportunity for the Defenders to recapture their former glory. To become Warriors again. But did Gurud even know what was driving him? What he was experiencing was hardwired into his caste, his genetic structure. If I was right, he'd fight – they'd all fight – even if they were hopelessly outnumbered and outgunned.

The road rose slowly, following the natural contours of the land away from the Inland Sea to the short plateau – a kind of pause in the landscape – before the final thrust of Treaty Mount, which was no more than a hill really, but the highest point in the city. We didn't see anyone as we walked, although the occasional Hegemony fighter flashed overhead. Our own ships were absent. We'd lost the air war. There must be Hegemony ground troops, but we didn't come across any, which was just as well. The way he felt now, Gurud would probably throw himself, howling, at them in a last act of defiance and we'd all be killed.

Isza looked back at me and I could tell she was picking up on some of my feelings even though she didn't know what I was thinking about.

There was something up ahead: I felt it before we saw anything. Something of what I was getting from Gurud, but less defined. Other emotions mixed in – fear mainly, and suffering.

The road levelled out and turned sharp left to a junction, and we saw others, a little ahead of us, all walking as we were. Some showed the signs of earlier battles, walking awkwardly, their chitin badly scraped or scorched. Others carried younglings or possessions, shuffling as if they had been carrying them for a long time.

"Come on," Gurud said. "We're almost there."

In his haste, we overtook the others. Some were too wrapped up in their misery to notice us. Others looked at us, hoping for some kind of help, but we had nothing to give.

Gurud walked faster. He would have leaped forward if he hadn't been holding onto Isza. I didn't see what the rush was about.

Treaty Mount wasn't going anywhere. Neither were the Hegemony.

A last bend and we came to the souk at the foot of the Mount. The square was half full of Kresz all making their way to the obsidian steps that led to the broad summit surrounding the Council chambers. Where were the Hegemony forces that they would allow this to happen unchallenged? There were so many Kresz up there. Many of them armed. They'd built barricades along the top of the steps. Obviously Kergis hadn't come to Treaty Mount in triumph yet. He was probably waiting in his shielded bunker on house lands until the Hegemony finished his work for him.

We joined the others climbing the Mount. I looked behind. It seemed we were among the last to arrive. Above us, the crowd was confused: everyone seeking news of loved ones, friends; a litany of shocks at hearing bad news; and bursts of happiness as family members were reunited. They spoke in hushed voices, the sharper sounds coming from the crash of body armour as people moved around in the now cramped space.

We passed through a gap in the barricade and waited by the edge of the summit. It seemed like madness to me: we were so exposed behind this wall made of furniture, doors, tree branches. One decent blast would breach it. If the Hegemony had wanted to herd us to one exposed spot to finish us off, they couldn't have done a better job.

"Gurud, we can't stay here," I said. "It's not safe."

"Nowhere's safe," he said tiredly. "The last House War ended here. It's fitting this is where our war with the Hegemony will truly begin."

I looked around. Our "army" was equipped with antiquated weapons, thick pieces of timber or metal, or nothing at all. We were no match for the invaders.

"All we'll do up here is die," I said.

A flash of anger. "Then at least we die together. As Kresz."

Isza laid her claws on Gurud's dominant arm. "Udun's right."

Gurud's anger increased for an instant, then subsided.

"This isn't sensible," Isza said. "We should get a transport, a speeder, anything. Make for our people in the deep desert. Some must have survived. We can hide out, gather our strength and plan. Then we fight, from a position of strength. On our terms."

"But what about these people?" Gurud said.

"You can't save everyone," I said. "Let's save ourselves. That's a start."

"This is where I must be. Where we all must be." He looked at me. "You are not going anywhere."

That look. What would happen if I did try to leave? Would he attack me? It felt like he would. But that was impossible.

There was a rasping behind me and I turned. A group of Defender caste, from different houses by their dress. One had drawn a long thin gaszti and was running the blade across the chitin of her larger claw. As a female she was the biggest Defender there. She glanced at me and then her eyes locked with Gurud's. Something passed between them. An animal heat that was almost lust. Isza felt it too.

"You will both stay here," Gurud said, and brushed past me to join the knot of Defenders. They greeted him with a clashing of body armour.

Other Kresz moved away from them, sensing the same danger from this group that I felt. That Isza felt.

"What is going on?" she said.

"I don't know, but I think they're getting ready to fight."

I could feel waves of rage, cold murderous intent and bravado. They were feeding on each other's emotions, using them to drive their own anger deeper into some kind of battle-ready mindset. We weren't a hive-mind species, but what I witnessed here was bordering on it.

"We have to get out of here," Isza said.

"Gurud won't come with us. Not now." He had pulled his own gaszti and was incising a pattern into his chest plate.

"I know." Two words, but I felt how hard it was for her to say them. "We'll come back for him. When this is over."

She took one last look at Gurud, then turned and pushed through the crowd. We'd drifted away from the gap in the barricade with the constant movement of people and now it felt like we were pushing against the flow of some great river. It was hard to keep up with her – bodies kept getting in-between us. I moved past them as gently as I could but Isza was less polite and I felt the momentary annoyances in those she pushed aside. All this against a clamouring fear, a deadly desire coming off the Defenders who were spreading out now along the edge of the barricade, and a silently keening desolation. And then everything stilled and became expectant.

"It may be too late to leave," I said.

There was a rumbling noise from below, growing louder. We were closer to the gap now. Isza, taller than me, looked down into the souk.

"What is it?" I asked.

"They're coming."

I pushed past a huddle of Cultivators who were trying to move away from the edge of the barricade. The rumbling stopped and was replaced by a sharp clicking, again and again, behind and to my left. I looked over. Gurud and the other Defenders were now ranged along the barricade. Each held a gaszti and they were slapping the flat of the blades against their carapaces.

Below, some kind of ground vehicle had entered the souk. A mobile cannon. Small, but with a large central bulge topped with a thick black tube that was lifting towards the top of the Mount. The gun was surrounded by ground troops. Their bodies were encased in their own type of armour, black and articulated; their heads fully enclosed in helmets of the same dull material but with a blue glow coming from the visors. They carried long sidearms and these too were raised towards us.

The Defenders' hoods were erect now. The slapping was replaced by a chant, taken up by others, not just Defenders. A meaningless but repetitive sound that seemed to worm its way into my brain, demanding a response. There was one simple deadly emotion linked with that sound. The whole hilltop reverberated with it, shared and amplified it. My world narrowed, my vision shrinking to see only the enemy below, my mind full of what we would do to them. Kill. Kill. Kill.

A laser bolt from the cannon blasted into the barricade to my right. A wave of heat washed over me. Bodies incinerated, chitin turning into flame.

The Defenders howled together, a collective death cry, as they stood at the top of the steps. Mantle energy leaped from them, flowing down the steps, crashing into the cannon and flooding the souk. Hegemony troopers fell to their knees, slapping at the ground where their legs were melting. The cannon didn't fire again. Its hull fell inward, the gun barrel tilting up at the sky. The black wave cleared and the souk was full of twisted metal and puddles of flesh. No one lived.

A shout went up from the hilltop. We tasted victory. It was hard not to be caught up in the emotion, but with the immediate threat past, I felt I could be me again. I held onto that.

Isza was beside me and I felt her confusion. Not two body lengths past her, the barricade was being rebuilt, the dead dragged away. How could we survive this and keep going? We'd go mad.

"We should leave," I shouted. "The Hegemony will be back. In greater numbers."

The space in front of us was clear. I walked to the gap in the barricade, but there was already movement below. I was about to move back when I saw what it was. And then I couldn't move. Four – no, five Kresz had entered the souk. None of them had mantles. They were walking towards us, arms outstretched, calling out words I couldn't hear yet. Two were Defender Caste, another two were Merchants, and the last was a Cultivator.

Their words came to me now. "Brothers! Help us!"

These Kresz had been excised. But they weren't criminals. The scars I could see were fresh, rusz still leaking from them and spattering the dusty souk. I was amazed they could still walk. How could the Hegemony … My mind refused to go any further.

Excisees who happened on civilised areas were killed if they didn't suicide. Was that what they wanted from us?

I passed through the barricade. Isza said something but I didn't hear her. I felt something in my mind tugging me back. But it was too weak. I took a step. Another step. I had no gaszti. How could I help them?

I was almost halfway down the stairs. The excisees had begun to climb – unsteadily. Soon we would touch. What would I feel?

There was a stinging sensation in my shoulder. A smoky smell I couldn't place. Then sound crashed in on me all at once.

"Udun!" Isza's voice. A huge shout – many voices from above. The sound of running, and the souk filled with Hegemony troops again.

The excisees reached out to me. Their feeder claws moved but their words couldn't carry above everything else. What were they trying to tell me?

Another sharp pain, this time in my upper thigh. I looked down. A small hole was burned through the chitin. My leg folded and I hit the hard stone.

"Udun!" Isza's voice again. I saw her break away from the others at the barricade. Flashes of blaster fire scorched the sky around her, from behind and from the souk below.

I felt that same strange group-mind building, but it was distant now. Uninvolving. My leg was fire.

Isza ran down the steps, ignoring the danger. I reached out to her. A hole opened up in her chest. I saw shards of chitin flying from her back.

She stumbled. Her eyes widened, looking right into mine. She took one more step and another hole exploded inwards beside the first. She fell forward, her face a claw span from mine. Her eyes looked through me, unfocused.

I couldn't feel her. Then I felt nothing at all.

23

Voss Space / Cygnus Sector / Hegemony

Denev was wedged into the scoutship's benchseat behind Rhees and Volmar. The seat wasn't rated for any flight longer than a couple of hours – certainly not in Voss Space – and he'd been sitting there for a whole day now.

There'd been no time to talk to Rhees alone since Volmar arrived. After the intel on the raiders' base had been fed to Denev's contacts, Volmar had insisted they head for the closest Voss Space junction that would lead them to the base. Now they were waiting, sequestered beneath a shadowy projection in the chamber wall, systems all but shut down.

The atmosphere in the cockpit was strained. There was a nasty dynamic playing out between Volmar and Rhees. She challenged him and he hated her for it. It wasn't going to end well.

Denev was trying to get comfortable for the fifty-first time when he heard Rhees breathe in sharply.

"They're here."

Ships started to stream into the chamber through the main channel. Brell, Sissilak and Totek ship configurations were all represented. The biggest ships were Totek by design but he'd seen nothing like them in HDC reports. Five heavy support carriers with long spines tapered at the front where the bridge was ringed by cannon and hung with segmented cargo and hangar sections for three-quarters of their length ahead of massive engines. These were interspersed with fifteen Sissilak and Brell destroyer escorts – the biggest ships allowed in system militias. They must be recorded somewhere but clearly the Hegemony auditors had become complacent about tracking their whereabouts. The Sissilak ships were sleek arrowheads; the Brell were similar but more organic, like the skull of a prehistoric bird with a razor bill. More surprising were the ten battlecruiser-class ships, six Sissilak and four Brell, which were completely outlawed and shouldn't even exist. Bringing up the rear were four Totek cargo transports, probably acting as fleet supply ships. Among all these flew more than fifty singleships: Sissilak Talon fighters and delta-wing Brell craft.

"I think the raiders have bitten off more than they can chew," Denev said.

Volmar grunted. "We'll see."

As the convoy traversed the chamber and moved into the channel that would lead directly to the raiders, he said, "Follow. Keep them in visual range."

Rhees brought the ship systems up and nudged the Voss Space drive over.

Denev couldn't guess how long Volmar had been aware of the raiders' location. He'd been kept out of the loop. Which meant his efforts on Herakli had been part of the game Volmar was playing with Rhees. Normally he would have met such news with equanimity. But something had shifted inside the careful wall he'd built between himself and the world. He felt used. He felt … angry.

He closed his eyes as they left the chamber and entered the channel in pursuit. He must have slept because the next thing he heard was Volmar saying, "Hold back."

They were on the lip of the channel where it opened into a new chamber crisscrossed with blazing energy bridges like columns of living lightning. The far walls were hard to make out against the glare, but he got the sense of huge distance.

By the dim glow of ship running lights he could see the rebel fleet was moving through this vastness in a close file … that began to break apart as he watched.

"What's happening?" he said.

"Look." Rhees was pointing at something high above. Cones of light glowed in the chamber's ceiling and shadows moved against them. "Those are other access channels. But …"

"Something's moving through them," Denev said. "At speed."

Explosions rippled across the main part of the chamber. Rhees brought up an overlay across the cockpit window, enlarging the glowing entry points. Ships were still streaming in. The unmistakable horseshoe-shaped raiders and with them larger craft, thinner and looking like a pistol grip. One of these fired a particle beam as soon as it emerged.

"Fighting in here," Rhees said. "They're fucking insane."

"Or very determined to win," Volmar said.

The image pulled back, amplifying the available light to show the full scale of the battle now raging before them. The ship column had completely broken up, with battleships and escorts moving into defensive positions around the heavy carriers and trying to cover multiple attack vectors. More raider missiles erupted in chains of light, some finding their mark, others just adding to the general mayhem. The side of a Sissilak destroyer escort split open, raked by laser fire, debris and bodies piling out into sudden brightness as the lightning bridges flared with rising field potential.

The augmented image dimmed to cut back on the glare. Then the rebels started to return fire. A battery of particle cannons on top of one of the Sissilak battlecruisers let fly at a group of incoming raider craft – but the beams diverged, sucked into a patch of dense darkness that swelled rapidly before shrinking into a bright bead and exploding outwards in a blinding annihilation that swamped the display's dampers. When the image cleared, the flight of raider ships was gone, along with the front half of the battlecruiser. Its hull spun wildly, smashing through a group of singleships that exploded in a cascade of flashes.

The light of particle weapons crisscrossed the chamber and more field anomalies grew and blossomed with quick death. Then the space itself began to twist and shift. Walls moved, closing over ship groups. Tunnels extruded into the chamber and whipped around, smashing through any ship unfortunate enough to get in their way. Reality seemed to judder. A flight of Talon fighters skip-stepped in and out of existence.

"We can't stay here," Rhees said, moving them away from the distending lip of their channel into the chamber.

Denev couldn't see there was anywhere safe to go. Small eddies in Voss Space marched across the display as the rebel ships escaped into normal space.

"We follow them," Volmar said.

"We could transit inside a —"

"Follow them!" Volmar shouted and slapped at the contact that activated the transit sequence.

The battle scene swam in the display and everything faded to black. Denev's breath came loudly in his ears and then they were in space.

∞

Alert telltales lit up across the board and space crashed into them. Rhees was jerked against her restraint, the straps cutting painfully across her chest. Behind her, Denev cried out.

The ship was spinning. A proximity alert blared. The powerful engines strained as Rhees fought to kill the spin.

"Gravity mass," she shouted against the shriek of engines. "We're in-system!"

The spin slowed, stopped. The display was full of debris. Some rebel ships had survived the transit but many had been pulled apart. A huge rocky planet loomed to port.

The ship's engines died.

"What's happening?" Denev said.

Rhees was glad he was still with them. "The transit fucked the engines."

She reset the primer. Closed the contact. Nothing. The ship's nose was turning towards the planet.

Volmar looked as if nothing was wrong.

"I warned you this would happen," she told him.

"I have complete faith in your piloting skills if nothing else," he said.

Reset. Contact. Still nothing.

"We have company," Denev said.

On the tac display a new wedge of untagged ships closed on the debris field. The raiders. Rhees struggled to understand what she was seeing. If they'd transited like the rebels most of them would be debris by now. But this was a large, intact force.

The main engines still weren't responding and the planet was starting to pull hard at them. It loomed dead ahead now, filling the forward view. On tac, the raiders were closing.

She still had attitude thrusters and the ship was fitted for atmos flight. It was a choice between certain death in space or probable death cracking up on landing. She fired aft thrusters and they leaped towards the planet.

"Can you get us down?" Denev asked, his voice strained.

"Down? Of course. In one piece? Let's hope so."

There was no more time to talk. She trimmed attitude and flattened their approach. The hull vibrated as the ship met the first tenuous wisps of atmosphere, then shuddered as it bit harder. She angled the ship down, streaking through the upper layers in a gout of flame, gaining speed. The sound was deafening. The ship jumped. Denev shouted behind her but she was too busy fighting the controls.

They burst through the cloud ceiling above a rocky plateau. Snow-capped mountains tore at the sky on the horizon. The ship dropped, lurched sideways and dropped again. She fired the thrusters, pulling them back onto the glidepath, shedding velocity.

The rock-strewn floor was coming up at them too fast. More thrusters. She wasn't sure she could actually pull this off. Maybe that would be okay.

She saw Petar's cracked-up capsule on the pitted asteroid. Fuck it. She didn't want to die on some nameless planet alongside Volmar.

They were almost down. She fired lateral thrusters, judging the windshear. The ground looked flat enough. Landing gear locked in place.

"Hold on!"

They hit, bounced. The gear held. Thrusters forward. Touching down again, jolting wildly but slowing. Slowing. Until finally the ship rolled to a halt.

She felt Denev's hand grip her shoulder. "Thank you," he said.

She turned to Volmar. "Have you sold us out?"

Volmar regarded her with hooded eyes.

Atmosphere was tolerable, so she keyed the lock open, slapped at Volmar's harness release, grabbed his arm and dragged him past a shocked Denev, out through the lock, and threw him to the rocky ground. The air smelled of sulphur.

"Answer me," she shouted. "There's no way those raiders could have tracked the rebels in Voss Space. And don't tell me it was just bad luck they ran into us. They had a whole other force waiting on this side."

"I don't have to answer to you," Volmar said. He pushed himself up off the rocky ground. "You're going back to the stockade for this, Lowrans."

As he rose, she punched him full in the face and he sprawled on the ground again.

"Might as well be worth it," she said. She walked away towards the mountains, not looking back.

"Wait!" Denev was running after her. She turned but didn't stop walking. "You can't just walk off," he said, falling in step beside her.

"Can't I?" She didn't stop. "How many people were on those rebel ships? Volmar just sacrificed another bunch of aliens and I'm not even sure he's working for the Hegemony any more."

"I don't know anything more than you do, but where are you going?"

"Away from him!" She stopped and turned to Denev, already breathing hard. The oxygen content in the air was lower than Earth normal. "How do you think the raiders knew exactly where to hit the rebels in Voss Space to drive them into the rest of their forces out there?"

"You're right. Volmar must have tipped them off. But that doesn't mean he's a traitor."

"Really? That's just SOP for the Corps, is it? I don't know what's worse: Volmar gone rogue, or Volmar executing an HDC-endorsed plan that sees Hegemony citizens fed to bloodthirsty raiders."

"We've been through this," he said. "Those citizens were traitors."

"So arrest them! Put them in jail, don't lead them into a slaughter. Do you really think Volmar did the right thing?"

He turned and gazed back at the ship. "No. It's not right."

Rhees looked up into the sky. "Oh, fuck."

A large raider ship was descending through the cloud cover.

She'd really fucked up now. And she'd dragged Denev into this whole mess. Better she'd gone to the stockade in the first place. But now ... She might just have cost them both their lives.

The vessel dwarfed Rhees's scoutship. A serious-looking plasma cannon hanging from the underside gimballed towards them. There was nowhere for them to run. No cover.

She saw Volmar climbing out of the scoutship. What the fuck had he been doing in there? He stood in front of it and waved to them.

Rhees looked at Denev. They started walking back.

The raider landed beside the scoutship, its hull splitting open and a ramp extending.

What the hell were they going to do? She had no sidearm and there was nothing in the ship they could use.

"Petar was wrong about you," she told Denev. "I was starting to like you."

Denev sighed. "No. He was right."

There was movement at the top of the ramp.

"We're not just giving up, are we?" he said.

"Fuck, no. But we need to pick our moment."

They both raised their arms, palms open and facing out. Volmar stood with a superior look on his face, but his right cheekbone was grazed and bruising. She could kill him with her bare hands if she had to. It may still be worth it.

Three aliens walked down the ramp towards them. They were short, biped and uniformly clad in tight-fitting clothing that had an oil-slick sheen to it. Their heads were large, dominated by a shaggy mane of golden fur, with dark skin, almost black, small dark eyes too close together and an equally small mouth. The way they walked was extremely fluid, as if their limbs were made up of multiple joints. They were all carrying blasters and they looked like they knew how to use them. Rhees noticed they also wore two black metal batons, one longer than the other, fixed side by side at waist level.

Volmar made a low growling noise, followed by a series of sharp clicks.

One of the aliens responded.

"What did you say?" Rhees asked.

"I simply asked if they were finished with killing and ready for talking. I work for the Diplomatic Corps you might recall."

Rhees knew better than to ask how he knew their language. It seemed Volmar was always several steps ahead of any other human.

"These are the Maagba," Volmar said. The three aliens reached the rocky ground and stood either side of the ramp. "Shall we go inside?"

Rhees didn't budge. "Have you betrayed us?"

He gave a short laugh. "Spare me," he said, and walked up the ramp.

Rhees glanced at Denev and followed Volmar into the ship.

The interior was unremarkable; the corridor ceilings a little lower than she was comfortable with. The level of tech looked comparable to the Hegemony.

They were led up to the flight deck. The commander had the same golden mane and uniform as their escort and the others sitting at stations set into the walls. He growled and indicated they should sit in acceleration couches near the back of the deck. While they weren't restrained, it was clear the Maagba wanted them to stay put. The three that had brought them on board stationed themselves behind the bank of couches, standing silently even through lift-off.

The vessel paused as it left the ground, hovering over the HDC ship and locking it to the underside of the hull, whether by grapples or some kind of force field, Rhees couldn't tell.

Volmar stared ahead, watching their departure on a large tri-D set into the bulkhead. Denev sat at Rhees's other side. His hand moved on the armrest, his fingers curling around hers. She felt at once vulnerable, but also strengthened by the contact. They'd face whatever happened together.

The ship was accelerating now, punching through the cloud deck and making best speed for orbit. Atmos fell away and the debris field of the rebel fleet spread before them. Hovering above the ruined vessels sat the Maagba force: a host of the familiar C-shaped raider ships, and behind them a megacruiser, as big as the biggest Fleet ship Rhees had ever seen. These Maagba were more than simple hit-and-run pirates. Where the fuck did they come from?

As they neared the giant vessel its hull split open, revealing a weapons bay. Their ship slowed, manoeuvring close, and then the walls of the bay were sliding past them as they were swallowed whole. There was a loud grating and the floor vibrated as the ship touched down on the deck, then the hiss of pressurisation.

"Great," Rhees said. "We're trapped on a hostile alien battlecruiser. Masterful plan, Volmar."

"Your days in the Corps were always numbered, Lowrans," Volmar said. "Your lack of respect for the chain of command is equalled only by your complete lack of faith."

"Faith and respect are earned where I come from."

Denev squeezed her hand and she looked in his eyes and saw a certainty there. He had her back. He let go as the Maagba behind them moved forward.

They retraced their steps to the ramp, their Maagba guard flanking them. On the deckplate outside, three more Maagba were waiting.

Volmar spoke again in their language, a sharp exhalation and a prolonged *krrrrk*. The middle alien on the main deck answered. Volmar, apparently satisfied, walked down as if he owned the place. Rhees and Denev followed.

They passed through another lock and then down a dim corridor, which intersected with another curving walkway. Volmar and the two Maagba escorting him turned left, but Rhees and Denev found that way barred. One Maagba held Rhees by the arm while another indicated she keep straight on with a sharp nod of its shaggy head. Denev was held by two other Maagba who were pulling him to the right.

Rhees planted her feet. The two Maagba with Volmar drew their blasters and pointed them at her head. There was nothing she could do.

"I'll see you soon," Denev said.

She nodded but felt far from reassured.

She let the Maagba lead her down the corridor. There was an opening in the sidewall. They pushed her inside and the door guillotined shut.

Rhees surveyed this new prison. The walls looked as sturdy as the door, and the floor was covered in some dense substance that gave slightly under her feet. There was a yellow oblong patch in one corner that gave a little more when she walked on it. It was roughly as long as the aliens were tall. She guessed it was a sleeping mat and sat down, back to the wall, facing the door.

There was nothing to do but wait and hope Denev was okay. It was strange to think it, but Denev was the only person she trusted.

Volmar had kept them both in the dark and there seemed to be no end to the depths he'd sink to. He'd withheld information on the raiders, then played the rebels against them with a callous disregard for life. How many Brell, Sissilak, Totek and Maagba had died in his latest powerplay? It was too simple to think he was working for himself. He already had all the power one man would ever need. No, this was pure HDC, another one of their dirty tricks. But HDC didn't operate in a vacuum. Central Administration knew exactly what they were doing. Which meant they approved.

Denev had called her naive. Maybe he was right.

24

I woke to an overpowering sensation of fear, as if someone was behind me, unseen, reaching out to do me harm.

"This one's awake."

A Cultivator was hunkered over me. My head and back were leaning against a wall.

"Where am I?" I said. There was a sticky wad of something on my leg, covering the hole. I touched my shoulder. Another lump, on my front and on my back.

"Don't touch that," the Cultivator said. "It's some kind of covering for your wound. The Hegemony put it there."

"Then help me get it off! It could be poison."

"I don't think so. Look." She had a knobbly lump on her forearm. "I was shot here. It doesn't hurt any more."

She was right. There was no pain.

I saw other Kresz standing behind her. We were packed into a room: mud-coloured walls, bare earth floor, nothing but a single ceiling light so we were all in shadow.

"Where are we? Where's Isza?" She looked blank. "My breach-sister," I added.

"We're still in Aktiuk. We were brought here after Treaty Mount. Those of us still alive. I don't know about your breach-sister. Sorry."

She was frightened. But she was kind. I was thankful for that.

I had to get up. Could I stand?

"Help me," I said.

Her long thin claws closed on mine. We paused in a moment of sharing but she pulled away. I couldn't blame her. We'd both seen too much horror. She'd lost someone too – I was sure of it from that brief contact.

I put my good arm behind me and shuffled until my legs were under me, then stood slowly. She hovered helplessly beside me. "Thank you," I said. My shoulder and leg were a little stiffer than usual, but that was all. I'd heal.

The room was longer than I'd expected and filled with Kresz. The far end was closed off with a thick mesh. I looked from face to face but recognised no one. Had all of these been on Treaty Mount?

"I'm looking for my breach-sister," I said loudly. "We were at the barricade together when the Hegemony attacked. Did anyone see what happened to her? Her name is Isza."

The mumbling conversations died and a robed Priest turned towards me. "She was shot when the excised came. I saw her fall. But after that …"

I remembered. The hole opening in Isza's chest plate. Her eyes looking through me.

"Did anyone else see her?" I called out.

They could feel how desperate I was, but no one spoke. They returned to their talk, the miasma of quiet anxiety falling over them again.

I wondered if there were other rooms like this. Maybe Isza was in one of those. Or she was dead. Killed trying to save me. I didn't want to think about that.

"I'm sorry," the Cultivator said again.

A youngster was with her; his shell was still a deep purple and his robes told me he was a pupil at the Academy. He stood close behind the Cultivator, peering around her. He was terrified.

"I'm Pet'la," the Cultivator said. She wasn't much older than her friend really, her shell a bright red. "And this is Chevket. We found each other when the ships came from the sky and started bombing. He doesn't speak much. In fact, all he's told me is his name."

I sent the greeting to both of them and felt it returned, tentatively from Chevket. I sat again, leaning against the wall, and Pet'la and Chevket hunkered beside me.

"You were both at Treaty Mount?" I asked. Pet'la indicated yes. "How long since the attack?"

"We were brought here right after we surrendered … after most of the Defenders had been killed. Maybe four hours. You were here when we got here."

I'd been unconscious the whole time. I tried to imagine what it had been like on the Mount when the Hegemony overpowered the remaining Kresz. They killed indiscriminately – I'd seen that. Why not kill everyone there? Or would that waste a useful resource? Were we to become a slave workforce under their domination?

Oh, Isza, I thought. Perhaps it's best if you're not alive to see this. Gurud would most certainly be dead. The way he was at the barricade, I couldn't see him surrendering.

"What are we here for?" I asked.

Pet'la looked sideways at Chevket. "I don't know."

She did know something. I could feel it. She just didn't want to say it in front of the youngling. He was frightened enough.

"They're killing us," Chevket said in a soft whisper. He pulled his thin robe tighter around his body and leaned into Pet'la.

"They've been coming since we got here," Pet'la said. "They take one of us, no more than one-two minutes pass. Then …" An image flashed in my head: the sky splitting apart. "I've seen enough death today to know what it feels like," she said. "If you don't believe me, you won't have long to wait to see for yourself."

The ceiling light went out and we were plunged into darkness. Chevket whimpered. My desert eyelid gave everything a dim blue glow. The jumble of bodies behind Pet'la began to find space to sit in the semi-darkness. Nothing, it seemed, was going to happen now. Night had fallen. The first night of the Hegemony's dominion over Homeworld.

There was a distant rattle. Then a sharp sound. The corridor beyond the mesh lit up and those around me stirred. Four Hegemony troops appeared, three with long sidearms. The third held a set of restraints.

They stood in front of the mesh and a section peeled back. The trooper with the restraints pointed at a Kresz near the opening. An old Priest. He shrank away at first, then stood and looked back into the room. We were all with him. Cultivator, Adept, Merchant, Scholar, House Czerag, House Ukat, House Dageru – all united with this single Priest who now walked upright through the gap in the mesh, holding his claws out so the restraints could be fitted.

The mesh rolled back. The Priest and his captors walked out of sight along the corridor. The light went out. Our comradeship faded, giving way to a jumble of despair, fear, anger, hope – not much of that.

In the darkness my desert eyelids flicked across again. I willed them to retract. I no longer wanted to see this sad room filled with a sense of waiting. I waited too, counting the seconds. One-two minutes – maybe a little more, maybe less – and I felt a sharp stab, an almost physical blow pushing me back into the wall. Then nothing. As Pet'la said, I'd seen enough death today to know this was what it felt like.

They came again, and again. The night became infinite. Blackness forever, punctuated by a flash of artificial light, a brief visit from our captors, blackness again and then death. More death. Death on death.

The room grew less crowded, until those of us left could stretch out on the floor. I tried to sleep through the eternal night that would be our last. And sleep did come at some point. I slipped into the worldmind and what a strange place it had become. Solitary. I floated alone in a multitude of dim points of light that sucked hungrily at the radiance they emitted, holding it back, trying not to be noticed. It was as if in our pain we were turning away from one another, because to do otherwise would reflect our miseries back on us again and again and again. I drifted in a kind of semiconsciousness, not wanting to give myself over to this strangeness but too exhausted to fully wake. It was the most unsatisfying sleep of my life.

In the morning, I was woken by a scream.

I was standing before I was fully awake. Other bodies were moving in the dim light. The scream came again, slicing through me.

By the mesh, Pet'la was bent over. Two, three long steps and I was beside her. She was huddled over a prone figure. Chevket. Lying face down on the ground, naked. His robe was bunched tight around his neck, twisted and passed through a gap in the mesh to twist around his neck again.

"He couldn't stand it any more," Pet'la said.

I kneeled beside her next to Chevket's poor body. "He's free now," I said. "Sakat has him."

I didn't know what I really believed but it felt like the thing people said at a time like this. Pet'la didn't respond. Poor Chevket. Was this all that was left for us?

There was a noise outside. The light in the ceiling came on.

Pet'la began to unwind the cloth from Chevket's neck. He had slid it through the gap in the guard plates over his larynx to press more firmly on the flesh beneath, stopping the flow of rusz to his brain. It would have been a gentle way to die. Perhaps better than what waited for us at the hands of the Hegemony. I helped Pet'la loosen the garment and unwind it from the mesh.

I heard the guards approaching, then booted feet appeared next to the mesh by Chevket's head. There was a grunting noise, translated almost at once by the Hegemony guard's voder: "Get back!"

Pet'la and I half-stood and dragged Chevket away from the mesh. The others in the room were all standing now and we joined them in the middle of the narrow space, Chevket lying between us. I looked at these Hegemony. Fur on top of their heads, unreadable expressions on their pale, soft faces.

A section of the mesh folded back. A sidearm muzzle came up, pointed directly at me. Another growl. "You're next. Come."

I looked at Pet'la and felt what little comfort she had left to give. Then I walked into the corridor between the guards. I was surprised my legs would carry me.

Behind me the others, very few now, sent their good feelings my way. My senses felt very sharp and I tasted all the subtle hues of that sending. The part that hoped they could walk when it was their turn and not huddle in fear. The part that was relieved it was my turn and not theirs.

It seemed I was going to my death. I wasn't a fighter and even if I tried to break free there was no escape. I'd die just the same. And what was left for me? Isza must be dead. Gurud too. Tzek, Czerag, Idke, Bvak. Surely none of them would be allowed to live when House Kergis or the Hegemony caught up with them. And they couldn't stay hidden forever.

We turned a corner. The corridor was lighter now, the floor smooth stone. A sign was on the wall near a door. It was written in Kresz: *Scholars Chambers*. A teaching facility?

We went through the door. More guards inside a small room with a skylight in the ceiling. It was day. And in the centre of the room, a metal table. It looked out of place. Wooden benches had been pushed aside to accommodate it. Metal coils hung from it. I stopped. Even though I was about to die I couldn't prevent my curious nature taking in every detail.

The guards that had led me here shouldered their weapons. Hands gripped my arms – I felt nothing from them. More Hegemony came forward. They were all dressed in their black body armour, but no helmets. They pushed me towards the table but I didn't want to move.

More hands grabbed me. They spoke to each other in their growls and pulled me to the table. There was another Hegemony there, not dressed in armour. It stood back watching, holding something metal in its hand.

My body was rigid, but they forced me face down on the table, my shell slapping on metal, and lifted me so I was sprawled along its length. The metal coils twisted around me, pulling tight, pressing me into the metal until I was trapped. I wished I could be facing the sky as they killed me, but all I could see was metal and a patch of floor.

A pair of booted feet walked into my field of vision. The Hegemony without the armour. Hands – I couldn't see whose – grabbed at my hood, pulling the mantle up and out over my head.

"What?" I said, and then the pain. Intense. Cutting into my back. I screamed.

A searing point moving. The smell of burning flesh. My flesh. Kill me, I thought. Just make it end.

Then the mindshock. Everyone. Gone. Like blindness.

I screamed again.

A slab of flesh fell onto the floor. The feet moved back out of the way. I saw my hood, on the floor, rusz oozing along the cut.

I went somewhere then. I didn't know where. Away from that sight. Away from that feeling. If I'd had the choice, I would never have come back.

The pressure on my body eased. A voice barked beside me. The voder spoke: "Come on, Kresz. We didn't cut your legs off."

There was more noise from the Hegemony. Untranslatable. Hands pulled me off the table, held me upright. Dragged me out of the room.

Now I knew what had happened to all those Kresz who had been taken from our cell one by one. They hadn't been killed. It was something much worse. Chevket had done the only sensible thing.

25

Sounds woke me. Not feelings. My eyes opened. I was lying on the floor in a small room. There was a large door. Noise from behind it. Echoing. An announcement. And other noises beneath that.

There were other Kresz here. Still sleeping. All excised. I couldn't see Pet'la. Her time would come soon, but there was nothing I could do for her.

Weak as I was, I stood. There were no guards here. Was I free to leave? Where could I go?

I walked through the large door and into an auditorium. "Welcome to the Hegemony," a voder voice boomed. "Please join a queue for processing and citizenship."

There were several queues. I joined the nearest one with a feeling of unreality. Nothing made sense. It seemed it didn't have to. The queue was full of Kresz. The room was full of Kresz. All of them hoodless. All of them "absent". Just as I was absent to them. It was like I was in space again, alone in my own mind. But Kresz were all around me. I couldn't reconcile the two facts.

No one looked up. No contact. No talking. Nothing to give. They were trapped, caught in grief or terror, and no one could feel what they were feeling. They couldn't express it either. They didn't have the language. None of us did. So we stood, not talking. And slowly moved forward in the line.

Up ahead was a row of tall thin desks, each with a Hegemony soldier. Their pink faces shone above the black of their armour. As I got closer I saw they stood on some kind of raised platform behind the desks so they were the height of the queuing Kresz. Each Kresz stopped in front of a desk, then moved on past.

I couldn't tell what expression was on the Hegemony's face as I approached. Scorn, hatred, anger, boredom? I couldn't imagine what it thought about the mutilations it had been party to. Were we just animals to it?

Then it was my turn. A speaker on the front of the desk spoke Kresz. "Name?"

"Udun of House Czerag," I answered automatically.

There was a whine and a sheaf of paper and plastic emerged from the top of the desk.

"Identity papers, curfew rules and a map of the curfew area," the speaker said.

I reached forward to take them and the soldier pressed a claw-sized box to my forearm plate. There was a snap and a thin line of smoke curled up from my arm. He drew the box away and I saw small marks incised into the chitin, a series of thick and thin lines. I couldn't read them.

I retrieved the papers and the speaker said, "Welcome to the Hegemony, citizen. Move on."

I walked past the desk and looked at the plastic card. It had my picture on it and characters I couldn't read. But some matched the marks on my arm. So I was a slave of the Hegemony now, marked as their property.

The map showed the inner city of Aktiuk. There was a red line running around the central part, and the area outside it was cross-marked. The same cross-marking covered Treaty Mount. I didn't read the other papers even though some were written in Kresz. I stuffed them into my travel pouch.

Another door ahead showed daylight. I walked through it into a large courtyard open to the sky. It was still the same: djel, sura and ataz shone down on us. The ground hadn't split asunder. The planet, the universe, went on despite what was happening to the Kresz people.

Excised stood all around me. Some stared at the papers they had been given, but not seeming to see them. Others just sat or stood gazing at the dust. Something so fundamental to who and what they were had been taken from them and they didn't know what to do. They didn't know how to live past this.

I didn't know myself, but I wanted to be away from this place where so much evil was being done by one "civilised" species to another. I walked out of the courtyard into the dusty street. There were more excised here, but soon I left them behind, guided by nothing more than the curve and downward slope of the road. I walked past broken walls, smoking houses, shops with their wares scattered across the ground.

I passed other Kresz who were intact. With the fighting finished, they had returned to their homes and businesses to pick over the ruins of their lives, trying to bring some order and sense to the world. But there was no order, no sense, any more. How could there be?

They looked at me, then looked away as if I wasn't there. I had become a ghost.

A turn in the road brought me into the area surrounding the souk. I hadn't meant to come here, and it made me feel all the more ghost-like. The market was set up as if nothing had happened. Gaily coloured shadecloths snapped in the breeze over stalls covered with sale goods. Kresz walked among the stalls as though yesterday hadn't happened. But as I looked closer I saw through the illusion. At the end of a row of stalls, the obsidian steps leading up to the Council chambers were cracked and slagged in places. Behind the closest row of stalls to me, many of the tables were empty.

And then I saw the Hegemony troops. Some stood around the cloistered walkway that surrounded the souk. But others were walking between the tables, looking at the goods on offer as if they were simply visiting our world. They wore no helmets and their weapons were slung casually on their backs. We weren't a threat to them any more.

A group of them clustered around a stall selling shell trinkets from the Inland Sea. They picked up the goods and casually threw them back down, talking all the while in their barks and growls. The stall holder looked at them, then at me. I couldn't feel anything from him, but I could see from his face he was terrified. He was trying to explain what the shells were, and what the trinkets were used for. One of the Hegemony picked a piece up and put it in a pouch of his uniform. The Merchant said he was welcome to it. No charge. His tone was so servile it sickened me.

I looked around. In the space of one day we'd gone from a proud, independent people to a beaten world of slaves and cripples. The market even smelled different. It smelled of them – their food, their waste. We had been completely subjugated. Those who fought and didn't die had had their bodies broken. Made useless. Cut off forever from Kresz society.

But perhaps it was a mercy not to feel the worldmind now. What would it be like? I imagined a horrible pool of despair, hateful and dragging at you until you couldn't think, couldn't act. The dead had been spared all this. I could spare myself too. I didn't need to see what was going to happen here any more than I needed to watch a gahe fruit fall all the way to the ground to know it would break open and spill its seeds on the bare earth. I would go to Cz'kras Park.

It was a strange feeling to have a purpose and for that purpose to be to end myself. Wasn't that against all genetic programming, all will for survival? From what I'd seen, survival was overrated. I wanted to be gone. I wanted all this to be over.

I walked past the stalls hurriedly and Hegemony troops turned to watch me. I supposed I didn't move like one of the broken excised. I passed close to some guards under the mosaic arch leading out of the souk. They clutched their weapons tighter, lifting the muzzles towards me. But what could I do to hurt them? I went through the arch and they returned to watching their comrades in among the stalls.

I would have run to the Park but I didn't want to attract attention. So I continued briskly down the winding roads, across a small aqueduct, through an open courtyard. It was the middle of the day and the heat was becoming oppressive. Doors and shutters were closed against it. But it wasn't too much further.

I turned another corner and stopped. A mesh fence ran straight across the road, taller than I could safely jump. It stretched to left and right along the crest of the hill that led down to the Park. I couldn't see the end of it. I didn't need to look at the Hegemony map to know this was the limit of where I could safely go. I had to break through.

Heat shimmered on the deserted road. I crossed the distance to the mesh and bent down. Sudden pain brought me to my knees: a sharp tear across my back, as if the movement had opened the wound where ... where my mantle had been. I put my claws up over my shoulder plate and touched the ragged seam where my hood had joined my body. My claws came away wet with rusz. But the wound didn't matter now. I rubbed the rusz off in the dirt and bent to the mesh.

Movement in the corner of my eye. I stood, looking for somewhere to hide. Panic gave me strength and I leaped, covering the width of the street in one jump. A shadowed laneway to my left, close to where I'd come out. I moved as quietly and quickly as possible and sank into the gloom there, pushing against the wall, looking out to the street.

I saw a pair of booted feet on the road, coming towards me. Hegemony, no doubt. A perimeter guard. I'd seen no obvious surveillance motes near the mesh, but perhaps there hadn't been time to set those up yet. Legs appeared, swinging in a slow, measured gait. If I had been discovered, this guard wouldn't have been walking so leisurely.

It came fully into view, still a way from my position. The head was fully enclosed in its helmet. I didn't know what manner of sensing equipment it might contain: movement detection, sound magnification, visible and non-visible wavelength capture? The guard carried a long weapon.

I could attack it, hope to be killed in the struggle. But there were no guarantees it wouldn't just maim me and throw me in a cell. I needed the certainty of death. I waited, calming any betraying signs my body might give, muscles relaxed until I was motionless, breathing slowed to a bare whisper through spiracles, the pulse points that moved rusz through my body dipped. That caused my vision to cloud a little, but I could still watch the approaching guard. Its head moved rhythmically left and right in counterpoint to its steady stride down the road. If it was bored with its duty, it didn't show it. It could have been a machine for all the repetitive precision it displayed in its progress.

Then it was beside my laneway. The head turned to look into the blackness. I waited. It moved on.

I waited some more, estimating the length of the road past my hiding place until it curved out of sight, and the speed of the guard's progress along it. When I thought enough time had passed, I tentatively looked out of the laneway. The road was empty again, but I couldn't be sure for how long. I ran to the mesh.

A portion of it was overshadowed by a tall endar tree standing at the crest of the slope. A break here would be less obvious. Although the mesh might be active and report a breach. I had to gamble that any response wouldn't be fast enough to stop me.

I bent again, favouring my left side this time, and my wound only complained a little. I took the mesh between my large lower mandibles. The wire was thin but stronger than it looked. I thought it wasn't going to give, and bit harder. It broke with a sudden snap. I bit another strand and another, conscious of a pressure on the back of my head, a feeling that a silent alarm would bring more than just one guard down on me any moment. Finally I was able to push the mesh apart. The opening was enough for me.

I scuttled through and turned to look back along the road. Nothing yet.

I pulled the mesh together. It didn't meet very well, but it was all I could do, then I was running full pelt down the hill, letting the slope push me along, dodging bushes and branches until I was at the bottom in thick undergrowth. I looked back up the hill. Still nothing. But the guard would be back. The hole would be discovered. They would come.

I moved off through the trees and into the Park. As a youngling, I'd played in these woods sometimes, bored while attending a ceremony for some old house member who'd died. These things were generally done back at the escarpment, but enough times we'd travelled into Aktiuk. I was never really sure of the reasons then. Perhaps whoever had died had worked in the city, or had a lot of non-house friends who lived here, or maybe just liked the park. It was beautiful, even now.

I emerged from the tree line onto grass stirred by a breeze off the Inland Sea. It was cooler here, even out of the shade. Groupings of trees dotted the expanse of the park with benches and tables in the shade beneath them. Each house had its own space and there were common areas too.

I saw the first of the spikes, beneath the nearest stand of trees, and stopped. There wasn't a spike that didn't hold a body; some had four and five – bodies piled on bodies, each new one pushing the others down below it, the flared steel spike cutting further into the carapace until the body at the bottom of the pile was split completely open. I walked into an oasis of shade, not wanting to look, but looking all the same. Every dead Kresz – and there were three-one of them in this grouping of five spikes – was excised, the ragged cut of flesh plain across their backs. Defenders lay on top of Adepts, Merchants beneath Cultivators; bright orange carapaces spilling rusz onto deeper red and black. All ages. All types. Joined by their excision and now joined in death.

I walked on and saw more groupings across the park. Clusters of bodies at each. I'd heard of criminals, lovelorn youngsters, others who had disgraced themselves, coming here in daylight or under cover of dark to throw themselves on the spikes: a dishonourable death with only ah'lok and other carrion eaters to feed on their flesh. It happened, but not very often. Not on this scale. These poor dead were like me. Excised. Their relatives and friends killed. Their houses destroyed. What was left for them? They offended Sakat. No one would breed with them. No one would help them. Death was a release; an end to their suffering. It made sense. No one should be expected to live like this. No intact Kresz would want to. We excised were at best an embarrassment, at worst pariahs.

"I'll join you soon," I whispered as I passed another group of impaled dead.

House Czerag's portion of the park was ahead. The closest group of spikes was relatively empty of bodies, unlike others nearby. I didn't look too closely at the Kresz there; I didn't want to recognise anyone.

The middle spike in the group had only one other body impaled on it. A Defender. His weight had slid him halfway down the metal. I climbed onto his back, muttering an apology for treating him that way, and hauled myself up to stand with the tip of the spike centred under the space where my chest plate overlapped my abdominal plates. I could feel the cold prick of steel on the hide beneath.

I held the metal tightly, ready to pull myself onto the tip and let gravity push me down onto the Defender's body. What last thoughts does a person have before they end their life? Do they think of something noble, some regret, or desire that would never be attained? Do they remember loved ones, times when they were happy – if they were ever happy? All I could think was that I wanted to be away from here. I'd always wanted to be away from here, but I'd always known this was my home. Home no longer existed; how could it? Now there was nothing. Nothing and no one.

I leaned forward, felt the tip press more firmly against my flesh.

"But why this mass suicide?" The voice spoke in mechanical voder tones.

I pushed back off the sharpened tip of the spike and jumped

to the ground, then slid under the Defender's body. Where had the sound come from? I heard footsteps on grass in the direction of the nearby trees, but I couldn't see anyone yet. Was it a patrol? Why couldn't they have come a few minutes later? I'd be dead then, like the rest.

"Sakat set us on the road to perfection." A Kresz voice. Familiar. "Whatever imperfections an ordinary Kresz may have are recoverable. We can all strive towards the perfect form Sakat embodies. But to be excised, or badly injured or born with some defect, is to be denied that path. There is no way these wretches can partake in Sakat's plan. And so they come here."

"It is a curious expression of your religion." The voder voice again.

There were two walkers only, a Kresz and one of the Hegemony. They were coming closer. I couldn't see them yet, but that Kresz talking – I couldn't forget that self-satisfied tone. It was Erdjis.

"We're better off without these," he said. "Kergis has seen the true way that we will embody Sakat's will. In time there will be only one house. You see, Homeworld was experiencing diaspora. The houses were beginning to become all things; traditional roles were being homogenised. Many saw this as progress."

"But not Kergis?" the voder asked.

"He saw the truth, but we weren't strong enough to act unilaterally. We could not have done it without your help."

"The Hegemony always helps its friends."

They were close now. I bent lower and peered across the rusz-stained grass. I could see heavily booted Hegemony feet and, beside them Erdjis's hoofs. I wished I had a weapon.

"You've proved that," Erdjis said. "Soon all Kresz will be one. Then there is no end to what we can achieve together."

They were walking past the group of spikes now, taking the rise beyond. I waited until I judged they were safely gone, then tentatively rose from beneath the Defender and looked around.

The park was deserted again. I climbed back onto the body and positioned myself over the spike.

All will be one. It was what the female had told me when I was kidnapped. How long had Kergis and the Hegemony been planning this? Had they been in touch even before the contact mission? It seemed likely. The Hegemony had provided the military might for Kergis to take on the house system. He was going to destroy everything – the houses, the lodges, the entire Kresz society – if the Hegemony let him.

What would replace it? Non-Kergis Kresz were being excised; they lay all around me, choosing death rather than face the horror of their situation. I was ready to join them, but what would that achieve except an end to my own suffering? Kergis was forming a new society unified under a single house founded on betrayal and hatred. Erdjis and his like were its exemplars. The way of the Kresz was changing for the worst. And this dead Defender I stood on; the others on nearby spikes, spilling their rusz into the soil – they were hastening this new way. Anyone opposing Kergis was excised, and those who couldn't live with that killed themselves. With every death, Kergis's dream came closer; the opposition dwindled to nothing.

I stepped back from the spike. I couldn't do it. I couldn't kill myself knowing it was exactly what Kergis wanted. These other poor wretches hadn't known what they were doing. But I knew, and I'd rather be killed fighting than just give up like this.

I felt a strength I'd never known before. Perhaps it had always been there. Isza told me once you never really know yourself until you've reached your lowest point. I hadn't understood what she meant. But I did a little now, though I was prepared to admit this may not yet be my lowest point.

My shoulder lanced with pain as I climbed down to the grass again. I had no idea what I was going to do, but I couldn't stay outside the curfew zone; I was bound to be picked up sooner or later. Erdjis and his friend had gone over the hill, probably to some checkpoint in the perimeter fence. I decided to go back the way I'd come and hope my own break in the fence hadn't been discovered. If it had I'd need to find somewhere else to break through.

I was weak from loss of rusz and hungry too now. I hadn't eaten since before leaving on the transport with Isza. Sakat, I missed her. But she wouldn't have wanted me to give up either. She'd want me to live.

26

Maagba Battlecruiser / Cygnus Sector / Hegemony

Rhees had been in the cell now for more than a day. No food. No water. Where the fuck was Volmar and what was he doing?

The door shot open and Volmar stepped through before it closed quickly behind him.

"So you're a prisoner too now," Rhees managed through dry lips. She paused to work some moisture back into her mouth. Prisoner or not, his uniform still looked immaculate. As if he'd just stepped out of his office.

"No," he said. "And neither are you. We are both honoured guests of Maagba War Leader Vatch, with whom I have just finalised a treaty on behalf of the Hegemony."

"You mean the attacks will stop?"

Volmar looked around for a chair, then leaned against the wall. "Absolutely. The Hegemony and the Maagba are on the same side. In fact, they will shortly become part of the Hegemony and provide us with assistance."

Rhees couldn't believe it. "What sort of assistance?"

"They'll be policing this part of the sector for us, mitigating the need for even a token Fleet presence and freeing up resources to be deployed elsewhere."

"You've given them control of Hegemony space?"

A humourless smile passed across his lips. "Black and white again, Lowrans? You are incapable of learning. The Central Administration approved the details by Voss relay a few minutes ago."

So she'd been right. Volmar's actions were completely sanctioned by the CA. "And what about the billions of Hegemony citizens they killed?"

"Aliens. The Brell, Sissilak and Totek have always chafed against Hegemony control." Volmar sighed. "You really don't understand how the system works, do you? While you chased your tail on Herakli, I was gathering hard data about the Maagba. Learning their language from intercepted broadcasts. Modelling their behaviour. Building a composite picture of them which was to prove vital in our negotiations."

So this was the end game all along. The Maagba were just another tool to Volmar, like the rebel ships the Brell and Sissilak nominally controlled. The whole thing stank, but she could see already how it would be sold to the people of Earth. The dead Brell would be downplayed, the treaty would be more of a capitulation by the Maagba, and the rest would be swept out of view.

"They're an interesting species," Volmar continued. "Not endemic to Cygnus Sector. They're more like itinerant marauders, living only to fight. They left their home world behind long ago and far away. However they came to hear of us, I have no idea. But they respect the Hegemony a great deal. They respect the control we exert over our region of space, and the will we possess to do whatever is necessary to maintain that control. In fact, they've wanted to join us for some time. But their culture prevents diplomatic overtures.

"You see, at heart they are a very basic race, brutal but quite easy to understand. They had to prove to us that they were worthy of joining the Hegemony as equals. Hence the series of raids to show their military prowess and provoke a large-scale armed response so they could meet us in open battle. The battle you witnessed. By defeating the 'forces of the Hegemony' they have proved themselves to be a match for us. I broadcasted the coordinates of the rebel flight plan knowing the Maagba would pick up the signal. I also laid down a challenge for them to engage our forces. The only way to facilitate their comparatively peaceful entry into the

Hegemony, and gain access to their military might and technology, was to allow them to win."

A smile spread across his face even though his eyes were cold and hard. "The alternative was a pitched battle with our own Fleet. Tell me, would you have had me sacrifice your one-time colleagues in such a venture just so we could open negotiations? I think not. The fact is, I did what was necessary for the good of the Hegemony, despite your dubious assistance. The Maagba will be a useful ally in the upcoming war."

"War? What war?"

"The war with the Hanloi of course. We didn't just lose contact with the diplomatic mission we sent out there. Those ships were deliberately destroyed. The Hanloi stand across major Voss Space routes towards galactic centre. We can't allow those to remain outside Hegemony control."

Plans spun within plans inside that skull, Rhees thought. And it all sounded perfectly logical if you held the lives of others cheaply. But she'd seen too much death and devastation at Volmar's hand up close. She looked away.

"I know you think your precious Fleet would have handled all this differently," he said. "More 'honourably'. But you're fooling yourself. We work *with* Fleet. Your own father signed off on the plan to use the Brell and Sissilak ships this way. The Fleet are already far too busy massing the attack force for the Hanloi campaign."

Her father ... Rhees stared at him. What the fuck was she caught up in? It felt like some horrible nightmare where everything she thought she knew was a lie.

She made to lunge at Volmar, but he pulled a small blaster from his pocket and levelled it at her. She sat back on the floor.

"So predictable. I had hopes for you, Lowrans, despite your obvious faults. I know you went behind my back on Herakli to contact Fleet. Yes, you thought you'd covered your tracks, but we're not fools. You're a loose cannon and a liability."

"Why are you telling me all this?"

"Another thing I admire about the Maagba: they believe the life of the individual is meaningless when compared to the collective. Each Maagba will gladly die if it benefits their leaders."

The door shot open and two Maagba entered. Volmar stepped back as they grabbed Rhees by the arms. She struggled, but it was clear after only a few moments that it would be impossible to break free. They pulled her roughly to her feet.

"So there's one more service you can provide for the Hegemony," Volmar said.

The aliens dragged her towards the doorway. When she refused to walk, they simply lifted her off the deck. She hung suspended between them, legs kicking helplessly.

"What is this?" she shouted.

"The Maagba culture demands a *raktaa* – a blood sacrifice to seal the treaty. There are Earth culture correlatives, but none quite so … extreme," Volmar said.

The Maagba carried Rhees into the corridor, moving quickly. "Get the fuck off me!" she shouted.

"Don't worry," Volmar called after her. "I'll tell your father you died in the line of duty. In the best tradition of the Corps. And rest assured I will continue to do whatever I think is necessary. For the good of the Hegemony."

She craned her neck to look back at Volmar. "You fucking bastard!" she screamed. But there was no response and as the corridor curved she lost sight of him.

She was helpless, suspended between these two hairy monsters. She tried thrashing around to throw out their centre of gravity but they held her too firmly.

At the far end of the corridor a door stood open. Another Maagba was waiting inside, standing beside a thick post set into the decking. The alien drew one of the longer black metal batons she'd seen earlier and activated it. A coherent column of energy extended from the business end and it vibrated loudly. Rhees didn't need a diagram. She had minutes to live.

Her two captors walked her through the door, dropped her to the deck and tethered her hands to the post with a long cable. One took a small hinged tube and closed it over the cable ends near her wrists. When the tube was removed the cable looked like a single piece. At least her feet were free.

The Maagba stood back, and the one with the baton silently raised the energy blade above head height. If this was a ceremonial killing it would be a quick one.

"So this is it? No speech about my noble death?" she said.

The Maagba hesitated.

"I'm not going quietly," Rhees said.

She flicked the cable into the air and pulled its loop down swiftly, passing it through the energy blade and severing the cord, then barrelled into the Maagba holding the blade, knocking it to the floor. The baton skittered away across the deck. She rolled on top of her executioner and grabbed its sidearm, kneeling on it to keep it down. She brought the blaster's beam up in a smooth sweep and the two Maagba who had brought her here fell to the ground dead. She shot the one struggling under her knee in the back of the head.

Her hands were still tied together. She couldn't angle the blaster to cut the cable close to her hands and be sure to have ten fingers afterwards.

She looked up. Another group of Maagba were tearing down the corridor towards her. She aimed and fired. Out of charge. She bent and swept up the baton, held it in front of her, the long energy blade humming loudly. It was all she had.

She stood with her back to the post as the Maagba ran into the room. They were all armed but none of them had pulled their weapons yet. Perhaps they wanted her alive so they could ritually kill her.

"If you want your raktaa," she said, waving the blade at the nearest Maagba, "it's going to cost you."

None of the Maagba moved.

Rhees's heart was pounding. "Come on!" she shouted.

Still no movement. Then the nearest Maagba took a step forward. Rhees adjusted her grip on the baton, but the Maagba was still out of range.

It pointed to its dead comrades. Blood was pooling on the floor where the beam had sliced through flesh. "Raktaa," it said, and then again more insistently, "Raktaa."

Rhees had no idea what was happening, but her heart was slowing, muscles unknotting.

The Maagba reached for its sidearm, but slowly, and laid it on the deck behind, then took a small device from a pouch near its waist. It was like the tube the other Maagba had used to tie Rhees's wrists. It held the tube up, then pointed at the bodies again. "Raktaa."

"This is the blood sacrifice?" Rhees said. "You don't care whose blood?"

Her arms were tiring and she dropped the blade so it pointed obliquely towards the deck. Fuck, she thought, maybe I'll live.

The Maagba stepped forward, one hand empty and open, palm towards Rhees, the other holding the tube between two fingers. Rhees brought the blade up again, but what was she going to do – slaughter all the Maagba on the ship with a fucking light sword?

Slowly the Maagba reached out and slid the tube over the cable tying her hands. The two ends fell open, and Rhees transferred her blade grip to one hand, curling the other so the cable unwound from her wrists.

The Maagba stepped back and said something to the others. They left. The remaining Maagba held a hand out to Rhees, then swept it towards the corridor and walked out of the room a few steps, before stopping and repeating the gesture.

Rhees followed, but she kept tight hold of the baton, and picked up the discarded blaster on the way. It wasn't much better than a sword against a shipload of uglies, but it made her feel better and the Maagba didn't seem to mind.

It kept walking, checking behind every now and then to see

that Rhees was still following. She didn't think she was being taken somewhere else to be killed. They could have overpowered and killed her in that room.

They walked along corridors and through too many doors. She didn't see anyone else. She wondered where Volmar was. The bastard was probably already on his way back to Herakli. But what about Denev?

Finally, the alien led her into a hangar. There was a row of ships on the deck: the small fast craft that had attacked the rebel fleet in Voss Space. The last ship was open, a small ladder hanging from its hatch. The Maagba pointed to it.

"Where's my partner?" Rhees said. "The man I came with?"

The Maagba spoke in its creaking language and pointed again.

She couldn't stay here, and she couldn't make them understand.

She found the cut-off switch for the energy blade, grasped the baton and blaster awkwardly together, and climbed the ladder into the small lock. She looked back. The Maagba was still standing on the deck, then it turned and walked back the way it had come.

Rhees operated the hatch mechanism. The short ladder retracted and the door closed snugly. She walked through the lock and into the cockpit, stowed the baton and blaster under the seat and sat in front of the controls. It seemed they were giving her a ship.

There was a single blast of a warning klaxon. Rhees tensed, but nothing was moving outside. Then the large hangar door began to move silently aside. The stars were waiting.

"Fuck me," she said under her breath.

The controls weren't too hard to work out. She fired up manoeuvring thrusters and, after a shaky rise from the deck, feathered the controls forward to glide along and out into space.

By the time she'd turned the vessel, the battlecruiser was already accelerating, part of a quickly receding group of ships.

∞

Denev was on his feet before the door was fully open. But it was only Volmar. The comptroller stepped into the room. The door remained open behind him.

"Relax, Operative. We can leave," he said. "The Maagba have agreed to work with the Hegemony. The whole mission has been a success."

Denev wasn't sure how to answer. He doubted the word "success" could be applied to anything that had happened since they left Herakli.

"Where's Rhees?" he said instead.

Volmar sniffed and looked down at the floor before looking up again. "I'm afraid Lowrans won't be joining us. She escaped her room sometime during the night and attacked one of the Maagba guards. They killed her."

Dead? Denev felt the familiar pain inside threatening to overwhelm him, but he couldn't let it. Not here in front of Volmar.

The comptroller was watching him intently. Denev had a strong sense that he was in more danger now than he had been during the battle between the Maagba and the rebels. The comptroller was a callous, heartless killer. A man that would sacrifice hundreds of lives. Just how far would someone like that go? He'd hated Rhees and threatened her on more than one occasion. Had she really escaped, or did Volmar have her executed to rid himself of an annoying complication?

"She was a woman of action to the last," Denev said.

Volmar nodded. "A regrettable trait. Come."

He turned back into the corridor, and Denev – with no belongings to gather up – followed, catching him up just outside.

Maagba guards were stationed at regular intervals. Volmar spoke to one in their creaking language as they passed by and received an answer that appeared to satisfy him. It looked like they were retracing their steps to the hangar and their ship.

"She betrayed us, you know," Volmar said as they walked. "Or tried to anyway. She contacted Fleet behind all our backs and erased the logs on the scoutship to cover her tracks. She could have ruined everything."

Denev was still trying to understand how Rhees could be dead. Was Volmar lying about that? But no. He couldn't see a reason why Volmar would want to keep her imprisoned on an alien ship.

"She wasn't Corps material, but I could see why my brother liked her," Denev said. "That wildness in her."

"Her fatal flaw," Volmar said.

They turned a corner and the entrance to the hangar lay open before them. The scoutship was ready and waiting, with what appeared to be an honour guard of Maagba lined up.

"Is Rhees's body onboard?" Denev asked. "She had a father, I think."

At the end of the line, the nearest Maagba held out the hand weapons they had been relieved of when they were captured.

Volmar handed Denev his gun. "I've spoken to her father, Admiral Lowrans, by Voss relay. There's no body unfortunately. The Maagba disintegrated her." He eyed Denev. "Our hosts have repaired the ship's engines. You *can* fly this thing, I hope?"

"I should be able to get us back to Herakli."

In the scoutship, Denev sat in what he still thought of as Rhees's seat. She'd tried to kick against the system and it had gotten her killed. But perhaps it hadn't all been in vain. She'd made him confront some ugly truths he'd ignored for a long time. He felt woken up by her.

Volmar took the seat beside him, and Denev checked the instruments and powered up the manoeuvring engines.

"You've done well, Antwer. So well that I think we may have a position for you on Earth. You're wasted on Prox."

"Thank you, Comptroller."

He doubted this was a reward. If Volmar had the slightest doubt about his loyalty he'd want to keep him close, but perhaps that was a good thing. It was time to find out what had really happened to his parents. Why had Volmar ordered their file sealed? Seeing at firsthand what kind of man he was made Denev wonder if Volmar had been involved in some way. On Earth he'd have direct access to the Datahive. There could be some digital fingerprint in the records that would provide some answers.

And then there was Rhees. If Volmar *had* killed her …

He'd bide his time and show Volmar what a good boy he was. And then Denev would decide what to do with the Troels Volmar.

27

Aktiuk, Homeworld / Kresz System / Lenticular

I scrambled halfway up the slope, trying to be as quiet as possible until I could see the fence. The suns were setting and the shadows had deepened along the roadway. It was hard to see where I'd broken through, which was a good thing. I couldn't see any guards or movement up there, though that didn't mean they weren't watching. But why would they? Why expect someone who broke out of the curfew zone to want to break back in?

Slowly I worked my way up the last stretch of slope to the fence, keeping under cover as much as I could. I came level with the road and looked to right and left. Dusk was falling. Nothing moved. I parted the ragged edges of mesh and pushed through. And stopped in agony as a wire strand scraped along the raw edge of my hood. I almost cried out but managed to stifle it. I backed up a little until the wire snapped back, then, favouring my wound as much as I could, pushed through again.

I pulled the wire shut behind me and ran into the lane I'd sheltered in before. It was much darker now and I followed it into the network of lanes between houses. The huge lethargy that had overtaken me after the excision was gone. I could think and function just the same as always. Well, maybe not the same – I was hardly an objective judge. But I didn't feel different to how I'd been on Telsus IV. For the moment, with no other Kresz around me, I could keep up the illusion that nothing was wrong. The capacity for the mind to fool itself is considerable, and I was grateful for that right now. There had been too many shocks crammed into the last two days.

It was fully dark now. I pulled out the instruction sheet the Hegemony had given me; it was printed in very formal Kresz. No one was allowed on the streets of the curfew area between the hours of three-five and one-two. Though I kept to the backstreets there was always the chance I'd be discovered or blunder into a patrol. I had to find shelter, but no one would take in an excisee.

I stuffed the instruction sheet away and looked at the map. The city was entirely enclosed. I couldn't shelter in the forests beyond. The desert was also forbidden to me. And even if I did break through the mesh again, there was too much open distance between me and House Czerag lands. I'd be easily picked up or picked off.

I wanted to do something to hurt Kergis and the Hegemony. Slow their progress somehow. Isza would say I'd know what to do when the time came. For now, all I had to do was stay alive. I kept wandering, and eventually came to the old Adepts area closer in towards the city centre. One of the larger houses had taken a hit from some weapon and the whole structure was a pile of rubble. I skirted the broken brickwork and saw a small opening between support beams that were still mainly intact. Perhaps I could stay here.

Gingerly I eased my body through the opening, careful not to jar my wound against the rubble, and sat. I couldn't lie down, not on my back, and there wasn't enough space anyway even if I twisted on my side with my legs pulled up. I wedged myself as far into the hole as I could and closed my eyes. I was still hungry, but there was nothing I could do about that. At least I could rest.

My thoughts drifted, but no worldmind opened up to take me into sleep. I tried to imagine I was off-world. That none of this had happened and I hadn't come home yet.

I didn't know what time it was when I woke, but it felt very late. I was freezing cold. My arms and legs were stiff and sore and the wound across my back was slowly throbbing. I couldn't stay here –

I'd die of exposure.

Painfully I crawled out of my hiding place and stopped dead as I saw light farther down the lane. Two blue lights swinging slowly over the cobbles and rubble, just as slowly moving closer. It had to be Hegemony.

As quietly as I could I scrambled in the opposite direction, keeping low, but trying not to let my calf plates or the hard shell on my hoofs scrape along the ground. Past the rubble of the house was a blank wall, untouched by the blast, smooth and with no gates or other openings in it. I risked a look back. The lights were still coming, but steadily. They hadn't seen me yet. A very high, rough stone wall abutted the smooth wall with no gaps between them. It too had no openings that I could see in the darkness. I had to keep going.

The next wall was smooth like the first, but there was a square hole cut into the ground at its base. I nearly fell into it. Steps led down to a door set in the masonry. I tried it. Unlocked. Inside was in darkness. The room felt empty of life. I shut the door behind me. Even if I was discovered, I was inside now during curfew. I was obeying their laws.

I couldn't sleep any more. The wound across my back throbbed too painfully. So I just sat there, too exhausted even to think. What felt like hours later, I crossed back to the door and opened it slightly, looking up at the line of sky between the buildings. Dawn. The curfew was over.

I climbed up the steps to the laneway. My legs felt suddenly weak and I kneeled, trying to work out where I was.

"There's one of them," a voice said.

Three Kresz, all intact, stood at the end of the lane. Cultivators, House Akczek by the white diamonds worn at their necks. Akczek and Kergis had always voted together. Was Akczek part of this too?

They walked up to me. I made to rise, but the one in front, about my age, shell deepening red, held out his claws.

"No. Stay like that. It's perfect." He pulled a long gaszti from a sheath by his thigh.

The other two, younger but just as large, flanked him either side, blocking the laneway.

I looked in the other direction. The walls at the far end had crumbled, spilling bricks across the path. I could jump over them if I wasn't so exhausted. Or wounded.

"What do you want?" I said, still kneeling.

"Only to do our duty," the leader said. "We will clear the Way for you. End your suffering."

"And did you do your duty when the Hegemony ships were attacking?"

He paused. "Fighting is not always the answer."

"Sometimes there's no question."

The knife blade pointed at me. "You are excised. You are outcast from Kresz society. You are not part of the Way."

The other two reached their long arms out and held me above the upper elbow on either side.

I looked at each of them. "What gives you the right to do this?"

"Quiet," the leader said. "Be at peace."

He held the blade in his left claws, backing the hilt with the flat of his right claws to thrust it when the tip was placed between my chest plates above the major pulse point. The thought flashed through my mind that I could just let them do it. But then I remembered the dead in Cz'kras Park.

The two accomplices were holding me loosely, attention focused on the point of the blade rather than on me. I pulled back hard and felt my excision scar rip open. The two Kresz were pulled inwards, crashing into each other and falling across me and down in a heap.

The other Kresz, startled, leaped over his friends, angling the blade down towards me. I grabbed his wrists, stopping the blade, but his full weight was above me, driving the point down. The two Kresz on the ground were thrashing to get themselves untangled. They'd be free soon.

The one with the blade stared into my eyes. I could see his fury even if I couldn't feel it. The knife edged towards my chest. My wrists were shaking, my attention divided between the blade, the others to one side, and protecting my hood stump.

"I can't. I'm sorry," I said.

I pulled down, shifting to one side and twisting his wrists at the same time. I thought my own would snap, but the blade turned at the last moment. The hilt hit hard dirt and the point, facing up now, pierced his chest plate just below the neck guard. He fell, still clutching the knife buried hilt deep in his chest. The other two, free now, froze in disbelief.

I ran for the open end of the lane and rounded the corner, listening for the slap of hoofs behind me. There was nothing, but I ran on as far as I could, unable to believe what had just happened. I had killed, or at best badly wounded, another Kresz. I'd hurt him and felt nothing. I didn't plan it – it was him or me. But I did it all the same.

Side street blended into side street. Those left alive were still indoors. The city was so empty it made me stand out. I slowed to a walk, imagining the two young Kresz still after me, or telling others about the murderous excisee and organising a search. I pushed that thought away and concentrated on another, just as unpalatable. I could function without the worldmind; I'd proven that in space, on other worlds, and finally here and now. But life was about more than simply functioning. There would be others wanting to grant me the "release" of death. It was just a matter of time.

I turned back towards the city centre. I needed to lose myself in a crowd, if that were possible now. And I needed to work out what to do. Was Homeworld completely subdued or were there still some areas battling the Hegemony? It seemed unlikely. Their advanced ships and sheer force of numbers had been overwhelming at the Point. But perhaps some resistance survived in secret.

And what of the Lenticular? There were such things as mutual aid agreements. Surely the Jantri'va, Telsans and Svestans would come in force when they learned of the invasion. Maybe not to save us primarily, but to prevent a similar incursion by the Hegemony against their own worlds. The longer they took though, the bloodier and harder it would be to force the Hegemony off-world. The invaders would fix the Point, more of their ships and troops would come, and they'd dig in and build ground fortifications, orbital platforms, deeprange warning systems – everything we should have had to stop this from happening in the first place.

By now, I was back in the Merchants Quarter. Half the storefronts were closed, or simply empty and abandoned, but those that were open were selling what little they had in a desultory fashion. People moved around in simulated normality. The suns were higher in the sky now and the day was becoming hot. I squatted in the shade of an empty shop out of the main thoroughfare and watched. I had become invisible again.

Other excisees passed through the crowd. They may as well have been walking ghosts for all the notice anyone took of them. On one level I couldn't believe such a thing would happen, but I also knew people needed the everyday in times of trouble. They'd cling to it with a desperate strength just so they could tell themselves everything would turn out all right, even when the evidence of their eyes showed them it wouldn't.

Across the packed-dirt roadway, an old Kresz fussed at the fruit set up in angled boxes along his shopfront. His shell was dark brown edging to black, and his left leg moved a little stiffly as he walked up and down, picking up jawna and polishing them, or sprinkling the lefa berries with water so they shone with a ruby lustre. He looked at me now and then. At me, not through me. I avoided his eyes. I didn't want pity, or to be ogled or despised. Whatever emotion he was feeling towards me, I was mercifully blank to it.

The suns moved around and I shuffled into the lee of the empty shop to keep in the shade. I think I slept off and on, hunched there. I couldn't be sure. I was tired, and hungry, and the hood stump was constantly aching now. It felt hot too.

I must have closed my eyes for more than a moment. When I opened them a pair of brown-black hoofs were in front of me. I tensed. Looked up. It was the fruit seller, a bunch of jawna in his claws. He held them out to me without speaking. Part of me wanted to ignore him. Did I look so pathetic that I would beg for food now? But I needed it.

I took the fruit and didn't know what to say. But he said it for me.

"Come into the shop when you feel like it. I have hot adza. You'd be welcome." Then he walked away.

The jawna were good. I ate the bunch quickly, leaving the skins in the dirt. The old Kresz was back at his shop, looking up and down the street, talking to the occasional passer-by. He didn't look my way again.

There weren't so many people on the street now. And I hadn't seen any Hegemony troops since I'd first sat down. I stood awkwardly, my legs stiff after squatting so long, and walked across the road. The old Kresz watched me approach, then turned and walked between two banks of boxes into the darkness of the shop. So I followed him, down a bare corridor stacked on one side with fruit crates and into a small bright kitchen with a stove and a plastic table and chairs.

He pulled one of the chairs out and walked over to the stove. I sat down.

"When I can't see you," he said with his back to me, "it feels like no one else is in the room."

I didn't need this. I began to stand. But he turned quickly for someone his age, his claws thrust towards me, urging me to sit again.

"Please, I'm sorry. I didn't mean to offend. You're tired and hungry. Please sit and honour my home."

I sat. Where else was I going to go anyway?

"I've never spoken to a ... one not of the worldmind." He turned back to the stove and lifted a long-handled copper pot from the flame. "I've never been to the Hub to see those aliens from the other Lenticular worlds either, or anything else like these 'Hegemony'. So many new things, you see. So forgive me. My name is Elrak. Please, welcome guest, what is yours?"

"Udun."

He poured the hot adza into two rough earthenware cups on a tray beside the stove, then felt in his hide apron and brought out a bunch of lefa berries and put them on the tray also. He deposited the tray on the table and sat opposite me with a sigh.

"So many new things," he said again.

I looked at his worn apron, his open-weave tunic beneath. "You don't carry a house sigil."

"Oh, I'm not really interested in the houses. I've lived in Aktiuk among Kresz of all houses and lodges too long for it to matter much."

"And you talk to excisees."

He pushed my cup of adza towards me. I took it and drank.

"Well, yes, there is that too. But there are so many of you out there, you see. It's unprecedented." He paused, thinking, then blinked. "Unprecedented, yes, that's the right word. Most of them walking around look like they barely know where they are. They're dead behind the eyes. But not you. If I'm so different, I think you might just be too."

"I'm used to being different," I said, failing to keep the irony from my voice.

"Well, there. It's a good thing, see. I've been different all my life. Strange ideas people used to say. Some of them didn't like it and ended up not talking to me. Some of my own house, for years. It didn't bother me much. I never lacked company." He pushed the bowl of lefa berries towards me. "Eat, eat."

I ate the whole bowl without noticing and then stared guiltily at the table when I realised.

"More where that came from," he said, rising. "Rest here. I'll be back soon."

"You don't think I should be euthanised?" I said when he returned with more berries and dropped them in the bowl.

"I'm a bit old for that. I think you'd have the advantage on me."

"Not you," I said. "You don't think it in general."

"Well, here's the thing," he said, sitting down. "There are a lot of your kind out there. And as far as I can see you're not doing any harm and you haven't deserved what was done to you. You fought these aliens, didn't you?"

"Yes, for all the good it did."

"But you fought. You fought for us, for those you love, and this was your reward. It seems to me you deserve something better, so how can I wish you more ill? I should be thanking you." He indicated the berries, the adza. "I am thanking you. Not very well, but I don't have much."

"Not everyone thinks as you do."

He looked at the scratches on my carapace. "I'm sure they don't, but as I said, I'm used to that. Here, look at my leg." He pulled back from the table. I saw that it hung unnaturally compared with the other, twisted a little. "If this leg had been much worse, I might have been euthanised and what would have been the good of that? How does my existence upset the natural order? If you want to live, then live. That's what I say. But the trick is to live well, live meaningfully. There's plenty of intact Kresz that do neither."

I'd never heard anyone talk like this, not even Tzek who was the most pragmatic person I'd ever come across. But Elrak seemed disposed to help me. And right now I needed help. I was exhausted, but on top of that I was sure I was sick. The wound wasn't healing properly and if it was infected I could die.

"Have you heard any news?" I asked. "Anything about the battle, or what's happened on any of the house lands."

He sat back, turning away a little, then glanced at me again. "I see the colour on your travel pouch. You're House Czerag."

"Yes. What have you heard? Please," I added, when he

remained silent.

"They took the worst I think. Worse than Aktiuk. An aerial bombardment. You live in the escarpment?"

"Yes."

"It belongs to Kergis now."

"Anything else from Czerag lands?"

"No."

Then the deep desert hideaways might still be safe. I hoped they were.

"There were similar strikes at many of the house strongholds," Elrak said. "Not Kergis of course."

"What do you know about him?"

"He's installed himself as a kind of ruler, if you can believe it."

I could.

"He's disbanded the Council. There was a broadcast. All very pompous. Old Kergis sitting in an empty Council chamber droning on about unification and Sakat and divinity. According to him the Hegemony is here to help! I'm as old as he is – older – but I'm not half as foolish."

"He means to rule us," I said.

"Then we're all in trouble. Nothing good comes from one person wielding more power than they should. Nothing good at all."

"Before the Hegemony took over, Elrak – was there any word about calling for help from the Lenticular?"

"I wouldn't know, Udun. I'm sorry. Sakat knows we needed it, but whether we'd ask for it …"

That was a worrying thought. And who would have sent a distress call anyway? It was a military decision, but it was hard to know if Resgtu, Dean of the Defenders Lodge, was part of the conspiracy and how far down the chain of command it might extend. There was a chance a signal wasn't sent, that no Lenticular fleet was coming to help. But even if that were the case, trade ships visited the Hub regularly; some may even have been docked when the attack started. Wouldn't they carry the news back if they got away? And even if they hadn't, how long before someone came looking for them?

There was a noise in the front shop.

"I'm closed," Elrak called. "Come back tomorrow."

I listened. Silence. Then a noise closer, steps in the corridor.

Elrak scowled and got up. "What is it n–"

Two Hegemony soldiers entered, long weapons slung across their fronts. Not pointed at us. Not yet.

"If you're closed then you won't mind helping us," the one who had entered first said through its voder. "Work detail. Outside now."

I stood with Elrak. The Hegemony moved aside and I followed the old Kresz down the corridor and out into bright sunlight. Others were outside: more Hegemony and two groups of Kresz. I saw immediately what divided them. One group was intact, the other excised. The intact group looked at me with barely concealed disgust. I walked to the other group and Elrak followed me.

"No," I said. "You'd better go with the others. I don't want to cause trouble for you."

"I don't know any of those idiots and I don't want to," Elrak said. "You're my friend. That's if you don't mind, I mean."

"I don't mind, Elrak." I felt touched by his words, more than I would have normally.

The intact group were clearly not happy to be here. They talked in angry whispers but there was nothing they could do. The soldiers had the weapons, and the hood power could not be used until the mantle was fully engorged. There would be time enough to shoot and kill an aggressive Kresz before that happened.

The excised group – there were one-four of us now – stood quietly, not looking around. Their eyes slid over me as I approached but there was no greeting there, or recognition. It was as if everything that made them distinct people had shut down.

"You see what they're like?" Elrak said. "Their bodies are here but their minds have gone elsewhere. The shock, I suppose. I – I can't imagine what it must be like."

"I hope you don't have to," I said.

The Hegemony trooper who had led us out of the shop activated its voder again. "Listen up! As Hegemony citizens it is your duty to assist in the reconstruction effort here. We will proceed to the spaceport where we have some work for you. At the end of the day you will be fed."

"I'm not working with those." A young Merchant, one of the intact, had spoken. He was looking directly at me.

The Hegemony soldier raised its weapon. "You'll work with them or you'll become one of them. It's your choice."

The Merchant was silent.

"Form a line and get moving," the soldier said.

We walked through the shop-lined streets and back into the residential area, covering in a more direct route the path I'd taken from the spaceport … how long ago? It felt like a cycle or two. There were one-three soldiers escorting us, one leading at the front, three on either side of the line, spaced along its length so there was no chance of escape, and two bringing up the rear.

Kresz on the street stopped to watch us pass. It was impossible to guess what was going through their minds. As a people we had kept our planet off-limits to aliens; now they walked among us at the invitation of a hierarch. They were stronger than us, their technology more advanced. The feeling of powerlessness that brought must have a deeply damaging effect. That and the mass excisions. It wasn't at all certain we could survive as a society. Kergis obviously had plans for what the Kresz people would become, but he was only one person and the Hegemony's invasion had already had a deep impact. With loss of pride came loss of identity. The longer the Hegemony stayed, the more likely it was that we'd become a vassal state with no culture of our own.

Elrak stumbled in front of me and I caught him. We kept walking, him leaning on me and favouring his stiff leg. I felt nothing at all from the contact. No empathic sense remained and I felt certain it was gone forever. Elrak was probably thinking the same thing but he was too polite to say anything.

"Are you all right?" I asked.

"Not used to walking so far and so fast." The breath whistled through his spiracles. "I'm glad you're here, Udun."

It was a simple statement but the words burned across my mind. Could my life still have meaning, crippled as I was? It was all a matter of choice, I realised. Choosing not to suicide in Cz'kras Park; choosing not to die at the claws of those intact Kresz in the alley. Choices could have negative consequences, but also positive. Elrak was glad I was here. Could I find a positive in this, not just for myself but for others? Sakat knew we needed help. Could I help?

We walked on, and Elrak leaned more heavily on me as he tired further. It made the going difficult for me too, but I felt a little stronger now; an inner strength.

Sura had reached its zenith by the time we made it to the spaceport. At the front entrance, our escort exchanged guttural growls with the Hegemony troops stationed there. I couldn't understand any of it but I think at one point they laughed. It wasn't anything like Kresz laughter. It was high-pitched and cruel-sounding.

We walked onto the main runway used by suborbital craft. The skystalk to the Hub touched down at the other end of the field and I could see its tensile thread stretching into the clouds. No cars ran there today.

Some way along the runway there was an odd assortment of walls backed by mounds of dirt and braced by metal supports. The strange construction ran across the centre of the runway, effectively closing it to any winged craft. As we came closer I saw that the walls didn't butt tightly against each other. They were built to overlap in two separate roughly circular arrangements. Our line halted close to the nearest wall.

The Hegemony soldiers put on their helmets, then took it in turns to check each other's helmet fitting and body armour.

The lead soldier spoke again. "All right. One of your ships cracked up bad on the runway here, behind these shield walls. They spilled their atomics all over the place and it's your job to clean them up so we can get this runway working again. There are shovels over there." It indicated a pile of tools I hadn't seen before: long poles ending in flat oblongs with curved-up edges on two sides. "Take one each. There are shielded boxes on the other side of those walls. Scoop the atomics up and into the boxes until they're all gone. Got it?"

The intact Merchant who had spoken earlier said, "Where are our shield suits? We can't take exposure to radiation."

"We don't have suits your size," the soldier said. "Do your job, and you'll get anti-rad shots after. The radiation won't harm you." It pointed its weapon at the Merchant. "You first. Move now."

The Merchant had no choice. None of us had. We picked up a shovel each and filed between the walls and the piles of dirt. In the centre was a wide space dominated by the rear half of the crashed cruiser I'd seen with Isza. It was tilted at a precarious angle above the remains of the shattered front section. There was a breach in the side of the hull nearest to us where the reactor had burst through and broken open. Drive pellets, highly radioactive, had spewed out the breach and were piled against the ship almost as high as my head. It would take a long time to clean them up.

"Are you up to this?" I asked Elrak.

"I'd better be. I don't think the Hegemony has much time or patience for 'citizens' who can't do their duty."

He held his shovel by the pole and pushed it into the pile of radioactives, lifted a load, swung it around and into a yellow cone-shaped bin, one of many dotted around the crash site.

I did the same, taking as large a load as I could, trying to speed things up, but half of the pellets slid off the shovel as I lifted it.

"Don't take too many," Elrak said.

Even with all of us working together without a break it would take several hours to clear the mess.

As we worked, the skin under my plates started to itch. I put it down to imagination until Elrak complained of the same thing. I knew from my studies at the escarpment that the pellets were fed in a steady stream into the reactor where they were annihilated. They contained an inhibitor to stop a bunch of them going critical, but I didn't know if that made them any less radioactive to us. The scar along my back began to complain too with the constant bending and flexing as I drove the shovel into the pellets and lifted load after load into the bins.

We worked on. Some of the Kresz were detailed to swap out the bins when they were full. The guards changed regularly, spelling each other to avoid overexposure I guessed, even though they all wore shield suits and hung back, away from the central mass of the pellets.

"Keep away from that," Elrak said, gesturing at the tail of the ship. "The weight of pellets must be holding it upright. It'll fall eventually. Just make sure you're not in the way when it does."

Shadows lengthened as the suns fell. The walls cast patches of dark across where we were working until the Hegemony brought in portable lamps on long poles that sat above the shielding. It seemed we were here until the job was finished, nightfall or not.

I started to weaken. Elrak looked terrible. His stiff leg made it difficult to bend and he wasn't able to lift much with his shovel any more, but when he sat down to rest the lead Hegemony soldier came up and prodded him sharply with its weapon, leaving a score on his chest plate.

"Up. Work," it said.

I helped Elrak stand and the soldier watched as he bent and lifted a pitiful number of pellets into the bin. His claws were shaking as he held the shovel to take another load. The soldier stepped forward again, then there was a clatter from behind and it turned in that direction instead.

The Merchant who had complained and two of the other intacts had thrown down their shovels.

"Pick those up and get back to work," the soldier said. Other soldiers were closing in, weapons at the ready.

The Merchant bent and scooped up his shovel again, but instead of obeying he threw it at the closest soldier and, bending low, jumped. He soared up to land on the very tip of the ship's tail section, which tilted, stopped, and then, with a shriek of metal, fell as he leaped again.

Soldiers scattered, some firing.

I grabbed Elrak and we jumped, falling side by side near the shield walls as the ship's tail hit the ground and threw dust, pellets and debris into the air. It was chaos. People were running everywhere.

I caught sight of the Merchant on the other side of the ship. Then the shooting started again. The soldiers fired indiscriminately at anything that moved. One of the excised screamed and fell not an arm's length from us. It was a massacre.

"We have to get out of here," I shouted at Elrak. "Can you stand?"

The air was thick with weapon fire, and somewhere nearby a siren was wailing. I saw the lead soldier near the pile of pellets, standing on a Kresz who had fallen. It pushed its gun into the Kresz's face and fired. The head disintegrated.

I got an arm under Elrak and heaved him up against me. There was a sound like a snap and Elrak groaned. I looked down at him. There was a smoking hole in the middle of his chest plate. He fell against me and we tumbled to the ground again.

"Go," he said.

"I won't leave you."

"Go! They're going to kill us anyway. I won't have you die for me." He grabbed at my neck guard, pulled me close. "Live meaningfully."

"If I'm going to live meaningfully, then I'm starting now," I said.

I laid him back on the dirt and got my claws under his dorsal plate. He was heavy but I managed to half-lift and half-drag him. There was an explosion to the right, throwing up more dust. Tiny rocks or perhaps more pellets rained down, crackling on my carapace. I shuffled us both into the shadow of the broken ship and looked around. Most of the work crew lay dead or dying. The Hegemony troops were walking among them, checking the bodies or looking for any survivors lurking in the wreckage.

Just then a group of the small fighter craft that had been so effective at the Point flew directly over the runway. Everyone looked up. I took my chance, heaved at Elrak with all my strength, and covered the short distance to one of the dirt mounds on the perimeter. Another heave and we were round the first ring of shielding. No one was there and no one, it seemed, had seen us.

I got Elrak through the second ring of shielding and laid him against the uprights. It was dusk now; only sura remained above the horizon. Ground cars were coming from the port control area, their lights flashing as they bounced along. I couldn't hear any more shots. They'd need another work detail to finish the clean-up. Would that group of Kresz have to clean up the bodies of those newly murdered?

Elrak groaned. "I can't go any further, Udun. Don't stay here with me. I don't want that blame."

I kneeled beside him. I didn't know what to do. Leaving felt wrong.

"Go!" he half-shouted, too weak to do more. "You've helped me more than I expected or deserved. The killing's stopped now."

"You're sure?" I asked.

The ground vehicles were nearly here. I grasped his claws and squeezed. Without my hood there was no empathic link, but the look in his eyes said he understood.

28

I kept low and followed the curve of the shielding round the other side until I was out of sight of the vehicles. Then I ran as fast as I could, ignoring the stiffness and pain in my back. I kept going until I was on the fringe of the main runway. Sura disappeared – the sky flashed briefly silver blue with its leaving – and full dark descended. Back at the crash site lanterns bobbed between the shielding as the Hegemony troops searched the area. I didn't hear any more weapons fire. They couldn't have missed Elrak so it meant he was all right. I hoped they would see to his wounds as they'd seen to mine after Treaty Mount. Ironically it was more than any Kresz would do for him.

I could do nothing here, that much was clear. Isza was gone. House Czerag was scattered. Elrak had taken me in, but he was the exception, almost as strange as me. If the Hegemony didn't work me to death or kill me, my own people would. I had to leave, find out what the Lenticular knew of the invasion and what their plans were. After all, I wasn't without friends there.

The problem was how to get away. There was no way I could ride the skystalk to the Hub, and had little chance of boarding a ship when I got there. The only other option was to hide onboard a ship launching from the spaceport. But I couldn't determine which ships were going where or when they might be leaving. I might end up on a short round trip to the Hub and back.

No lanterns shone my way so I moved again, heading towards a group of dark shapes midway between the spaceport administration buildings and the sea. These were the warehouses Isza and I had landed near. The last time we were here, there was a large number of transports parked together on the other side of the warehouse facility. I kept close to the building's walls – the whole structure was in darkness – and when I came to a corner, tentatively looked round it. My desert eyelid penetrated the darkness, showing a blue-toned image of rows of transport ships parked there. There didn't seem to be any method to their distribution. Old transports – looking like they'd been mothballed ready to take the final flight out to the Czerag tekla-reclamation facility – sat next to newer models.

I couldn't see anyone on the apron, so I left the side of the building and moved quickly to the stubby landing legs of the nearest transport. Very cautiously I moved along the nearest row, running from one set of landers to the next, stopping in the shadows and looking around as much as I dared, straining for any detail that might single out one transport above another, something that showed it would be leaving soon and hopefully travelling out-system.

I'd gotten maybe halfway along the row of ships when I saw movement up ahead. I crouched behind the nearest transport leg, moving to get the barest glimpse of the next ships in the line. There was a fuel tanker parked between this line of ships and the next one over. A large Kresz, a Cultivator by the height of him, was securing a refuelling tube from the tanker to the underside of a transport. Lines ran from the tanker to four other transports. The Kresz walked back to the tanker and pulled down levers above each of the tubes. So, here were five transports refuelling.

I looked at them more closely. The nearest was small, turbines only, so fitted for atmospheric flight alone. The one beside it was the same. Over from them in the next line of ships was a larger transport, newish, turbines and spacegoing. That was a possibility. The next one along on my line was older, but the same series as the other spacegoing transport. The problem was, these were mainly used for Hub runs: they carried cargo that couldn't go on the skystalk for safety reasons.

That left the last transport connected to the tanker. Sitting in the next line over, it was bigger than any of the others. It also looked like it was well past retirement, with deep scrapes where docking arms had grabbed it off centre too many times, and dents and patches around the cargo-bay hatch. Most of its bulk was taken up by an antiquated but still powerful-looking set of tenspace engines. I could board this transport or wait for a more likely opportunity. But that might not happen before dawn, and I couldn't afford to be caught out here in daylight. At least this one looked like it was going on more than a Hub run. Exactly where was impossible to tell.

Refuelling took place after cargo had been loaded – I knew that much. So these transports would be leaving soon; maybe at dawn after the pilots had their morning meal. I waited till the Kresz at the tanker began to push the levers back up on the fuelling control. While his attention was focused on unlatching the hoses from the smaller ships, I covered the distance to the nearest transport opposite in an odd gait to stop my hoofs from clacking on the runway surface. I ducked behind the transport's landing gear and waited.

The Kresz dragged both hoses back to the tanker and began folding and stowing them. I moved silently, keeping in the darkness, and stopped behind the thick leg of the medium-sized ship that was also being refuelled. I heard the Kresz grunt as he pulled at the docking ring, and then he was dragging the hose back to the tanker.

I had to move a little round the landing leg to keep out of sight as he dealt with the last two ships, stowed their hoses, started the tanker engines and drove off. Then I made my way to the landing gear on the large transport and walked aft. There was a hatch with a ladder extending part way to the ground. I reached up almost to full extension, gripped the bottom rung with both claws and pulled my body up. The wound across my shoulders lanced with pain. I felt sure it had opened again.

I got my hoofs up on the ladder and climbed the few steps to the door. The control panel set in the hull showed the door was unlocked. There was another device near the control though: a circle of small lights flashing in sequence round and round. It could be some kind of Hegemony alarm or sensor. I had no idea how to disable it but I couldn't wait out here any longer. I activated the hatch and it hissed up, too loudly to my ears. But no one came.

The ship seemed to be empty. I went inside and the hatch hissed shut. The inner door opened and automatic lighting came on in the corridor. The floor plan was similar to Bvak's ship, except on a larger scale. I stood in a central gangway, which led to the flight deck on the left, and to the aft kitchen and sleeping quarters on the right. I turned right, and stopped at an elevator door. When I touched the call pad the lift opened immediately, and carried me down to darkness a few seconds later. The desert eyelid swept across my vision, showing a dirty corridor with lubricant and other unidentified liquids pooled on the floor. Doors to individual cargo holds opened off the corridor to left and right. I chose one far enough away from the elevator so I would have time to hear anyone approaching.

The door sliced up and I had to bend a little to get through. Cargo podules were stacked on either side, held by restraining nets. There was a narrow gap between two stacks that looked big enough for me. I crawled into the space, tilting my body so my shoulders would fit – and almost cried out as the hood stump scraped on the lowest podule. The pain was intense and I vomited on the deck.

I moved further into the gap, favouring the wound on my back as much as possible. My arms shook with the effort. I lay down and the shaking moved from my arms to the rest of my body. I felt hot then cold and had to swallow the urge to vomit again. My back throbbed with pain, punctuated by sharp twinges where the hood had been. My skin tingled, whether from the imagined effect of radiation poisoning or something more serious, I didn't know. And the hunger that had become a constant for me was joined now by a deep thirst. I could die here, I thought. They'd find me when they unloaded the cargo and just dump my body. No one would ever know what became of me.

∞

The deck vibrated beneath me and I realised we were in flight. I'd missed lift-off. I shifted and felt the floor wet beneath me. The wound had opened in my sleep. How much more rusz could I lose before I passed out and did not wake up?

I heard the hold door open and two sets of hoofsteps.

"He said it's in this one or the next. A weight imbalance. Enough to throw us off." It was a Kresz voice, joined soon after by another.

"Why isn't Kdan doing this? He stowed the podules."

"Let's just get it done."

It sounded like they were moving down the corridor nearest the entrance. I heard them tapping podules, pausing to shift some of them, perhaps reading the manifest coding. They were being thorough and that gave me some time. My mind was racing, desperately trying to work out a plan. Perhaps if I was quiet enough, I could move as they moved, staying out of sight. It was a large hold with lots of podules. But I'd have to be completely silent.

I crawled out into the access way between the stacks. The two Kresz were in the next row back towards the door, about halfway to the bulkhead wall. I lifted my hoofs, careful not to scrape them along the deck, and moved in the opposite direction. I came to the end of the row of podules. The exit was to my right. I moved left, two rows over, and started towards the bulkhead end. The others were still making steady progress along the rows. They hadn't heard me yet.

"Do you smell rusz?" one of them said.

I stopped. This wasn't going to work. I looked back the way I'd come. A trail of rusz spatters marked my progress. They'd find it soon enough and follow the rusz to me. I'd be caught, questioned and killed.

I retraced my steps to the other end of the row. The entrance was to my right. But I'd have to cross the mouth of their row to get there, and then where to?

I walked as briskly and quietly as I could. Still no sound of discovery. But the entranceway was shut and they'd hear it open. I got ready to run and activated the door. It shot up with a hiss.

One of the Kresz cried out, "Who's that?" He appeared at the end of the row of podules. His friend joined him.

I ran into the main gangway, turning right. They were behind me. I jumped, keeping low in the confined space, managed to keep my balance as I landed and ran on. I'd gained a bit of space.

The gangway was a dead end. Then I saw the round access hatches set into the bottom of the bulkhead wall. Without slowing I lunged, hit the deck on my side and slid straight through the hatch, catching the purge lever as I fell through into a pod's globe-shaped interior.

Alarms sounded behind me, cut off as the hatch closed over. Then I was thrown back as the emergency pod thrusters pushed away. Light flared through the window, a blue and twisting arm of energy. We were in tenspace still.

The ship fell away behind me, but I was coming up fast on the tenspace wall. If I hit, the pod would be crushed.

The transit control was beside the purge lever. I pulled it and the universe smashed into me. I screamed.

When I could open my eyes again, I was in realspace. The pod was tumbling wildly, then the dampeners kicked in and it levelled out. I couldn't strap myself into the crash-chair because of my hood stump. Instead I kneeled on it and held the straps in my claws, as if I was riding some crazed beast. Through the pod's ring of ports all I could see were unrecognisable stars. Then a steady beeping started up.

I looked around, trying to locate the emergency transponder. It was keyed to send out a distress signal automatically. If the transport had followed me out of tenspace …

I found the panel above my head. There wasn't an off switch;

who would want to silence a distress beacon? I punched up into the panel, then again and again. The metal parted and I pulled at wiring inside. The beacon finally silenced, or the internal alert did. For all I knew the thing could still be broadcasting. I looked at the panels and controls in front of the crash-chair. The left screen was filled with diagnostics. One flashing line made me relax: *distress beacon inactive.*

Ahead of the pod lay an asteroid field, the individual rocks composed of some purple mineral the same colour as a youngling's carapace. Ordinarily it wouldn't be wise to enter, but I wasn't sure what the ship I'd just left would do. It didn't seem likely they'd just let me go.

I was travelling too fast at the moment to enter the field. The controls of the escape pod were simple; they had to be so anyone could use them. There was a lever set into the floor in front of the chair marked "thrust". I grasped it and pulled back gently, and through the port saw a puff of propellant. The pod slowed and I held the strapping with my free claws to stop from falling forward against the curving wall. Still too fast. I pulled the lever again, holding it back as a steady stream of propellant slowed the pod to what felt like walking pace.

As I released the lever and cut the flow, the pod drifted between two asteroids at the edge of the field, both of them bigger than my vessel. The left screen threw up a flashing set of words – *ship transponder identified* – then a string of numbers ending with the character that marked it as one of ours. So they'd followed me out of tenspace. We must have been near a transit junction, which made sense. My emergency transit should have killed me. But it meant they were able to backtrack in realspace.

I couldn't see the ship yet, and hopefully they hadn't seen me, but it wouldn't take a genius to work out where I was. There was nowhere else to hide. Heedless of the risk, I pressed the lever forward to take me into the asteroid field.

It was hard to keep track of all the rocks around me. They were generally moving with the same speed and orientation, but there were variations brought on by minor collisions that sent them spinning or moving against the flow until more collisions set them back on course again. Something scraped along the top of the pod and the burst of strength that had helped me escape the ship suddenly deserted me. My vision clouded and I felt I was going to pass out.

I couldn't. Not here. I jammed a claw into the wound across my back. I cried out, but the pain focused me and the faintness passed.

How much longer could I keep going like this? Dying here or dying on Homeworld made very little difference. I'd been lucky – if you could call it that. But trapped in a tiny escape pod with limited fuel in an asteroid field – and now no distress beacon – was where that luck must surely run out.

Through the port, I thought I caught a glimpse of the transport ship just as I passed behind a larger asteroid. I grasped the control lever and slowed the pod, matching speed with the large rock, keeping it between me and where I thought the transport was. Had they seen me? I didn't know what type of sensors the transporter had, or if it was equipped with weapons. They could be scanning for biological signs, or the concentration of metal in the pod hull. They could model the movement of individual rocks in the field and look for any anomalies.

This rock my ship was travelling with might shield the pod and my own presence – it was certainly large enough. If I stayed with it, matching velocities, I might survive. But for how long and to what purpose?

Because it's what Isza would do, I thought angrily. Because as long as I'm alive I can act.

29

Rhees had seen for herself that the ship had Voss Space ability. And she knew roughly where she was. But where the fuck could she go? Volmar would denounce her if she turned up in human space. And any Fleet ships would likely attack first and sift through the wreckage later. She was piloting one of the infamous raider ships after all.

Besides, she didn't want to go back even if she could. Her father had condoned the HDC action out here. She believed Volmar on that. He had no reason to lie to a dead woman. Rhees couldn't understand it. Even though they weren't close, she'd at least thought she knew what her father stood for. Fleet upheld the law with judicious use of force. If there was a fight to be had, the reasons for it were clear and the fighting happened out in the open. By contrast, no one she'd known had a good word to say about HDC. But Fleet and HDC were two sides of the same coin, both serving the ultimate aims of the Central Administration, which sanctioned wars and murders and anything else they deemed necessary for the good of the Hegemony. Was this really the way humanity chose to survive? How had things got so fucked up?

She thought Denev was starting to see things her way. But there were twenty billion people on Earth, and billions more spread across Sol system. Most saw the Hegemony as necessary after the war with the K-Chaan, but not everyone on Earth was happy with the status quo. Denev had accused her of sounding like an Inclusionist. She'd never really thought about politics before but maybe she was. Through chance, circumstance and her own pig-headedness she was on a new path now. She had no idea where it would lead, but she'd promised to live meaningfully. She wasn't about to give up.

Ahead, space was rippling, the stars seeming to wobble in place. She blinked, rubbed at her eyes. She was too exhausted to see straight.

When she opened her eyes again she was nose to nose with another ship. It hung directly ahead: a down-curved front section sweeping back and out into an equally curved delta wing enclosing a saucer. It was big. Big enough for a crew of forty or fifty. Humans, that was.

Fuck, she thought. Not again.

They hadn't fired on her. Yet. It made for a welcome change of pace.

She opened comms and tried standard hails, running up the frequencies. No response.

The other ship was too close. She brought forward thrusters online, building power ready to back away. Still nothing over comms from the newcomer.

She engaged thrust to back away slowly, watching the other ship all the while. But the view of it wasn't shrinking. Was it following? She increased engine power. Sensors said the other ship wasn't moving. Nav said neither was she.

Main engines. Full reverse. The cockpit shuddered, engine noise building to a tortured roar. No change. The ships still sat nose to nose.

She looked at the array of controls, identifying functions, and brought weapons online. Gun ports rolled open. Missiles showed ready. Would they let her go before she fired?

The cockpit was plunged into darkness and engines shut down. Controls were offline. Weapons systems dead. At least she still had life support. She sat back in the chair. There would be no escape.

The other ship moved closer, the curved nose then the wing

passing slowly over her cockpit bubble. It stopped above her and she heard the docking ring engage. There was still nothing on comms.

She unstrapped from the chair and walked aft into the small chamber between cockpit and main engines. There was a secondary lock above her head. That was where the other ship had engaged. She could hear the metal of the hatch door ticking as the cold vaccum of the outside was replaced with some kind of atmosphere. The indicator set into the door displayed a running set of characters in whatever alphabet the Maagba used. She had no control over ship systems, but whoever was on the other vessel did.

There was a final *thud* and then the hatch door swung down, a ladder extending. Rhees stepped out of the way until it locked in place on the deck beside her.

She went back into the cockpit. The energy sword under her chair wouldn't be much use – she was no swordsman – but she felt better with the blaster in her hand.

She climbed up into the narrow lock chamber. The outer door stood open above her head. She could see the roof of the other ship's lock entry but couldn't hear any movement. The space felt empty. She climbed through the opening one-handed, keeping her blaster pointed to the floor but ready.

The lock on the alien ship was unremarkable. The inner door was open in front of her, showing a short corridor with walls angled outward so the space was roughly like an isoceles triangle standing on its point.

"You won't need your blaster." The voice seemed to come from everywhere. "We're not going to harm you. And its energy cell has been neutralised."

Fuck. She dropped the blaster on the deck. "Who are you?" she said. "Show yourselves."

"We will. We don't want to frighten you. Your kind haven't encountered us before."

"If you're trying to reassure me, it's not working."

"Follow the light track. It will direct you to a room where we can talk. I'll join you shortly."

On the floor in front of her a solid purple line glowed, leading to the end of the corridor ahead and disappearing round a corner to the left. She had no other choice; she followed the track. If they wanted to talk, well … talking was good. Sometimes it led to dying but not always.

Round the corner she found what looked like an elevator. The door irised shut behind her. There was no sensation of movement, but when the door opened again she was looking down a much longer corridor, the glowing track still laid out ahead of her. The corridor was empty of life. They – whoever they were – were keeping out of her way. Or maybe there weren't many of them onboard.

The track ended halfway down the corridor at another door. The room inside was unremarkable and furnished with a single chair beside a table on top of which rested a glass of what looked like water. She sniffed the liquid. It smelled like water too, but she wasn't about to try it.

The door closed as she sat and she stood again immediately. The door opened. She looked out into the corridor. It was still empty. The message seemed to be "you're not a prisoner". Except she was. Her ship was disabled.

She sat and the door shut again.

Minutes passed. She looked at the glass of water. She was thirsty but she still wasn't going to drink it.

The door slid aside and a figure stood in the opening. It wore what reminded her of marine-issue space armour but it was more angular, and marines favoured sensor-neutral, non-reflective black for obvious reasons, not shiny gold. The figure was much bulkier and taller than a human – over two and a half metres tall. The faceplate was clear but she couldn't make out any features inside, just a mist that sparkled like fireflies in smoke.

"I am Nok of Jantri'va," the same voice as before said.

The figure moved to stand opposite her, then bent and locked into a sitting position. The engineering was superb. She couldn't see any obvious joins or weak points. But it showed her this alien's body plan was at least close to human.

"I'm Rhees of … well, nowhere really," she finished and nearly laughed. She was feeling a little overwhelmed by the unreality of all this.

"Everyone is from somewhere. Do you want to go home?"

"What?"

"It's a simple enough question. You come from Sol system. Do you want us to take you home?"

"You couldn't get within ten parsecs of Sol," she said.

"You don't know what we can do. Or we could release you to fly home in your Maagba fighter."

Her laugh was short. "I'd be just as much of a target."

"You do want to go home, don't you?"

She wasn't prepared to answer that. "Who are you?"

"I'm Nok of Jantri'va."

Which was no help at all. She tried another tack. "Why am I a prisoner?"

"You're not."

"Right. So I can leave now. You'll release my ship."

The silence stretched.

"We haven't finished our conversation yet, but some things are clear," Nok said. "The Hegemony ship you arrived in left without you. Your release from the Maagba ship was entirely unexpected. Despite being given a vessel you did not set course for a Hegemony-controlled planet. And right now you exhibited strong resistance to the suggestion of going home."

"Are you reading my mind?"

"No. But we've been gathering baseline data on your emotional state and responses since you came onboard."

There was nothing to say to that. They were reading her even now. But what game were they playing?

"I think," Nok said, "that your relationship with the Hegemony is … complicated. And, no, this is not some kind of trick, though I don't expect you to believe me now. But we may be able to help each other."

"I very much doubt that," she said.

She was completely alone and at their mercy. Which meant she couldn't afford to show weakness. Nok wanted something from her – most probably intel. That meant she had something to bargain with. She had to use that, and build on it if she could. She needed intel of her own.

"Jantri'va is your home planet?" she asked.

"Yes."

"And where is that exactly?"

"You don't expect me to tell you?" Nok asked.

"I suppose not."

"So I will."

He – she supposed from the voice it was a he – held out a gauntleted hand, palm upward. It must contain a holoprojector because a swathe of stars appeared in the space between them. She recognised Hegemony space. One star was blinking. From the position she guessed it approximated where she'd emerged from the Maagba ship.

"Our worlds are in the Lenticular," Nok said.

The holo shifted, tracing a path in along the galactic arm to what Rhees judged was the midpoint and a collection of stars forming a loose ellipse.

"You're a long way from home," she said.

"As is a small attack force from your Hegemony."

"I don't understand."

"There is a planet in the Lenticular. The indigenes simply call it 'Homeworld'. The people there are insular and peaceful, although their internal politics can be volatile at times."

The starfield disappeared, replaced by what Rhees assumed was one of the planet's natives. It was tall and heavily armoured, like a cross between a crab and a lobster but with only two arms and two legs, although these were strangely jointed and much longer than a human's. The eyes too were human-like, even if the thing's mouth looked like a horror show.

"This is a Kresz," Nok continued. "As I said, peaceful for the most part. They certainly didn't deserve to have their capital city destroyed by Hegemony forces, their people slaughtered."

More death and suffering, Rhees thought. The Hegemony Central Administration doing what it did best.

"You see this cowl behind the head?" The image rotated and Rhees saw what she'd missed before. It reminded her of a cobra's hood. "This organ is unique in all the species we've encountered. It provides the Kresz with an empathic sense: the ability to instantly understand the other in any situation. It's the bedrock of their civilisation."

The image disappeared, and Nok's hand dropped to rest on his suited knee. Rhees gazed into his faceplate.

"The Hegemony harvested the hoods from every Kresz that opposed them. Many who survived the procedure suicided, unable to live with what was done to them. Those still alive are barely functional for the most part." The glow behind the faceplate brightened. "This is not simple occupation and suppression. It's beyond even calculated murder. It's the malicious destruction of the soul of an entire people, something only a species that has lost its own soul could contemplate. This is the human race."

Rhees looked away, but she couldn't unhear what the Hegemony had done. She knew Nok was telling her the truth; the Hegemony was more than capable of what he'd described.

"The Hegemony is still on Homeworld," Nok said. "The Kresz are still suffering."

"Why are they so far out?" It wasn't so much a question for Nok as for herself. It didn't make sense.

"We don't know. We suspect a prelude to a larger invasion."

"So you want intel on the Hegemony," she said. "You could

torture me for it."

"We could," Nok said. "But we won't. We don't just want information on the Hegemony. We want you to help us defeat them."

Rhees sat back in the seat. She'd happily betray Volmar. But was she so lost that she'd betray her own species?

Hegemony
Diplomatic
Corps

343-34/6444890-1

Hegemony Diplomatic Corps

Species Report: Kresz (343-34/6444890-1)
Eyes only: Troels Volmar, Comptroller Hegemony
Diplomatic Corps

Report on interrogation of Kresz subjects – document #88(0)-1

Following the covert capture of the Kresz deeprange vessel *Might of Gnow*, a full interrogation of survivors was undertaken.

The species physiology is highly compartmentalised, able to survive significant amputation and damage short of major trauma to the head or torso. As a result physical torture was limited in efficacy, with better results afforded through full-spectrum psychotropic drugs augmented by cephalic probes.

None of the subjects survived. The following report covers a number of aspects of the Kresz civilisation.

1. Creation myth and associated beliefs

The Kresz believe that their homeworld was drawn from their primary sun by *Sakat*, which trink tech translated as "god of death" with a 78% accuracy rating. Sakat moulded the sun-stuff into a ball and placed it in orbit. The sun-stuff cooled and solidified, but its atmosphere was poisonous so nothing could grow or live on it. It was locked in this form, unchanging, until Sakat moved across the face of the world and sucked all the poisons from it. Where Sakat passed, life sprang up, and Sakat was pleased, because without life there can be no death. This legendary act by Sakat seems to have had a significant effect on the Kresz psyche, setting up a powerful relationship between cleansing, life and death. The Kresz believe that the first life was very simple, and as it grew and prospered, it changed and gave rise to more complex forms.

After many thousands of years passed, the first Kresz sprang up on the planet. As these proto-Kresz grew and differentiated, Sakat cut down those that were deformed or otherwise weakened so the Kresz would become stronger and stronger. In this way the Kresz stumbled upon a faith-based theory of evolution.

It was the prophet Tlonat who divined Sakat's purpose over 5000 standard years ago. Tlonat believed that as each new form of life was born more complex than the previous, Sakat had set the world on a path to develop perfect living organisms which would be free from disease, all-wise and all-powerful. It followed that the Kresz, as the only sentient species existing, were to be the fulfilment of that goal, so to ensure they continued to develop as a strong race they took on the work of Sakat. They killed any Kresz born deformed because this was an indication that those individuals were unfit. Likewise the sick or injured were left to either recover or die "at the will of Sakat". As a result the Kresz never developed any form of medicine or healers. The fact that they seem amazingly resistant to a range of disease pathogens (as released on test subjects) points to a genetic advantage gained as a result of thousands of years of careful selection. Euthanasia is practised as a matter of course in modern Kresz society. The advent of the communion (see section 4: *Language*) is seen by the majority as further proof of the divine evolution of the Kresz species.

As a side note: this also explains their insular nature. Kresz do not seek out alien contact because they see alien life as "not on the path of Sakat" and therefore unable to become perfect beings.

This striving for perfection also finds its way into the reproductive habits of Kresz. For a full report on this aspect see section 2: *Social structure and politics* and section 3: *Physiology and sexual reproduction*. Once a Kresz foetus has been initiated, the hierarch of the house visits the female and introduces a string of his own DNA into the partially fertilised egg. The child then has donor DNA from the father, the mother and the hierarch. This is believed to give the child a genetic advantage because the hierarch, as leader, is seen as the most perfect Kresz of that generation. The hierarch insemination is also necessary as a determinant of the caste, or body type, that the child will inherit. It is said that the hierarch has a degree of control over this, although the exact mechanism is not known as no hierarch was present amongst the test subjects.

This belief in evolutionary perfection and euthanasia could provide valuable leverage for HDC operations. Further analysis is recommended.

2. Social structure and politics

Kresz society is a strictly ordered hierarchy in which social standing depends on a mixture of function and lineage.

There are six houses to which all Kresz belong by virtue of birth. These six houses own the entire landmass of the homeworld, with the exception of the capital city of Aktiuk and its surroundings which was deemed neutral territory during the first of the house wars 3500 standard years ago. As well as the six houses, there are also six lodges representing the main streams of employment in Kresz society. This means that the normal citizen will be represented by their house hierarch, on the grounds of their familial connection, and by their lodge dean by virtue of their profession.

The hierarch of each house and the dean of each lodge holds a seat on the council, which is the ruling body for the Kresz people. Leadership of the council rotates regularly between the houses and lodges. Each house and lodge also has its own internal council which advises the hierarch or lodge dean on matters and assists in the administration of house/lodge affairs.

The Kresz hierarchy is organised along the following lines:
1. House hierarchs, lodge deans and their functionaries
2. Scholars
3. Adepts: professional disciplines such as scientists, lawyers, administrators
4. Cultivators: agents of agriculture and fishing
5. Merchants: agents of manufacturing and commerce
6. Priests
7. Defenders

The six lodges are consequently Scholars, Adepts, Cultivators, Merchants, Lodge of Sakat (which comprises the priesthood) and Defenders (official name of the warrior lodge).

The six houses and their hierarchs are:

Kergis. The Kergis hierarch holds the title of protector and commands the combined Kresz armies and fleets in war.

Ukat.

Akczek. The Akczek hierarch controls lands with an abundance of gemstones and precious metals; consequently they have much to do with the Merchants Lodge and strong ties with the military.

Czerag.

Haketiug.

Dageru.

There is a small underclass of criminals, who after repeat offences have their mantle surgically removed (see section 3: *Physiology and sexual reproduction* for further information) and are banished from Kresz society into the desert wildernesses to die.

Kresz body types differentiate according to function, which is determined by the hierarch on secondary insemination (see section 3: *Physiology and sexual reproduction*).

3. Physiology and sexual reproduction

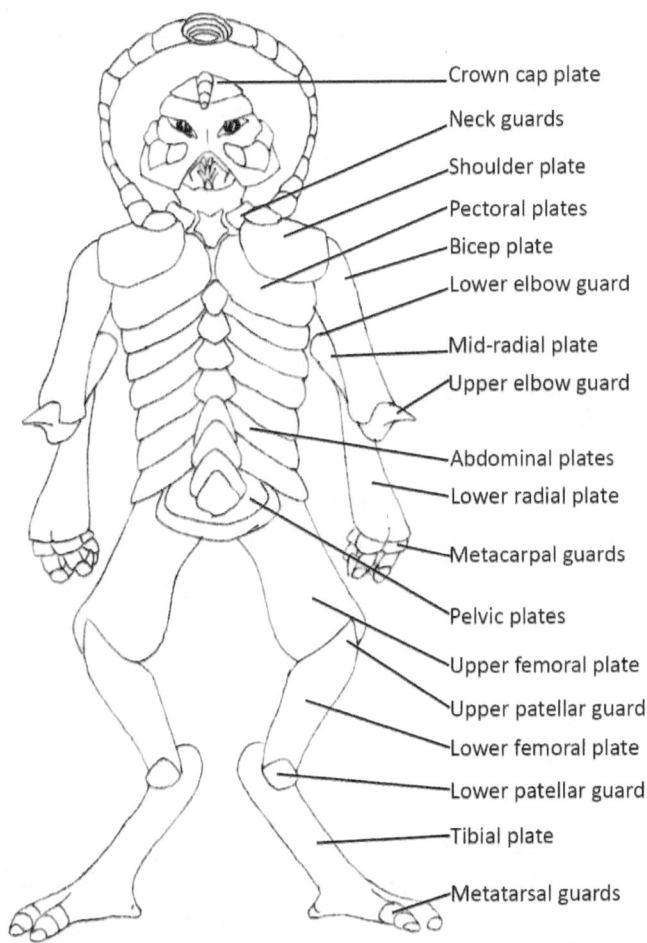

Typical armour arrangement (non-Defender)

Kresz males stand on average 2.8m tall. The females are generally larger, averaging 3m. The exception to this is Kresz that differentiate as Defenders. Both Defender males and females average 3.5m. Merchant class are shorter. Cultivators have longer arms that extend to the ground, the upper body and arms being more ridged and less smooth than other castes. Further information will be supplied when more test subjects are available.

The Kresz homeworld has a gravity equivalent to 1.4 terrestrial standard gravities. Consequently the Kresz have both an endo- and exoskeleton. The endoskeleton is composed predominantly of calcium, while the exoskeleton is chitinous in nature, and continues to thicken and change colour throughout the life of the Kresz.

The chitin forms a series of interlocking and overlapping plates over a tough scaly hide which is completely covered by the chitin, in effect forming a living armour. Tests demonstrated the chitin of a fully grown Kresz is effective at deflecting small-arms fire and diffusing energy weapons up to and including level three.

The Kresz foot is akin to a terrestrial dromedary possessing two toes which spread flat as pressure is applied. Much of their homeworld is desert, and it is thought that this affected Kresz evolution significantly. As further proof, the eye is complex but possesses two eyelids: one fleshy; the other of clear cartilage which not only provides protection from sandstorms but is shaped to provide an additional lens that enhances visual contrast and distance vision.

The Kresz leg has two opposing knee joints, the upper much like a human knee and the lower canted towards the rear as in terrestrial birds. Musculature running under the chitin is well-developed and subjects demonstrated an ability to jump up to 4 metres vertically and 10 metres horizontally under extreme circumstances. Bipedal in nature, the Kresz's pelvis and vertebrae are similar to human forms, however the arms have a double elbow in the same arrangement as the leg joints. Consequently both the arms and legs are significantly longer in proportion to the rest of the body than in humans.

Kresz hands possess two clawed fingers arranged opposite an opposable thumb. This is believed to be the reason for their base six numbering system (see section 5: *Numbering and time systems*).

The Kresz mouth most closely resembles that of a terrestrial crab with a number of overlapping jointed feelers. The various mouth parts have a number of different functions including feeding, olfactory and taste sensors, and verbal communication.

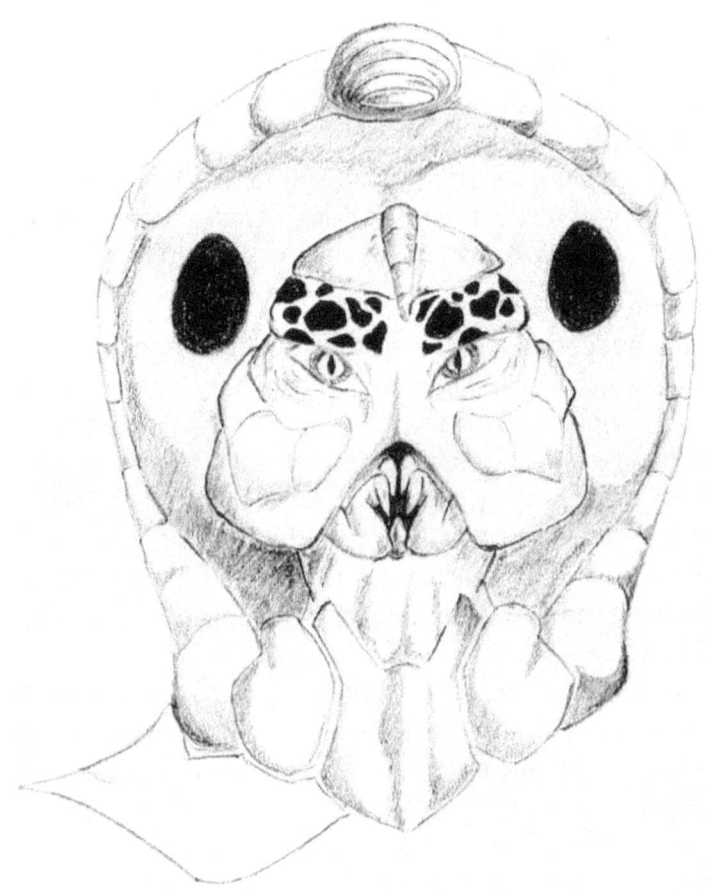

Kresz appearance (with mantle engorged)

Internal organs

Internally Kresz share much with insect-type creatures. Kresz breathe a mixture of gases within terrestrial tolerances but they breathe through spiracles: tiny tube-like structures in the secondary hide.

The Kresz lungs, fed by air intake through the spiracles, have more in common with the book-lung structure of terrestrial locusts. Oxygenated fluid is pumped through the lungs to the extremities by a number of independent "hearts", six in all: two in the chest, two in each upper arm, and two in each thigh. These can independently shut down to restrict fluid loss following major trauma; e.g. the loss of a limb.

Their excretory systems bear out this resemblance to insects and their early evolution in a desert environment. Various reabsorptive functions, such as volume reduction, regulation of individual electrolytes, adjustment of osmotic concentration and pH regulation, which are associated with distinct renal segments in the mammalian kidney, all occur simultaneously in the rectum of the Kresz.

The Kresz mantle

The mantle, or hood, is a unique organ never before encountered by HDC. It is a fleshy cape-like organ which hangs from the shoulders and covers the upper back of the Kresz. When engorged it inflates behind the head of the Kresz and resembles a terrestrial cobra-hood. It is an extra-sensory organ which allows the Kresz to "pick up" on the empathic state of other Kresz nearby. The Kresz worldmind and "communion" that has resulted was described by subjects as a gestalt experience; however, the Kresz do not appear to share a hive-mind mentality.

The mantle has an older function which pre-dates what the Kresz call "the Emergence". Over short distances it can concentrate and loose electromagnetic energy which appears to have offensive potential. Further investigation of this function is required as a priority when additional test subjects are supplied. A risk advisory has been dispatched to Fleet Command.

Sexual reproduction

Despite the insect-like features of the Kresz physiology, reproduction is similar to mammalian reproduction with insemination of an ovum in the female by the introduction of male sperm following penetrative sexual intercourse. Prior to intercourse the female produces a chemical which acts as a pheromone to the male and also softens the chitinous covering to her sexual organs. The pheromone provokes a cascade of chemical changes in the male also, softening the chitin that protects his sexual organs and enabling penetrative intercourse to ensue.

As mentioned above, fertilisation of the egg is a two-fold process. Initial fertilisation is by the chosen male, but the differentiation of the ovum will not progress past a certain point until the introduction of a second set of sperm by the house hierarch. This sperm contains the information to enable the fertilised ovum to differentiate into a particular caste or body shape. Subjects indicated that the hierarch can consciously control the type of sperm he produces in order to choose the caste of the ensuing child.

4. Language

The Kresz language is relatively standard in structure and syntax. But by Hegemony standards it is fairly blunt and basic with a limited set of phonemes:

a	b	c	d	e
ad | ag | ah | ak | al | ar | as | at | az	bv	cz (ch)	da | de | di | dj (ji)	e/eh | el | ek | er | es
g	h	i	k	l
ga | ge | gi | gu	ha | he | hi | hu	id | ig | ik | il | ir | is	k | ka | ke | ki | kl | kr | ku	la | le | lok/luk
r	s	t	u	z
ra | re / reee| ri | ru	sa | se | sg | si | sk | st | su | sz (sh)	te | ti | Tz (ts) | tu	ud | ug | uk | ul | un | ur | ut	z | za | ze | zi | zr | zu

Yet the Kresz social structure and civilisation appears to be as complex as many others we have encountered. The reason for this variance is believed to be due to the existence of the Kresz empathic sense. Consequently nuances which in Earth society would be expressed in language are communicated through empathic means in Kresz.

5. Numbering and time systems

The Kresz use a senary (base six) numbering system. Terrestrial equivalents include ancient Sumerian.

Base 10

100,000s	10,000s	1000s	100s	10s	Units

Base 6

7776s	1296s	216s	36s	6s	Units

Their language expresses numbers as compound phrases, so where

0	=	ri
1	=	ek
2	=	sa
3	=	alak
4	=	ruz
5	=	djah

a number such as 154_6 is expressed as ek'djah'ruz.

36s	6s	Units	
1	5	4	$= (1 \times 36)+(5 \times 6)+(4 \times 1) = 70_{10}$

The Kresz time system varies markedly from Hegemony Standard, relying as it does on the Kresz numbering system and the diurnal and annual motion of their homeworld.

Kresz Time Periods			Heg Time Equivalent	
1	"second"	=	0.6	seconds
1	"minute"	=	0.36	minutes

1	"hour"	=	1.296	hours
1	"day"	=	1.944	days
1	"week"	=	1.666	weeks
1	"month"	=	2.499	months
1	"year"	=	1.2497	years

The Kresz "year" or cycle, which is the closest translation available for this time period, is based on one rotation of the homeworld around their trio of suns.

The year contains six distinct seasons which correspond roughly to the six month divisions.

6. Technological index

The Kresz species is space-faring and possesses a form of Voss Space drive – though the term they use is tenspace. Their world is serviced by a beanpole-type space elevator. While their technology is equivalent to late 21st century terrestrial, they have access to more advanced technology through local trading partners (see section 8), including limited access to gravitic generators.

7. Military potential

Although proud of their war-like past, the Kresz lack easy access to technology equivalent to that of the Hegemony which means they are not considered a military threat. The empathic bond they share could be exploited in a combat scenario, and is the reason why wars and violent crime have all but died out on their planet.

8. Contact with other species

While the Kresz are an insular species they have limited trade arrangements with a number of other alien species in a nearby area of space called "the Lenticular". Little was known of these other species by the subjects interrogated. Further intelligence on the Lenticular is required.

Jang Hollis
Diplomatic Corps Information Exchange Officer

GLOSSARY

Adjubon	Capital city of the main landmass on the planet **Herakli**.
ah'lok	Kresz small, feathered reptilian flying creature.
Ah'lokna (season)	Kresz season when the ah'lok swarm and mate in the desert reaches. Weather is dry and hot.
Aktiuk	Chief city of the Kresz Homeworld. The Treaty City where the houses made peace after the **Emergence**.
Aphsan	Lenticular sentient species, resembling cone shape mounds with a thick brow ridge of sensory tissue. Close trade partners of the Telsans.
ataz	Largest of the Kresz Homeworld's three suns; golden yellow in colour.
auto	Hegemony term for automobile or small, personal ground vehicle.
Battle for Earth	A pivotal moment in the Earth–K-Chaan war, when the enemy penetrated the Solar System and almost invaded Earth before being driven back.
Betlaan	A peaceful planet and home to **Atalna**. Due to political infiltration by the Hegemony, the rightful government was overthrown and replaced with a puppet government controlled by HDC.
Brell	Cygnus Sector alien species from the Brell Conglomerate. Bipedal but horse-like. Tall, covered in fine brown hair, long-necked and long-headed with long ears. Their home planet is **Brell Prime**.
Central Administration (CA)	The executive governmental body of the Hegemony.
communion	A full empathic sharing between Kresz.

compensator	Hegemony ship device that assesses the stability of a Voss Space chamber in three-dimensional space and selects an exit point out of Voss Space.
Cygnus Sector	A region of space that was annexed and settled by the Hegemony shortly after the defeat of the K-Chaan. Home to the **Brell**, **Sissilak** and **Totek**.
Cz'kras Park	An area of Aktiuk set aside for Kresz house funeral ceremonies.
Datahive	HDC headquarters and main surveillance and analysis facility, situated on Earth in Cape York Conurb.
datanook/nook	Immersive data conduit for HDC operatives. It connects directly with the operative's mind, establishing a **synapse link** that enables them to interface directly with the data architecture in cyberspace. The nook imposes a **neural brake** on the user during interface with the datastream to still any involuntary muscle movement while connected.
dean	Title for the head of a Kresz lodge.
Defence Force	The combined Kresz defence fleet, comprising all ships owned by Kresz houses and lodges and controlled by the Defenders Lodge when required.
djel	Second in size of the Kresz Homeworld's three suns; red in colour.
Elysem	A domed city on **Telsus IV**.
Emergence	The moment in history when the empathic link manifested between all Kresz.
endar	A type of tree on the Kresz Homeworld with blue foliage.
Endikar	A **Brell** colony in Cygnus Sector.
gaszti	Kresz traditional weapon – a long knife, carried in a sheath.
Hanloi	An alien species that inhabits galactic centre. A Hegemony mission to Hanloi space was lost, presumed destroyed.
Herakli	Hegemony-settled planet in Cygnus Sector.
Hierarch	Title for the head of a Kresz house.

House Akczek (Kresz)	House colour: white; house lands: the northern reaches of the planet. The Akczek hierarch controls lands with an abundance of gem stones and precious metals; consequently they have much to do with the Merchants Lodge and strong ties with the military.
House Czerag (Kresz)	House colour: brown; house lands: the escarpment and the deep desert. The Czerag are traditionally nomadic, producing much of what they need in hidden areas of the desert. Their main trade item is tekla, an ore which they mine and refine. It has good properties for spaceship hulls particularly for Voss Space craft.
House Dageru (Kresz)	House colour: red; house lands: the southern reaches. The Dageru lands occupy the southern pole and extend around a major proportion of the far southern landmass. Dageru lands produce textiles and electronics.
House Haketiug (Kresz)	House colour: yellow; house lands: plainlands to the east of the Inland Sea. The Haketiug are traditionally agriculturists.
House Kergis (Kresz)	House colour: green; house lands: the equatorial belt of tropical rainforests. The Kergis hierarch holds the title of Protector and commands the combined Kresz armies and fleets in war.
House Ukat (Kresz)	House colour: blue; house lands: the Inland Sea and the southern shores. The Ukat hierarch oversees cultivation and harvest of the Inland Sea.
Jantri-va	Lenticular sentient species. From a highly radioactive planet. Always wear radiation armour when interacting with other species.
Kareee (season)	Kresz season of rains. The drought breaks and, particularly over the Inland Sea coastal regions, there is heavy rainfall. Temperatures begin to fall. Planting begins for the growing season.
Kedisz Ocean	Kresz Homeworld's southern ocean.
K-Chaan Empire	Aggressive alien species in the Earth–K-Chaan war.
Kresz caste: Adept	Professional disciplines such as scientists, lawyers, technicians, pilots etc.

Kresz caste: Cultivator	Agents of agriculture and fishing. Cultivators have elongated limbs and are taller than most Kresz, except for female Defenders.
Kresz caste: Defender	Defenders are the tallest of males, despite lacking a second knee joint and mid-calf. Their armour plating is thicker and they have an oversized arm – usually the left – which ends in a massive pincer. Prior to the **Emergence**, Defenders were a warrior caste who fought for their house hierarch.
Kresz caste: Merchant	Agents of manufacturing and commerce.
Kresz caste: Priest	The priests are devoted to maintaining the teachings of the Kresz god, **Sakat**.
Kresz caste: Scholar	Academics, researchers and scientists, Their claws are thin and delicate and their feeder claws are similarly longer, used for manipulating delicate instruments as much as for eating.
luk'ah	Kresz fish and a valuable food source. Also the name of a Kresz-style singleship similar to a ramcraft.
Luk'ah (season)	Named after the indigenous luk'ah fish which is the primary food source from the Inland Sea. Luk'ah is the period when these fish are harvested. The cooler weather is coming to an end. Temperatures are rising as the rain ceases to fall.
luk'ri	Larval stage of the luk'ah fish.
Luk'ri (season)	Named for the larval stage of the luk'ah fish which develops along the shores of the Inland Sea at this time. The weather is hot but changeable and thunderstorms predominate.
neural brake	See **Datanook**.
podule	A standard-sized cargo unit used across the Lenticular.
processor	Kresz computer.
Prox Base	HDC intelligence gathering post, second only to the **Datahive** in importance.
raktaa	Maagba term for agreement by blood sacrifice.
realspace	Kresz term for space, as opposed to **tenspace**.
rikla	An edible Kresz fern, the heart is considered a delicacy.

Rikla (season)	The season of drought. Harvest occurs during the first few weeks before the heat and lack of rain take their toll. The season is named for the rikla fern which withers at this time.
rusz	Kresz blood analogue. Thick and yellow.
Sakat	The Kresz 'god of death'. Also the name of the season at the end of the Kresz year associated with rebirth.
Sakat (season)	The season of rebirth. Crops benefit from cool days and mild nights and regular rainfall.
setzla	Kresz animal. A predator, the size of a large dog. Known for its cunning.
shield metal	A dense bluish metal that blocks Kresz empathic signals when of sufficient thickness. It is used to line the offices of house hierarchs and lodge deans and other sensitive facilities.
Sissilak	Cygnus Sector alien species. A reptilian analogue, resembling human-size snakes but with four arms. The scales that cover their bodies are thick like an armadillo's plate armour.
skystalk	A space tether and orbital elevator between the Kresz Homeworld city of **Aktiuk** and the **Hub**.
stonewood	A type of tree on the Kresz Homeworld known for its strength.
sura	Third and smallest of the Kresz Homeworld's three suns; blue in colour.
Svestans	Lenticular sentient species. Methane-breathers, large, covered in thick bony skin bristling with spines. Aggressive.
Talos III	Barren world in neutral territory used as a ceasefire meeting place in the Earth–K-Chaan war.
tekla	An ore mined only on the Kresz Homeworld. It has unique insulating properties over a wide range of temperatures and is favoured in ship-hull construction and mining and other heavy industrial applications.
Telsans	Lenticular sentient species. Small, furry and sharp-toothed. Generally brusque in nature.

Telsus IV	A molten world in the Telsan system. The Telsans scoop the abundant minerals from its surface in floating manufactories. They have also constructed cities such as **Elysem** and other habitable areas on suitable floating plates of the rocky crust, covered with crystal atmosphere domes to keep out the deadly air.
tenspace	Lenticular word for **Voss Space**.
Totek	Cygnus Sector alien species. Look like walking kettle drums; communicate by rapping a beat on tightly drawn skin across the top of their body.
trink	Hegemony tech. A translator link, worn in the ear, that provides instant translation of programmed alien languages. See also **voder**.
voder	Ubiquitous Lenticular tech. A voice decoder that enables instant translation of Lenticular languages for the wearer. See also **trink**.
Voss Space	Also known as **tenspace** by the species in the Lenticular. A space that exists above/below/between space – dimensions other than the four dimensions of spacetime. Access to Voss Space enables ships to travel to other parts of space more quickly than by conventional means.
vuscreen	Kresz term for visual display.
yoq	Kresz animal. A beast of burden similar to a buffalo.

THE LENTICULAR

BOOK TWO

TRAITOR'S BARGAIN

AN EXTRACT

1

The transport ship was hunting me and I had no way of knowing where it was. I was going to die.

I nudged the thruster, bringing the pod I'd stolen closer to the asteroid's rough striated surface. A flash of brilliance to my left, and a smaller rock burst apart at the far edge of the asteroid field. Debris smashed into neighbouring rocks, setting up a rippling cascade of collisions. The direction of the burst gave me a momentary fix on the transport's position.

I eased the pod around the asteroid, so close now the hull scraped across it. A wave of dizziness took me and my vision faded.

∞

I lay on the table where they'd excised me. But my mantle was already gone. What more could they take?

Bright lights. Alien voices. But no pain this time. No sensation at all.

∞

I jerked awake as the light from another blast blossomed silently near the centre of the asteroid field. I was still sheltered against the large rock, but if I blacked out again …

The next explosion was closer, but behind me. The pod's hull rang with an ominous sound then another long scrape. A second asteroid had been pushed against the pod. I was trapped on both sides. If I moved again I'd disturb the rocks I was nestled between and the transport would find me.

The best thing to do was sleep. Conserve air.

I got as comfortable as possible, then concentrated, slowing the rush of air through spiracles. I felt my pulse points slow in response and let exhaustion take me.

∞

"Udun?"

The voice that spoke my name sounded odd. Attenuated, like sound through a door. Like I was the door, vibrating in sympathy.

White walls glowed with their own inner light. Someone spoke again. But they were too far away to hear me answer.

∞

I woke. A light flashed on the control array. The air supply was almost gone but I hadn't been asleep that long. Whoever owned the escape pod hadn't kept the tanks filled. If I drifted back into comfortable unconsciousness I'd suffocate. But each second I survived made me hungry for another and another. If I was going to die, I'd die doing something.

I eased the thrusters back and forth, gently pushing against one asteroid then the other. There was a disconcerting scraping noise, but it was working. The gap between the rock faces opened until I could see stars above me. I sent the pod moving up. As I cleared the rocks, I looked through the ports front and back, to the side and above, trying to spot the transport. I wanted to see the ship if it was going to fire on me.

No killing shot came. But the transport might be on the other side of the field, manoeuvring towards me.

"Come on," I said, my voice hoarse and desperate. Where were they?

A chime sounded. My air was exhausted.

I floated above the asteroid field, close to the centre. The thin air wheezed through my spiracles. I blinked as a darkness deeper than the starfield closed around my vision. I was losing consciousness.

The pod turned. There was movement out near the edge of the field. A ship. Or maybe my imagination.

∞

"Udun." The same voice spoke my name.

I opened my eyes, but they refused to focus even with the desert eyelid. A shape moved closer. I tried to speak but something was clamped to my feeders. I made to lift my claws to brush it away. My arms were bound at my sides. My hoofs couldn't find purchase.

"Udun, it's Emba. Calm down. You'll hurt yourself."

I pulled harder but I couldn't move. I was submerged in liquid, but a liquid I could breathe.

The shape moved again. Hard to see. Emba? We'd met on Telsus IV when I was setting up the secret trade deal for Hierarch Czerag. Emba had introduced me to Atalna, who'd warned me about … the Hegemony. The invasion. I had to warn him but the thing around my feeders made it impossible. I kicked and my hoof hit something. There was a dull ringing. I kicked again.

"Stop! You'll smash the tank. Wait."

My body was pulled down and I touched bottom. The liquid was draining into the floor.

"Just wait," Emba said again. "You've been sick. Injured. We had to put you in a coma while you healed. The tank's cleansed the radioactives from you."

The liquid continued to drain and the level dropped past my eyes. I blinked, the inner eyelid flicking over, and saw Emba through the crystal wall of the tank.

"You're healed now," he said.

But I'd never be completely healed. I still felt the laser searing away my mantle flesh. When I closed my eyes I could see my sister Isza blown apart on Treaty Mount steps.

My arms were released, but as the liquid sucked away gravity fully asserted itself and I slumped against the tank wall, barely able to stay upright. The crystal slid aside and the cold air stung the hide beneath my plates.

Emba tried to help me stand but I was too heavy for him. I fell forward, taking him with me, and we landed together on the floor.

He wriggled out from under me.

"Emba," I rasped, "I have to warn y–"

"You have to help me get you into bed. Then you can warn me." He scuttled behind me and helped me to sit up. Then he grabbed at my torso plates and dragged me backwards. "Come on. We need to do this together." He grunted as he gave another pull. "I told the house staff to take a holiday when I knew you were coming."

I pushed with my hoofs against the carpet and in this way we slid across to the bed. With his help I was able to haul myself up on to the broad platform. Finally, I lay across the mattress, out of breath, but I couldn't wait any longer.

"The Hegemony – they've invaded Homeworld. You have to warn the Lenticular."

Emba was puffing as he sat on the edge of the bed. "Save your words, Udun. We know what's happened on Homeworld."

I lay back ready to hear more, but Emba was silent. "And?" I asked finally.

"And nothing. Hierarch Kergis contacted the Lenticular Assembly and explained that there's been a regime change on Homeworld. Trade is unimpeded and life goes on. It's not for us to interfere in internal politics."

Kergis. I remembered the battle at the Point. The Hegemony ships streaming through, being met by our own forces. And then the Kergis ships pulled back and fired on the other Kresz Defender ships. Betraying us.

I tried to push myself up, but my arms were too weak and I collapsed back onto the pillow. "There's been an alien invasion by highly aggressive forces from outside the Lenticular," I said. "Doesn't that worry you?"

"It's highly unusual."

He wasn't making any sense.

I tried again. "My people are dying. You need to help them. The Lenticular needs to help them."

"Kergis has assured the Assembly that the Hegemony is no threat to the wider Lenticular," Emba said.

"And you believe him?"

His snout wrinkled, showing sharp teeth. "Of course not. We're on high alert. But there's nothing to be gained from attacking them on Homeworld. If they move against us, we'll be ready. Right now it's a stalemate." He stood. "You need to rest, Udun. We can talk about all of this when you're stronger."

I tried to push myself up again, but it was no good. "Does anyone know I'm here?"

"No. You were delirious when they picked you up, but you had enough wit to say my name. The freighter captain is a friend of mine. He contacted me and we felt it more prudent to bring you here with a minimum of fuss."

Prudent. This wasn't the time to be prudent. I closed my eyes and saw the Hegemony ships boiling out of tenspace and our Defender craft exploding in gouts of flame. And then on Homeworld, the Hegemony troops firing at us on the runway of the spaceport, killing indiscriminately. Even forewarned I'd been unable to prevent the invasion. I should have done more to convince Czerag to alert the other houses.

"It was harder getting the tank installed when the doctors told me you needed one," Emba continued. "But you can –"

"I want to see Atalna."

Emba stared at me. "That's not a good idea."

"Pl–" My voice failed me. I tried again. "Please. Bring him here."

At least the Betlaan would understand what we were dealing with. He'd already suffered through a Hegemony invasion on his world.

"All right. But only if you promise to sleep."

I felt I could never sleep again.

∞

When I woke, the light filtering through my eyelids felt wrong. The wall beside me glowed blue-white. Of course. I was in Emba's house.

Without thinking, I rolled onto my back and realised there was no pain. I reached around to feel the ridge of flesh where the Hegemony had cut off my mantle. I'd become so used to the constant nagging ache or sharp shock if I jarred it, but now the skin was puckered but firm.

The room was empty except for the bed and the tank I'd woken in. The tank looked out of place here, its crystal door still open, pipes and cables snaking from its sides across the carpet and into the wall.

I pushed the bedcovers back and stood slowly. No dizziness. My muscles were tired but I felt I could walk a little.

The door opened into a short corridor that ended in a blank wall with a sparkling piece of sculpture composed of shifting light and not much else. To my right the corridor led into a wide, low room with a long table and a sitting area with padded chairs. A crystal wall ran the length of the house and through it I could see a garden, illuminated by overhead lights set into a transparent dome. A gravel driveway separated the house from a central flower bed dominated by strange, many-stalked plants with fat pods on the end of thick, curling branches.

The house seemed empty. I remembered Emba saying he'd sent the servants away. Right before he told me his government knew about the invasion of Homeworld. Why weren't they and the other Lenticular governments planning a counterstrike? Were they all too scared to act? Or – worse – had they struck their own bargains with the Hegemony, just like Kergis? I needed information. Even a lie would tell me something.

I heard the whine of a turbine, then a vehicle ground along the drive and came to rest in front of the window-wall. The vehicle's door axed up and Emba climbed out.

I stepped forward and the crystal wall split and moved aside. The air was warmer outside and smelled of growing things.

"Udun. You're up," Emba said as he went to the far side of the transport and helped his passenger stand.

"Atalna!" I called, and walked out onto the rough gravel to meet him.

The Betlaan turned stiffly, his leg obviously paining him, but I was by his side and supporting him while Emba closed the vehicle door.

"You're well?" I asked.

"I bear my scars. As I see you now do, Udun. It is good to see you."

Emba bared his teeth at the two of us. "It seems I have a weakness for looking after lost souls."

"I was on Telsus when Emba sent word," Atalna said as we walked together into the house. "He organised a fast transport here."

"This isn't Telsus Prime?" I asked. But then a gout of smoke and flame flared up through the bushes, and I saw past the lights in the dome that the sky was a dark blanket of brown and yellow cloud reflecting a red glow from below. This was Telsus IV.

"We're at my estate," Emba said.

"Udun, you look like you've been through a terrible ordeal," Atalna said as I helped him to a chair at the long table. "I'm sorry that my fears of a Hegemony attack have been fulfilled more swiftly than even I imagined." He glanced towards Emba. "If only I could have done more."

I pulled up a stool and sat opposite him without replying. I could plot my own "if onlys" all the way back to when Sakat sucked the poisons from our world and set the first proto-Kresz to live there. There was no use in "if onlys".

Emba noted my silence and changed the subject. "Udun, you haven't eaten since you got here. And you've slept around the clock since we talked last. It's time for breakfast."

He crossed to a wall of cupboards and pulled out plates of fruit, bread and some kind of cured meat that he placed on the table before us. I was hungry and piled berries and slices of dark bread onto my platter.

Emba poured us all a drink from a crystal ewer filled with a green liquid. "It's goja juice. Try it."

He took a long gulp, exhaling loudly as he finished his own glass, and refilled it. "So, Atalna," he said, "you're well? How is the dwelling?"

"I am well, thank you. And the house you found me meets all my needs." Atalna turned to me. "Emba provides me with a stipend. Far more generous than I deserve. I have money enough to live. And it's peaceful there."

"I could do the same for you, Udun," Emba said. "I have more than enough resources. You know I'd be happy to help."

The piece of bread I was chewing felt suddenly thick and too salty on my feeders. Some juice helped and I swallowed the mouthful. "Have the Hegemony surrendered or withdrawn?" I asked.

Emba's snout dipped. "No. Everything is the same. But you escaped. You were lucky to get away alive."

"Others were not so lucky," I said.

Emba glanced at Atalna again, then sighed. "It was clear from the first moment I met you that your hierarch was playing a dangerous game and the political situation on your world was far from stable. Your side has been out-manoeuvred and you've been caught up in the consequences of that."

"This is more than some internal power struggle," I said.

"But is it? Kergis chose to get help from outside. Unconventional for a Kresz, but not difficult to understand in the scheme of things. Now he's formed a new government which is making all the right noises to my political masters and the rest of the Lenticular. The Point is being rebuilt. Though the Hub has been damaged by terrorists acting against the legitimate government –"

"It sounds like Betlaan all over again," Atalna said.

"The point is, things are calming down," Emba finished.

"You're talking as if all the killing that *will* be done on Homeworld *has* been done," I said. "As if all the suffering has passed. Kergis is destroying our way of life and anyone who stands in his way is put to death. How long till he decides to execute anyone who's not House Kergis just to be rid of an inconvenience? I can't stand by and watch that happen."

"What can you do?" Emba said. "You're one Kresz and not even … well … an injured one at that. It's over for you. You survived. Come to terms with that, because if you don't it will only end in your death. Either you'll throw your life away on some foolishness, or you'll make such a nuisance of yourself Kergis will reach out from Homeworld and crush you." Emba leaned over and touched my claws. "I can help you. You want a place to live, somewhere you can feel safe. Somewhere you can stop running. Somewhere the Kresz and the Hegemony will never find you. I can do that for you if you'll let me. The fight is over. Be kind to yourself."

I pulled my claws away. "Have you forgotten what Atalna told us? The fight is never over with the Hegemony. You can sit here and fool yourself you're safe, but eventually they'll come here and take everything you have too."

"I brought Atalna here to show you there are alternatives to fighting and dying." It was clear Emba was struggling to keep his voice calm. "He escaped the Hegemony. They're still out there, but Atalna has found peace."

There was a grunt from the other side of the table. "Friend Emba, you have made my life very comfortable, but I cannot say I have found peace. Not the peace that comes from knowing that justice has finally been done. The people of Betlaan are enslaved. The fact they are light years away does not alter that fact, and there is not one second of every day that I do not think of them and wish I could make their suffering stop. I ran, and that is my shame. But

I could see nothing else for me. I stopped running because, again, I was weak. I do not want you to think I am ungrateful for your help. But I would throw myself into the fight against the Hegemony again in an instant if I could only see some way I could hurt them. Even if it cost my life."

Atalna hesitated. Emba's face was unreadable. "Again I'm sorry, Emba. I do not mean to toss your kindness back in your face. But I think I understand Udun more than you can." He grasped my claws across the table. "Don't become like me, Udun. The daily bread of life is poor feeding when you can't share it with those you love."

I grasped his hand back. "Believe me. I will not give up until the Hegemony is gone from my world."

Emba slammed his glass onto the table. "You are both as insane as each other."

"I pray you don't get to share in our insanity when the Hegemony comes to your world," Atalna said.

"Emba," I said quickly, "you want to help – I know that. You are genuinely a friend. One of the few I have left. Please. I'm asking you for the sake of our friendship, for the dead and suffering Kresz on my world, for the sake of your own loved ones. Please help me."

"I thought I *was* helping you," he rasped. "I don't know how else I can. What do you want, Udun? No one cares about your world enough to intervene."

His words hurt but they were true. The Kresz had never bothered to make alliances beyond expedient trade links with the Lenticular.

"Just do one thing for me," I said. "Arrange it so I can speak to the Lenticular Assembly. It's not a small thing, I know, but I hope, I pray, you can do it. Let me help them see what I have seen. Give me a chance to change things."

Emba stood. He looked like he'd lost his appetite. "Finish your breakfast," he said. "I'll make some calls." And he went out of the room.

"He'll be all right," Atalna said. "He has a habit of doing the right thing. It's unavoidable for him. And this is the right thing."

I blinked. "I don't know. Emba's right that I'll be putting myself in harm's way again –"

"You are doing the right thing," Atalna said. "Believe someone who relives the consequences of his actions every day I draw breath. The faces of my dead family never leave me. Let me help you. You won't have to fight the Hegemony alone."

"I …" I stopped; I didn't know what to say. "Thank you," I managed, and squeezed his hand again, embarrassed by how much his words affected me.

⊒

The combined Brell, Totek and Sissilak force was strung out in a column across the dark Voss Space chamber: massive, illegally armed support carriers interspersed with destroyer escorts and equally outlawed battlecruisers, accompanied by a swarm of Sissilak Talon fighters and delta-wing Brell singlecraft. Rhees froze the recording, then spun the holo to orient her view at ninety degress to where she knew her Hegemony Diplomatic Corps scoutcraft had been, hanging back on the lip of the chamber as she, Denev and Volmar followed the rebel force.

She hadn't seen the attack ships transit first time around, but she was looking for it now. Maagba fighters, shaped like horseshoes standing on end, phased into the chamber at its apex. They speared down on the convoy, which was already breaking apart as limited sensors registered the intruders. A series of explosions rippled through the disintegrating column, and ships veered madly to escape destruction.

Another wave of Maagba ships and more missiles, and then the Sissilak, Totek and Brell began firing back. Lasers and particle weapons lanced out and dark bulbs of energy formed as the Voss Space field reached criticality then exploded in searing plasma blasts, burning ships out of existence. In the mayhem, the pace of attack stepped up and the Voss Space chamber began to break down, walls shifting and tunnels extruding to crush unlucky ships, singlecraft stuttering in and out of existence. That was when Volmar had insisted they transit.

The image shifted to space. Rhees could see her scoutship, mostly disabled and too close to the planet. While she was crash-landing – heavy on the crash, not so good on the landing – the other half of the Maagba force that was waiting safely in space mopped up what was left of the rebels sent to attack it. Sent by Volmar – although the poor rebels hadn't known he was the source of the intel Denev had fed them through his network on Herakli.

The Brell, Sissilak and Totek had only been defending themselves from a series of attacks from the Maagba that had already killed billions. But somehow they'd hidden their own considerable attack force from the Hegemony auditors. It was far more than they were allowed for a local militia. They still didn't deserve to be sacrificed by Volmar so he could make an alliance with the raiders.

Rhees fast-forwarded the images. She knew what happened next. The Maagba had captured them on the planet – but only after she'd punched Volmar in the face. That at least had felt good. Then Volmar made whatever slimy deal he'd been planning all along with the Maagba and offered Rhees up to them as a blood sacrifice to seal the bargain. That shouldn't have surprised her. Volmar had been looking for an excuse to get rid of her ever since she'd been thrown out of Fleet for killing her boyfriend – Denev's brother – in a training exercise and ended up in HDC. Except the Maagba hadn't killed her. She'd won her fight with them and they'd gifted her a ship. Something Volmar and Denev didn't know.

She watched to the end of the recording, saw the HDC scoutcraft she'd piloted leaving without her, heading back to Hegemony space. The sensor channel running along the bottom of the image showed the ship contained two humans. So Denev had survived. She hoped he was still safe.

She'd been picked up by the Jantri ship and Nok a few hours later. The alien had offered the recording when Rhees had asked if he knew what had happened to her companions, though she didn't give a shit about Volmar. She hadn't expected to see such a comprehensive record of Volmar's treachery. Now she wondered just how long the Jantri'va had been observing Cygnus Sector, and did their surveillance extend deeper into the Hegemony?

We don't just want information on the Hegemony. We want you to help us defeat them. She hadn't been able to sleep since Nok had dropped that bombshell.

Part of her felt it was the perfect solution. What she'd seen of the Hegemony Diplomatic Corps, Volmar and the ruthless acts of the Central Administration disgusted her. The species bigotry she'd witnessed on Herakli, and Volmar's deal with the Maagba – a plan her father, Fleet Admiral Gart Lowrans, had signed off on – were shining examples of how low Earth had sunk. So if the Jantri wanted her help to defeat the Hegemony and free humanity and every other species in its grip ... Why not?

But could she really support a bunch of powerful aliens who wanted to attack Earth? Twenty years ago the K-Chaan had come close to wiping out the human race and the Hegemony had been created to make sure that never happened again. Since then though, the Central Administration had lost its way, seeming to believe any action was justified in order to maintain control. The majority of humanity thought itself safe and secure, but that safety came at a terrible price. Privacy was just a word. No secret was left undisturbed under the gaze of the HDC. Freedom was another illusion. It was freedom with hard barriers. Freedom to do whatever you wanted as long as it accorded with what the Central Administration judged was right and good. Meanwhile, HDC and Fleet moved out into space and subdued, threatened and corrupted any alien species they encountered all in the name of keeping the peace. But that wasn't how lasting peace was won, was it? Even a Fleet brat like Rhees could see that.

And now HDC had stirred up a bunch of aliens from a star system she'd never heard of. From what she'd seen of this ship and Nok's armour, the Jantri'va looked at least equal to the Hegemony in technology – and may be more advanced in some respects. There would be other species in the Lenticular who were equally unhappy with the Hegemony's incursion. HDC was already picking a fight with the Hanloi out towards galactic centre. Just how many battles on how many fronts did they want to start?

She shifted on the mat, still far from sleep. Her gaze took in the table where she and Nok had sat. There was no way she could afford to trust him – it – whatever. But they were already aligned in one respect. The Jantri'va wanted to stop the Hegemony encroaching on their space; she wanted to change the paradigm under which the whole Hegemony operated.

She barked a short laugh. When had she developed such lofty ambitions?

But she knew she was right. It was important to protect Earth, yes. But do it through cooperation, alliances, friendships, not fear, suppression and – what did Nok say? – by destroying the souls of entire species.

If she worked with Nok, she would be branded a traitor. There were those who would never forgive her. Her father, who she'd had little contact with growing up, already saw her as an unreliable hothead. This would put her beyond the pale.

There were also no guarantees she'd be able to influence how the Jantri'va ultimately acted. It was easy enough to aim a weapon and fire the kill shot. It was far more difficult to pull your aim to simply wound your adversary, and then hold back from firing again. Especially when a wounded foe was the most dangerous of all.

But what was the alternative? Run away? Fuck that.

She stood, feeling like her brain was wrapped in cobwebs. The door opened at her touch – Nok had insisted she wasn't a prisoner – and as she stepped over the threshold, a light track set into the deck strobed sequential lights leading away to her left and around the corner. She was being shepherded again. She almost turned right in defiance, but she was too tired for games.

She followed the lights, taking everything in: the walls, ceiling, control panels, ducts, doorways, other passages, trying to get a feel for the internal topography. Finally she came to a broad entrance. The lights disappeared as the door scissored open. Nok stood there, or at least the suit did.

"I'd like to hear more," Rhees said.

"Come inside," Nok said.

There were two other suits in there, operating wall stations. Maybe they were robots. Maybe Nok was too. As she entered, she was surrounded by a web of light: wildly looping beams all connected into a network floating around and above her. She raised a hand tentatively, brushed at a light trace with the back of one finger. She heard a low hum and the light felt cool against her skin.

She joined Nok in the centre, ghost fingers of light brushing against her face and arms.

"This is the – Voss Space, you call it – network for the galactic arm," Nok said.

"All of it?"

"As much as we've mapped, which now reaches into Hegemony space and back past the Lenticular. Speaking of which." He caught a loop of light in one gauntlet and pulled it towards them. The network shifted, expanding along the line Nok was following. "This is near-Lenticular space. And this intersection is where your Hegemony emerged to attack the Kresz Homeworld. As you see, the local branchings open into a much larger passage that leads through the rest of the Lenticular. We detected another, much larger Hegemony force advancing on the same corridor a few days ago. We feared a further invasion force, to consolidate their hold on Homeworld before launching an attack on the rest of the Lenticular. It was certainly a large enough group. But instead ..." He expanded the view of the main Voss Space corridor crossing that part of space. "They passed right through the heart of the Lenticular and kept going. They're currently passing a gravitational anomaly at the far end with no sign of slowing. There's another similar Hegemony force heading to the Lenticular now. It's not clear whether they'll follow the others or stop once they reach that part of space."

Rhees plucked at the main passageway. It felt slippery against her fingers, like soap. She rotated the view, turning it end to end, studying the branchings. The anomaly Nok mentioned was impossible to miss. Voss Space bent round it in a distinctly ungraceful way, and beyond it was a local network of crosspaths that opened into another, much wider chamber extending further into the arm towards galactic centre. That second Hegemony force had to be the Hanloi attack group. Volmar had said the Hegemony was going to war. Which meant the destruction of the Kresz was simple collateral damage. The poor bastards were just in the way.

She could tell Nok about the Hanloi, but she wasn't ready to share just yet.

"So what's the plan?" she asked.

The suit was silent. Was it reading her? Did it know she was holding back information?

"We are not ready for a plan yet," Nok said eventually.

"They're already killing your Kresz friends. Don't you want to do something about that?'

"Any unilateral plan to attack and subdue the Hegemony in the Lenticular has already been considered and discounted. The K-Chaan learned that lesson and the Jantri will not repeat it."

So the Jantri knew about the K-Chaan. Just how long have they been studying us, she wondered.

"Any solution must be owned by those it most directly affects," Nok continued. "We are not saviours, we are facilitators."

Rhees shook her head, then wondered if the gesture would be understood. "That's just an oblique way of justifying not doing anything. What happens if 'those it most directly affects' are too beaten to see a way out or fight back?"

Eddies of gas sparkled behind the Jantri's faceplate. "Then they will be trapped in the situation."

Fuck. She'd been about to say that was inhuman. But look at what she was talking to.

People were being crushed but who was worse – the group

doing the crushing or the group that stood by while it happened? The Hegemony had stripped itself of its humanity. The Jantri had none to begin with. But they'd chosen her to help. Why?

"But we don't believe that's the current situation," Nok said, bringing her back to the present.

"So you wait? For what?"

"For the necessary elements to align."

"And how long will that take?"

This was insane. Should she cut and run? Could she? They wouldn't just let her leave. And there was no way she could outrun this ship. But she needed space around her.

"I need to get outside for a while," she said. "I think better out there."

The faceplate looked down at her, unreadable.

"You said I'm not a prisoner. Where's my ship?"

Nok crossed to a door at the far side of the room. As it opened, his head – disconcertingly – turned one-eighty degrees on his shoulders to face her. "The hangar is below, but we have something better than the Maagba craft you brought."

She followed him into a large elevator, and the car dropped a long way. The doors opened onto a blindingly white hangar. Rhees blinked, not able to get a sense of how big it was. The vessels studded along the deck – including her "gifted" ship – looked like toys.

"You can take your own ship out if you like, or you could try one of these." Nok pointed a gauntlet towards the nearest of a long line of singleships.

The hull was featureless grey, shaped like an ellipse, pointed at the front and flowing up and back into a sleek hump. It didn't look like anything Rhees had ever seen but somehow reminded her of a dolphin, or an artistic abstraction of one.

"Gravity drive, of course," Nok said, "but it also generates an inertial field I think you'll find interesting. Far more manoeuvrable than Hegemony ramcraft and no need for you to be entombed in a gel coffin."

"For someone who's only recently encountered the Hegemony, you know a lot about them," Rhees said.

Them, she thought. Not *us*. She'd crossed a line. In her head, at least.

Taking one of their ships guaranteed she couldn't just run. But the pilot in her was intrigued. "How do I …"

The hump of the ship split open, flowing back like putty. The interior seemed made of the same material as the hull, some of it bulging into the approximation of a crash-seat. She glanced at Nok but he said nothing. The floor of the cockpit was spongy, giving beneath her weight as she climbed in. The chair moved around her as she sat, and the hump flowed back over her head, plunging her into darkness.

Control faces lit up around her – lightboards floating in space – and she forced herself to relax. The seat supported her, easing back a little, and a view of the hangar opened up just above the controls. Then … it was as if she'd blinked very slowly and opened her eyes on a new way of seeing. She couldn't still be looking through her eyes, but it didn't feel like the synaptic shunt of immersion either. She could see the hangar all around her, the controls superimposed on her view as if the ship hull wasn't there. But that wasn't all of it. Somehow she had a complete three-sixty-degree view. She saw everything without turning her head or focusing on a particular area. It was like suddenly being given a third arm – weird but obviously useful. Especially for a combat pilot. She'd used broad-range sensors before but this was more immediate, like it was a part of her. And instinctively she knew her sight extended far beyond the visible spectrum now. She also realised she knew exactly how to fly this ship.

Nok was standing patiently by the hangar entry. Rhees activated the launch sequence – a moment's concentration on the blinking icon – and headed for a new opening in the larger vessel's hull.

The stars waiting beyond were tinged slightly green by what her augmented senses knew was a force curtain holding in the hangar's atmosphere. She punched for full thrust as soon as she was clear. She knew exactly how fast she was accelerating, and Nok's ship dwindled to a pinpoint in less than a second, but she may as well have been sitting on the bed in her apartment. Inertialess. Intellectually it was impressive, but her body missed the rush of the ramcraft. Still, that would mean …

She plotted a series of manoeuvres that would pancake a ramcraft pilot even in the most advanced gel coffin, and activated commit. Three seconds later she was back where she'd started, and the craft had traversed the six planes of a cube five hundred kilometres on an edge and executed twenty-four ninety-degree turns at the vertices. She hadn't felt a thing.

There wasn't one ship in the Hegemony she couldn't fly rings around. But flying was only half of it. Her view expanded, magnifying local space and shifting into ladar. There. A tight cometary swarm, way out on the long orbital axis of whatever sun it visited in an epochal cycle. Weapon interfaces shouldered into her awareness. Pretty impressive armaments.

She imagined her ship from outside: a dolphin pausing for a moment, sonar penetrating the depths in search of prey, then diving in a flash of fin and tail for a glittering shoal. Again, she couldn't feel the acceleration, but she saw the comet swarm leaping towards her and sensed the tightening in her chest and belly.

There were six cometary masses. Dirty accretions of rock and water-ice, packed so close the tenuous gas halo enveloped them as one. She was headed straight for the centre, counting down seconds to impact.

This is the last thing Petar saw, she thought. She'd never be able to forget the sight of his gel coffin burst apart. But she pushed the ship faster, the wall of ice rushing to meet her. She screamed. Almost broke off at the last moment.

Then weapons engaged – laser clusters breaking out along the length of the ship's body, an expanding shell of missiles, the harsh grunt of a rail gun mounted in the nose. The rushing ice vapourised ahead, and around her each rock and pebble freed from the conglomerate was tracked and slagged by lasers or burst into dust by pinhead rockets, the gas halo lighting up like an aurora. And then she was through, with nothing bigger than a grain of sand left in her wake.

She brought the ship to a full halt and let out a long breath. Going by the holo records she'd seen, it was clear the Jantri had been observing the Hegemony for a long time. Nok might be content to wait for the 'necessary elements to align', but she needed to know everything the Jantri knew. There *was* no going back, no matter how many caveats she put on it.

∞

When she stepped out of the dolphincraft, Nok was waiting by the door as if he hadn't moved the entire time.

"I'll work with you," she said. "But only as far as our goals align. I'm not handing over everything just because you want it."

"That is acceptable."

"The Hegemony forces you've been tracking. They're not interested in the Lenticular. They're heading further out to engage the Hanloi at galactic centre."

Nok's faceplate glowed the same as always. "I see."

"I need to know everything they're doing," she said.

"Follow me."

They re-entered the elevator and got off at the same level as before. Rhees followed Nok down a series of corridors. She was expecting him to take her to some kind of surveillance hub crammed with listening tech. Instead he led her back to her room.

"Everything you need is here," he said.

The room filled with light – coherent interfaces floating in midair, control surfaces that Nok pulled into place, arranging them around his visor. Rhees moved to stand beside him, already recognising some of the functionality.

"These can be reconfigured any way you want," he said. "And

you may as well be comfortable while you work." He pointed at the mat she'd failed to sleep on and it twisted and folded to form an angled chaise longue.

Rhees settled herself on it. "Got anything worth eating onboard?"

"I'll see what we can find," he said, and left her to it.

ABOUT THE AUTHOR

Keith Stevenson is the author of the science fiction thriller *Horizon*. His short fiction has appeared in *Andromeda Spaceways Inflight Magazine*, *Aurealis Magazine*, *Oceans of the Mind* and the Agog! Press anthology *Agog! Fantastic Fiction*. He's a past editor of *Aurealis – Australian Science Fiction and Fantasy Magazine*, hosted the Terra Incognita Speculative Fiction Podcast, and edited and published *Dimension6*, the free Australian speculative fiction electronic magazine.

WWW.KEITHSTEVENSON.COM

ALSO BY KEITH STEVENSON

MURDER AND BETRAYAL IN SPACE
WITH THE FATE OF HUMANITY IN THE
BALALNCE

TRY A HOPEFUL APOCALYPSE
FOR A CHANGE

available as print and
ebooks

The Lenticular Series

Two outcasts. One goal. Stop Earth.

Coeur de Lion

www.ingramcontent.com/pod-product-compliance
Lightning Source LLC
Chambersburg PA
CBHW020259120726
47904CB00001B/269